DRAGON DAY

Also by Lisa Brackmann

Rock Paper Tiger
Getaway
Hour of the Rat

DRAGON DAY

LISA BRACKMANN

FINKELSTEIN MEMORIAL LIBRARY SPRING VALLEY, NY

Published by
Soho Press, Inc.
853 Broadway
New York, NY 10003

Library of Congress Cataloging-in-Publication Data

Brackmann, Lisa.
Dragon day / Lisa Brackmann.

ISBN 978-1-61695-345-4
eISBN 978-1-61695-346-1

I. Title.
PS3602.R333D73 2015
813'.6—dc23   2015001857

Printed in the United States of America

10 9 8 7 6 5 4 3 2 1

To my mom, Dorothy Carol Brackmann Galante,
who taught me to love books, baseball, politics and cats,
and has the best laugh I have ever heard.

DRAGON DAY

DRAGONS AND CHINA. IT'S the biggest fucking cliché. If you ever go looking for books about China, you know how many of them have "dragon" in the title? Like all of them, practically.

Thing is, dragons are a big deal in China. The emperor's symbol was a dragon. Dragons are all kinds of good luck, and super powerful. They can control weather, especially the kind that involves water. Your village keep flooding? Maybe you pissed off the local river dragon. Dragons can hide among clouds, disguise themselves as worms, or grow as big as mountains. Out of the twelve animals of the Chinese zodiac, Dragon is the one you most want your kid to be. Dragon babies are attractive, smart, natural leaders, bring good fortune to the family. Yeah, I know all the other animals are supposed to have positive characteristics, but come on. You're telling me you'd choose to be a Sheep over a Dragon?

Me, I'm a Rat. Obviously I'm not winning any zodiac beauty contest. Sure, they say we're clever survivors, and that's useful, I guess. It's true I've survived some pretty crazy shit.

On the other hand, if I'm so clever, why do I keep walking into it?

If you believe in any of this Chinese astrology, it's way more complicated than just the animal year you were born in. There's an animal for your birth month, for your birthday, for the hour you're born, and there's all this other stuff having to do with the four elements—or maybe it's five—and stems and pillars, and I have no idea what any of that means.

All these things have to do with your luck, or lack of it, and what kind of person you are. Because it's not like every single baby born in a Dragon year turns out to be smart, good-looking, and destined to rule, right?

So maybe you're born in a Dragon year but on a Sheep day. And maybe some of those Sheep have Dragons inside.

CHAPTER ONE

I'M EYEING THE BOTTLE of vintage Moutai on the table and wondering if it would be unforgivably rude of me to pour myself another shot.

I don't even like Moutai. But Sidney Cao singing "Feelings"? I definitely need something.

We've finished the Château Mouton Rothschild ("Genuine one," Sidney promised), and there's nothing else left on the table to drink except Pepsi.

"Feelings . . . nothing more than . . . feelings . . ."

I'm sitting in a private room in what I'm told is one of the three most expensive karaoke bars in Shanghai. The weird thing is, it's not in a super-upscale neighborhood like the Bund or Nanjing Road, the French Concession or the riverfront in Pudong. Instead it's this area west of the Shanghai train station that looks pretty typical: grey high-rises, broad streets choked with traffic and torn up by subway construction, nothing green in sight except for the occasional strange paint job. Vendors selling socks and DVDs and steamed buns crowd the sidewalks, along with bicycles and electric scooters.

This place though, outside, it's a façade pretending to be marble that's slathered with neon, fiberglass columns, and turrets surrounding tall, fake-bronze doors. The cars double-parked in the street are Beemers, Mercedes, Ferraris, a Rolls, and a Bentley. On the inside there's a huge lobby four stories high that you have to go through a metal detector to enter, and when you do, you're surrounded by the fronts of fake buildings, like a movie set of a European village, all painted white, and everywhere you look, there are gilded planters and gold chandeliers, Plexiglas kiosks advertising luxury goods, giant ornate mirrors, and the kind of fussy carved furniture that belongs in a Three Musketeers movie with dudes wearing long powdered wigs, except instead of being white like it usually is, the furniture's painted peacock blue and neon green.

Also grand pianos. There are several in the cavernous lobby, black Steinways, sitting beneath a painted sky hanging four stories up that gradually changes from sunny blue with popcorn clouds to a garish red sunset.

No pianists, though. Maybe the pianos are just for decoration.

Our private room is pretty cozy, with fake Renaissance paintings on the red-flocked walls, which I have to say do not go very well with the peacock blue and neon green Musketeers furniture. But whatever.

I'm sitting next to Lucy Wu on one of the couches. Lucy, my sometime partner in the art business, owns a Shanghai gallery, and she dresses the part. She wears crazy designer stuff a lot, but tonight she's outdone herself outfitwise. It's this short, sleeveless, white dress with daisy-shaped cutouts and a halo of wispy white ostrich feathers, paired with red leather boots. Her shiny black hair is cut in this blunt anime style, and she's wearing bright scarlet lipstick, thick mascara, and eyeliner like on a cartoon Cleopatra.

"Feeeeelings . . . Oh, oh, oh, feeeelings . . ."

"One more chorus," she says to me, all the while keeping a big smile on her face.

Sidney really can't sing. I mean, I can't sing either, but I'm not the one standing up there with the microphone. So far this evening, Sidney has regaled us with "Yueliao Daibiao Wode Xin" ("The Moon Represents My Heart"), "Home on the Range," and "Sailing the Seas Depends on the Helmsman"— "Cultural Revolution favorite!" he explains with a big laugh.

I'm just about to reach for the Moutai when the song ends. Lucy smiles, showing her perfect tiny teeth, and claps. I smile and nod and clap.

Vicky Huang, the fourth member of our party, sits straight backed, not smiling, because this is serious stuff apparently, and she's staring up at Sidney and applauding like she's witnessing the Second Coming.

Sidney beams and approaches our little group of couches, microphone in hand. As he does, our very own private waitress, dressed in a French maid's outfit, emerges from the shadows of the back wall, where she'd blended in like one of the paintings.

Smiling, without saying a word, she refills the tiny crystal flutes reserved for the Moutai.

"*Ganbei!*" Sidney says, raising his glass.

"Oh, thank God," Lucy Wu murmurs in my ear.

I lift my glass. We clink. And Lucy, who is about the size of an anorexic hobbit, downs hers in a single "*Ganbei.*"

I don't do as well. I know this is expensive stuff and prized in China, but it's about 110 proof and tastes like sweet and sour paint thinner, with maybe a dash of soy sauce. The Moutai catches in my throat, and I cough.

"Now, Ellie, I think it is *your* turn!" I look up, and there's Sidney holding the microphone in his outstretched hand.

"Oh, no, that's okay," I say. "I'm . . . you know, I can't really sing."

"Everyone can sing! You only must express what's in your heart!"

Believe me, buddy, you don't want to know.

"I . . . uh, my throat's kind of sore."

"Then you should have more Moutai!" He doesn't even need to raise his hand. He merely flexes his fingers, and the waitress rushes over to refill our glasses.

"Just sing something!" Lucy hisses in my ear.

"Why don't *you* sing something?" I hiss back.

"Because he asked *you*."

"What shall you sing, Ellie?" Sidney asks.

I really don't want to sing. But a good rule of thumb? Don't piss off Chinese billionaires.

Especially don't piss off Sidney Cao.

I mean, it's not like he *seems* scary. He's wearing his usual golf shirt, slacks, and ugly designer belt, this sixtyish guy with prominent cheekbones, a bony nose, and crooked teeth. Which he could obviously fix if he wanted to. But he doesn't seem to care.

"I . . . um, where's the book? I'll take a look."

The waitress quickly fetches the Big Book of Karaoke Tunes, a red leather binder with an embossed gold crest on it, some kind of made-up coat of arms. I start flipping through it. I have no freakin' clue what to sing. "My Heart Will Go On"? I don't think so.

"While you decide, I will sing," Vicky Huang announces. She rises.

I think of Vicky as Sidney's enforcer. I doubt that she'd actually break my kneecaps, but she'd know who to call. Like the dude in the nice suit standing sentry by the door. There's nothing about him that sticks in your head. He's just this slightly taller-than-average Chinese guy with a thick neck and a crew cut.

Vicky, on the other hand, stands out. She's wearing an outfit that might look cute on a young, thin, twenty-something girl: brown leather hot pants over black leggings and a tight, fuzzy pink sweater. On a middle-aged, chubby woman with a cloud of teased, dyed black hair sporting red highlights, not so much.

Sidney hands her the mike like he's passing a loaded gun. I drink my Moutai, which I've decided is not so bad, at least situationally.

She takes her place in front of the giant flat-screen karaoke monitor. Stands there with this deadly serious expression, like she's facing a firing squad or has otherwise found Jesus.

The music begins. Swells. Building up to something big. On the screen there are random nature scenes and a young couple sitting on bright green grass, staring at each other, holding hands. Cartoon hearts drift up into the pixelated sky.

Vicky Huang opens her mouth, and out comes, *"The hills are aliiiive . . . with the sound of muuuusic . . ."*

What I wasn't expecting: Vicky Huang can actually sing.

Sidney claps wildly.

L u c k y   m e ,   V i c k y   g e t s on a roll and sings four songs, and by the time she's done, Sidney's ready to bounce. This whole long night, he hasn't said one word about why he wanted me and Lucy to meet him in Shanghai for karaoke, but that's the way business gets done here a lot of the time.

When we gather in the lobby, next to a Lucite display advertising Rolex, the fake sky is black, with a full moon and clusters of stars. A jazz combo plays around one of the grand pianos, a song that would be kind of mellow if it weren't amplified to the point of distortion.

"Thank you for the lovely evening," Lucy says to Sidney. "Please let me know if there's anything I can do for you while you're in Shanghai."

"Of course, of course! We will talk. Perhaps tomorrow?"

Vicky Huang consults her iPad. "Two P.M." It is not a suggestion.

Lucy doesn't miss a beat. "I believe I'm available." She turns to me. "Ellie?"

"Oh. Yeah. Sure." I mean, what else am I going to do, other than try to score soup dumplings? Which sounds like a great idea, actually.

I'm the one who hooked up Lucy and Sidney. And even though Lucy thanks me for the connection, I feel a little queasy about it. Because I like Lucy a lot. We work together. She's a friend. And getting involved with Sidney is a really mixed bag.

"Shall we meet at the gallery?" Lucy asks. "I have a show up now with an emerging artist who may interest you."

"Of course, of course." Sidney sounds distracted. "Vicky will arrange."

Sidney Cao, in addition to being a ruthless billionaire guy, is seriously obsessed with collecting art. He has a collection that blows a lot of museums out of the water. Everything from Vermeer to Warhol. More recently he's gotten into contemporary Chinese art, which is how our paths happened to cross. I manage the works of an important contemporary artist: Zhang Jianli, my friend Lao Zhang. "Lao" means old, which he's not; he's maybe forty, but it's also a term of respect and friendship.

A lot of people respect Lao Zhang.

My ending up as his representative was kind of an accident,

and though I've come around to thinking that the art gig isn't bad in theory, some of the complications—drinking tea with Domestic Security, karaoke marathons with a homicidal billionaire—are starting to wear on me.

Okay, maybe "homicidal" isn't fair. Maybe he just told his muscle to do whatever it takes to arrange a meeting with me to discuss Lao Zhang's art a couple of months ago, and what it happened to take was . . . well, killing people. Stuff happens, right?

Besides, I'd probably be dead if he hadn't. I was in the middle of some serious shit at the time, and the people his men killed weren't exactly my friends.

"Can I drop you at your hotel?" Lucy asks me. She drives a cute MINI Cooper.

"That'd be great." I'm staying at my usual Shanghai rack, this funky, sprawling nineteenth-century hotel at the north end of the Bund. It's getting kind of pricey, over seventy bucks a night, but I have this thing where I get comfortable someplace and that takes the edge off the ol' PTSD hypervigilance, especially in a city as crazy big as Shanghai. This hotel, I know where it is, how to get there, I know the menus at their bar and café, even a couple of the staff, who recognize me when I check in. I feel, if not exactly safe, safer.

"Ellie, do you still have time tonight?" Sidney asks. Suddenly. "For a night*cap*?" Emphasis on "cap." He giggles. As if he's nervous.

Sidney, nervous? I've never seen *that* before.

I'm not liking this at all. And I'm past ready to go to my familiar hotel and burrow under my queen-size comforter.

Don't piss off the billionaire.

"I, uh . . . Sure."

★ ★ ★

WE END UP AT some club over in Pudong, driven there in
Sidney's Bentley, the driver a rent-a-thug I don't recognize, the
plain-wrap bodyguard riding shotgun. The club is in the penthouse of a crazy high-rise that looks sort of like a giant bottle
opener, on the bank of the Huangpu River. Floor-to-ceiling
windows a couple stories tall. A huge aquarium that takes up an
entire back wall, containing a pair of sea turtles, a stingray, and
a hammerhead shark. I guess they all get along.

Sidney and I sit in a high-backed, private booth up against
one of the windows overlooking the river. I have to admit it's
a pretty cool view, the old, restored European buildings on
the Bund, science-fiction skyscrapers lurking behind them like
invaders from another planet, obscured by mist. Boats tool up
and down the river.

The whole time on the ride over here, Sidney made small
talk—about his museum plans, about art he wants to buy.
Whatever it is he wants to talk to me about isn't something he's
willing to bring up in the backseat of his Bentley. Apparently
it has to wait for another overpriced drink in some pretentious
hangout for assholes with too much money.

"What can I get you for drink, Ellie?" Sidney asks.

"Whatever you're having," I say, and immediately regret it.
Because what if it's more Moutai?

Instead the waitress, a drop-dead-gorgeous woman wearing
a skintight black dress, brings us this fancy cut-glass bottle of
liquor the color of bloody amber. She pours two glasses—snif-
ters, I guess they're called—about a quarter full.

"Courvoisier L'Esprit," Sidney announces, holding his snifter up to the table lamp, this glowing, egg-shaped thing that

I guess looks pretty cool but that doesn't cast enough light so you could actually read a menu by it.

I lift up my snifter, too, wait for Sidney to clink and take a little sip.

Well, okay, this tastes pretty good. Like smoked apricots and honey.

"I am investor here," Sidney explains. "So they keep a few things I like for me."

"It's really delicious," I say.

He turns and stares out the window. The mist has thickened, making everything seem out of focus. Unreal. I look the other way and watch the hammerhead shark slowly cruise the length of the aquarium with a couple flips of its tail, one rubber black eye peering out in our direction.

I read somewhere that hammerhead sharks are actually pretty harmless—they just *look* deadly.

"Maybe you wonder why I want to talk to you this evening, Ellie," Sidney finally says.

"I, uh . . . art?" Because I figure it must have something to do with Lao Zhang. Sidney's been dying to get a few of Lao Zhang's pieces for his collection. Like I found out a couple of months ago, he's willing to go to a lot of trouble to get them. The problem is, because of some recent complications with China's Domestic Security Department, I can't really sell him any. We made this arrangement where I donated him one (long story), but now I'm thinking one wasn't enough. That he wants a different piece, maybe one I can't donate in good conscience, one of Lao Zhang's major works that could bring him a lot of money—if he were allowed to sell it anyway.

"No," Sidney says. "It's because of Gugu."

Gugu?

CHAPTER TWO

"GUWEI," SIDNEY SAYS, SHAKING his head. "I must correct myself. Gugu was his child name."

"Your son?" I ask.

"Yes. The younger one."

Sidney has three children. For a guy as rich as Sidney, China's official one-child policy is more like a mild suggestion.

Two boys and a girl. That's all I knew about Sidney's kids. Now I know that one of them's named Gugu. Guwei, that is.

"Oh," I say. "So Guwei, he's interested in contemporary Chinese art?" Because I can't think of anything else I'm involved with that a son of Sidney's might care about. It's not like I have connections with Ivy League colleges, or Wall Street firms, or really much of anything, other than Beijing dive bars and cheap dumpling restaurants.

Sidney sighs and lifts his hand. Immediately the waitress appears. She pours us both more of the fancy cognac.

"No," he says. "He does not care for the art. He cares for the expensive cars and clothes. Girls. Things like that."

Not my MOS, that's for sure.

Sidney leans forward. "I think maybe he falls into some bad company." A reluctant confession.

"I see," I say, but of course I really don't. So the kid's a spoiled little emperor, driving hookers around in his Ferrari or whatever. What's that got to do with me?

"I warn him, but he doesn't listen. I tell him maybe I take away his money, but he already has his own. 'I can make more,' he tells me. 'I don't need anything from you.'"

The way Sidney hangs his head, I feel a little sorry for him. A guy so rich he owns his own ghost city, and he still can't get his kid to listen up. Which doesn't answer the essential question: Why me? Because I'm such a fuckup that he thinks maybe I can give him advice on how to deal with another one?

"I think it is because of this *American*," Sidney says suddenly. Like it's a curse word. "I think he is the bad influence on my son."

"Oh," I say. "Sorry." Maybe I'm supposed to be apologizing for the sins of my countryman.

"I investigate him," he says, jabbing a finger in the air. "He is a businessman. A *consultant*." He spits that last word. I kind of don't blame him. It's harder to be a total con-artist foreigner than it used to be, but there are still plenty of sketchy white dudes calling themselves "consultants," or "market-intelligence strategists," or whatever.

"What does he want with Gugu?" I think to ask.

"Don't know. Gugu won't say."

And all of a sudden, I'm getting a feeling why Sidney invited me out tonight.

"So . . . of course I'd be glad to help. But . . . it's not like I have any connections who can tell me about this guy. *Wo meiyou zheyangde guanxi. Nide guanxi bi wode geng hao.*"

My *guanxi*, my connections, aren't as good as yours. Not even close.

Sidney waves his hand, as if he's swatting a mosquito. "Not about *guanxi*. About moral character."

"Okay," I say. "Moral character. But, um . . . I don't know that I'm . . . I mean . . ."

"You are American," he says, jabbing his finger again. "You are the better judge. You can tell me, his, his . . . *shenqian*."

His intentions.

My head is spinning. And not because of the Courvoisier.

Okay, maybe a little.

"But . . . if Gugu won't talk to you . . . why would he talk to me?"

"Gugu likes foreign girls," Sidney says, with a smile that I am thinking is not about finding something funny or pleasurable. "And he is staying in Beijing now."

"But—"

"Vicki will arrange."

Oh, shit.

If there's one thing I've learned, it's that when Vicky Huang arranges something, it stays arranged.

"ON THE ONE HAND, it's good to have a powerful patron. On the other . . ." Harrison Wang pauses as his *ayi*, "Annie" from Fujian, brings out two steaming mugs of coffee.

"*Yili, ni hao*," she says to me. She's a middle-aged woman, small, thin, all tendon and bone. "*Ni xihuan chi shenme?* Omelet? French toast?"

I'm really not hungry. Mostly I'm tired after an overnight train from Shanghai, where as usual I didn't sleep much. "Just coffee, thanks."

The coffee is amazing, of course.

"Micro-lot, single-estate, from El Salvador," Harrison

explains. "Fresh harvest." He sips his. "I'm investing in a new coffee business. Something a little more specialized and upscale than Starbucks. We're opening first on Doujiao Hutong and then in Sanlitun if the demand is there."

I got back from Shanghai on the overnight train around 9:00 A.M., dropped my bag off at my apartment, and headed to Harrison's place. After the karaoke marathon with Sidney the night before yesterday, I called Harrison to arrange a meeting.

I never wanted to get involved with Sidney Cao, but he didn't leave me much choice. He'd wanted a piece of Lao Zhang's art, and he was going to get it no matter what it took. If that had been the end of me and Sidney, I'd count myself lucky. Maybe even have a few warm fuzzies for the guy, since he did kind of save my ass.

But that wasn't the end, and now I'm getting tangled up even deeper. I don't like the feeling.

Harrison and I sit in the breakfast nook of his penthouse apartment in central Beijing, on the southern edge of Chaoyang District. He's dressed for business meetings, which means slacks and this beautiful button-down shirt so totally, absolutely black that it's like staring into a black hole, looking for stars that aren't there, or that you can't see. Which is pretty much Harrison's MO.

"So what's the other hand?" I ask.

"His power is connected to certain factions in the government. If those factions lose out in the coming leadership transition . . ." He sips. "I think these beans may be a little overroasted."

This whole thing is making my head hurt. "Well, *you're* powerful."

Harrison laughs shortly. "Not like Sidney Cao."

Harrison is my boss, sort of, at a distance. He set up the foundation that I use to sell Lao Zhang's art. Or *was* using, before Domestic Security got on my case. Otherwise he's a venture capitalist/patron of the arts with an interest in "concepts of community in postnationalist societies emerging from the New World Disorder."

This is from our nonprofit's mission statement. I didn't write it.

"Who's he connected with?" I ask. Not like I'm any kind of expert in Chinese politics, but I've paid enough attention to get some idea about the Chinese Communist Party's different factions. That the CCP *has* different factions anyway. I couldn't tell you much about what any of the factions stand for. Just that some of them go back to family feuds from before the Cultural Revolution.

"From what I know, Tuanpai—Communist Youth League. But I've heard he has some contacts with the Shanghai gang as well. And of course there are the *hong er dai*."

The "princelings"—children of the original revolutionaries. Richer than shit, a lot of them.

Harrison takes another exploratory sip of his coffee. "Anyone with his amount of wealth obviously has some high-level relationships."

"What do you think I should do?" I ask.

"Well, it will be hard not to go along with him for the time being."

I don't need this. I don't need to get any more involved with Sidney Cao than I already am. I mean, he has people killed. It's not relaxing to be around.

"Great."

Now Harrison puts down his cup and focuses on me. "What

I recommend is that you do as little as possible to fulfill your obligation. Meet his son, meet this American, offer your expert opinion. That's all he's asked of you. Don't volunteer anything else."

Like I'd do that.

I'M HEADING TO THE nearest subway stop, thinking about a nap. The last thing I want to do is think about all the potential complications with Sidney and now his kid.

I'm sleepy, and I'm distracted, so when the door of the black Buick parked with two wheels up on the curb opens in front of me, my first reaction is just to step out of the way.

Then two guys get out, two muscular guys with short haircuts and nondescript clothes.

My heart pounds in my throat. Not this again.

"*Qu liaotianr,*" one of them says. Let's go for a chat.

"Just for tea," the other says, smiling.

CHAPTER THREE

"I ALREADY TOLD YOU. I don't know where he is."

Pompadour Bureaucrat leans back in his chair. He doesn't sigh or anything like that. Just gives me a look over his steepled fingers before picking up his glass teacup and blowing on the steaming water, pushing around the leaves that float on the surface till they sink to the bottom.

"Nothing has changed?" he finally asks.

"No. Nothing."

Which of course is a lie.

Like before, he's interrogating me about Zhang Jianli—my former sort-of-not-quite-boyfriend and current client. Lao Zhang, who got into trouble with the government a year ago for having the wrong friends and creating a community that helped like-minded people find one another. "Government doesn't care for it when too many people get together," he told me once. As far as I know, he hasn't actually been charged with anything. Not yet anyway. That isn't how things work in China. First they decide you're a threat. Then they find a label for it.

And also like before, I'm sitting in an anonymous room in an anonymous "business" hotel that reeks of stale cigarettes and fake-flower-perfumed room deodorizer. This time the hotel is somewhere in west Beijing, in Fengtai. I know this because of the billboard we passed that said, in English, WELCOME YOU TO FENGTAI! LEADING EXAMPLE OF AN URBAN-RURAL INTEGRATION DISTRICT AND AN ECO-FRIENDLY RESIDENTIAL DISTRICT. FULLY INVOLVED IN THE DEVELOPMENT OF A BRAND-NEW CITY IMAGE OF AN ENVIRONMENT-FRIENDLY BEIJING!

You'd think in a city like Beijing, Rising China's capital, full of shiny new architectural wonders by famous avant-garde architects, high-speed trains and freshly built subway lines crisscrossing the city like a spider's web, with luxury malls displaying endless amounts of Gucci and Prada and designer crap, that they would have worked a little harder on fixing the Chinglish.

Not so much.

I have time to be thinking all this because Pompadour Bureaucrat is fond of long silences as a part of his interrogation method. Like if he sits back and blows on his tea long enough, I'm suddenly going to break down and confess all.

I'm not naïve enough to think that's all he's going to do. At some point things have to escalate, right? And it's not like I'm some badass who's going to hang tough if things get really bad.

This is the second time Pompadour Bureaucrat and the Domestic Security Department have asked me to "drink tea"— that's cute secret police talk for "interrogation, off the record."

He did offer me actual tea, for what it's worth.

I don't know this guy's name. I don't know his title. I assume he works for the DSD, but for all I know, he could belong to some other Chinese security agency. It's not like he's going to show me his credentials or explain himself to me.

The only thing I know for sure is that he has the power to fuck with my life.

Now Pompadour Bureaucrat does sigh. A long exhale that

sinks the remaining floating tea leaves. He's a middle-aged dude with that swept-back, dyed-black hair that just about every Chinese official seems to favor, wearing a black suit, a white shirt, and a red tie with a pattern of white dots. More formal than the last time I saw him. Maybe he got a promotion. Maybe he's inspired by the 18th Party Congress coming up, 'cause he's dressed like every single one of those Standing Committee guys you see displayed in awkward lines in the official photographs.

I focus on the tie. If I stare long enough, the dots look like they're moving.

"You know, your status here can change at any time," he finally says.

Like before, he speaks to me in Mandarin. I don't know how much English he understands, if any. My spoken Chinese isn't bad, but I'm not sure it's up to this.

"*Wo zhidao.*" I know.

I try to hide the shiver. Because he could just mean, *We're revoking your visa and kicking you out of the country.* Which would suck. But lately I've been thinking about leaving anyway. It's just getting too weird here.

But he could also mean, *We're throwing your ass in jail.* An official prison or a black jail, off the books.

And that whole prospect, I don't do so well with that.

"I can only tell you what I know," I say. "I know Zhang Jianli's email address. I already gave it to you."

"But you manage his art." He smiles, baring his teeth. "Hard to understand how you can do this without knowing where he is."

We've been over this before.

"He left me instructions. It's not so hard."

"You sell his art, then."

"I *sold* some art," I correct. We haven't sold a thing since February. When this whole "fun with the DSD" game started.

"You sell his work," Pompadour Bureaucrat repeats. "Then how does he get paid?"

My heart thumps harder. This is a sensitive subject. "I just collect the money. He hasn't taken any yet."

A frown. "But this is a little strange. This is his money, after all. His work. He behaves . . . almost like a man who is no longer alive."

Oh, shit.

I do not like where this is heading.

"All I know is what he told me. What I told *you*. He wanted some time away from Beijing, so he could work. Get fresh ideas. Too many distractions here." I risk a tiny smirk, 'cause I just can't help it. "See, he likes coffee. He's not so fond of tea."

I STUMBLE OUT OF there in the late afternoon, into the yellow-grey haze of a hot May afternoon. Smog mingles with the dust of a construction site, where this huge jackhammer thing rises like an insect on steroids above temporary metal walls covered with photo murals of new, modern China: sleek high-speed trains, spaceship skyscrapers, and, to show proper respect to tradition, and tourism, the Temple of Heaven.

I'm pretty sure it's a subway they're building. They're building them everywhere. I wish it were done, so I could ride down some long escalator, past ads for Lancôme and real estate and cell phones and socialist modernization, into some shiny new train that would whisk me away, underground, below all the traffic and noise, and I'd emerge in my own neighborhood, safe at home, like magic.

Yeah, well, that's not going to happen.

I limp past a yellow Home Inn and signs for some sports complex left over from the '08 Olympics, and I can see a line of tall, straight trees in an empty field at the side of an expressway, maybe a ring road, but I don't know which one, because I've hardly ever been to Fengtai before, except for the Beijing West Railway Station, a place I hate that's hard to avoid: ugly Soviet mainframe built like a cheap brown suit topped with Chinese pagodas. I'm a lot deeper into Fengtai than that, though, right at the edge where it turns into crumbling old villages and farmland.

A taxi, I think. I need to find a taxi.

Either that or a drink.

I buy a bottle of Nongfu Spring water at a newsstand and take a Percocet.

I NEED THEM, I tell myself. It's not like I'm some addict who just wants to get high. I'm in pain most of the time. The Percocet takes the edge off. I mean, what else am I supposed to do? I've tried acupuncture. It helps, sometimes. So does exercise, sometimes. Tried smoking pot or hash, which helps, too, but, you know, it's technically illegal, and with the rising tide of shit I'm already in . . .

I feel like the little boat that's about to get swamped.

I sit in the back of the taxi and tell myself to think about something else. Something that doesn't make my heart pound and me break out in a cold sweat.

Like, what *am* I going to do when I run out of the Percocet stash that my mom brought me from the States? That's really gonna suck.

Another good reason to leave the country.

If they'll let me.

I stare out the window at the barely crawling cars on the Third Ring Road, at banks of skinny high-rises, whatever colors they once were bleached by smog, their rusting balconies crowded with laundry.

Well, at least they let me out of that cheap-ass hotel.

ANOTHER REASON TO LEAVE: the fucking construction in my neighborhood.

This big stretch of Jiugulou Dajie is torn up, with temporary walls and those blue-trimmed white construction dorms and giant machinery pounding away at the earth, and I swear I feel like I'm living inside a fucking drum sometimes. Another subway line that's going to hook up with Line 2 at my stop, Gulou, and while I'm totally in favor of subways, this is really starting to suck. All my favorite snack stands are gone, swept away for no real reason that I can see. I mean, they aren't digging the line down there, I don't think—they just decided to knock a couple blocks down because . . . I don't know why. No one does. Shit like this happens constantly, and you mostly have to guess at the reasons, because no one is going to tell you or ask for your opinion.

'Cause if they had, I would have said, *Whatever you do, keep that* yangrou chuanr *guy! He makes the best mutton skewers in Beijing!* I used to love to watch him work, carefully dusting the chunks of meat with red spices, rotating them just so, and it was good meat, not some tiny, gristly hunks of who-the-fuck-knows-what animal. It was weird, because he was so into it, so happy doing this simple thing, it seemed like. I would stand there sometimes, waiting for my skewers, wanting to ask him, *So what's the secret of life?* Because I was pretty sure he had the answer. Something to do with taking pride in doing simple things well or some bullshit like that.

Now he's gone, and I don't know where. I never had a chance to ask. No warning. I just walked down the street one day and all those guys were gone—all the stands in front of grey old *hutong* buildings, all those blackened metal grills, the little signs for *chuanr* made from tiny red lights on twisted wire frames. The old buildings, too. All gone. Replaced by temporary metal fencing, with slapped-on billboard murals of high-speed trains and the Temple of Heaven.

Fuck this, I think, unlocking my apartment door. If I can't sell Lao Zhang's artwork, I'm not going to make enough money to pay for this place anyway.

There's an explosion of happy barks and yips. My dog, Mimi.

I open the door and she's dancing around: a medium-size, long-haired yellow dog with a dark muzzle and a feathered tail. She sees me and puts her paws up on my hips, but gently, looks up at me with this *Omigod, I love you more than* anything! expression.

She needs a walk. I can tell. And in spite of the fact that there's major serious shit I need to deal with, in spite of the fact that what I really want to do is drink two or three large Yanjing Drafts (because that's what it takes to get any kind of buzz off the weak-ass beer here), what I decide to do is take the dog for a walk.

First things first, right?

We walk around the *hutongs* behind the Bell Tower a little while, past the community hospital and the police station hiding in the narrow alleys, by the industrial-looking grocery and butcher where everyone's lined up at a window to buy fresh *baozi*, past a trendy-looking bar/restaurant where you still have to use the public toilet across the alley. Finally Mimi does her business (a two-bagger). "We'll go to the Drum Tower later, okay?" I tell her. Lots of people in the neighborhood like to bring their dogs out to the plaza between the Drum and Bell Towers, but not until after dark, when all the tourists have gone. It's a big problem here, finding any kind of open space where your dog can run around a little. Another reason to leave, I think.

But where would I go? This is the question that always stops me.

I'd better think about what's on my plate right now, I tell myself.

So while Mimi sniffs at some interesting stains on a grey brick wall, I get out my iPhone. Stare at it. I don't exactly want to send this email. I'm really not ready to deal with the person on the other end.

It's not really a choice, I tell myself.

I launch the VPN on my phone, open up my email, and type: *"Do you have time to meet?"*

CHAPTER FOUR

"SO WHERE IS IT you're going?"

"Just to visit a friend."

My mom pauses in the middle of her chopping—chicken, for tacos. "And you don't want dinner?"

I shake my head, even though I love my mom's tacos and she's making three kinds tonight ("Chicken, potatoes *y rajas*, and I thought I'd try mutton") and even has enough ripe avocados for guacamole.

"How much pepper for salsa?" Andy asks.

"Oh, throw in a few more of these little ones and another bunch of that cilantro."

He nods and starts chopping. Their knives fall into rhythm. He's not much taller than she is, and they're both a little stocky.

If I were a better person, I'd think it was kind of cute.

Zhou Andian, "Andy," lives next door. My mom's boyfriend. I mean, no point in pretending otherwise. She spends as much time over there as she does here, but she likes our kitchen better for cooking. I figured the thing with Andy would end up being one of her typical flameouts, which would have been all kinds of awkward, given that we're neighbors, but five months in, it shows no signs of fading.

Andy's . . . not bad. He's into this weird Christian house-church, but it seems pretty harmless—they're not setting themselves on fire in the middle of Tiananmen Square anyway. My mom shares the whole Jesus fixation, so it gives them something to talk about.

Otherwise he likes to help. He's quiet, even-tempered.

Added bonus: he's not a drunk or a meth addict or an asshole.

And he really likes my mom.

"What time will you be home, hon?" she asks.

"Not sure," I mutter. "Don't wait up."

She's about to pop the quiz, I can tell, so I hustle myself out of there.

How the fuck did things end up like this?

I had my own apartment. I was making decent money, and I was even doing something kind of cool, representing "emerging" artists. No DSD on my ass or anyone else trying to fuck with me. I can't say I left the war behind—it's always going on in my head somewhere—but I wasn't thinking about Iraq so much. I had this brief period where I wasn't scared all the time, or numb. I was thinking maybe I'd actually found a place for myself.

But that wasn't the main thing, I realize. The main thing was, I felt free.

I'd gotten over my ex-husband, Trey, sort of. I didn't have to worry about whether I was Lao Zhang's girlfriend or just one of a number of girlfriends he fucked, or if that was something I was even entitled to care about, because wherever he was, he wasn't around—and when I interacted with him online, in a chat room, he was pretty much the perfect boyfriend.

And I sure wasn't worrying about what lie to tell my mom *this* time.

I was unattached, and I liked it.

The army shrink, the guy I had to talk to after I got blown up, would probably tell me that I was "isolating" or something.

I sit on the subway, thinking about all this, surrounded by texting twenty-somethings, stylish women carrying shopping bags from Apple and Starbucks, migrant workers with browned faces hauling overstuffed duffels made from plastic grain bags.

I *hate* thinking about this kind of shit.

To GET TO WHERE I'm going, I have to take the Line 2 to the 13 to the 15. When did Line 15 happen? I can't even keep track anymore.

The segment they've built runs northeast, from Chaoyang District to Shunyi District out around the Sixth Ring Road, but not as far as where I need to go.

I don't know this part of Beijing very well. When you get out close to the airport, it's villa land, where a lot of the wealthier folks live, Chinese and expat alike. I've met with collectors out here a couple of times: "I want a piece that compliments my color scheme!" kind of people.

Line 15 runs aboveground on this leg. In the dark what I see are flat, empty stretches of land, patches and lines of ghostly trees, remains of older villages surrounded by construction cranes, half-built high-rises, clusters of gleaming mirrored skyscrapers. At one point I glimpse a golf course.

I get off at the end of the line, at Houshayu station. Ribbed grey ceilings, rows of industrial spotlights casting white dots on the grey marble floors, broken up by red columns, all shiny and new. Not many people. It's just past 9:00 P.M.

No taxis either.

"Come on," I mutter. Why are there no taxis? Don't the folks who live past this subway stop need to get home?

They probably all drive their Audis or Beemers or whatever.

On the north side of the station, there's a parking lot. An expanse of cars, most of which look new. I guess they belong to the fancy car dealerships across the street. A ways farther, there's some stadium-size mall thing that might sell furniture.

On the other side of the station, a bank of trees and a broad street, with signs pointing to the Airport Expressway and some other highway. Is this the Sixth Ring Road?

There's a bus stop, but I don't know which bus to take.

I could make a phone call and ask for a ride. But I don't want to do that. Because when it comes to attachments I'd rather not be dealing with, this one is high on my list.

I start to walk to the bus stop when I hear a high-pitched honk.

"Miss! Miss!"

I turn. It's a *modi*, a motorcycle taxi: basically, a three-wheeled motorcycle surrounded by a tin box, the kind of transport you take when you're too broke for a taxi. Not what I'd expect to see out here in Expatlandia.

The driver is an older guy wearing People's Liberation Army cast-off camouflage. He mimes a steering wheel. Even though it's a motorcycle with handlebars.

These things are so totally unsafe.

Oh well, what the fuck.

I stare out the little square window of the *modi*, low enough to the ground so that I'm at eye level with the wheels of the massive blue trucks roaring past us, bouncing up and down on the wooden bench with every little bump in the road. It sounds like someone's hammering on the tin-can cover surrounding me, but maybe that's the backfiring two-stroke engine. We skid around a traffic circle, spraying gravel.

Maybe this was not such a good idea.

But finally we turn off the highway.

New construction. Cranes. A couple rows of old village buildings surrounded by a crumbling brick wall. Clusters of villas, low-rise housing. Developments with names like "Yosemite" and "Palm Beach."

My destination: Fiji Palace Estates.

I'm hoping for hula girls in grass skirts and maybe some tiki torches, but no. It's a cluster of high-rises, maybe ten or twelve stories each. Only two of them look completed. The others are still wrapped in green netting.

I'm looking for Number 5.

There's a guard in a box by an unfinished wall, and once he sees a foreigner inside the *modi*, he barely looks at me, just waves us through.

The landscaping isn't done, but there's a line of skinny young trees in front of an artificial lake and, around the lake, finished town houses with designs that look like a drunken hookup between a Greek temple and a Bavarian castle.

The driver pulls up in front of Number 5.

I pay him. Grab the flimsy metal doorframe for balance, plant my good leg on the ground, and haul myself up and out. Take in a deep breath.

"*Man zou,*" I tell the driver. The Chinese equivalent for "Drive safely," but what it actually means is "Go slowly."

Too late for that.

"YILI."

"John."

He steps aside, and I step across the threshold. I almost stumble, which I tell myself is because my bad leg's still cramped up from the ride in the *modi*. He reaches out to steady me, seems to think better of it. His hand drops.

I steady myself on a low wooden cabinet in the entry and kick off my shoes. Not because I'm comfortable with John. Far from it. But it's rude to walk around in a Chinese home with your shoes on, and I guess I've been here long enough now where it's habit with me, too.

"Slippers," John says. He points at a shoe rack across from the cabinet. Like the cabinet, it's plain, dark wood.

I find a pair that look to be my size. Quilted black cloth, with embroidered flowers on them.

John doesn't look at me, and I don't look at him. I walk past him, into the living room.

Like the rest of the complex, it doesn't feel finished. The walls are white, bare except for one large framed piece of calligraphy, black ink on white paper in a black frame. The floors are some kind of blond wood, or maybe bamboo, or most likely Pergo. There's a couch. Black. Plain. A table by the kitchen, with two black wood chairs. All the same stark design as the stuff in the entry.

"Nice place," I say.

John shrugs. "You like some tea? Maybe beer?"

He knows me. He knows what I like, and it isn't tea. I'm tempted to ask for it anyway, just to fuck with him. But I don't.

"Sure," I say. "A beer would be great."

I watch John retreat to the kitchen. He's wearing fitted black jeans and a T-shirt, his usual. Trim, taut, with some muscle. If I got up close, I'd see a white scar cutting across one eyebrow, a slight shadow of beard framing his sharp cheekbones. A good-looking guy.

His business card says his name is Zhou Zheng'an. I doubt if that's his real name.

Either way, he'll always be Creepy John to me.

Blame it on the first time we met. There I was, thinking I was maybe going to mess around with a cute guy at a party. I had no fucking clue what his agenda really was and what would end up happening between the two of us.

He comes back out with a large Yanjing Draft and two glasses. Hesitates. Then gestures at the table.

Good. I don't think I want to sit on the couch with Creepy John.

He puts the glasses on the table as I limp over there, then goes back into the kitchen. Brings out a second beer. And black-and-red lacquer coasters.

He *would* have coasters.

We sit. He pours. I drink.

"So is this your apartment?" I ask.

John shrugs again.

"Pretty upscale neighborhood," I continue. "I didn't think they paid DSD spies that kind of money. Or are you just on the take like every other cop in China?"

He looks at me. I see anger, but only for a moment. He takes a big swallow of his beer.

I can't help it. I keep going: "Has your ex-fiancée been over? She sees this, maybe she'll change her mind."

He puts down his glass with a thud. On the coaster. "Enough," he says.

Now it's my turn to shrug. Okay. I'll drink, then.

I think about getting hauled away by fucking DSD

plainclothes to a crappy hotel in Outer Fengtai and about how I might not just walk away the next time.

Yeah, I'm pretty pissed off.

"So you wanna hear about my day?"

"Of course. I know you must want something. Otherwise you wouldn't text."

He does a good job sounding like he really doesn't give a shit. Hey, maybe he doesn't. Which is more than fine by me.

Except that I need him. To help me with this DSD situation, right?

"Maybe you already know," I say, and I sound like a total bitch, even to myself.

He shakes his head.

Cool down, McEnroe, I tell myself. He's not going to help you if all you do is try to piss him off.

Which is kind of too bad, because pissing people off seems to be one of my stronger skills.

I tell him what happened. It takes me the entire beer to get through, plus part of his. He doesn't say anything; he just listens, watching me with a level expression. I mostly don't look at him. Instead I stare at my hands.

When I finish, I notice my hands are trembling. Weird. I got through that whole experience without losing my shit, but I feel like I could fall apart right now, just dissolve into a million pieces.

"Do you want another beer, Yili?" John finally asks.

"Sure." My voice cracks. "Thanks."

He returns with the beer. Fills my glass. Hesitates and then fills his. Abruptly sits.

"That guy . . . he is such an *asshole!*" John says, and then he drains about half his glass.

I don't know why this makes me laugh, but it does. "Yeah," I say. "A total asshole."

John doesn't laugh. He's lit up, like someone's flipped his switch, his dark eyes bright, everything about him tense and alive. Angry.

"People like Zhang Jianli, making art, people who say truth in newspaper or on Internet, he wants to arrest people like that. Why?" His voice rises. "Why? Because they threaten China? No. Because of corruption. Because he benefits the way things are now. He doesn't care about real security, for China. He doesn't even know what that means."

"Wow, John," I say. "Keep talking like that, maybe *you'll* be drinking tea with him."

Now he chuckles. "Maybe. Maybe not. He is not even very important. Just a . . . a little man who wants to be a *da wanr*, a big shot. He thinks bothering you and bothering Lao Zhang can help make his name big."

"So what do I do?" I ask. Because I can laugh at John, I can do my best to piss him off, and there's no way that I trust him, but I still need help. And out of everyone I know in China, for this situation? He's the best person to ask.

"Stay out of trouble. Don't do foolish things. I think, if I have some time, I can maybe do something about this guy."

"Do something?"

He waves his hand, that dismissive gesture I see Chinese men make combined with a little head shake, like when you try to get a taxi driver to take you someplace he doesn't want to go.

I probably don't want to know.

"Yili, but I must ask . . ." He hesitates.

"What?"

"Zhang Jianli. You really don't know where he is?"

He stares at me, his dark eyes steady, his expression concerned.

"No. I don't." I stand up. "Thanks for the beer. And fuck you."

I head for the door.

"Yili, please, wait."

I half turn, and I see him reach for me, and he catches my wrist. I pull away.

"Wait," he says again. "I just—"

My hand's on the doorknob, and I'm twisting it to open, and his hand grabs the fleshy part of my shoulder, and he pulls me toward him. I stumble a little, and my tits brush against his hard chest, and then we fall into each other. Before I know it, his mouth finds mine, tongue slipping between my lips, and I'm trying to slip my hand beneath the waistband of those snug jeans. Finally my fingers find his nice, firm butt cheek.

I so was not going to do this.

At least he bought a bed. Okay, a futon, but it's a queen. By the time we land on it, my shirt and bra are off, and he's got my pants pulled down below my ass and his fingers hooked on the band of my panties. I am looking forward to those fingers. I know what he can do with them. Meanwhile I'm trying to slide his T-shirt over his head, but it's caught on one arm, thankfully not the one with the hand that's tugging down my underwear.

I get his shirt off at about the same time that my panties reach my knees, and I'm sucking on his nipple while his fingers stroke and probe, and meanwhile I'm doing my best to release his brave little soldier from the confines of his jeans and boxers.

"Yili," he manages. "No, wait—"

"Would you just fuck me?" I say. "I don't want a marathon tonight, I just—"

His finger thrusts, and I shut up.

WELL, THAT WAS DUMB.

I'm lying on the futon next to John, both of us sweaty and spent. His hand rests lightly on my breast, like it's a shy cat that he wants to pet.

John is not your boyfriend, I tell myself. He's not even a friend with benefits. You can't trust him. The last thing you need to be doing is sleeping with him.

It felt pretty damn good, though. I'm sure way more relaxed than I was when I got here. I don't even feel the need for a Percocet.

"I'm sorry," he murmurs.

"Huh?"

"For asking. About Zhang Jianli."

Things are so much better when he doesn't talk.

I let out a sigh. "If I did know, I wouldn't tell you. But I don't."

We're facing each other now. "I just ask because . . . I need to be sure," he says.

I laugh softly. Because it occurs to me that maybe John doesn't exactly trust me either.

Fair's fair, I guess.

"So are you? Sure?"

He slowly nods. "I don't want anything bad to happen to him. I'll help him if I can. But . . ." He reaches out his hand and touches my cheek. I feel his fingertips there, warm, a little rough. "If it's you or Zhang Jianli, I help you."

My stomach does a kind of flip. Part of me is mad, hearing him talk that way about Lao Zhang. Another part of me feels all teary, because, you know, I believe him. Which means he really likes me.

Don't go there, McEnroe, I tell myself. Just don't.

"I don't want you making some kind of deal," I say. "I mean, me for Jianli. I don't want that."

"I know." John rolls over onto his back. "Anyway, you don't know where he is, no deal to make."

I lie there and think about what I'm going to say next. My heart's pounding. Because I don't know where he is, but I do know something.

What I say is, "Why do they even care? He's an artist. He's not trying to overthrow the CCP. You know that."

"Maybe because his work has political theme."

"Come on, lots of Chinese artists do work with political themes."

John stares at the ceiling. "What they do with Zhang Jianli, it's just a way to remind everyone who is master. Like with dog. With Mimi you have that leash, the kind you can let out and make long. Dog can run around. But you always can control. Can bring the dog back. She can only run so far."

Silence fills the room. There's this big thing that we both know that neither of us is saying.

So finally I say it.

"What about the Game? Did you tell them about it?"

The Game is a video game. Sword of Ill Repute. Kind of like World of Warcraft, based on Chinese mythology, with a lot of magic swords, wise dragons, and flying monks. Completely harmless, right? You create an avatar for yourself and go storm castles or whatever.

Except Lao Zhang figured out a way to use the Game to talk to people privately. To organize.

It wasn't supposed to be anything political. At least that's what Lao Zhang told me later. "The Game, it is another community. A place where you can express your personality, make friends, have common goal. No one say you have to go on quest, collect treasure. Instead maybe you can build something else. Make art. Talk about ideas. Use this Game to play your own."

Lao Zhang was Upright Boar. I was Little Mountain Tiger. Before the Game was compromised.

John had been there, too. And I still don't know the whole story. Whether it was all about spying for the DSD or if he really believed some of it.

And right now . . . I don't know if I want to know the truth.

He lets out a sigh, a hiss between his teeth. "I had to tell them."

I guess I'm not surprised. I'm not even really disappointed. It's what I expected.

He turns to stare at me. His dark eyes look liquid, like water at night.

"I tell them it's just a game."

There's this hard knot in my gut, and I feel like it's uncoiling. I resist it. You can't relax, I tell myself. You gotta keep your guard up.

"Why?"

"You need to ask me this?" He sounds pissed off.

"Well . . . yeah." I sit up. My tits are bouncing around, which I figure maybe is not best for a serious conversation, since John seems to find them distracting. I pull up the sheet. I'm a little cold now anyway.

"Look, do I have to remind you about the night we met? About our first 'date'?" I make the finger quotes. Because now

I'm kind of pissed off. "Everything you told me was a lie, and then you just kept lying. So why am I supposed to believe you now?"

At this he bolts up, tense and angry again, and I shiver a little and try not to show it.

Sometimes I forget, he's kind of a scary guy. And here I am in bed with him.

"You and me, together like this, and you still think I lie to you?" He sounds insulted. Or like he can't believe it.

"I . . ." I take in a breath, and I ask myself, what *do* I think? I have no clue.

I manage a shrug. "So we fucked a couple of times. You know what that means in my life? Either nothing or a great way to get screwed." Tears are starting to dribble down my face, which makes me even madder. I throw off the sheet. Catch a glimpse of the familiar scars on my leg, the missing chunk of flesh, purple in the dim light. "I need to go."

John doesn't say anything. He watches me pull up my jeans, fumble around for my bra, turn my T-shirt right side out. My panties I wad up and stuff in my pocket—I'll throw them in my bag, wherever that is. In the living room, somewhere, with my jacket. My shoes . . . ?

"Hard to find a cab now," John finally says.

"I'll find something," I mutter.

"I'll take you. Just to the subway, if you want."

I almost say no, just out of habit. But it's closing in on ten thirty. I might not even make the last train home.

"Okay," I say. "Thanks."

HE ENDS UP DRIVING me all the way back, in his nice shiny Toyota, because yeah, I missed the last train. As long as he doesn't try to come upstairs, I think, as long as he doesn't do that and my mom doesn't see him, because my mom thinks he's cute and nice and that I should be going out with him. Hah. She has no idea who he really is. I'm thinking about what he did to me the night we met, and what the fuck is wrong with me for ending up in bed with him not once but twice? That's just beyond fucked up, I think.

Though he did wash my dishes. And save my ass. And take care of my dog.

At least he doesn't talk on the long drive back. It's like a replay of the last time, I think. We have some fun—I mean, it's weird, but basically good. He acts like it's a big deal. I get mad. He gets mad. Then we end up not talking to each other and finally go our separate ways.

This is bad, I tell myself. I have to stop doing shit like this.

We're almost to my place, heading west on Dongzhimen, the red lanterns in front of all the hotpot restaurants on Ghost Street still lit, when John breaks the silence.

"I will do what I can, about this situation." He sounds formal. Like it's the end of a business meeting or something. "Just remember what I tell you. Give me some time. Don't look for trouble."

"I don't exactly look for it," I mutter.

John actually snorts. "No. Always these troubles just find you."

I almost snark back. Yeah, like that whole thing with Lao Zhang and the Uighur and the Game was something I looked for. Like I wanted to get blown up in Iraq, or get involved in my ex-husband's shit, or even come to China in the first place.

But then there's the other stuff, the stuff I did seek out, or when I stumbled on it, I didn't run far enough or fast enough.

Like I needed the buzz.

"Believe me, I don't want any more trouble," I say.

It's not until John turns up Jiugulou Dajie, the main street that leads to the *hutong* where my building is, that I finally have to say it. I'm not sure why I feel like I do. Just . . . I don't want to be keeping so many secrets anymore.

"Zhang Jianli says he's coming back to Beijing."

John's head whips around, and he almost misses my alley. "What? You talk to him?"

"Email." Which is only sort of a lie. "I don't know where he is. I really have no idea. But yeah, we email sometimes."

"*Tamade.*" Your all-purpose Chinese expletive. John scrunches up his face like he's getting a sudden headache. "Why? Why does he come back?"

"He felt bad I was having problems, I guess."

"He is here now?"

"I don't think so. Not that I know of anyway."

"If he is somewhere safe, he should just stay away."

"I know. I told him not to come. He won't listen."

"Did you tell him what happened today?"

I shake my head. "I tell him that, it'll just make him come back faster."

We've reached the gate in front of my building, manned by the usual night guard, a middle-aged guy named Dongfeng with a thatch of greying hair and sleepy eyes who spends a lot of time playing Angry Birds on his smartphone.

"When he comes back, Yili, you have to tell me," John says.

"Why? So you can turn him in?"

John stares straight ahead. "I don't want to."

"But you will."

"*Someone* will." He grinds the heels of his palms against

his temples. Maybe he really does have a headache. "I have to think of way . . . think of way we can be safe."

"Who? You and me?"

His hands drop. "All of us."

I almost believe him.

"But mostly you." Now he does look at me, but it's so dark that I can't really see his expression. "Because you have connection to Zhang Jianli, if they think you lie . . ."

I shudder. And then I shrug it off. "They'll kick me out of the country. Whatever."

"Maybe," he says.

Or maybe not.

Getting kicked out of China could be the best-case scenario.

"Maybe I can find out what they want from Zhang Jianli, what they say he did," John says, and he's making an effort to sound calm. Like it's no big deal. "He is just an artist. Maybe it isn't so bad."

I don't know who he's trying to convince: me or himself.

"It doesn't matter what he did." Suddenly I'm so tired that I can't even hold my head up anymore. "It's whatever they want it to be, right?"

Because if there's anything I've learned, it's that sometimes there's no reason for any of it. Sometimes it's just wrong place, wrong time. Somebody with power gets a bug up his ass. Like that musical where the hungry guy steals the loaf of bread and the cop gets the hard-on of all hard-ons over it.

John rests his hand on mine, just for a moment, then pulls it away, like he's embarrassed.

"Try not to worry, Yili."

Right.

CHAPTER FIVE

THIS IS THE KIND of place I fucking hate.

First off: I've been warned by Vicky Huang that where I'm meeting Gugu is going to be expensive.

"Dress up!" she told me over the phone, and to make it abso-fucking-lutely clear I get it, she sends me a package via FedEx—clothes.

Expensive clothes. Designer clothes. Armani and Marc Jacobs and Stella McCartney. I know this because I check the labels, also because you can just tell with expensive things, the way they're cut, the way they feel.

When I put them on, I can't help it, I go to the bathroom to put on some mascara, see myself in the mirror, and think, Okay, I look kind of hot. We went through this whole thing before, how to dress me for my first meeting with Sidney, and the rule seemed to be if it costs a lot, it's probably okay. This outfit looks pretty much like the last one: a black jacket, skinny low-rise pants, and a button-front shirt that's pretending to be a men's shirt, except it's not (there's more cleavage involved)— in black this time. "Slouchy boyfriend cut," according to Lucy Wu, which is actually a real high-fashion description. Who knew?

But you need to be careful accepting people's gifts.

Just go there, I tell myself in the subway. Meet Gugu. Meet

this American guy. Try to get a read on his "moral character." Pop smoke and go home.

"There" is a Beijing club that I've heard of but had managed to avoid—Entránce.

Entránce is in Chaoyang, near Workers Stadium, a part of Beijing that's all wide roads and big buildings, nothing that really sticks in your head, except for things such as a huge neon sign for MY LIKE AESTHETIC PLASTIC HOSPITAL GROUP stuck on the side of a building that resembles a giant plastic footstool, like the ones you'd find in a preschool. The kind of area where crossing the street is a major hike because it's six or eight lanes wide.

Normally I wait for a pack of other pedestrians to cross with, safety in numbers and all, and I feel like they have a better sense of when it's safe to go, given that traffic laws are still a little more theoretical than actual a lot of the time here, but it's already 11:00 P.M., and there aren't all that many people on the streets around here after the end of the business day.

I hump it across, my leg throbbing. Not like I'm going to get a pain-free evening when I have to do something I really don't want to do, right?

I should have taken a cab, I think, except sometimes you can't get a cab to drop you where you want to go because it's too much of a hassle for them to turn around in the traffic, where so many streets have iron barriers.

Cars speed by me, a couple of them making illegal left turns, and I grip one of those iron fences, waist-high, painted white, take a moment to wait for a gap in the rushing cars, to catch my breath. For some reason I'm thinking about this time in the Sandbox when I was the convoy medic and we were stuck because this bus had gotten blown up in the middle of the intersection, a couple of cars, too, and we couldn't get through. So all of us stop, the Humvees, the KBR trucks in between. And we wait. And it's so fucking hot, and I'm staring out a rippled safety window from the backseat of a Humvee at the busted asphalt and these painted cement buildings with rusted balconies. There are no people around. They're out of sight, hiding. Waiting for something else to blow.

Cross the street, desert queen, I tell myself. Nothing's going to blow up here. I've had some bad shit happen in China, but none of it involved things blowing up.

I make it across the street.

From the sidewalk there's nothing much to Entránce, just a sparkling white dome kind of entrance thing backing up against an anonymous wall of squat glassy buildings that occupy the block.

Inside the dome is a metal detector flanked by two bouncers—a Chinese guy and a black guy, both with shaved heads and bouncer-size shoulders. Great. Now I have to worry if the titanium rod and screws in my leg are going to set off the fucking metal detector. Usually it's fine, but every once in a while . . .

"Private party tonight," the black guy says in English. He has an accent, African, but I don't know from where.

"I'm invited."

Lucky me, I'm on the list, and I don't set off the metal detector. I hobble over to the escalators heading down into the club proper, bass thumping louder as I descend.

Someone could blow up Entránce and I wouldn't be too upset.

Everything's all white, plastic, and shiny. A dance track shakes the floor, bass vibrating through my rib cage, the highs loud enough to cut glass. My ears already ring from getting blown up and all. I don't need this.

I find a cocktail napkin and tear off a couple strips, roll those up, and stuff them in my ears.

There are two or three levels to the club, a main pit with a couple of bars and a stripper platform and pole in the middle of it all—I know it's a stripper platform/pole because there's a white woman, Russian maybe, wearing a fringed bikini thing and platform shoes, gyrating on it. Upstairs is filled with white egg-shaped booths wedged up against a Plexiglas wall topped with chrome. The guests are mostly young. They look like too much money. I've seen plenty of rich people in the art crowd, but this is different—more obvious bling—designer labels, the real thing, not *shanzhai* rip-offs, diamond-studded iPhone cases, outsize jewelry, and two-thousand-dollar watches. There are guys in white shirts and black jackets with headsets all over the place, keeping tabs.

I look for where the headsets are clustered the thickest, figuring that's where I'll find Gugu and his inevitable posse.

Sure enough.

In the main pit surrounding the stripper pole, a waiter deposits an ice bucket of champagne in front of a group of guys. Yeah, there are women around, too, but most of them are on the periphery—chairs pushed back from where the men gather, talking mostly to one another. Glasses of red wine sit in ranks on an adjacent table.

I recognize Gugu right off—Vicky emailed me his photo. Early twenties, wearing a two-hundred-dollar T-shirt under a military-style jacket, except the camouflage pattern is done in acid-bright greens and reds. Some designer bullshit, no doubt. He's a pretty boy, long bangs hanging limply over one eye like a teen idol, but when I look closely, I see Sidney's bony nose and high cheeks. There's a girl hanging on his shoulder who looks like she's about sixteen, wearing a rhinestone-studded trucker cap with skull patches, ED HARDY embroidered in red on the brim. Next to her is another girl with pigtails who looks even younger, dressed in some kind of designer sailor suit— high-fashion anime.

Sitting on the left is a white guy. Thirty-something. Maybe older. Dark hair, broad face. Good-looking, I guess. Heavy-lidded eyes, like he's half asleep or drunk. Full red lips, curved in a slight smile.

The "bad influence." A guy by the name of Marsh Brody.

I really don't want to do this.

"Introductions taken care of!" Vicky told me. "You just tell Gugu that Mr. Cao wants him to look at art, for museum project. It is his filial duty."

I mean, how lame is that?

Especially because the whole museum thing was actually my idea—an art museum in Xingfu Cun, the ghost city Sidney Cao built.

When I say the museum was my idea, what I mean is it was a line of bullshit I spouted to get myself out of a jam, nothing I'd thought of in advance or knew anything about or had any intention of doing. I was just trying to appeal to Sidney's ego— "Do something for your legacy." Meaning, *So your three kids won't just sell off your billion-dollar collection after you die.*

It worked at the time. I got out of the jam. But shit like this always comes back and bites me in the ass.

Case in point.

Gugu turns toward the girl in the rhinestone baseball cap, smiles, and pours her some champagne. Marsh leans back in his chair, watching the two, eyes at half-mast, still with that little smile. Sailor Girl drifts over to him, glass of champagne in one hand, cigarette in the other. He grins, reaches up, and puts his arm around her, hand brushing her sideboob. She perches on his lap for a moment. I can't tell if she's comfortable there or not.

Just get it over with, I tell myself.

But maybe have a drink first.

I grab a glass of wine off the tray of a passing waiter and take a slug. Although I'm not the world's most educated wino, I can tell this is pretty good stuff. It's the kind of thing you get an education in, hanging out with rich people.

Slow down, McEnroe, I tell myself.

I find an empty spot against the railing, where I'm not in Gugu and Marsh's direct line of sight but I can still keep an eye on them, and sip my wine. The music pounds, the beats slamming into my chest, light show keeping time, like synchronized fireworks.

I really want to get out of here.

I drink some more, about two-thirds of the glass, just enough to feel the beginnings of a comforting buzz. Put the glass down on the bar and approach Gugu's table.

"*Cao xiansheng, ni hao,*" I say, practically shouting over the music. "Sorry to bother you."

He looks up. Pushes his limp hair off his face and stares at me.

"I'm Ellie McEnroe. Your father wanted us to meet."

Gugu continues to stare. His bangs start drifting back over one eye. I'm thinking either Vicky Huang screwed up this introduction (unlikely) or he wants nothing to do with me.

"To discuss the museum project," I say, feeling my cheeks flush.

He sweeps his hair off his face again and finally nods. *"Qing zuo,"* he says, indicating a chair across from him and to his right.

Please sit.

I do. He tilts his head at Rhinestone-Cap Girl and mutters something I can't hear. She straightens up, grabs a glass of wine from the table, and hands it to me. Behind her, Sailor Girl covers her mouth with her hand and giggles.

"Xiexie," I say. She responds with an eye roll. I'm guessing she doesn't much like playing waitress.

I sip the wine. "Very good," I say, because it is.

Gugu shrugs.

Boy, we're having some fun now. I wonder how long I'm obligated to do this.

Meet his son, meet this American, offer your expert opinion.

"So," Gugu finally says, in English. "You're involved with my father's museum."

"Yes," I say. "Yes, I am."

"And he wants you to talk to me."

I nod.

He tosses back his drink. Lifts his hand to call a waiter. "Why?"

"Well, I represent some emerging contemporary Chinese artists," I say, and I'm kind of proud of myself for remembering the proper art lingo. "Your father wanted to get your opinion on some of the work. To see if it belongs in the museum."

Gugu snorts. "What do *I* know about it? Why ask me? I'm not even interested in these things."

"Well . . . uh, he wants you to be involved. Because it's kind of a big deal. You know, it's his legacy and all."

He stares at me with the eye not covered by the hair curtain. "If *I* am involved, then why not my brother and my sister?"

I sip my wine. It's a good point.

So I fake it.

"They will be involved, too. This is just my first meeting."

I say this, and I'm thinking, Oh, great. Because getting involved with one of Sidney Cao's kids is bad enough, and now I've opened the door to the other two. It's like what you're not supposed to do with vampires, right? Invite them in.

"I see," Gugu says.

The waiter arrives with his drink. Some amber stuff in a tumbler. Gugu tosses it back. Beads of sweat rise on his forehead. I'm guessing he's getting pretty plastered.

"So what do you want?" He hiccups. Leans back in his chair, legs splayed. "Meaning, what does my father want me to do?"

We didn't exactly cover that part of the plan. So once again I fake it.

"Just like I said. Look at some work. And talk about the . . . the philosophy. And the goals. Of the museum."

Gugu laughs. "The goals are whatever my father wants them to be."

"Yeah." I drink some wine. I really suck at this—being all undercover. Getting people to tell me what I need to find out.

Besides, I know he's right. This whole museum thing is about Sidney's ego. Even if Gugu did get involved, decided he really gave a shit about art, and about a museum, and about his dad's legacy, I'm pretty sure if he and Sidney disagreed about something, Gugu would end up on the losing end of the decision.

"I think he's just hoping you'll take an interest," I finally say. "Because, you know, someone will need to be in charge after he's gone."

"Fuck that," Gugu pronounces. He holds up his hand for

the waiter. "Let Tiantian or Meimei take an interest. I have better things to do."

Tiantian, the older brother. Meimei, the girl in the middle.

"Like what?" I think to ask.

Gugu shrugs. "Maybe movies." He leans over and mutters something to Rhinestone-Cap Girl again. She pouts a little. Tilts her head at Sailor Girl, who grabs another glass of wine off the table and brings it to me, pausing a little to execute a sort of bad charm-school curtsy.

I take the glass. "Thank you."

"I'm Celine." Now *she* tilts her head at Rhinestone-Cap Girl, who has resumed her barnacle duty at Gugu's side. "That is Betty."

"I'm Ellie."

"Very happy to meet you."

"Likewise."

She giggles. She seems to do that a lot. "This is such an interesting party. Don't you think?"

"I, uh . . . yeah."

"You don't really think so?" Her head's tilted down, and she's looking at me through thick mascaraed eyelashes, a little smile on her face.

"Celine, why are you bothering her?" Gugu snaps.

"She's not bothering me," I say, because I don't want any trouble and besides, he's being kind of a dick.

"Sometimes Gugu is too polite," Celine says. "He doesn't really know how to have fun." She blows a thin stream of cigarette smoke in Gugu's direction.

Okay, maybe she's kind of a bitch, too. But looking at Gugu's sweating face and bored expression, I have to wonder if she's right.

"Movies, huh," I say to Gugu. "You want to make them?"

"Sure, why not? Culture and soft power are part of the new Five-Year Plan." He laughs.

Next to him Marsh laughs, too.

The guy I'm supposed to be evaluating for his moral character.

I turn to him. Put on my best fake smile. Which I'm pretty sure isn't very good. "I'm Ellie McEnroe," I say.

He smiles. "Marsh Brody." He's got a gunmetal shadow of beard outlining his broad cheeks, shading his jaw. I'm guessing he's the kind of guy who cultivates a two-day stubble.

We shake. His hand lingers. One of his fingers strokes the back of my palm, ever so lightly.

Yeah, that kind of guy.

"You live in Beijing?" he asks.

"Uh-huh. You?"

He tilts his head to one side. "Part-time. I'm back and forth between here and LA."

"LA. So are you in movies or TV, something like that?"

"Something like that." He thinks to smile again. "I do a few different things. Mostly I try to connect Western businesses with the right Chinese partners."

"Oh, yeah." I smile back. "You're a consultant, right?"

"Right."

We stare at each other. I get the feeling he's irritated. But it's not like I called him an English teacher.

"Hey," Gugu says suddenly, his hand flopping open-palmed on one thigh, "let's go somewhere. This is boring."

Rhinestone-Cap Girl, Betty, rests her head on his shoulder. "But this is your party," she says with a pout.

Behind her, Celine smiles.

"So? It can go on without me. Marsh, you want to leave, right?"

Marsh nods.

Gugu turns in my direction. "You want to come along?"

"I, uh . . ."

Have absolutely no desire to go anywhere with these guys.

"Sure. I just, uh . . . need to go to the restroom."

FUCK.

I hold my hands under the automatic sink, bow my head, and watch the water circle the drain, and I wonder how I'm going to get out of this. All the alarms I have are pinging, but bugging out has risks, too. Because the last thing I need to do is piss off Sidney. We're friends now. I'm pretty sure I don't want to be on his enemies list.

I exit the bathroom.

Unlike the rest of the club, this part's done in black: black paint and black vinyl. Tiny spotlights guide me back out into the main room. I start to follow them.

"Hey."

He's come out of the men's room just ahead of me. Marsh.

"Hi," I say.

He stands there for a second, blocking my way down the hall. "You coming?"

He takes a few steps forward. All of a sudden, he's standing too close, and I back up without thinking about it, trying to get some space. My butt touches the black wall.

"Aren't you with Celine?"

"Define 'with.'"

Marsh is right in front of me. He stretches out an arm, places his palm flat against the wall, right by my head.

"Why don't you come along? It'll be fun. Promise."

I can feel his hot breath on my ear. My heart's thumping hard.

"I don't think so," I say.

"Too bad." He shrugs and backs off. "Next time."

FUCK THIS, I'M GOING home.

"Yeah," I say to Gugu, "it's getting a little late for me. I've got some appointments in the morning, and anyway, maybe we can meet in the next couple of days to . . . uh, talk about the museum. See some artists."

We're standing over by the stripper pole, where Betty, Celine, and a bunch of other girls are dancing to Lady Gaga. They look like kids.

"Sure," Gugu says with a yawn. "Maybe you can meet my brother and sister." He snorts. "We can all plan this museum together."

"Sounds great. I'll give you my card."

Not like he needs it, I'm pretty sure Vicky Huang would tell him how to get a hold of me. But I do the polite thing anyway: reach into my shoulder bag for my card case, pull out a business card, hold it in both hands, and extend it to Gugu. Maybe it's corny, but why take the chance?

Gugu grasps the card with both of *his* hands. Gives it a cursory glance and places it in the breast pocket of his psychedelic fatigues. So he has *some* manners.

Behind him, Marsh lifts his hand. "Don't I get one?"

Like I want to give this asshole my card.

What difference does it make? I ask myself. If he wants to find me, he will.

I extract another card and give it to him, one-handed. He takes it, smiling, and slips the card into his jeans.

By now Celine and Betty have drifted over. Celine smiles at me. Reaches into her tiny clutch purse and pulls out a gold card case. Extracts a card of her own.

"Here is mine," she says. She also holds it out with both hands. Almost like she's making fun of the whole ritual. I take it. In the dark light of the club, I can't really see what it says, but it's red, with yellow characters.

"You can look at my website, and my Weibo," she says. "You know Weibo, right?"

"Sure." Weibo is like Chinese Twitter.

There's something sly about her smile. "Maybe you can learn more about modern Chinese culture."

"Great," I say. "Thanks."

Whatever.

Now I have to give her a card back, and since I give her one, I figure I'd better offer one to Betty, too.

Betty actually studies it, like you're supposed to, which kind of surprises me, given that she's been kind of bitchy the entire time I've been here. She nods a little awkwardly, the rhinestone ball cap concealing the expression on her face.

BY THE TIME I make it back to my apartment, it's past 1:00 A.M. Mimi slides off her spot on the couch with a thump and trots over to greet me. Somehow she knows when it's me coming in. She never barks. Maybe she can hear my limp.

There's a note from my mom stuck up on the fridge, held there by a magnet with a portrait of Hu Jintao done up like Colonel Sanders, below his face the slogan PRC—I'M LOVIN' IT!

"At Andy's," the note says. *"We walked Mimi around midnight. Hope you had a fun evening!"*

Oh, yeah, it was a blast.

"On how many levels of bad was that?" I say to Mimi.

She whines softly.

"You want a treat? You been a good dog?"

I grab a hunk of dried beef from a jar in the pantry. I am way too paranoid to buy her any of the premade doggie treats from here—too many food-contamination issues. "Sit! *Zuo!*"

She sits. Holds up one paw like one of those Japanese ceramic cats. "Good girl!" I give her the treat. "Let's go watch some TV, okay?"

First, though, I'm getting out of these clothes. I go into my bedroom and start to undress, and all of a sudden I can't get out of them fast enough.

I throw on some sweats and a T-shirt. Grab a cold beer and a glass and head for the couch.

Maybe I shouldn't have bailed. I didn't really complete the mission. I'm going to have to tell Sidney *something*, but what?

Marsh is trouble, I'm pretty sure, and I guess I can tell Sidney that, but on the other hand, given Sidney, do I want to be responsible for what might happen to Marsh without being *really* sure?

Though I'm sure he's a total douche.

This picture flashes in my head, a Roman-emperor dude like from a cheesy gladiator movie giving the thumbs-down. Then some other pictures, about what happens to people who get in Sidney's way.

The problem is, there are too many bad pictures in my head just waiting to show themselves.

I sit on the couch with my dog next to me, her head resting on my good leg, and I sip my beer. I'm feeling kind of sick, that cold nausea I get deep in my gut when I fuck something up really bad.

Somehow, when Sidney asked me to do this, all I could think about was what he could do for me—or *to* me, depending. I didn't really think about what might happen to Gugu's "bad influence." I mean, I thought about it in the abstract, a little. But now there's a living, breathing guy in my head. And even if he *is* a scumbag . . . do I want to be responsible for that?

First do no harm, right?

You haven't fucked it up yet, I tell myself.

I'll think of something. Play things with Sidney and/or Vicky as best I can. Tell them I don't know enough yet, that I need more time. Maybe I'll actually do some work on this museum project, who knows?

Right now I'm just glad to be home with my dog and a Yanjing Draft.

The evening those guys are having, it's the kind that ends up with somebody running over a migrant vendor with a Ferrari, or with said Ferrari smashed to pieces against a freeway abutment—with or without dead hookers. It's how the *fu er dai*, the second-generation rich, tend to roll.

Bugging out was the right thing to do.

CHAPTER SIX

I'm sitting in bed with my laptop checking the English-language China gossip sites like I do a lot of mornings, this time with a little more interest than usual, because hey, what if Gugu and Marsh *did* crash a Ferrari into a concrete wall?

But if something went wrong last night, it hasn't made it onto chinaSMACK yet.

I take another sip of strong, black coffee. Not as good as the stuff Harrison served up the other day, which is one of the problems with hanging out around rich people—they always have better stuff than I do.

Or maybe that's *why* I hang out around them.

I glance over at the designer clothes heaped on this armchair that I never actually sit on—it's just where I throw clothes. They're wrinkled, and I can smell the cigarette smoke on them from here. Discarded lizard skins.

I drink more coffee. At least I'm not hungover, just tired and headachy and dry-eyed from all the smoke and the noise and not enough sleep. But I'm still feeling all mature for not doing anything totally stupid last night.

That is, until my iPhone rings.

"Vicky Huang. I have Mr. Sidney Cao for you."

Fucking great.

"Hello, Ms. Ellie!" Sidney, as usual, sounds weirdly cheerful.

Though maybe it isn't weird to be cheerful when you can buy anything you want. "I hope you had a nice evening?"

"Yes. I did. Pretty much."

"And how was Gugu?" He's still all Mr. Happy, but it's forced this time. Because yeah, actually, you *can't* buy everything.

"He seems . . . I don't know, pretty good." I mean, what else can I say? *He seems like a bitter, drunk parasite?* Which, you know, might be a little of a pot/kettle scenario, but I'm at least doing no harm, right?

"And you meet this friend of his? This American, Marsh Brody?"

My heart starts pounding. "I did."

"And what are your thoughts?"

Stay Hippocratic, McEnroe.

"You know, it's a little hard for me to say. It's not like I really got to know him. There wasn't enough time. And it was, kind of . . . loud."

"I see." He no longer sounds cheerful.

"We're going to meet again," I say quickly. "To talk about the museum. With Meimei and Tiantian."

"All three of my children?" I can hear a cautious little happy note under the surprise. And I'm thinking, Oh, shit, I have stepped in it again. I mean, I have no idea what the relationship between the kids is like, except from what Gugu said last night—it sounded like he wasn't close to the other two. Who knows if I can actually get the three of them together to discuss Sidney's art obsession? If Sidney has some kind of fantasy about a family reunion and I don't deliver . . .

"So this . . . this Marsh Brody. He is interested in art?"

"Yeah. Well, movies, I think."

"Movies." He snorts. "Those are not art."

"Well, you know, some contemporary artists, they've been really influenced by film," I manage, and I'm not sure where I pulled that little gem from, but it sounds credible, right?

"Maybe, in older days of classics. Now just men in tight underwear and things blowing up."

"Right."

"Vicky can help arrange this meeting," he says, and I can tell I'm being dismissed. "After, you can tell me your impressions."

"Sure. Great. Looking forward to it."

Shit.

I flop down on the bed, my laptop balanced on my pelvis, wondering if it's too early for beer.

It's 10:45 A.M. That's too early.

Out in the kitchen, I hear the scrape and squeak of the steel door opening and Mimi's toenails skittering and dancing on the vinyl kitchen floor, along with an excited little "Woof!"

Must be my mom.

"Well, hello, Mimi! Are you a good dog? Are you a good dog?" Now Mimi's nails are clicking on the floor like a flamenco dancer. Of course she loves my mom, who always gives her scraps from the taco projects.

I lie there a moment longer with my arm over my eyes. I'm so not ready, not for any of this.

But my door's open, so my mom pokes her head in. She's wearing one of her Christian T-shirts, one that says HOT MESS WITHOUT JESUS.

"Hi, hon," she says. "You want some breakfast?"

"No, that's okay."

"You sure?"

"Yeah."

"Late night?" She smiles.

I have to push down the rush of anger. I don't know whether she thinks I was out having fun or what, but it's none of her fucking business, and anyway, it wasn't fun.

"Yeah, kind of." I'm not a great actor, but I've gotten better at faking things the last few years. Mostly by shutting up and nodding a lot.

Lucky for me, sometimes my mom is pretty oblivious. Or she's acting, too. Tell you the truth, I'm not really sure anymore.

"Andy and I were thinking about driving out to Miyun in a little bit. Do you want to come? The weather's supposed to be nice today, and the air's better out there."

She's looking at me with that same look Mimi gives me sometimes, the liquid eyes asking for something, some kindness, maybe.

Or a treat.

I'm such a shit.

"I'd like to," I say. "I've got some stuff I gotta do. Maybe if things don't get too busy."

"Okay. Just let me know. We have some time." She turns to go, then stops. "You sure you don't want some eggs? I have pork belly."

"That sounds good," I finally say. "Thanks."

After she leaves, I lie there a few more minutes. I tell myself I need to get up. To do something. But what?

I can't sell Lao Zhang's artwork right now, given this whole DSD situation. They're already looking at him for "economic crimes," tax evasion, something like that—whatever they can use to make a case—and Harrison thinks we'll only compound the problem by continuing to sell his work. Or anyone else's work, for that matter. Because even if it's all about getting

Lao Zhang, I'm the one whose name is on the paperwork as "Director of Operations."

If I can't sell any artwork, I'm not going to be able to afford this apartment much longer. My craptastic disability payment doesn't come close to covering it. And my lease is up in a month. If they raise the rent on me . . .

There are other jobs I can get, I tell myself. I used to be a bartender. I could do that again. Or, given Harrison's new coffee project, maybe I could be a barista.

That is, if I don't get arrested.

Why am I staying in this country again?

Because there's nothing left for me back in the States. No job for me to do. No future that I can see.

Because for all the enemies I have here, I have plenty there, too.

I finally sit up.

Sure, I'll have some breakfast. Maybe I'll even go to Miyun with Mom and Andy. It would be good for Mimi to get some exercise, to breath some semi-fresh air.

Good for me, too.

Instead what happens is this: First, my phone rings again. "Pressure Drop" by Toots and the Maytals. The ringtone I use for Vicky Huang.

"Tonight you can go to meet Meimei," she tells me.

"I can?"

"Yes. At seven P.M. For dinner. She is in Beijing today. She has favorite place. I send directions."

"Okay," I say, figuring it's pointless to argue.

"Expensive." Vicky nearly hisses the word. "Wear nice things."

I glance over at the pile of smoke-soaked clothes on my chair. "Will do."

I fall back onto the bed again. I guess this means I probably don't have time for an outing to Miyun with Mom and Andy. Which on the one hand is a relief.

On the other I kind of wanted to do it. For the clean air and all.

The next thing that happens is I hear the chime that tells me I have incoming email.

Honestly, I don't even want to sit up again. Because it's probably junk mail, or if it's relating to the art business, there's nothing I can do about it anyway.

But I do sit up, because I figure I should take one of my fancy shirts to the laundry and see if they can have it ready for me in time for this fancy dinner with another one of Sidney's insane children. I mean, I have to figure she's insane, based on my experiences with the family so far.

Whatever. As long as she pays the tab.

I'm not expecting the email that's landed in my inbox.

"You Cannot Miss This!"

My heart starts to thud, before I even take it all in.

"This is our Pick of the Year! We don't see this slowing down! We know many of you like momentum!"

Spam, you'd think, right? For some bullshit phony stock. But I've gotten this email before. It's a signal, and I know what it means.

"WHAT DO YOU THINK?"

My mom hovers near the table, clasping her hands in that way she does when she's nervous.

"Really good."

She's made these spicy eggs with bits of pork belly, chives, and her homemade pico de gallo, stuffed into something that's a cross between a flatbread like you'd find in Xi'an and a thick corn tortilla.

I'm not lying. In spite of the fact that the last thing on my mind right now is eating, I actually have to stop and savor what she's made, because it's delicious.

"I wish I could find more avocado," she says. "It would be good with some avocado, don't you think?"

"Everything's good with avocado." I shovel more into my mouth.

"It's not exactly Mexican food, but it's better than most of what I've had here. I don't understand why you can't find good tacos. I think Chinese people would like tacos. *Andy* likes them."

"Mmm." I glance at the clock on the microwave. I need to get going. "So I can't go to Miyun with you guys. Something's come up. A meeting."

"On a Saturday?"

"Yeah, well, you know. Artists," I mumble, and I push the rest of the eggs onto my fork with the last piece of flatbread.

"Oh well, I understand."

"Thing is . . ." I look up. She's still standing there with her hands clasped, like she hasn't moved. I can feel my cheeks reddening, and I'm not sure why. "Can you take Mimi with you? You know, so she can get some fresh air?"

I mean, why should I be embarrassed? Mom and Andy love that dog.

"Sure, we could do that." She frowns a little. "There really aren't a lot of places for dogs in Beijing, are there? You'd think with all the dogs here, they'd have a dog park or two."

"Yeah, well, the whole pet thing is pretty new. Lots of places in China, they still think of dogs as taco stuffing."

My mom shudders. "I don't know," she mutters. "I really do like it here, but . . . there're some things I just can't get used to."

I shrug. I could say the same thing about anywhere.

I TAKE THE SUBWAY to the Yonghegong stop and find a coffeehouse south of the Lama Temple, past the gilt-embellished peaked roofs that rise above the red-washed walls. Typical coffee place—menu drawn with multicolored chalk on a blackboard, scarred wood tables, mismatched chairs, curling black-and-white photos of old Beijing and Red Guards stuck up on burlap walls with thumbtacks. The brewed coffee here sucks, so I order an Americano. Get out my new MacBook Air, launch my virtual private network, and open a browser.

The spam stock email was a signal from Lao Zhang, telling me to log on to the Great Community.

No network is safe. Anything on your computer or on the Internet can be accessed. Hacked. I know that. But I at least don't want to make it easy.

I copy the string of numbers from the bottom of the email that look like random computer gibberish, place it into my browser's address bar, put periods in the right places, and hit ENTER.

And find myself on the "Welcome" page of the Great Community.

On a beach, where choppy grey waves crash against the sand, an animation that looks like it was done in brushstrokes. A three-legged dog that barks at an incoming wave. The giant Mao statue, which before was faded and half buried in sand, looks even more battered now, encrusted in barnacles that have climbed up to the top button of its tunic. It's about to fall over, propped up by the outstretched arm holding a Little Red Book. Farther up the beach, one of the Twin Towers *has* toppled. The other one sways in the pixel breeze.

It's a virtual community, a secure environment that Lao Zhang created after he disappeared from Beijing last year, where he could make art, where it was safe to hang out and chat. I don't know who hosts it, where the servers are, who's paying for it. Better not to know, right?

At first it was just for the two of us—at least that's what he told me—but I don't know if that's really true. Other people showed up pretty quickly. Other artists and musicians and writers. He kept adding to the place, and so did the newbies, until there was a whole virtual village, with galleries, houses, nightclubs, stores, bizarre sculptures, performance pieces. A safe place to say what you wanted, be who you wanted.

Funny thing is, I never spent all that much time here, especially after it got busy. I never even gave my avatar a cool outfit. Just the same jeans and white T-shirt she was created with. There wasn't all that much for me to do here, other than chat with Lao Zhang. Some of the concerts were okay, and some of the art, but I wasn't making any art. Wasn't playing any music. The Great Community was just another place where I stood around and watched other people do stuff.

I figure I'll take the path along the cliffs that leads directly to my house. Usually the three-legged dog runs ahead, stopping now and again to wag its tail and bark, until I catch up.

This time the dog does something different. It turns inland, on a different path, the one that leads to the town square.

The last time I was here, there was lots of stuff going on. All kinds of avatars, text boxes popping up faster than I could read them. A poetry reading by a fountain that spouted multi-colored sprays of gems, butterflies, stars. A couple of dinosaurs lumbering through the plaza. Who knows why?

Today it's empty. Hardly anyone here. The fountain is motionless, a pool of standing water. A lone avatar dressed in a samurai outfit stands by a building that looks like a cross between a cathedral and a rocket ship. As I pass, the building suddenly pixelates. Then vanishes. Just like that. Deleted.

The samurai avatar stands there for a moment longer. Then he, too, disappears. Pop. Gone.

I shudder. The real me, I mean. My avatar continues to trot through the deserted town, following the three-legged dog to the path that leads to my house.

THE HOUSE LOOKS THE same.

Same stone house, same wooden deck, same pine trees around it. The orange cat sleeps in a spot of sun by the front door. Purrs when I cross the threshold.

Same as always.

I go inside. The lights come up as usual. I sit my avatar down on the couch facing the wall-size window that looks out over the animated beach.

There's no time for even the giant goldfish animation before the knock at my door—this script has sound, two hard raps on hollow wood.

I click on the door to open it.

In the Great Community, he's called Monastery Pig. My friend, Lao Zhang.

YILI, NI HAO, appears in a text box above his head.

Like me, he never did anything fancy with his avatar. Just cargo shorts, a black T-shirt, and a beanie skullcap—the hat changes, from time to time. I've seen him in baseball hats, Mao caps, even in a cowboy hat once. But today it's the beanie.

NI HAO, I type back.

His avatar hovers by the couch.

QING ZUO, I say. Please sit.

He does.

It's weird, you know? It's like we're sitting next to each other on a real couch and I'm watching the whole thing outside my own body. Staring at a screen. And I know that he's somewhere—who knows where?—staring at a screen, too.

WHAT'S GOING ON HERE? I finally ask.

I'M COMING TO BEIJING. IN A WEEK OR SO.

WHY?

Truth is, I already know why. Or at least what he told me. He said he felt bad about the position he'd put me in.

IT IS JUST TIME.

YOU SHOULDN'T, I say. IT'S NOT A GOOD IDEA. ANYWAY, I'M FINE.

I NEED TO, he says. TIME TO FINISH THE PIECE.

WHAT PIECE?

THE PERFORMANCE PIECE. THE BIG ONE. MADE UP FROM ALL THE LITTLE PIECES. THE WHOLE CYCLE.

WHAT THE FUCK?! I type.

I mean, I know Lao Zhang used to do performance art. Painting himself red and strumming a ukulele on top of the Drum Tower, singing the chorus to Nirvana's "Smells Like Teen Spirit." Steering a little boat through the Houhai lake with a statue of Chairman Mao in the prow. Whatever it meant. I wasn't always sure.

This time I don't have to know what the new piece is about to know that it scares me.

DON'T DO IT, I type, pounding the keys. JUST DON'T. IT'S NOT WORTH IT.

OF COURSE IT IS.

We sit there in silence for a minute.

WHAT'S HAPPENING HERE? I type. WHERE IS EVERYONE? WHY ARE THINGS DISAPPEARING?

I TOLD THEM THEY SHOULD GO. IF THEY BUILD IT, THEY SHOULD DECIDE WHETHER TO DELETE IT OR LEAVE IT.

BUT WHY SHOULD THEY GO?

BECAUSE MAYBE THIS IS NOT SAFE PLACE ANYMORE. OR WON'T BE SOON.

Like after you get yourself arrested for some dumb-ass performance art? I want to scream.

But I can't scream. I can only type it with the CAPS LOCK on.

A series of laughing emoticons appears in Lao Zhang's text bubble.

I PROMISE IT WILL NOT BE DUMB-ASS, he says.

Finally I have to ask it. Even though I kind of hate myself for asking. Because what's the point? I know it's not going to end well.

CAN I SEE YOU? I type. BEFORE?

There's a long silence. His avatar blinks on the couch.

MAYBE NOT A GOOD IDEA.

WHY? I type. Though I think I already know.

BECAUSE MAYBE THEY ARE WATCHING YOU.

I snort with laughter.

Yeah, you think?

CHAPTER SEVEN

FUCK, FUCK THE FUCKING fuck.

I walk out of the coffee bar, and my head's spinning.

Sure I'm being watched. By my very own personal spy.

Do I tell John about this?

I know Lao Zhang, I say to myself. Whatever it is he's planning on doing—his final "piece," I mean—he wouldn't hurt anyone. He's not going to try to blow something up or anything like that, right?

He wouldn't. That's not who he is.

Not who he *was*, anyway. I haven't seen him in over a year. I don't know what he's been doing, what he's been going through.

How well did I really know him before, for that matter?

Don't go there.

If I can't believe that Lao Zhang's the man I thought he was, what has the last year of my life been about?

I pass the rows of little shops selling incense and Tibetan Buddhist tchotchkes: gilt statuettes, sandalwood beads, prayer flags, and cards. I bet at least a couple of them have postcards of the Dalai Lama behind the counter.

Whatever it is that Lao Zhang plans on doing, it's got to be some big, stupid gesture that gets him into trouble. I mean, he's already in trouble, right? By coming back, it's like he's giving up. He knows what's going to happen. Maybe not the details, but that it's nothing good.

I'm getting teary-eyed, which I really hate.

And for all he said it was about taking the pressure off me, well, I know one thing about so-called superpowers—they hate being embarrassed. There's no way I'm not going be on the receiving end of some blowback from this.

By the time I'm on the escalator heading down to the Number 2 subway, I'm really pissed off.

All this time I've been doing what Lao Zhang wanted me to do. First, going on that crazy hunt through China last year, following clues he'd laid down for me, getting my ass kicked from one end of the country to the other. Then managing his art. I'm still not sure why he picked me for that.

Yeah, he told me he thought it was good for me. That I needed something to do. Which, okay, was true. I needed a mission. Something to take my mind off the Great Wall of Bullshit that had been my life to date.

But how is *this* going to help me? Being the front woman for a dissident artist determined to get himself in deeper shit than he already is.

So he thinks he's going to make some big gesture and that it's going to mean something. Like those Tibetans lighting themselves on fire to protest the regime. Does any of that help? Does it change anything?

And fuck it, I'm not Chinese. This isn't my country. It's not my business trying to change it.

And further, I'm sick of being a good soldier on someone else's mission.

You know what I could really use? A guy who's actually there for me when it counts. Not some flaky artist who—okay, I know he cares about me, at least I think he does, but I'm never going to be first. Or even close to it.

I swipe my card at the turnstile and take the escalator down to the platform. Stand there and feel a wash of stale air from the tunnel. It's not too crowded at least. Middle-school kids in tracksuits, a couple of European tourists examining the map enclosed in Lucite that details the exits, a cluster of PLA soldiers in square-cut, baggy fatigues who don't look much older than the middle-school kids. A subway worker, an older woman in a blue uniform with gaudy gold buttons, sweeps the tiles with a straw broom.

Too fucking late, I think. I already signed up for this.

I swear, if I make it through, this is the last time I go out on someone else's mission. Next time I'm working my own.

Like I have a clue what kind of mission that might be.

I'M PRETTY SURE THAT my mission of choice would *not* be meeting Cao Meimei for dinner at a pretentious restaurant on the top floor of a five-star hotel in the Central Business District.

The name of the restaurant is Estasi. Italian, maybe? I can't tell from the decor. It's just a lot of bullshit marble, fancy lighting, dark wooden alcoves with carvings of grapes and vines.

Just going into the hotel lobby made me want to run the other way. Marble everywhere, more gold trim than the Lama Temple, perfectly conditioned air, and the faint hum of Muzak. There's an atrium that goes up a few stories with a giant fountain in the middle puking illuminated sprays of water. Rich people hanging out in the lobby, checking in, meeting for drinks in the downstairs bar, wearing well-cut suits and cute little dresses and hundred-dollar T-shirts, branding themselves with Gucci and Vuitton and Coach.

I'm hoping that Meimei beat me to Estasi. She has a reservation, and I'm supposed to join her. Otherwise I guess I'll sit at the bar and nurse an overpriced glass of wine, because it's not like this kind of place serves the local Yanjing Beer.

I approach the hostess station. A marble desk surrounded by a carved wooden screen depicting cherubs toting bunches of painted grapes.

"*Ni hao,*" I say to the hostess, your basic young, elegant, gorgeous Chinese woman. "I'm meeting a friend who has a reservation. Cao Meimei."

It's funny to watch. The hostess, already a paragon of good posture and polite attitude, still manages to straighten up, put a brighter smile on her perfect face.

"Welcome," she says. "Please, follow me."

We weave our way through the restaurant. Past plush wooden booths and more public tables that are covered in linen and decorated with silver candles and delicate sprays of fresh flowers. I'm wearing my designer duds from Sidney, last night's shirt still wrinkled and smelling like cigarette butts. Maybe it's dark enough so no one will notice.

Finally we reach what has to be the best table in the house. A table for two against a huge expanse of window looking out over the lights of the CBD.

The hostess clasps her hands and does a little bow to the figure sitting at one end. "*Cao xiaojie, ninde keren laile.*" Your guest has arrived.

If I didn't know better, I would've thought Meimei was a teenage boy, a pretty one, like a Korean pop star. She wears a white silk suit with a silky sky blue T-shirt beneath it, her short hair slicked back from her face.

She smiles and gestures at the seat opposite.

I sit, trying to do it gracefully, trying not to groan. I manage with a wince and a grunt.

"What would you like to drink?" Meimei asks.

I stretch out my leg. She has a wineglass to her right, half full of something white. Next to the table is a silver ice bucket on a stand with a partly submerged bottle inside.

"Whatever you're having would be great."

Meimei turns to the hostess. *"Zai lai yige jiubei."*

The hostess nods and quickly retreats. I swear it's less than a minute before a waitress hustles over with a wineglass and pours me some of whatever Meimei's drinking.

Meimei lifts her glass. She's lounging in her chair with one arm draped on the chair back. I lift my glass in return. Sip.

It's wine. White. Tastes great. That's all I need to know.

"I hear you are a soldier," Meimei says.

This is not what I was expecting.

"I was in the National Guard."

"Is this not a soldier?"

I shrug. Take another sip of wine. A large one. "We're supposed to defend the home front. Bunch of us ended up in a war instead."

"Ah." She sips her wine. "So you were in combat?"

I'm twitching like I'm hooked up to a live current. I hate talking about those times. "I was a medic."

"But you got hurt. How did that happen?"

"Mortar."

"I see." She looks a little disappointed. Why? Because I wasn't out killing bad guys when I got blown up?

"I was outside the wire plenty of times," I mumble. Like that matters. Like that makes me some badass.

Outside the wire wasn't where the worst shit happened anyway.

"I envy you this experience."

I feel this rush of anger so strong that I'm sure it shows on my face. I swallow hard. Don't fuck this up, McEnroe, I tell myself.

"There's nothing about it to envy," I say. And I drink.

She leans forward, her face lit up with a weird enthusiasm. "But you serve your country. You prove yourself in challenging situation, like a man. I think this is admirable."

If she knew what I did during the war . . .

"It's not what people think it's like," I finally mutter.

I glance to my right, at the view of the CBD and the night sky. Lights and neon, giant characters and logos, skyscrapers like ghosts, softened by smog. For a moment I feel like I'm floating in space.

"I fly small planes," she says. "In fact, I have thought about applying to China's air force."

"Oh, yeah?"

"Flying is wonderful." She pauses abruptly. "Shall we order appetizers?"

"Sure."

What I want is another drink. I'm feeling rattled. I guess I shouldn't be surprised that she knows something about my history. Sidney's got the money to hire any kind of private detective or private spy he wants. So does Meimei, I'm guessing. She would've had to have worked fast, but with all the information that's out there on the Internet? It wouldn't take much time.

I let Meimei order the appetizers. I'm not hungry, and I don't know what half the stuff is anyway. ("Duck Liver Terrine with Sweet Kaffir Lime Liqueur." "Truffled Capicola with Lenticchie di Montagna and Chopped Preboggion." "Crispy Sweetbread and Lobster Ragu.") It all tastes good, but mostly I just want to drink.

Except not too much. I can't afford to lose it.

"So you help my father with his museum project," Meimei says after doing the swirl-sniff-taste of a new wine, a red one this time. She nods at the waitress, who pours fresh glasses for both of us.

"I'm . . . consulting." Which seems as good a way as any to put it.

"Interesting. I know that you represent some modern Chinese artists here in Beijing."

I nod. I've got this hollow feeling in my gut, like she knows all about Lao Zhang and the trouble he's in. If she had me checked out, she'd have to know something. There've been a few articles, here and there, about the "disappeared" Chinese artist, the rumors surrounding that, and I've sure been asked about it enough times. *Is he in jail? Is he in hiding? Is he in trouble? Do you know where he is?*

Meimei holds her wine up to the table light, tilting it and watching the rivulets of wine run down the inside of the glass. "The legs," Harrison explained to me once. Though he never did explain why anyone was supposed to care about this.

"Art is not really an interest of mine," she says. "Of course I like to have nice things. But my father is really obsessed about this. Don't you think?"

"He's . . . uh, an enthusiastic collector."

For the first time, she smiles in a way that suggests she

might actually be amused. "Yes. I think he always hoped Gugu would take an interest in this, too. Art is not for Tiantian. And it is not for me. But Gugu, he has this artistic temperament."

And here's where I need to think fast. Because this whole thing started as a pretext for me to evaluate Gugu's creepy American friend, Marsh, and now, somehow, the whole crazy family's involved in a museum project that I pretty much pulled out of my ass.

"I think your father would just like to see the three of you work together on this, a little. I mean, it's his life's work, and it's not like it needs to be yours. But he sees it as . . . you know, his legacy, and you're his children, and . . ."

Which is where I totally run out of things to say.

"Yes, yes," she says with a dismissive wave. "I can call Tiantian. Even though he does not approve of me. Shall we order our *primo*?"

"Sounds good." Whatever it is.

MEIMEI PAYS FOR DINNER. No big surprise there. I thank her as enthusiastically as I can fake.

"It was my pleasure," she says, taking my hand. "You are an interesting person, with interesting experiences."

"Not really," I manage. "That's nice of you to say."

She lets go. I reach into my little black leather messenger bag, another gift from Sidney (Vicky didn't dig the old canvas one I usually travel with) and pull out a card case, extract a card. "In case you need to get a hold of me," I say, doing the two-handed handover.

She studies it politely. "I think I will. For our meeting with Tiantian."

★ ★ ★

WHAT A FUCKING WASTE of time.

I mean, I don't particularly want to meet Tiantian. I don't want to work on Sidney's museum project. I especially don't want to spend any more time evaluating Marsh for his moral character. Yet for some reason, I need to do all these things to fulfill my obligations to Sidney Cao. Who, okay, it must be said, did save my life, or his people did anyway. But with Lao Zhang coming back to Beijing, my life just torqued into another level of complicated.

I'm thinking all this the next morning while I'm taking Mimi out for a walk. We're doing our usual thing, wandering through the *hutongs* around the Drum Tower and the Bell Tower, and on top of everything else I'm feeling all kinds of guilty for not taking very good care of my dog. I mean, I'm not terrible. She gets her walks. She gets as good dog food as I can find here, and lots of people food for treats. But it's not like I take her out for a long time or she gets to run around much. My mom and Andy probably spend more time with her than I do.

Face it, I'm not very good at taking care of much of anything.

I'm thinking this as she trots ahead of me down a narrow, grey-walled alley, then stops to sniff what must be a really interesting lamp pole from the attention she's paying to it.

I stare at a tangled nest of wire hanging under the eaves of a grey-washed *siheyuan*, one of the traditional Beijing courtyard houses that are almost all gone now, bulldozed for high-rises and subways. A couple strands of the wire nest are plugged into some kind of power box, but what are the rest of them for? I seem to wonder about this kind of shit a lot. But I hardly ever get answers.

Mimi tugs at the leash. I look up and see her tail wagging. And then I see why.

"Yili."

"John."

He stands there in his black jeans and black T-shirt and leather jacket, weight on the balls of his feet, fists loosely clenched. It looks like he hasn't shaved today. His beard's not that heavy. Just a light black shadow that outlines the hollows under his cheeks, the circle of his chin.

I admit, I'm kind of a sucker for that.

Mimi noses his thigh, then his crotch before she rises up on her hind legs and puts her front paws on his hips. He scratches behind her ears as her tail swishes back and forth.

"Can we talk?" he asks, except it's barely a request.

I shrug. "Sure. Fine."

WE GO TO A bar/café tucked back in the *hutongs* that's nearly empty and big enough to find a private space. I mean, someone could be watching, I guess. There are surveillance cameras all over Beijing, and you never know. I see the black dome of one when we enter. But John takes a look around the newly remodeled, faux-industrial space and nods. Apparently Mimi's no problem either. She trots by my side, hugging my hip, and no one says a thing.

We sit at a table in the back, underneath the factory-style staircase done with galvanized metal, black rubber treads, and thick cable railings. John orders tea. I order a Mexican coffee. The waiter, your typical slender young guy with lank hair drifting over his collar, knows what that is, but I'm kind of hoping John doesn't.

Though why should he give a fuck, really?

The waiter brings us our drinks. John waits for him to retreat to the bar. Then:

"What are you doing with the Cao family?"

I shrug again. "Consulting on a museum project."

"I told you to stay away from trouble." I swear, his jaw's clenched so tight that a muscle's doing a little tap dance. "Yet you have dinner with Cao Meimei."

I take a slug of my tequila-infused coffee. "Yeah, well, she's part of the project."

"The Caos are completely corrupt! Rich people like them are parasites!"

"True, but they're the ones with money for museum projects."

"Parasites," he repeats, as though he didn't hear me. "Especially the *fu er dai*. They don't work themselves, just get everything from their parents. And they all profit off the backs of the workers."

"Spoken like a true Communist," I mutter. But it's not like I disagree. "So you've been spying on me?" Which is not a huge surprise either. It's what John does, right? The dude's a professional stalker.

John stares at me with that black-eyed intensity that's either creepy or sexy—I can't decide. Which pretty much sums us up.

"I only look out for you, and you already know why," he says.

I wish I did. I wish I could be sure. But no matter what John says, no matter how much he claims to care, I still don't know what his game really is. I mean, he's a Chinese secret service agent Taoist sex freak who may or may not support antigovernment dissidents and who really seems to enjoy fucking me. Or with me. Another thing I can't decide.

"Besides, Cao Meimei may be lesbian," he adds darkly.

"Wow, that would be shocking. Your point?"

"Just what I told you." He's wearing his concerned face. "You must be careful with people like these."

CHAPTER EIGHT

ANOTHER NIGHT, ANOTHER PARTY. I think about buying myself a new shirt.

This time Tiantian's the host.

Meimei called me herself to give me the invitation, the afternoon following our dinner. It's going to be at a house Tiantian owns. And it's happening tomorrow. "Oh, yes," she said with a laugh. "As soon as Tiantian heard that you meet with our father, Gugu, and me already, then of course he couldn't be left out."

Great. The last thing I need is to get involved in some kind of weird Cao-family sibling rivalry.

But does that mean I need a new shirt? Because the new black one is too dirty to go a third night, and the white one I got in Xingfu Cun I wadded up and threw in the hamper after karaoke with Sidney in Shanghai.

"That's a lot of late nights for you," my mom says when I tell her about my plans tomorrow night. She's distracted. She's experimenting with making tortillas again.

"Yeah. Can't be helped."

Maybe I'll resurrect my old T-shirt with the weeping black-and-white cartoon cat that has the caption BLACK CAT, WHITE CAT, IF IT CATCHES MICE, IT'S A GOOD CAT. It's a Deng Xiaoping reference. But maybe that wouldn't go over well with Tiantian.

Now, if it were Gugu's party, it would probably be okay. He might not like contemporary art, but he sure seems to be into the hipster aspect of it all.

"Do you think I could get one of those *jianbing* grills?" my mom suddenly asks.

"What?"

A *jianbing* is like a Beijing breakfast burrito—these egg-crepe things with chives and sort of a crunchy fried skeleton of a savory waffle, spread with hot sauce and folded up into a little bag that you can take with you to keep your hands warm in the winter.

"You know, those round, stone . . . I don't know, griddles? The things they cook them on. Where they spread out the crepe."

"Oh. Yeah. Sure. I mean, I'm sure you could find one. Andy would know."

"Because I'm wondering if I could use it to make tortillas."

"Yeah, I mean, why not?" I'm still thinking about the whole shirt issue. I decide against the T-shirt. Too risky.

THE WEIRD THING IS, Tiantian's place isn't far from me, just a subway stop over off Guozijian, where the Imperial University is, right next door to the Confucius Temple. Both of them are museums now. I went to the Confucius Temple once, in the dead of winter, with my ex, Trey. We wandered through these ranks of white stone tablets with engraved calligraphy on them that looked like stretched-out tombstones, freezing our asses off in the bitter winds that were blowing down from Mongolia. We were holding hands with our gloves on, and I remember the texture of the scratchy cable-knit yarn pressing against the skin where Trey's fingers circled mine. I don't know why I remember those details so specifically. It's not like I care about the guy anymore.

Now it's spring, and the weather changes from day to day. A warm night tonight. I'm already sweating into my black Sidney shirt (I had it cleaned) as I limp through the *shanzhai* Ming-dynasty gate that frames the entrance to Guozijian.

They've restored this street, added some polished granite markers and wall plaques explaining the history of the street, and spiffed up some of the surrounding *hutongs*. Just past the expensive but historic teahouse from the Ming or Qing dynasty (as usual, I forget), I take a turn down an alley and then down another one that breaks off at a sharp angle. Easier to find it myself than to ask a cabdriver. I wander a bit farther until I see the fancy stone lion dogs with one paw resting on a drum. A red gate with brass fittings. A murmur of *erhu* music from the other side.

Tiantian's place.

The real giveaway's the guys in black suits wearing earpieces standing on either side of the door. The Caos tend to travel with a security detail.

They check my name against an iPhone app that has my photo on it—shit, for all I know, it takes a retinal scan. I pass, apparently, because one of them tugs on the thick brass ring to open the heavy red gate.

Well, okay, it's a Chinese palace. Of course it is. Not a huge one, just your basic Chinese minor-prince kind of size. Behind the gate is an entry hall open at the back. I jog left then right, toward the main gate that faces north. Limp up the two granite steps that lead to the entrance to the courtyard I know is on the other side and step over the red wood that cuts across the bottom of the double doors. There's a huge black-lacquered screen with gold calligraphy on it that's almost as wide as the entrance and as tall as the ceiling. You have to go around the screen; you can't just walk right into the place. I think it's maybe supposed to stop bad spirits, because they can only move in a straight line.

I walk around the screen. Before I even turn the corner, there are young women in *qipaos*, and not cheap restaurant polyester ones either. These are beautiful, form-fitting dresses, red with silk embroidery. One of the women holds a lacquer tray bearing tiny crystal flutes. The other makes a polite little bow and hands me one.

Moutai. Of course.

I smile and nod and hold it up to my mouth, because it would be rude not to, and I'm actually almost getting a taste for Moutai, you know, if I drink it quick enough.

On the other side of the entry hall is a courtyard with three more halls in a U shape around it—your classic Beijing *siheyuan* built for a wealthy owner. In the center of the courtyard, there's a big granite boulder, all jagged and knobby, a dozen or so feet high. I've heard these things called "strange stones." Usually there's some calligraphy on them, some proverb about wisdom or changing seasons or whatever. Spaced around that are small twisted pines in marble planters, party guests, and more serving girls in *qipaos*. All the girls are pretty, I notice. That's not surprising either. China has a lot of pretty girls, and guys like Tiantian can afford to pay for them.

There are halls left, right, and center, single- or two-story at most, grey stone and red wood and glazed curved roof tiles. I spot the source of the *erhu* music, now mingling with a *pipa*, a *yanqin*, and the occasional slap of percussion: a quartet set up on the other side of the strange stone. While it's true that your basic subway *erhu* player often sounds like he's strangling a cat, a badass player can shred with that bow and two strings. I've also heard some amazing stuff on a *pipa*, which is sort of like a medieval guitar—a lute or whatever. These guys sounds pretty good, if you like that traditional stuff. I swear I've seen the *erhu* player jamming with a punk-rock band at Mao Live House. Maybe the *pipa* player, too.

"Oh, so you came."

I jump a little. Marsh.

He's wearing all black: slouchy black jacket, black jeans, black boots, and a designer black T-shirt. It goes well with his designer stubble.

"Yeah," I say. "I was invited."

"I'll bet." He sips his drink. Whatever it is, it's not Moutai. Something amber, in a tumbler.

I shrug. "You know, it's this museum project."

One of the waitresses approaches with a platter of appetizers. Tiny designer *jiaozi* nestled in paper cups.

"Dumpling?" she offers. "Pork and black truffle juicy?"

"Sure," I say. Whatever. I take one and bite into it. This intense, almost buttery mushroom-and-pork-fat flavor explodes in my mouth. I manage not to drip the juice on my shirt. Barely. Only because I don't want to waste it.

I look up, and I see that Marsh is watching me.

"*Xiaojie.*" He halts the waitress with a light hand on her elbow and grabs a dumpling off the tray. "Have another," he says, extending his open palm out to me, the dumpling perched on his fingers.

I so want another one of those dumplings.

"That's okay," I say. "You should try it."

He smiles and shrugs. Pops it into his mouth and chews

with a satisfied smirk. Flicks a glance to his right. "Interesting crowd."

"I guess."

I mean, I guess it is, actually. A weird mix. There are a lot of thirty-, forty-something people dressed in expensive designer gear, the conservative kind, like they came from an after-work function or an awards banquet. Some of them are wearing interpretations of traditional Chinese clothes: silk mandarin-collar jackets, sleek versions of *qipaos*. Tiantian's posse maybe.

Then there's Gugu's group: giggly younger women in sequined T-shirts and denim short-shorts and fuck-me stilettos, guys with wispy goatees, fedoras or sideways ball caps, and visible tattoos.

I'm not sure which Meimei's crowd is. If she even has one. Maybe the athletic twenty-somethings hanging around the edges or the ones wearing high-fashion labels, all that Gucci Pucci crap that looks like money.

Funny thing is, I realize that Marsh and I are dressed almost exactly alike.

"You enjoying yourself?" he asks.

"It's okay." I shrug. "I'm not that into parties."

"But if they have good drinks and nice food and rich people who might throw a few crumbs your way . . . you'll drag yourself here. Right?"

He's got his tumbler in one hand, and he lifts it in a sketch of a toast before he brings it to his reddened lips and tosses the rest down.

"Like I said. It's this museum project."

He snorts. "Right." Raises his empty glass. "*Xiaojie*," he calls out, a little louder this time, so he can get his drink quickly. Then he leans toward me.

"Don't tell me you don't like it," he says. "I recognize those labels you're wearing. Don't tell me you don't like nice things."

I stare back. Lock my gaze on his hooded, bloodshot eyes, and I don't look away.

"Yeah, well, it's a recent development." I toss my head in the direction of the main hall. "Excuse me," I say. "I need to find the head."

M O T H E R F U C K E R .

Okay, I'm pretty sure this guy is bad news, and I'm not just saying that because he's right about my recently liking nice things.

What do I tell Sidney?

First do no harm. That's been my mantra since I got any leftover gung-ho bullshit blown out of me in the Sandbox.

If I tell Sidney what I think about Marsh, what kinds of consequences am I willing to shoulder?

On the other hand, there's *my* ass to think about. I have to tell Sidney something.

I head toward the hall on my left. Not the main hall, if I remember how places like this are laid out—that would be the one perpendicular, the northern house, and the grounds here look big enough to have additional buildings behind that.

This one's shutter-style wooden doors are flung open, welcoming you inside. Even with the open doors, they're running some kind of air conditioner that feels more like a cool breeze blowing from inside.

A few guests have drifted in here. A big rectangular room with high ceilings, framed in wood and a lot of black and red and lacquer. Worn stone floors dotted with old, expensive-looking woven rugs. Chinese brush paintings and scrolls hang on the walls. Expensive ones, from what I know, not that I'm an expert. Sometimes you can just tell. One of those green-and-yellow Tang-dynasty horse statuettes, which I'm guessing is a real one, sits on a fancy inlaid cabinet. Some classic Chinese furniture and some modern interpretations of it, because you know those Chinese chairs and benches look cool, but they aren't all that comfortable. Hardwood chairs grouped around small square tables and this giant carved wooden bed thing with a little table on top of it. A couple of hipster types lounge on the bed thing, smoking something in long-stemmed pipes, their drinks on the little table. They're not wearing shoes, and I wonder if I should take mine off, too.

I approach one of the servers, who's rearranging the glasses on her tray.

"*Xiaojie.*"

She starts a bit, rattling the little crystal glasses. Turns toward me, the friendly smile mask already in place. Another pretty one. Big brown eyes and plump painted lips.

"*Nimende xishoujian zai nar?*" I continue. Like I told Marsh, I'm looking for a bathroom.

"That way, miss." She points toward the north end of the hall. "Go out."

At the back corner of the room, there's a screen, this carved, lacquered thing with white birds painted on it—cranes? I spent some time at a bird sanctuary not very long ago, but I still suck at identifying them.

Behind that a hallway.

I go out.

I'm guessing it was added on, even with the aged grey on the outside wall. Plenty of places that got knocked down in these neighborhoods to salvage it from. Little lights in the ceiling cast yellowish circles on the worn stones. There's a door made of wood and frosted glass at the end.

Just as I get there, the door's flung open. I jump. Out comes a woman, one of the thirty-, forty-somethings, in a black sheath dress and fancy heels. Louboutins, which I know only because of Lucy Wu. Polished more than pretty, with a designer bobbed haircut. Her face is redder than the soles of her shoes. I can't tell if she's been crying, is furious, or has been slapped.

"*Duibuqi,*" I say. Excuse me.

She looks at me like, *What the fuck are you doing here?*

Good question.

With barely a nod, she storms down the hall, her heels click-ing on the stone like taps from a hammer.

I go into the bathroom—fancy, of course, more stone and rustic wood, with a shower off to one side. Do my business. There's another door on the other side, and I decide to go out that way, just because. I'm thinking about a Percocet. I'm thinking about a beer. I'm thinking, What do I have to do here before I can leave?

Find Tiantian, I guess. He wasn't in the first hall, so maybe he's in this one up ahead: the north hall, the main house. I mean, that's where the lord of the manor is likely to hang out, right?

The second door opens onto the side courtyard, a narrow rectangle between the west house and the north house. The smaller wing of the north house is closed up, though I can see lights inside. I'll have to go over to the main entrance if I want to go in and check it out.

"Hello!"

I flinch a little, but everything has me jumpy tonight. A

young woman with pigtails, wearing a sort of designer baby-doll outfit. She looks familiar, but I can't quite place her.

"From Gugu's party," she supplies. "I am Celine."

"Right. You have a website." The one she said I should read to learn something about modern Chinese culture. I think she was giving me shit, but I'd actually meant to check it out.

"Yes. And I hear some things about you." She gives me a look. I think she's amused, but I'm not sure why. Just 'cause I'm funny, I guess. "I hear you work with artists," she says. "Some interesting ones."

"Yeah," I say. "Are you interested in art?"

"Recently I become more and more interested. I even work in a gallery sometimes. Artists say fascinating things about society. Don't you think?"

"I do," I say. I have to admit, not what I expected from a twenty-something club kid. Is she talking about Lao Zhang?

I try to think of something to say, something to ask about what artists she finds particularly fascinating, but she beats me to the next question.

"Do you like this house?" she asks.

"Sure. It's pretty. I mean, it's traditional Chinese, right?"

"Yes. Tiantian likes such styles. He always says China culture is over five thousand years old—what does rest of the world have to compare?" She giggles. "But he likes some modern things, too."

Am I supposed to ask? Ever since I started hanging out around the younger Caos, I feel like everyone's speaking in some kind of code all the time and I'm not really deciphering it.

"Like what?" I ask. "Fancy cars? New plumbing?"

She leans forward. "Modern girls," she says, peering at me through her eyelashes. "Did you see Mrs. Cao just now?"

"Tiantian's wife?" I think about it. The only person I've seen just now was the angry and/or crying woman in the bathroom. "Maybe."

"She is unhappy with Tiantian, because he has this modern taste," she says, fumbling a cigarette pack out of her tiny purse. "And she is *hong er dai,* so it is better if she is happy."

Hong er dai. Second-generation red. The sons and daughters of the revolution, born into privilege.

She taps out a cigarette. "Smoke?"

I shake my head. I haven't smoked since the Sandbox. Though I still get the itch sometimes.

"They are Panda." She shows me the pack. Two pandas on a sea-foam green background. "Deng Xiaoping's favorite."

"Is that why you smoke them?"

"No. It's because I like pandas. *Zhen ke ai.*" She flicks her lighter and inhales, then blows out a dainty cloud. "Very cute."

I don't really want to make small talk with this girl, but it's not clear to me what else I should be doing, other than organizing a museum or something.

"You're here with Gugu?" I ask.

She lifts one shoulder. "He is here, and I am here."

"Oh. I haven't seen him yet."

"So is Betty. My friend you meet before."

Rhinestone baseball cap. "Right."

Then it occurs to me that I could actually do something productive. "And Marsh is here."

She chuckles, a little belly laugh bottled up behind her closed lips. "Yes. I saw you talk to him."

"Yeah. He's . . . I don't know. Interesting."

"Yes. Interesting." She takes a draw on her cigarette. "Sexy, I think. Don't you?"

"Not really my type." Which is true and not true. He's nobody I want to get anywhere near, but he's got that kind of creepy charisma that some bad boys have, in part because you don't know what they'll do. It's the kind of thrill you get in your gut going up a roller coaster that might actually be nausea.

"He likes to think he is dangerous," Celine says suddenly.

"Oh, yeah?"

Come up with something smart to say, dipshit, I tell myself.

"So is he?" I manage.

She blows a few smoke rings into the dark. "I think he is just acting. But maybe he forgets this sometimes."

OKAY, I TELL MYSELF. You need to go meet Tiantian. Pitch the museum or whatever and then get out. No reason to waste a lot of time. Because it's not actually going to happen, right?—the kids all getting together to support Dad's ego monument.

I'm here to evaluate Marsh, download to Sidney, and *di di mao* the fuck out. I tell myself this as I limp up the shallow, broad steps that lead to the entrance of the main house.

Two *qipao*-wearing serving girls stand by the entrance with trays holding glasses of wine. I take a red. One Moutai, one glass of wine. Doing okay, I tell myself. Even though my leg's throbbing, this pulsing nerve in the middle of my thigh that feels like an electrical fire, and I really want a Percocet.

After I meet Tiantian, I tell myself.

It's going to suck when I run out of Percocet.

Another lacquer screen. I walk around it and through the little entry and then into the main room.

There's this low, almost yellow light. More carved Chinese

furniture, antique urns and scrolls, black lacquer chests, red silk hangings, chunks of pale green jade. It kind of looks like *Crouching Tiger* exploded.

I pick my way through the Chinascape. Knots of guests watch me pass, or maybe it's my imagination. But there aren't a lot of foreigners here. There's Marsh, and there's me.

"So you came."

I turn and see Meimei, lounging on one of those carved wooden bed things with the little table, smoking a Chinese brass water pipe, the kind with the chamber that fits in your hand and a long curved stem. She's wearing a take on a men's silk jacket with a mandarin collar, her hair slicked back like last time, and a pair of antique-looking round gold-framed spectacles with the lenses flipped up. China steampunk.

She extends the hand with the pipe. "Care to try?"

"What is it?" I ask.

"I don't know, maybe just some tobacco."

"No thanks."

"You can always have something else if you'd like."

I don't know what she means, but man, am I tempted to ask.

Don't be stupid, I tell myself. "I'm good," I say. "Got my wine here."

"Have you met Tiantian yet?"

"Not yet."

She swings her legs off the side of the bed and hops to her feet in one nimble move. "I will introduce you."

I limp after her.

We walk to the back of the main hall. There's an exit that leads to a narrow courtyard and, like I thought, a two-story hall behind that. As we step up the three stairs that lead to the entrance, this random factoid flashes into my head, that the back house was where the unmarried daughters used to live. I don't know if that's true or something I'm just making up.

Whatever the truth is, this doesn't look like a home for cloistered daughters. It's more like an upscale man cave. Leather, glass, and chrome furniture. The biggest TV I've ever seen embedded in one wall. A living room, I guess. There are a bunch of men sitting around, some obvious rich guys but also a few who remind me of Pompadour Bureaucrat, wearing polo shirts and ugly designer belts, others dressed in subdued black suits. The women who are here are mostly younger than the men. Of course they're cute. Of course they're wearing expensive outfits with short skirts and high heels and carrying rhinestone-studded designer purses. They perch on the arms of the couches, hanging around the edges.

"Hello!" Meimei calls out in English.

Everyone turns and stares. It's like one of those scenes in an old western, where the gunfighter walks into the saloon. The music doesn't stop playing, though. Too bad, as it's this cheesy Mandopop, and I have a low tolerance for that shit.

One of the men stands abruptly. The girl hovering next to him has to step aside, and she totters on her candy-red heels, and for a moment I think she's going to fall back on her ass. But she grabs the arm of the couch and steadies herself.

The guy has to be Tiantian. In his thirties, a little heavy through the hips and gut. He's wearing a black jacket, a grey shirt, and black slacks, and even from across the room I can tell that the clothes are expensive, but for some reason they still don't fit him quite right, like his sort of dumpy build defies all the custom tailoring.

"I've brought Father's friend Yili," Meimei says.

"Ah." Tiantian smiles briefly and bobs his head. "A pleasure to meet you," he says to me in English. He doesn't speak it as well as Meimei or Gugu.

"*Hen gaoxing renshi ni,*" I offer back. Nice to meet you, too. "Thank you for your hospitality."

He waves that off. "You're my father's friend."

I can see the resemblance to Sidney—like Gugu, Tiantian got dad's bony nose and high cheeks. His face is broader, more like Meimei's. Maybe they got that from Mrs. Cao, whoever and wherever she is. It occurs to me that I've never seen Mrs. Cao, never even seen a photo, never heard Sidney or Vicky or anyone say a word about her.

Tiantian gestures at the chair to his left. "Please, sit. So we can have a talk."

I hobble over and sink into the chair. The leather is as soft as velvet. Meimei perches on the arm of it, rests one dainty ankle on the other knee.

Tiantian sits in his chair. Jerks his head to one side and snaps his fingers. One of the serving girls rushes over. The same one I bumped into earlier, I think, or maybe she just looks like her. I mean, they're all pretty. All in *qipaos*. All with their smiles in place, anxious to serve.

"What will you like?" Tiantian asks, his lips curving up as if they're being lifted by tiny hooks.

It's a good question. What will I like? I mean, how do I even know until I've tried it?

"Uh . . . wine. Thanks."

"That wine you have now, we can do better." He raises his hand to his mouth and mutters something to the *xiaojie*. Something about "*tebie hong putaojiu.*" Special red wine.

I sip the one I've got. Tiantian watches me, that fake smile frozen in place. Am I supposed to say something? Make small talk? I suck at small talk. But one thing you don't tend to do in China is get right to the point.

Plus, I'm not even sure what the point is. The museum project I made up to save my ass? Marsh Brody?

I settle on, "This is a great house."

"A traditional Beijing *siheyuan*. You know this kind of house, I think." He's proud of this place, I can tell. Well, who wouldn't be? It's a fucking expensive piece of real estate, for one thing.

"Yes. I've lived in Beijing for a few years. Not too far from here."

"By Gulou, I think, yes?"

Great. Well, it's no surprise that he could find out where I live.

"Right."

Sidney's family is from Anhui Province, and when Tiantian speaks, unlike Meimei and Gugu, I can still hear the Anhui in his accent. He's older than the other two by nearly a decade, I'm guessing. I figure Tiantian, being the eldest, was probably raised in Anhui, way before Sidney built his ghost city, Xingfu Cun, maybe even before Sidney made his billions.

What's the draw for Tiantian in Beijing, aside from traditional courtyard architecture?

I look around the room, at the guys in polo shirts and plain dark suits, and think, *Party members*. Officials. Somebody has to be in the capital to represent the family. Tiantian's the eldest. Of course that would fall to him.

"I like it a lot," I say, remembering that I should be making small talk.

"Yes. Beijing is still a culture center. Traditional Chinese culture." He shoots an unsubtle look at Meimei. "Not like Shanghai."

Meimei chuckles. "Shanghai is more modern. And clean." She looks around the room, at all the guys in suits and polo shirts, and smiles. "It's too dirty here."

The *xiaojie* has returned with the special red wine and some glasses on a tray. Tiantian nods and points at me. She trots over and holds out the bottle, like she's highlighting a product in a commercial. I'm supposed to pay attention to it, I guess.

So I do. Make a show of studying the label, which looks like your typical snooty French wine label, with a little castle engraving on it and a name that starts with "Château." Except it's from Ningxia.

"Wow, Chinese," I say.

"Yes. It is good quality. We can do this as well as France."

Meimei rolls her eyes. "Not yet. Maybe someday."

"*Zhen, zhen!*" Tiantian snaps at the serving girl.

She hastily hands me a glass and pours me a taste.

I do the sniff-and-swirl because I've seen Harrison do it enough times, and I'm trying to be polite, though about all I usually get out of it is, "Hey, smells like wine."

I taste, and it's not bad. But I've drunk enough of the good stuff thanks to Harrison and Sidney that I've had better.

"Very good," I say.

"You see?" Tiantian shoots a glare at Meimei. "You just prefer Western things because they are Western."

"And you just prefer Chinese things because they are Chinese." With that, Meimei slips off the arm of the couch and springs to her feet, like some androgynous little ninja. "I will go find Gugu. So we can discuss this museum."

"Great," I say. "Looking forward to it." I take a gulp of wine, in the interest of further politeness.

Tiantian leans forward. His face is flushed, probably from the wine. "So you have seen my father's collection."

"Yes. It's amazing." Which is one response that I don't have to fake. I mean, the dude has van Goghs in his basement.

"Huh." Tiantian tosses back a gulp of his special wine. The serving girl hastily refills his glass. "Some of it I like. Some of it I think is nonsense."

"Well, you know, it's . . . um, all about how you respond to a piece. If you don't like it, that's okay."

Tiantian frowns. "I don't like it because it is *nonsense*," he says, jabbing a finger at me.

I don't think he's loaded, not the way Gugu was at the club, but he's had enough to drink where maybe he's letting his inner asshole off the leash. Or maybe he's always like this.

"Okay, but by international standards everything he has is, uh . . ."

I can't think of how to put it without sounding insulting, not in Chinese, not in English.

"Significant," I finally manage.

"Significant." Tiantian snorts. "It's nonsense. My opinion is this modern Chinese so-called art is worst of all."

"Oh. What makes you say that?" Because contemporary Chinese art is fetching a metric crap ton of money in the international market, and increasingly in the domestic one, too. I figure if nothing else, Tiantian would appreciate a good investment.

"It simply copies decadent Western notions. It ignores Chinese traditions, or it mocks them."

"You don't think maybe some of them use Chinese traditions to comment on modern circumstances?"

Hey, I've learned *something* after doing this art gig for over a year.

Tiantian stares at me, and for a moment I have the weirdest feeling, like he's just going to lose his shit right there, spring out of the chair and try to beat the crap out of me.

But he doesn't do that. Instead he leans back, and it's like somebody's flipped a switch—he's all relaxed and jolly, the good host.

Maybe I was just imagining it.

"Perhaps. Perhaps my problem is simply that I prefer China's traditions to the modern circumstances." He turns to the serving girl. *"Kuai nalai hai yi bei putaojiu."* Quick, fetch another bottle of wine.

Yeah, and if it weren't for China's "modern circumstances," you wouldn't be a *fu er dai* sitting here in however many million dollars' worth of Beijing real estate, asshat, I think, but I figure I'd better not say that.

Instead I sip the wine I've got and wonder when I can get the fuck out of here. Go home and pet my dog.

That's when the pissed-off woman from the restroom strides in, the one in the black sheath dress and designer heels. Her head swivels around, and she takes me in, sitting at Tiantian's left.

"Is this another one of your *biaozi*?" she says in a low, cold voice.

"Hey," I say, because though I may be a bitch, I'm sure as shit not *Tiantian's* bitch.

"Ta shi wo babade huoban," he snaps at her. My father's business associate.

"Really." She takes a step back from him and turns to me.

Stares me up and down, her eyes glittering. "You don't look like a businesswoman."

"I represent artists," I say. I wonder if she's on something, or ill. Aside from the crazy eyes and weird paranoid hostility, she's pale and sweaty, and one of her hands is trembling.

"Artists." A snort. "I won't put up with this anymore," she says, in a voice loud enough to catch the attention of a man in a dark suit chatting up one of the polo-shirt guys. He turns and stares. Sixtyish, with hound-dog cheeks, baggy eyes, and a frozen smile.

"*Bie xiashuo,*" Tiantian says in a low voice, with a forced smile of his own. Stop speaking nonsense.

The man in the dark suit takes a few easy steps toward our circle. In control. "Dao Ming, are you feeling all right?" he asks. "You look a little uncomfortable."

Crazy Lady, Dao Ming—Mrs. Tiantian, I presume—stops in her tracks. Blinks a few times. "Yes," she says. "Yes, I'm not feeling well, Uncle Yang. Forgive me."

Uncle Yang offers Dao Ming his arm. "Let's go, so you can have a rest. *Xiuxi yixia.*"

Dao Ming nods, the glittery fury in her eyes giving way to clouds of exhaustion. She rests her hand on his and allows herself to be led off.

"My wife has an illness," Tiantian says after she's out of sight. "Please don't take any of her nonsense to heart."

"No worries," I say. I sip from my glass. "This is great wine." Because that's the only thing I can think of to say. It's like I'm in this beautiful house, surrounded by all this money and all this nice stuff, and I have this weird sense that there's some kind of black hole in the center of it all, pulling us toward it.

"I can't find Gugu." Meimei has returned, her steampunk lenses flipped down.

"You called him?" Tiantian snaps.

"*Dangran.*" Of course.

"Did you ask Marsh?" I say. "His American friend?"

Because I might as well work the mission, right? The real mission. Find out what I can about Marsh Brody. Even though I don't know what I should do about what I might find out.

Meimei shakes her head. "Didn't see him either." She's not giving me anything. No real reaction. I can't tell if she's acting or if she just doesn't have an opinion.

"Oh. Maybe they went someplace else. The two of them."

"Maybe." She turns to Tiantian. "Why don't we have this meeting later? When it's more convenient. Maybe go out for dinner, just the four of us." She turns to me. "What do you think?"

"I think . . . that sounds great." Because if it means I can go home now, I'm all for it. I'm getting that twitchy feeling again, like I did when I went out to the club for Gugu's party, like something bad is going to happen, and I don't want to be here when it does.

"Okay." Meimei pulls out her iPhone. "I will arrange something."

"Great." I take a last slug of wine. "Thanks so much for your hospitality," I say to Tiantian. "I really appreciate it."

He nods, not looking at me, distracted. I guess I would be, too, if I were him.

"Okay, then." I brace myself on the arm of the chair and push myself to my feet. My bad leg cramps up, and the pain that shoots through it is enough to make me gasp. I hide that as best I can. I don't want to show weakness in front of these people. That's how I've tried to operate since I got blown up. Don't show them the soft spot where they can hurt you.

Though who knows? Maybe I'm better off if they think I'm weak. Harmless. Because it doesn't matter how strong I might be. These guys still have all the power.

I get a business card from my little card case and hold it out to Tiantian. "My card," I say.

Now he does look up. Takes my card with both hands and pretends to study it.

"I hope we keep in touch," I say.

"Yes, yes," he says. "That will be a pleasure." He manages that fishhook smile and lays my card on the end table.

IT'S STILL TOO WARM out in the courtyard, but there's a breeze and it's outside, away from all that weird-ass shit. I stand there by the *erhu* combo for a minute, take a few deep breaths, and sip the remains of my wine, thinking, What the fuck was all that, and do I really want to know?

Much as I hate to admit it, I'm feeling like John was right—I don't want to be anywhere near any of these people. But what are my options for getting away from them? How do I tell Sidney Cao that I don't want to have anything to do with him, his kids, or his museum? I mean, I tried saying no to Sidney before and ended up with his hired killers stalking me. Though I also did get a few free rides in his fancy private jet. I kind of liked that part.

You can't think that way, McEnroe, I tell myself. You gotta figure out how to disentangle yourself from this guy. Without totally pissing him off.

"Still here."

I flinch and try to cover it. Marsh. He stands too close to

me, as usual, close enough so that I catch the scent of scotch on his breath.

"Yeah," I say. "I was waiting on Gugu. We were supposed to have a meeting, but he never showed." I shrug and take the last slug of my wine. "I'm heading out now."

"He's around." Marsh gestures toward the east house. "I'll take you."

"That's okay," I say, maybe too quickly. "We're going to reschedule."

"You don't want to pay your respects? Wouldn't be too polite, to come to the party and not say hello."

He's got that shit-eating grin on his face, and I know this is some kind of setup, some kind of joke he wants to play on me, or worse.

I shrug again. "Yeah, well, sometimes that's just the way it goes. I'm sure he'll understand."

I start to pull away. Marsh taps my shoulder. Lightly.

"Hey," he says.

I turn. He's staring at me with a kind of confounded expression. "Are you afraid of me?" he asks. Like it's a real question.

"No," I say. It's possible I sound defensive. "I just . . . uh, I need to get home."

He lifts his hands. "Look, I'm not gonna rape you or whatever it is you're worried about. I just thought you wanted to see Gugu, and he'd probably like to say hello to you, too. But if that's not something you want to do, hey, fine with me."

He might as well have said, *I double-dare you.*

I hesitate, but only for a moment. Because I don't want this guy to think he has any power over me.

"Okay," I say. "I just can't take too long. It's getting late, and my dog needs a walk."

I figure we're only walking over to the east house. There's a limited amount of trouble I can get into between here and there, right? I'll just keep him ahead of me, and watch my back.

We walk past the strange stone, through a little garden with more weird-looking rocks and water fountains. Not as many guests over here, no serving girls in *qipaos*. Not a lot of light.

Stay frosty, I tell myself. It's not paranoia when they're really out to get you, and given my experiences of the recent past, I'm probably not paranoid enough.

"So . . . movies?" I ask.

"What?"

"Movies. You said you work in Hollywood. And Gugu's into the movie thing, right?"

Marsh nods. "Yeah. We're putting a deal together. Historical. Easiest thing to do as a coproduction. That and rom-coms. Otherwise you run into all kinds of bullshit politics. No horror, that's supernatural, and we can't have superstitions in a modern socialist society. You wanna do a caper film? Well, don't suggest that crime's a real problem or that the authorities don't have a handle on it. You're better off setting something in the bad old days, before the revolution. Then you can do just about anything you want."

His face is in shadow, and I can't see his expression. But it's the first time he's talked to me like a normal person and not some supercreep with a chip on his shoulder.

I'm thinking, Okay, maybe he's not a bad guy, and I can tell Sidney that and be done with this whole mission. Let him and Gugu spend Gugu's money and make their own money. What's it going to hurt?

As we approach the entrance, I notice there's a muscle guy

standing there. Yeah, no girls in *qipaos*. My nerves start pinging again.

I do a kind of stutter step without meaning to. Marsh notices. "Something wrong?"

"No, just got a text." I reach into my little leather bag and grab my phone, unlocking the screen so it's lit up like maybe someone texted me. Bring up John's number. Okay, so he's in my Favorites. It's in case of an emergency.

I don't call him, I don't text him, I just have his number ready.

Marsh walks past the muscle without a look or a nod.

I hesitate. Think, Okay, if you back out now and this really is just a "Let's go say hi to Gugu," you're going to look like an idiot.

If that's *not* what this is . . .

Hand on my iPhone, I follow Marsh.

This wing has the look of an upscale hotel. Anonymous furniture and dimmed key lights. Quiet. Maybe it's where Tiantian stashes his guests. We walk through a sitting room with heavy black furniture. No one's here.

"Look—" I say. Marsh turns and puts a finger to his lips. He heads down a hall at the back, gesturing for me to follow.

"Fuck," I mutter. Here I am again, doing something that I'm pretty sure is a bad idea. Why do I keep doing this shit?

I follow him anyhow.

We walk down the darkened hallway, past a couple of closed doors. Sconces cast soft fans of light on the walls.

The door at the end of the hall is cracked open. We get closer, and I hear a low moan.

Either someone's hurt or someone's having fun.

I'm kind of hoping someone's hurt. Because I am not in the mood for fun with Gugu.

Marsh pushes the door open a little wider. Peeks inside.

Draws his head back and turns to me, his eyes squeezed shut, his expression a grimace. He takes a couple steps back to clear the way and gestures at the door.

I take a step forward. I don't want to look, but I do. It's this thing where I have to know, no matter how bad it is.

I'm aware of Marsh standing just behind me, this solid presence radiating heat, and I think that if this is some kind of trap, I need to be ready. Stomp on his foot. Grab his balls and twist.

I take a look inside.

My eyes are already adjusted to the dim light, so I can see that there's a big bed against the wall to the left. A woman sitting on the bed, propped up against the headboard. She's a little heavy. She's topless, or maybe naked. Who knows? I don't get that far. Because there's Gugu sprawled across her lap, and he's sucking on her tit. Which is, you know, whatever. Except that her tits are swollen with milk. I see this when Gugu lets go for a moment and milk dribbles down his chin.

The woman stirs, turns her head toward the door. Stares at me for a moment. She's not that young. Her face seems hard. Then she looks away, back at Gugu, who's too out of it to notice. I see her hand, going up and down.

Okay, that's as much as I need to see.

I turn, and there's Marsh standing in front of me, practically convulsing in silent laughter.

Marsh's gaze drops down to my own rack. Lingers there.

"Got milk?" he whispers.

I stare at him. "Fucking hilarious," I mutter, and I walk away.

"COME ON, CAN'T YOU take a joke?"

I stop in my tracks. We're in the sitting room of the east house, and I'm heading for the door.

"What kind of friend of his are you anyway?" I spit out. "Showing me that?"

Marsh raises his hands. "Hey, I didn't know he was gonna be doing . . . that."

"Bullshit," I snap.

"Okay, I thought maybe he was with a girl, not with some . . . wet nurse from Anhui." He snickers. "It's a trending thing, I hear. Supposed to be good for you. The milk, I mean. All the rage in Shenzhen."

"Good luck on the movie. I'm out of here." I turn to go.

"Wait."

He's standing there, palms out, and even in the dim light I can see that he's doing a pretty good impression of contrite. "Look, I . . . I saw it and I thought it was funny. Okay, so I'm an asshole. And I'm kind of drunk. I'm sorry."

I let out a hard sigh. "Whatever. Tell Gugu I hope to see him soon."

As I turn to go, the last I see of Marsh he's still in that same pose, palms open, asking for forgiveness.

CHAPTER NINE

I'M RIDING THE SUBWAY one stop to home, and I keep saying to myself, That's it. No more stupid stuff.

I need to stop drinking so much. I need to exercise more. Figure out how I'm going to manage my pain without Percocet.

Or how to get more Percocet.

And I need to stop doing stupid stuff.

I just have to keep pushing things to the edge. Why do I do it? I'm starting to think maybe I really do want the buzz.

Or maybe I just don't give a fuck if I keep pushing and one of these times I fall off the cliff.

Ever since the Sandbox, ever since I got blown up, I haven't been able to get my head on straight. Before that I was so young, who knows what kind of person I'd be now if I hadn't gone to war? Maybe I'd still do stupid stuff. But it's like I never got the chance to actually grow up, like a normal person.

Of course, what are the odds that I would've grown up normal anyway?

WHAT WAKES ME UP the next morning is Mimi, barking.

I freeze, heart pounding. Listen.

Happy barking.

Okay, then. I settle back into bed and try to relax.

"Who's a good dog? Who's the *best* dog?"

My mom.

I reach around for my phone, which is somewhere on my bed, I think. My fingers brush against its shiny glass.

It's 11:51 A.M. I guess I can get up now.

I mean, I walked Mimi hours ago, for about five minutes. Which I guess is not really a "walk." But after last night . . .

It's not like I had that much to drink, for me. Just the wine, and then a couple of beers when I got home. My mind wouldn't stop going for a while, after that party.

John's right. The second-generation rich are a creepy bunch. And if Dao Ming, Mrs. Tiantian, is a *hong er dai* with connections to the Party leadership . . .

These are really not people I want to be hanging out with.

I mean, I already have my rich friend Harrison and a Party friend . . . spy . . . whatever he is, John.

That's enough.

There's a Chinese proverb I learned once. Something about when tigers fight, you sit on the mountain and watch.

What you *don't* do is make friends with one or both tigers. Pick the losing tiger, you're fucked. Try to make friends with both, one of them's bound to eat you.

I drag myself out of bed. My head feels swollen. I didn't have that much to drink, I tell myself. The atmosphere over there was poison, that's all.

"What am I doing?" I say out loud. "I have to stop doing this."

I'm not sure what "this" even is.

"SEE WHAT ANDY GOT me?"

My mom is standing in the living room. There's a big, round, cast-iron griddle sitting on top of a box next to the dining-room table.

"Was it here last night?"

"No, it just came. It's a *jianbing* griddle." She peers at the box. "I think the other thing's a stand and a propane tank."

"Oh, yeah." I limp over to the kitchen. I'm thinking coffee. It occurs to me to ask, "You want to make *jianbing*?"

"Tortillas."

"Oh." I get out the coffee, scoop some into a filter. Another thing occurs to me.

"You're not going to cook in here with *that*, are you? I mean, a propane tank?"

"Only if it's safe."

Deal with this later, I tell myself, pouring water into the coffeemaker.

Mom waits until I sit down at the table with a fresh cup before she says, "Andy and I have been talking about opening a restaurant."

I have coffee in my mouth, so I can't answer that right away. When I do, the best I can come up with is, "A restaurant?"

"A Mexican restaurant. Tacos mostly. Nothing too complicated."

"Do you really think that's a good idea?"

"Well, I think there's a real market for it," she says, and it's hesitant enough to sound almost like an apology. "The ones I've tried here aren't very good. I know I can make better salsas. I just have to get the tortillas right. And find enough good avocados for a decent price."

I take another gulp of coffee, because this time I don't really *want* to answer right away. I swallow.

"Mom, opening up a business here, it's very tricky for a foreigner. With restaurants people've even had them *shanzhai*'d.

Copied. The original owners thrown out and the business taken over."

"I know you need a reliable Chinese partner," my mom says. "That's why it makes sense to do it with Andy. Andy has some money. Or he can *get* some money. He owns a few apartments. Plus, he has a friend who might want to invest."

I don't even know where to start with this.

"Okay, you've known Andy *how* long?"

Mom scrunches up her face like she's calculating. "I think it's been almost four months."

"Do you even know what he does? *Why* he has money?"

"Some kind of state job? I think? He might be partly retired. He doesn't seem to have to show up all the time. He said he bought the apartments back when they were cheap. I know one of them's in Qingdao."

"What happens if the two of you break up?"

There's a long pause. Then a sigh. "Well, I hope that doesn't happen. But the thing is, Ellie . . ." She sits down across from me. She seems . . . I don't know. Weirdly calm. "Both of us want to try something new. We think this could work. And sometimes you just have to go for it."

I study her. Her face is slightly flushed. She looks good, I think. She's been exercising, she and Andy, ever since we got back from Yangshuo, where they bicycled and did tai chi classes together.

I think about this, about my mom being fifty-one and trying to make a fresh start yet again.

"Yeah," I say. "I guess you do."

What else can I say? And maybe she's right.

"Andy and I are going to get lunch. And, after that, check out a few potential locations." She twists her hands together, uncertain again. "Do you want to come? It'd be great to get your opinion."

I realize, all of a sudden, that the uncertainty isn't about what she wants to do, with the restaurant and with Andy. It's with me. Like I'm this cat that might respond with a hiss and a scratch.

"Yeah, I'd . . . I'd like to. But I have some things I need to do."

I really am a shit.

She doesn't look surprised, or even disappointed. It's probably what she expected me to say.

"Maybe, if you want, we could look at some places in a couple of days?" I offer.

She smiles. "That sounds great, hon."

She probably thinks I don't really mean it. Who knows? Maybe I don't. But I could. I could be a little nicer. Pretend like I'm a grown-up, even if I'm not.

Mimi dances around my mom like she's about to get a walk. "Sorry, puppy," my mom says, ruffling the fur at her neck. "Some of these places probably don't like dogs much."

"Except on the menu," I mutter.

My mom rolls her eyes.

"I'LL TAKE YOU FOR a walk, I promise," I tell Mimi after she leaves. "I just have to do some stuff first."

What stuff, I really don't know. Check email. Shower maybe.

Decide what I'm going to tell Sidney about last night.

We haven't had the museum meeting yet, I tell myself. I could try to put it off a little longer.

Why do I keep putting it off?

Marsh is a creep. But does he deserve to get whacked by

Sidney for that? I mean, who's the worse influence here, Marsh or Gugu?

Like I'm going to tell Sidney about Gugu's milk fetish.

Maybe I'm overreacting here. Maybe Sidney won't actually *kill* Marsh. Those guys his men smoked a couple of months ago, that was a little different, right? They were bad guys, hired guns who nobody much was going to miss, and it was kind of a kill-or-be-killed situation. Like combat. You engage the enemy. Someone's going to end up in a glad bag.

I'm thinking all this, and someone pounds on my door.

This time Mimi barks and bares her teeth.

I grab her collar. "Quiet. Sit." I brace my hands on the table and push myself up. "Stay."

I hobble over to the door. Peer through the keyhole.

A guy in a uniform and a man in plainclothes behind him.

I'm on the fifth floor. There's nowhere to run.

And this whole drill is starting to feel almost routine.

So I open the door. I don't even bother to say anything.

"Ellie McEnroe?" It's the plainclothes guy in the back. Fortyish. Slacks, white short-sleeved shirt.

"Yeah?"

I'm thinking, more tea with the DSD.

Except the uniform in front has a patch on the shoulder of his light blue shirt with the Great Wall and the olive leaves that says 警察 and then, in English, POLICE.

Regular cops, more or less.

This is confirmed for me when the guy in plainclothes says, "We are from Beijing Municipal Public Security Bureau. I am Inspector Zou. This is Sergeant Chen. We think perhaps you can help with our investigation."

"Sure. Okay."

I open the door wider and step aside.

I mean, what else am I going to do? Ask for a lawyer? This is China.

The two of them walk in. The uniform, Sergeant Chen, stations himself close to the front door. He's tall, young, lanky, all angles, like a jointed puppet, and has a messenger bag slung across his shoulder.

Mimi stands by my side, neck arched, tail up high and stiff. Ready to attack.

"No, Mimi," I whisper. "Be a good dog."

The man in plainclothes, Inspector Zou, leans back on his heels, a little freaked. "Will he bite me?" he asks. "I do not know dogs well."

"Oh, no," I say, because I'm having these nightmare scenarios where they shoot her or drag her away and sell her for hotpot. "She's just nervous with people she doesn't know." I ruffle the scruff around her neck. "Right, Mimi? Don't bite Officer Friendly."

Mimi's tail relaxes. A little.

Sergeant Chen approaches us. Her tail stiffens again.

Oh, fuck. Please do not shoot my dog.

"Sit, Mimi," I say. She doesn't. She hugs my hip, and I can feel her muscles tense.

Sergeant Chen crouches in front of Mimi, so he's at her level. Cautiously extends his hand, palm up, even lower, so it's practically scraping the floor. His expression never changes. Not scared, not happy, just neutral, as far as I can tell.

She sniffs his hand. Her tail relaxes. Slowly swishes back and forth.

I guess he smells okay.

"I'm just going to put her in the bedroom," I say. "Come on, Mimi. You can sit on the bed if you want."

WHEN I COME OUT of the bedroom, Zou is strolling around the living room, his hands clasped behind his back, peering at the stack of DVDs on the coffee table, at the books on the bookcase behind the couch. He's shorter than Chen and a bit stocky, with buzzed hair that looks as if it would grow in like brush bristles.

"You are . . . *Jidujiaotu* . . . ? Christian?" he asks.

I shrug a little. "My mother." I'm not going to bust out the Mandarin yet. Sometimes it's better to act like you don't understand. Play dumb. Besides, his English is pretty good.

Zou nods. "I see. Your mother lives here, too."

Which you must already know, I almost say. Because she had to register with the PSB when she came to stay with me.

But apparently we are doing small talk before we get down to police business.

"Would you like some tea?" I ask. "Maybe a beer?" I'm kind of snarking but figure he can't necessarily tell.

Zou pauses in his wandering. Tilts his head up, like he's seriously pondering this.

"It is . . . very hot today. The . . . *kongtiao* . . . the cold air . . . in our car . . . is broken. So. Yes. I would like some beer." He grins. "Officer Chen is the driver."

WELL, OKAY, THIS IS weird.

The three of us are sitting around the dining-room table snacking on spicy peanuts and shrimp chips. Inspector Zou and I have Yanjing Draft in little glasses, the open bottle and a fresh one on the table. I gave Sergeant Chen a Coke.

"This is . . . nice apartment," Zou says. "Do you like this area in Beijing?"

"Yes. Yes, I do. Very convenient."

Zou nods. "Not so many places like this left, with the *siheyuanr*, the old kind of houses," He says it with an "r," like a proper Beijinger. "When I was a boy, my family live in *siheyuanr*, near Dazhalan. You know it?"

"Sure." Dazhalan's down by Qianmen, an old neighborhood south of Tiananmen that mostly got *chai*'d for the Olympics, the main street rebuilt into a Disneyfied version of itself, a fancy pedestrian mall that's half empty.

"Very dirty, really," he says. "Toilet outside house in *hutong*. I don't miss this part."

Zou pauses for a sip of beer. I refill his glass. He drinks. Puts his glass down with an audible thunk.

"So." Zou suddenly slaps his hands on the table. "The investigation." He tilts his head toward Sergeant Chen. "*Chen Jingguan, gei wo zhe zhang zhaopian.*"

Sergeant Chen, get me the photograph.

Chen reaches into his messenger bag and pulls out a manila folder. Opens it, extracts a glossy piece of paper. Hands it to his boss.

Who lays it on the table in front of me with a small, satisfied smile, like he's flipping over his hole card.

A dead woman.

"This woman, do you know her?" Zou asks.

She's young. Chinese. The shot is a close-up of her face. It's bruised. One eye swollen shut, the other clouded and flecked with dark red specks. Nose broken, shunted to one side, dried blood covering her split lip. Below her jaw, around her throat, more purple bruises.

"No," I say.

"You are certain?"

I shake my head. "I don't recognize her."

I want to say more, something like, *It's possible I met her once, but the way she looks now, how could I tell?* Except I haven't had enough beer to say something that dumb.

"This does not disturb you?" Zou asks.

Oh, I'm supposed to gasp and cry or something? Go all to pieces over a photograph?

Maybe I should feel something, but I really don't.

"I was a medic in the Iraq War. I saw dead people in person. This is just a picture."

"I see."

Fuck. Maybe I should've pretended. But I'm not a very good actress.

"If you are a . . . medic? Is that a doctor?"

"No. More like . . . we're first responders. We help people on the scene, when someone's hurt. Do first aid. Stop the bleeding if we can." I try to gauge his reactions. I'm not sure if he's understanding me, but one thing I'm pretty sure of: he's not stupid.

"But still you are a medical person. So. How is she dead, then?"

"You mean, what killed her?"

"Yes. In your opinion."

I look at the photo some more. "I couldn't tell you from a photo. No one could for sure. Not even a doctor. Not unless it was something really obvious. But someone beat her up. Maybe choked her."

"Choke?"

I put my hands on my own throat for a moment. "This."

"Ah."

We fall silent. The photo sits between us on the table, a piece of paper that suddenly feels like it weighs a ton.

"Why are you asking me about her?" I finally say.

Zou crooks his fingers at Chen, who makes a show of shuffling through the manila folder before he gets out another piece of paper and hands it over to his boss.

Zou studies it for a moment, then looks at me. Lays the paper on the table and slides it across.

That's when I realize: *This* is his hole card. Because the Xeroxed image on this piece of paper is a business card.

My business card.

I feel myself flush and then chill as I break out in a sweat.

"Yeah," I say. "It's mine."

Zou eyes me like he's monitoring every twitch, every drop of sweat. "Do you have something else to say now?"

"Yeah. Where'd you get it?"

"You don't know?"

Asshole. I feel a little rush of anger. It almost feels good, that surge of chemicals, and suddenly I can focus again. "Actually? I don't usually ask people questions when I already know the answer."

"Ah." Zou allows himself a small grin. He points at the photo of the dead girl. "This card was on her body. In her pocket. So you can see why we want to talk with you."

I don't feel anything right away. Just blank. Like any thoughts I had just got sucked out of my head.

What I say is, "Makes sense."

I pick up the photo of the dead girl. Study it again. If I know her, I don't know her well, not well enough to make up for how the swelling and bruises and busted nose have distorted her features.

"I really don't recognize her," I finally say. "Maybe she's someone I've met, but the way her face looks now, I just can't tell."

"Then how can she have your card?"

"I don't know. Look, I give my card to a lot of people. At galleries and openings and parties. She could be someone who was interested in an artist I represent. I have no idea."

I push the photo back toward Zou. "Are you going to tell me who she is?" I ask.

"Ah." Zou straightens up. Has another sip of beer, like this is a happy social occasion. "You see, this is also why we want to talk to you. We don't know. She has no purse. No . . . no *zhengming*."

No identification.

Nothing but my card.

Now my heart's pounding, and I'm thinking, It's a setup, it has to be, but who—and why?

Marsh. Or maybe Tiantian. Someone at that party.

Okay, McEnroe, slow down, I tell myself. You can't just assume that.

"Can you tell me when she died?" I ask.

"Why you wish to know?"

He's still smiling, but the way he says it isn't friendly. Like I have no business asking and it's suspicious that I'm doing so.

"Because she's dead and my card was in her pocket," I snap back. "So maybe she got my card not too long before she died. It might help me narrow it down."

Or she'd stuck it in her jeans or whatever she was wearing, forgot about it, and it was still there when she put them on again.

I push that thought aside.

Zou draws in a deep breath. Crosses his arms over his chest and pats his elbow with an audible slap.

"Sometime last night or early this morning. We still wait for . . . the study." He uncrosses his arms to sip more beer. "Some workers find her out near Sixth Ring Road. In some . . . some trash. This big trash mountain by an old village they . . ." His forehead wrinkles. He can't come up with the word. "Very embarrassing," he mutters. "My English."

"Your English is very good," I say automatically.

What I'm thinking is, She died last night or this morning.

Ding, ding, ding—we have a winner.

Meanwhile Zou's tapping something on his phone. A dictionary, I'm guessing. I have one on mine. "Demolish," he says with emphasis.

But Marsh wasn't the only one at that party who had my card. I'd given one to Gugu and to Meimei and . . . did I give one to Tiantian? Yeah, I think I did, right as I was leaving.

All three of the Caos. If I tell Zou that . . .

What's Sidney going to do if I tell a cop about his kids?

I think some more, back to the night of Gugu's party. I handed them out to that girl, the blogger, to Celine, and to her friend Rhinestone-Cap Girl—Betty.

Could the dead girl be one of them?

I don't think so, but I can't be sure.

"Does this give you any idea?" Zou asks.

A few too many, I'm thinking, but I don't say that.

What I say is this: "I was at a party last night. I don't think I gave my card to anyone there, though."

It's only a small lie.

Along with a big omission.

"A party. How late you stay?"

"Mmmm, about midnight?"

"And there are people from party to . . . to . . ." He checks his phone dictionary again. "*Verify* this?"

I shrug. "Sure." I hope.

"Who?"

Oh, shit. But there's no way around it. If I don't say where I was, Zou's going to have an even bigger hard-on for me.

"The name of the host is Cao Tiantian," I say. "I can give you the address."

LUCKY ME, I DON'T end up handcuffed in the backseat of a squad car or in some unmarked sedan with a bag over my head. Instead I pour out the rest of the beer, like a good hostess, and Zou finishes his glass. Then he stands. Sergeant Chen rises with him.

"If you can think of something to help us, please call me." Zou reaches into his little man bag, pulls out a card case, and gets a card. Hands it to me with both hands.

I make a show of examining it. Chinese on one side, English on the other.

Chief Inspector Zou Qiushi.

I wonder if he had these made himself or if this is the Beijing PSB's attempt to be all hip and modern?

"I will," I tell him. Who knows, I actually might.

I look at the Chinese on the back of the card. I still don't read as much as I speak, but I'm getting better.

"Qiushi—you know the meaning of this name?" Zou asks suddenly.

"I, uh . . ." Dumbshit, I say to myself. Way to show you know the language. Well, that and the Chinese dictionaries in the bookcase.

He probably already knew anyway.

"Seek truth, right?" I say.

He beams and nods. "Yes. And you say *qiushi* a different way, can mean 'jail cell.'" His smile broadens. "I like this name of mine."

I've just told a Beijing homicide detective he should check out the people at Tiantian's party. What's going to happen when Sidney finds out? I don't think he's going to be happy.

The idea pops into my head I could just tell Sidney that Marsh is a bad element, and whatever ends up happening because of that . . . well, all I did was tell Sidney, right?

But I can't. Marsh might not have anything to do with it, and I'm not going to have that on my head. Anyway, even if he does, would Marsh's getting whacked by Sidney solve *my* problem? Because even though I haven't been arrested, I can't assume I'm off Zou's suspect list. I'm pretty sure the PSB would love to pin this on a decadent foreigner.

"Fuck," I mutter, and I go to the fridge and get another beer. I shouldn't, I know I shouldn't—I mean, I'm already a little buzzed, and it's barely lunchtime, and I'm having a hard time thinking this through as it is.

Oh well.

I open up the bedroom door, beer in hand, and Mimi trots out, still on alert, eyes wide open, ears pricked forward.

"They're gone," I tell her. "Let's go sit on the couch. You can help me figure this out."

I pour out a little glass of beer and sip, and I think about what makes the most sense for me to do.

Okay, actually? The most sensible thing would be to just hit the eject button on this country.

To leave China.

Except where would I go? It's not like I can expect a warm welcome in the good US of A.

I sink back against the couch cushions and pat the seat next to me. "Come here, Mimi," I say.

She clambers up in that stiff-legged way dogs have.

If Marsh *did* do it, I could go to Sidney and suggest that rather than having his rent-a-goons kill him, Sidney use his money and influence to make sure Marsh gets arrested. That could work. It would get *me* out of trouble, right?

But what if Marsh didn't do it? What if this has nothing to do with the Caos at all?

Then what could I do that might be productive but that probably wouldn't get someone else killed or falsely thrown in prison?

Okay, I think. Okay. I gave cards to Gugu, and Meimei, and maybe Tiantian. Marsh. Celine and Betty.

There's a dead girl.

So candidates for Dead Girl that I gave my card to would be Celine, Betty, and Meimei.

Therefore first order of business would be find out if any of them are dead.

I refill my little beer glass, kind of proud of myself for figuring this out so logically and all.

I lift up the glass. And it suddenly occurs to me I can't do this right now. I need to stay frosty. I've got stuff to do.

I take one final sip of beer and put the glass on the coffee table.

★ ★ ★

MEIMEI FIRST, BECAUSE I don't have to reach too far to come up with a reason to call her.

She picks up after about five rings. *"Wei?"*

"Cao Meimei, ni hao. Shi . . ."

"Of course I know you are Ellie McEnroe," she says with a hint of amusement. "This is why I answered the call."

That's a good thing. I guess.

On the other hand, she's a Cao, and who knows what she's after?

Well, she's not dead anyway.

"Did you enjoy the party?" she asks.

"Oh. Yeah. Sure."

She laughs. "Oh, I forgot. My brother's wife was very rude to you. But you shouldn't care too much. She is crazy."

"Good to know," I say.

"You are calling about our dinner?"

"Yes," I say, relieved, thinking, Cool, I didn't even have to bring it up. "Because I need to go out of town maybe, and I wanted to make sure that we scheduled something first."

"I see." A pause. "Let me talk to my brothers. I think we can arrange something soon. Then you can go out of town if you like."

That went well. I think.

NEXT CELINE.

Unlike Meimei, she doesn't seem to recognize me. So I continue with the introduction: "I'm Ellie McEnroe. We met at Gugu's party."

"Ah!" I can picture her wide-eyed smile on the other end. "The family friend of the Caos."

The way she says that, I'm pretty sure she's mocking me. I

want to tell her, *Hey, so not my choice to be a Cao family friend. The Caos make me nervous.* But I don't say any of that.

"I wanted to talk to you about your website," I say.

"My website? Oh, you like it?"

"I haven't seen it yet. That's why I'm calling. I have an artist who's interested in . . . a collaborative project that involves, uh . . . the impact of social media on . . . discourse centered on female sexuality." Whatever. "And I thought she'd be interested in your website. But I lost your card."

"Oh." A pause. "That first part, that was . . . *yidianr buqingchu.*" A little unclear. "You mean some kind of artwork?"

"Yeah, sure. Maybe. It's more . . . research to . . . to inform the work."

"Okay." I'm guessing she's still *yidianr buqingchu* about the whole thing. Which, given that I'm just spouting bullshit jargon I pulled off the top of my head from a bunch of different art magazines, is not too surprising. "So you want my website's address?"

"Right."

"Okay. I can text to you." I can hear her long nails tapping on the screen of her phone. "Funny, though," she adds.

"What?"

"You have my phone number. But you say you lost my card."

Oh, well, shit. She's not dumb. "Yeah. I put your number in my phone. I must have gotten interrupted, because I didn't put in the address of the website, and now I don't know what happened to the card."

"Ah. I see."

I'm not sure whether she buys this or not, but I don't really care, because she's not dead, and that's all I need to know.

"Do you have Betty's number?" I ask.

"Betty?" I don't think I'm imagining the suspicion in that one word. Why would I want to call Betty? I don't have a good explanation. But one thing I've figured out lately. Sometimes if you just act like you're entitled to something, you'll get it.

"Yeah. We talked about getting together for coffee. But I forgot to ask for her number."

There's a silence on the other end, and I can picture her again, maybe taking a moment to light one of those Panda cigarettes while she considers what to do.

"Sure. I can text to you."

"Thanks. Looking forward to checking out your website."

"I think maybe some topics I write about might interest you," she says. "I hope you have a look."

"I definitely will," I say. "Thanks again."

We disconnect.

I'm thinking about what I should say to Betty, if she isn't dead, when the bamboo chime on my phone announces an incoming text.

From Celine. It says, LettersFromTheDeepYellowSea.com. Celine's website.

Huh. Not a .cn address. I wonder if her site's hosted outside of China? Makes sense if she's posting anything even a little sensitive. I really should check it out.

While I'm looking at that, another text. A cell-phone number, with the name in caps: BETTY.

I've really got nothing to say to Betty. I barely said two words to her, and she didn't seem to like me much. But does it even matter what I say? The only thing I care about is whether she's alive or not.

So I touch the number on Celine's text until the phone starts ringing.

"*Wei?*" Her voice sounds small. Shaky.

"*Ni hao, shi Betty ma?*"

"*Ni shi shei?*" Who are you? And I realize what that note in her voice is: fear. She's scared.

"*Duibuqi. Wo buxihuan mafan ni.*" Sorry. I don't want to bother you. "It's Ellie. Ellie McEnroe. We met at Gugu's party."

If I thought this was going to calm her down, it pretty much does the opposite.

"Why are you calling me?" There's a ragged edge to her voice now, like she's barely holding it together.

I almost hang up, because I don't know what to say. I should have thought of something. Should've planned it better. But I wasn't expecting *this*.

"I . . . uh, sorry. Just, I . . . I'll call you later. It's not important."

And then I do hang up.

SO HERE'S WHAT I know.

Meimei, Celine, Betty, not dead. Betty's scared. If that really *was* Betty. I barely talked to her at Gugu's party.

That's about it.

I sip the very strong cup of coffee I made. Think it through, McEnroe. Think it through.

How does this help me?

It doesn't, I conclude. Not really. None of the women I gave my card to who were at Tiantian's party are dead, assuming I just talked to the real Betty. The dead woman could be someone else who was at that party—shit, maybe even Milk Lady—and I have no way of knowing. Or she could be someone who wasn't at the party at all.

I already told Inspector Zou where I was last night. If I tell him more than that, like who I gave my cards to, there's going to be Cao-related blowback. Count on it. Bad enough I had to tell him about Tiantian's party.

Maybe once he finds out who he's dealing with, he'll lay off. You don't want to go after people like the Caos. Not unless you've got your own powerful backers who want to see them brought low.

It would be a hell of a lot more convenient to go after someone like me. Never mind that I had nothing to do with it. Forget that I have absolutely no motive or that I don't even know who the girl is. They could just make some shit up. Close the case, wipe their hands, and that's that.

Is there any kind of bone that I could throw Zou that isn't going to get me in even deeper?

I could tell him about Betty, or whoever it was who answered Betty's phone. She was scared of *something*.

"Fuck," I mutter. Because I don't want to sic the cops on Betty. I don't know what her connection to the Caos is, other than that she hangs out with Gugu. She could be another *fu er dai* or *hong er dai* for all I know, with her own powerful *guanxi*.

So what do I do?

I could call John.

I slump back against the couch. I call John, what's he going to say?

That I should have listened to him. I should've stayed away from the Caos.

Like I really had a choice.

What happens when somebody connects the dots? When Inspector Zou finds out I'm in deep shit with the DSD?

Because he *will* find out, sooner or later. And watch me go from person of interest to the perfect scapegoat.

Pompadour Bureaucrat would be the happiest little totalitarian ever.

CHAPTER TEN

"DON'T SAY IT."

John grimaces. It's as if holding back his "I told you so" is physically painful.

"Okay, you know that *chengyu*? That proverb? The one about how once you're riding on a tiger, it's really hard to get off?"

"*Qi hu nan xia,*" John mutters.

"Yeah. That's where I am with the Caos."

John halts in his tracks, and he just can't contain himself anymore. "But *why* you get on tiger in the first place?" He's punching the air with his fist as he says this.

We're wandering around the Yuanmingyuan, the Old Summer Palace, which he picked because it seemed like a good place to meet where neither of us would attract much attention, its being a tourist destination and all, but a low-key one. And it's not that crowded today, but this isn't exactly turning out to be a discreet conversation, which is what we're supposed to be having right now.

I didn't give him a blow-by-blow. Just, this girl turned up dead yesterday morning with my card on her body. And oh, yeah, whose party it was that I went to the night before last.

I lean against the metal railing that circles what used to be a decorative pond, or maybe a fountain. It's hard to tell. The

Yuanmingyuan was sacked and burned "by the Anglo-French imperialist forces" in the middle of the nineteenth century, during the Opium Wars, and what's left is all these big blocks and pillars of granite, the remains of marble bridges and stone boats, almost like the pictures you see of ancient Greek ruins, just the skeletons of something that used to be really grand. Really powerful.

"Listen. I didn't ask to get involved with the Caos. Sidney came looking for me. And the problem is, I owe him, big time."

A six-pack of Chinese girls, college age, are posing for pictures around what must have been the centerpiece of the fountain, this giant scallop-shell thing that looks more European than Chinese. They're cocking their heads to one side, kicking out their feet, making peace signs. They don't seem too concerned with the outrage committed by the Anglo-French imperialist forces.

"He got me out of a really bad situation," I say. "And there doesn't seem to be anything I can do to make us even."

John stands rigidly still, the muscle in his jaw still twitching. Looks down at his sneakers. Black leather Pumas. If they're fakes, they're good ones.

He nods, still staring at his shoes. Then he looks up.

"I can help you. I have some ideas," he says.

"What are you planning on doing?" I cut him off before he can object, before he can tell me to let him handle it. "If you're going to help me, I need to know."

A shrug. "Simple. I just go to this Inspector Zou and tell him I have interest in the case. He must tell me his progress. He has no choice but to obey."

Hearing this makes me feel slightly sick to my stomach. "Then he'll *know* I have a DSD problem."

"Yes. But this way he can just report to me, not my bosses. I can make a suggestion, maybe he should arrest someone else."

I think about it. The plan's simple and kind of brilliant in a way: Do an end run around the DSD's getting involved by being the DSD guy in charge before the bosses find out about the case.

But this is the Cao family we're talking about, the Caos and their *hong er dai* connections. With people that powerful, if Zou pursues any of them, if they're in any way connected to a murder and that gets out, what are the odds that Domestic Security gets a call? Either from the Caos or from one of their enemies?

"I don't think it's a good idea," I finally say. "This goes wrong, you could get in a lot of trouble."

"Not if we solve it quickly. Then I am just doing my job."

"Solve?"

"Find the right one to blame." His face darkens. "All those Caos, they are all guilty of something."

Hoo, boy.

It's possible that I just made things a lot worse.

On the way home, I stop at a dumpling place I like on Andingmen to pick up a late lunch. I get it to go. I don't feel like eating in the restaurant by myself, and besides, I need to get home to my dog.

This place is popular, and it's usually crowded, but right now, just after 2:00 P.M., the lunch crowd is gone. I sit on a hard wooden bench by the entrance and wait for my dumplings. A bunch of *fuwuyuan* eat their lunches at a round, plastic-covered table in the back, kitchen workers in white, waitresses in cheap embroidered jackets, "traditional" style except done in neon shades of pink and yellow and turquoise. A few more lounge around by the drink cooler in the back, yelling at a soccer game on the TV. Chinese soccer is a pretty corrupt business, or so I'm told, and I guess the national team sucks, but they still really get into it.

I shouldn't have told John. If he starts digging around looking for dirt on the Caos . . . what are the consequences likely to be? It's not like I care if he finds out that Tiantian or Meimei or Gugu or even Sidney is a corrupt fuck. I mean, that's kind of the default setting if you're *fu er dai*. It's more that poking the hornet's nest isn't a good idea. Believe me, I know. I've done it when I didn't even know that was what I was sticking my hand into. But John doesn't have that excuse. He has to know that going after the Caos is asking for a shitstorm. And I know John. He's a gung-ho mofo. He's not going to stop until he completes the mission.

Or someone takes him out.

I get my dumplings.

I walk home along Gulou Dongdajie. Normally it's one of my favorite streets—old-style grey brick buildings, two or three stories high, traditional signboards, funky little boutiques and coffeehouses. Today, though, I'm tempted to flag down a cab. It's not that far, but my leg's just killing me. I stop at a little snack stand, buy a bottle of water, crack it open, and take a Percocet, wondering like I do every time I take one lately how the fuck I'm going to manage when I run out of them this time.

I could try a doctor here, I guess. But everyone I've ever talked to tells me it's almost impossible to get an outpatient prescription, and if you can, they're pretty stingy with the pills and they cost a fortune to boot.

I'm standing in front of a guitar shop. For whatever reason, this stretch of Gulou Dongdajie has a bunch of music stores. You can buy guitars, drums, violins, traditional Chinese instruments, whatever. The whiteboard in the window of this one lists some of the guitars they have to offer, in English (THE NATIONAL STEEL COUNTRY BLUES GUITAR), and below that, also in English, these lines: KEEP ANGER, KEEP REVOLT! FUCK THE WORLD! FUCK THE GOVERNMENT! FUCK THE RED LAND!!!

Rock and roll, dude.

I keep walking.

I pass some fancy-ass private club—I mean, I'm assuming it's fancy; I've never been inside. But it has discreet lighting, a traditional red door trimmed in brass, and a couple of very pretty hostesses standing outside in *qipaos*, I guess in case any princelings happen to stop by for happy hour.

Nice *qipaos*, I think. They remind me of the ones I saw at Tiantian's party: Classy. Expensive.

I think about that house and that party and the kind of money it would take to have that place and throw that little get-together, and all it does is piss me off. Why do assholes rule the world anyway?

And then I think about something else. The serving girls at Tiantian's party. The ones in the fancy *qipaos*. There were a lot of them. All young. All pretty.

I wonder if maybe one of them didn't make it home that night.

OKAY, GRANTED, IT'S A long shot.

Assuming that the dead girl is connected to Tiantian's party and the Caos—which my gut tells me is the case, but hey, my gut's been wrong before—she could have been a chicken girl, a hooker. Or one of the guests. But I figure a guest, someone with money or family connections, that kind of person doesn't stay unidentified for long.

A *fuwuyuan* at some kind of high-class catering company? That's a different story. Because I'm guessing it's just a dressed-up version of your basic restaurant businesses. A lot of girls from all over China come to Beijing for work. They get hired in a restaurant. Their families are far away. They don't show up for work one day, the employer may or may not give a shit. She's moved on to something better, that's what he might think. Or she's just moved on.

So how do I find out if I'm right?

"VICKY, HI. IT'S ELLIE McEnroe."

"Ellie McEnroe. Do you have report for Mr. Cao?"

I sigh between gritted teeth. Vicky's like, like . . . I don't know, a bloodhound or something, or maybe a leopard. I heard on some nature show that leopards fixate on their prey and you can't break that focus until said prey is hunted down and killed. Or maybe it's jaguars. Either way.

"I have dinner with the children soon. Meimei is arranging it."

"So you report after this dinner?"

"Yeah," I say. "Sure." Maybe. "Actually, I was calling about something else. There was a catering company at Tiantian's party. *Yige yinshi fuwu.*"

"Yes?"

"I might have to organize an art opening, and this catering company was very good. I wondered if you know someone I could ask for their name?"

"Of course, I have it." An uncharacteristic chuckle. "You think Tiantian runs his own house?"

Score. This is going better than I hoped. I thought I'd end up with another name, Tiantian's housekeeper or something like that, or if my luck was really sucking, Dao Ming, Mrs. Tiantian. But I can picture Vicky Huang keeping an eye on things if Sidney's money is involved.

"Would you mind sending the name to me?"

A hesitation. "This company . . . is very expensive."

"I'd like to talk to them. My client might be willing to pay."

I get the feeling Vicky Huang's of the "knowledge is power" school and she's reluctant to part with any of it. Or maybe I'm right, and something happened last night, and she knows about it.

She's silent for another moment.

"Deng yixia." Wait a minute. I hear her fingernails tapping, probably on her iPad. "I email it to you."

THE NEXT THING I do is call John.

"I have an idea who the dead girl might be. But you'd be able to find out a lot easier than I could."

"Okay, good." He sounds cautious, measured. "So tell me."

"If I do, I want you to promise me something. That you tell *me* if I'm right. After you find out but before you go do anything about it."

"Yili, maybe it's better—"

"No." I take in a deep breath. "You're the one who's always saying I should trust you. So okay, you want me to trust you? Then do what I'm asking."

This is it, I think. He'll turn me down, or he'll agree, and if he agrees, then all I can do is hope that he keeps his word. Which is no sure thing.

"Okay," he says. "I will tell you what I find out."

★ ★ ★

HERE'S MY THINKING. JOHN is in a better position to go to the catering company and get a useful response. All he has to do is show that DSD credential—I mean, assuming he has one in his capacity of undercover nark. And while tracking down the identity of the dead girl is still likely to bring him into the Cao's kill zone, it might be more surgical than if he just goes after any and all Caos. Maybe the blowback won't be as bad.

Because I guess I like John, and I'd rather see him not get into trouble.

And if he can actually figure out who this girl is and who killed her, maybe *I'll* be off the hook.

CHAPTER ELEVEN

HE CALLS ME THE next day.

"Can we have lunch?" he asks.

"You found something?"

"Maybe."

WE MEET AT A Sichuan place out in Haidian, the sort of typical large restaurant that has nothing distinguishing about it: round tables covered by oil-spotted red plastic, beige and faded green decor, blocky radiators and drink refrigerators, the kind of bathroom that you really have to need to use to make yourself use it, and as loud as a football game: shouted conversations, plates dropped on tables, and the clinking of beer bottles. My kind of dive.

Since it's Haidian, the university district, there's a bunch of foreigners here, so John and I don't attract any particular attention. Just a couple of pals out for some *mapo dofu* and *yuxiang rou si*.

John waits until we've ordered. Rather till *he's* ordered. It's a Chinese-guy thing. Sometimes it's irritating, but in this case he knows what I like, and he doesn't bother to ask.

After the *fuwuyuan* brings our Yanjing Draft beer and some vinegar peanuts with spinach, John reaches into his jacket pocket and gets out his smartphone. Unlocks it and finger-swipes a few times. Then holds it out to me.

I take it. My fingers brush against his, and yeah, I'm still feeling those little electric shocks, and a part of me is thinking maybe we could go someplace after lunch.

Bad idea, McEnroe, I tell myself.

I look at the phone screen.

On it is a photo of a young woman. Almost a mug shot, except she's smiling. She's wearing a sort of uniform smock with a plastic badge that has a name and a number on it.

"Her name is Wang Junyi. She worked at Cao Tiantian's party," John says. "And she does not come to work the next day. They say maybe she has just left for a better job."

I shiver a little. I study that smiling face, and it's a broad smile, one that looks real, and I think, God, I *hope* you left for a better job.

Please don't be that dead girl with the bruised, shattered face.

"Did you find out where she lives?" I ask.

He nods.

"Did you go there?" My mouth's gone dry, and the words catch in my throat. I swallow some beer.

"Not yet." John looks up at me. There's something soft about his dark eyes. "I promise you I tell you first."

Oh, man. My heart's beating hard. It's like he's trying to make me really like him. And it's maybe even working.

"So . . . after lunch. Can we go there?"

Because, yeah. I just have to push it.

He closes his eyes and does that little grimace I've come to know so well. "Why?" he asks with a sigh.

I shrug. "Just . . . because."

The truth is, there's no real reason I should go at all. I just want to see what he'll say. Maybe I want to make him mad, I don't know. So he can turn me down and I can go back to a safe distance, where I don't have to trust him.

"Okay." He picks up a mouthful of spinach and peanuts with his chopsticks. "We can make up a story to tell them, I think."

Well, shit.

TURNS OUT HER PLACE isn't that far from the restaurant. It's right near the Line 13 *qinggui* stop for Da Zhong Si, the Big Bell Temple, which John once told me was near his childhood home. I never did find out if that was the truth or not. I did visit the temple once. It's now a "bell museum." The front courtyard selling souvenirs: bells and Buddhas, T-shirts, kites, and toys. The temple's surrounded by a forest of tall, skinny high-rises painted in this color scheme of yellowish cream and brick red that you see everywhere in China, built a couple decades ago and now washed over with grey grime and black soot.

We drive in John's silver Toyota, down a major road, three lanes each side. Pass this giant . . . I don't know what it is. A shopping center? Multistory pink walls and green tubular trim, an entrance resembling part of a mammoth Lego set. The whole building looks like it's surrounded by scaffolding, some kind of metal latticework to hold up huge signs for products I've never heard of.

"You really grew up around here?"

John nods, scanning the road for something, an address maybe. "Different now," he says. "Used to be farms not far from here. Fields."

We turn right. A smaller street than the near highway we were just on, only four lanes across. Blocks of high-rises with businesses on the first few floors that face the street. The usual stuff. Electronics and cell-phone stores. Restaurants. Barber-shops, some of which are sex joints. All lit up by the afternoon sun, filtered through a yellow-grey haze.

"I liked playing in the fields," John says suddenly. "We had all kinds of games. Mostly Chinese Red Army against the Japanese devils. Of course the Red Army always wins."

We turn down an alley. To the left there are steel barriers marking off a small parking lot, I guess for the high-rises in front of and behind it.

"Here," John says.

He shoehorns the car into half a space by driving the front wheels up onto a curb. We get out.

It looks like a pretty nice complex, actually. A few trees that aren't dying, a couple of stone benches beneath them in a little quadrangle in the center of a cluster of apartment buildings that look to be twenty or so stories high. The exteriors stained and speckled with black grime and trickles of rust. Closed balconies where the windows are permanently fogged by the pollution. But, you know, nice.

John looks at something on his phone. "This one," he says, pointing to one of the buildings that fronts the sidewalk.

We go into the lobby. It's not bad. Finished granite floors, wood-grain wallboard, a little flat-screen TV beaming ads between the brass-trimmed elevators, a couple of decorative plants.

John's studying the mailboxes that line the wall across from the elevators.

"Looks a little pricey for a *fuwuyuan*," I say. "Even one who's working for a high-class caterer."

I'm thinking maybe Wang Junyi has a little business on the side.

John nods. Looks at his phone again. "This house number . . . not here."

"What do you mean?"

He points at the mailboxes. "All the numbers have floor, then house number. So tenth floor, house number five, is 1005. Her number is 41."

"Maybe it's the first floor?"

"No. First floor start with 'one.' And no floor has forty-one apartments."

"Huh."

I think about what this might mean. Maybe she gave her employer a fake address?

John meanwhile strides to the lobby door and heads outside. I follow him as he approaches a stout older woman in a dark blue smock and pants who is slowly sweeping the cement path with a straw broom. *"Laodama,"* I hear him say. Auntie. I hear bits and pieces of the conversation, John asking about the apartment number, about Wang Junyi. I hang back, listening to the cars honking on the street behind me, to a thin stream of music, some Chinese pop with a high-pitched chick singer, and I feel a sudden shiver in the warm, yellow afternoon. I don't know why.

"Hao, hao. Xiexie ninde hezuo."

Thanks for your cooperation.

When he reaches me, his expression is neutral. "Okay," he says. "I know how to find her place now."

We walk around the building. A narrow alley runs along one side, the ragged cement blackened with soot and worn-in grease, from the Xinjiang restaurant next door, I'm guessing. I can smell the roasting lamb and charcoal and lighter fluid.

There's a heavy steel door, painted beige and dented in

places. John opens it. He doesn't wait for me to go first. Instead he steps inside, holding the door open but standing in front of me like a shield.

I cross the threshold. He lets the door close behind me.

We're at the top of a stairwell. Unpainted cement, lit by a single fluorescent bulb. John points at the stairs.

We go down a flight, pass the first landing we see, and head down the next flight. Long, steep flights. When we get to the bottom, I figure we're two stories below the first floor.

There's a corridor, harshly lit by a couple more fluorescent lights in bare, rusting cages. Seeing them reminds me of something else, a place I was at back in the Sandbox, a place I never want to see again but still can't get out of my head.

Some people can just forget shit. Why can't I?

"Something wrong?"

I wipe my forehead. It's covered in sweat. "No. Just hot down here."

Pipes run along the ceiling, water pipes that drip, plus electric conduit and tangles of loose, frayed wire. There's a sign next to a junction box warning of danger, with a little black silhouette of a man getting zapped by a black lightning bolt.

We walk a ways. On one side there's more machinery: boilers and stuff, I guess, plus a jumble of crates and dusty boxes, mopeds and bikes. On the other it's flimsy wallboard, interspersed here and there with those dented blue tin panels they use to make temporary fences at construction sites. We turn right, and then it's wallboard and blue metal panels on both sides.

I catch the sweaty scent of hot, packaged noodles before I really get it.

"People are living down here, right?"

John nods. "Rat tribe," he mutters.

I don't know if it's an insult, calling them that: the legions of Beijing's workers who serve and cook in the city's restaurants, who clean its fancy hotels, the migrants who come here to make money and who can't possibly afford a real apartment in the city, the college grads and dreamers and artists who've ended up in tiny cubicles in the basements and subbasements of high-rises and former fallout shelters. I mean, there are worse things than being called a rat in Chinese culture. I was born in the Year of the Rat, and everybody says that means I'm a clever survivor.

So, hey. Embrace the suck.

I don't get the feeling that there are that many people here right now. No conversations. No laughing, or shouting, or crying. If I listen hard, I can hear a faint strain of some Chinese pop music, so quiet it's like I'm almost imagining it, like maybe I'm hearing something else, a pump or a rattling air conditioner, and I'm conjuring music out of it.

I guess most everyone's at work this time of day. Or sleeping.

We walk down the makeshift hall, John checking out the numbers stenciled and in some cases scribbled in thick black marker on the wallboard. It's pretty dark, with the only light coming from behind us. No hint of daylight anywhere. How could there be? We're in a fucking basement fallout shelter.

John stops about halfway down the hall. Points at a blue construction panel. It's a makeshift door, I finally realize, with holes drilled on one side and thick wire running through those and into the wallboard. Light leaks out around it like a glowing frame.

I think, Okay, there's light. So she must be there, right?

Someone is anyway.

John raps on the door.

There's a rustling sound, someone moving, and then, *"Shi shei?"* A young woman's voice.

John jabs a finger at me.

Me? I mouth.

He nods, with that hint of irritation I've seen on him before, like I'm missing something obvious.

Whatever. *"Ni hao. Wang Junyi ma?"* Hello. You're Wang Junyi?

The door rattles, then opens a crack. She's got some kind of chain on it, which is pretty funny. A couple of good, hard shoves and you'd rip the wire "hinges" right off this "door."

"Bushi. Ni yao shenme?" No. What do you want?

Shit. I really should've made something up ahead of time.

"A couple of nights ago, I went to a party," I say in Mandarin. "Wang Junyi was working there. She left something. I wanted to give it to her."

John nods, this time with something close to a smile. Like I'm not such a bad liar after all.

He should know.

"You saw her?"

"Yes." Which, you know, I probably did.

The door opens a crack wider. "You're a foreigner," she says.

"Right."

More rattling.

The door opens.

I can't see her that clearly, with the light coming from behind her. She's young, I'm pretty sure. Short, a little stocky. She takes a step back, her body rigid.

"Who's he?" she asks.

"A friend."

"He was at the party?"

"No."

She hesitates. I can't tell what she's thinking. It's hard to see her face.

"Come in," she finally says.

IT'S A LITTLE CUBICLE with white walls. The floor space is almost entirely taken up by a couple of twin mattresses. There's a pole running above our heads from one side of the room to the other that's hung with clothing, a couple of salvaged shelves piled with shampoo and cosmetics, stacks of magazines, some folded T-shirts, a laptop, and an electric kettle, the plug for that stuck into a power strip plugged into an extension cord that runs up to the single ceiling light. There's stuff on the walls, a plastic poster-size slick ad for Lancôme cosmetics that looks like it came from a subway station, the face of a beautiful woman holding up a tiny bottle like it's got a genie inside. A picture of Rain, the Korean pop star, next to a mountain landscape that looks familiar but that I can't place.

"Huangshan," she explains. "We both come from Anhui. Do you know Huangshan?"

"I've never been there, but I've heard of it," I say.

"Most beautiful mountain in all of China. You know the saying in China: 'Once you visit Huangshan, you would not want to visit any other mountain.'"

"I did not know that," I say.

John and I sit on one of the mattresses while she makes tea. "Juliet is my English name," she tells us. She has one, even though she doesn't speak more than a few words of the language. "I saw the movie with Lai'angnaiduo Dicapuliao. *Luomiou yu Zhuliye.*"

It takes me a minute. "Oh. Leonardo DiCaprio. *Romeo and Juliet*," I say in English.

She nods vigorously, smiles a little. "So romantic." She hands me a glass with some loose leaves floating on top. "Be careful," she tells me. "Hot." It is, almost too hot to hold. "But I think I'll change my name soon."

"Why?"

She shrugs as she hands John his tea. "It is a silly idea. Dying like that for love."

Finally she sits on the mattress across from us. "So Junyi's belonging, what is it?"

I squirm a little. The glass really is hot. I put it on the floor in front of me.

"Her identity card," John says. "So we want to give it to her personally."

It's a good lie. They use that card, the *shenfenzheng*, for all kinds of things in China. Buying train tickets. Opening a bank account. Applying for a job.

Juliet nods, staring at the floating leaves in her glass. She twists it around in her hands, which I notice are reddened and chapped. "I don't know where she is," she says at last. "She hasn't come home since that night. I call her phone, I call her work, I call her friends. No one has seen her."

I get that horrible, collapsing feeling in my gut. Because I'm pretty sure that *I've* seen her since that night. A picture of her anyway.

"Did you contact the police?" John asks.

Juliet snorts. "The police? What for? We don't have Beijing *hukou*, why would they want to help us? Anyway, the police are useless."

John blushes a little. I doubt Juliet would notice, but I do.

"But if she is missing . . ." he says, almost gently.

Then Juliet starts to cry. I hate it when people cry. I never know what to do.

"We are friends from Anhui," she says between sobs. "We came to Beijing together to make money. I don't know what to do."

John reaches out and pats her on the shoulder. "I am sorry," he says. "But you must go to the police. Tell them she is missing. I know a detective. You can go to see him."

Juliet looks up. Her face, like her hands, is red and blotchy. Her body is suddenly tense, like she might bolt, or maybe attack. Fight or flight. I can't tell which.

"Why do you care?" Her voice shakes, and I'm not sure how much is anger and how much is fear. We could be anyone, and maybe we're not here to help. "What do you really want?"

"Justice," John says.

"She called me from that party. She said if she worked late, she had a chance to make more money."

I guess Juliet believed him. But then, John's pretty convincing when he wants to be.

Maybe he even means it.

"When she said this, how did she sound?" John asks.

"What do you mean?"

"Angry? Happy? Scared?"

Juliet frowns a little, pursing her lips. "Just . . . normal. She said she was tired. But she was happy to have a chance to make more money. This is why we came to Beijing. To make money."

John nods. "I understand. This company she works for. Do you know anything about it?"

"Just that they like pretty girls." She shrugs. "Junyi is very pretty. Not like me. I could never work there."

They were all pretty girls, the ones working at that party.

"How long has *she* worked there?"

"Not long. Maybe . . . two months."

"Does she like it?"

Juliet snorts. "She likes the money. Much more than her last job. She says maybe we can get a better apartment soon, because the money is good."

"Has she worked late before?" I ask. Because I'm wondering what that might have involved.

"Only once."

I hesitate, because I really don't know how to put this. And while my Chinese has gotten pretty decent when it comes to the basics of talking to people, I don't exactly have much skill in the way of nuance.

"What did she say, after that first time?" I ask. "Did she tell you about it?"

"No," Juliet mumbles, rubbing her roughened hands, not meeting my eyes. "I already went to sleep."

"Huh."

Her head snaps up. "Anyway, what does it matter? Why are you asking all these questions?"

"I told you," John says. "I have a friend who is a detective."

She stares at him. I'm not sure if she's buying it. "You came to bring her identity card. You can leave it with me."

John shakes his head. "Since she is missing, it must go to the police."

Her eyes are tearing up again.

"Here." He produces his wallet, pulls out a business card. Looks like the same card he gave me once, the one for his supposed company, "Bright Spring Enterprises," where his name's Zhou Zheng'an.

I'm pretty sure it's not a real business either.

He holds out his card to her. "You can call me if you want. I will tell you what the police say."

She doesn't take the card. She squeezes her eyes shut, like she doesn't want to see it.

I get it, I think. If she calls him, maybe she's going to hear something she doesn't want to hear.

"If there's news, you want to tell her parents, don't you?" he asks softly.

Finally she nods and takes the card.

"So what do you think? The catering company has 'girls selling smiles' after hours?"

He's been quiet during the ride back to Gulou. Distracted.

"Maybe so. Or maybe someone just has this expectation."

"Yeah, could be," I say, thinking of Milk Lady, a little detail I have not told John about. I mean, for all that the guy is great in the sack, in a freaky kind of way, he's got a moralizing streak a mile wide, plus he seems to have a bug up his ass about rich people in general, the Caos in particular.

"What now?" I ask.

"I thought you want to go back to Gulou."

"No, I mean . . . Okay, so we think we know who the dead girl is. What happens next?"

"Hmmm." His forehead wrinkles. "We can tell Inspector Zou. But maybe we can wait a little while." His eyes get that dark look again, the one that kind of scares me. "I think I want to meet these Caos first."

I slump back in the seat. This is not going to end well, I'm pretty sure.

CHAPTER TWELVE

D INNER WITH THE C AOS is at a place called Tea.

I checked it out online. From the photos the place looks so perfectly elegant and minimal that it makes my teeth hurt. And according to an article on CNN, it's one of the most expensive restaurants in the city.

"You sure you want to go, John? What if you end up with the bill? They give you that kind of expense account?"

John pauses in the middle of straightening his tie and shoots me a glare.

We're in my apartment. John's in the bathroom, giving himself a once-over in the mirror. He's wearing a suit—something I've never seen him wear before—and though I'm no expert, I'm pretty sure he, or somebody, spent some money on it: a kind of silvery grey that drapes just so over a perfect white shirt. He's put a styling gel in his hair that makes him look like some kind of movie star for the teen-idol set. I have to say he looks pretty good. Way better than a guy who's hanging out with me should look. I mean, shouldn't he be with some cute, perfect, dainty Chinese girl? What's he doing with a train wreck like me?

Probably spying, I remind myself.

Mimi sits there half on his feet, staring up at him with a look of utter adoration. She's always loved John.

I thought dogs were supposed to be loyal.

John smoothes his coat and turns to me. Looks me up and down. I'm wearing one of my Vicky Huang outfits.

"That is nice," he says. "Though why do you never wear a dress? I think you will look pretty."

I want to smack him. Instead I shrug. "Busted-up leg, not so pretty. Look, can we just get out of here and go to this fucking dinner?"

Mimi thumps her tail. Like she thinks we're going for a walk. I lean over and ruffle the scruff around her neck. "Sorry, pup. I know you're not getting enough walks. Tomorrow, I promise."

Assuming I don't get arrested.

TEA IS IN A *hutong* area just north of the Forbidden City, close to the National Art Museum and Jingshan Park. Not all that far from where I live, but the traffic sucked, and there was an accident on Di'anmen, and by the time we get close, my leg's hurting and I'm twitching like a meth head, feeling like the longer we sit in this car, the more of a big fat target I am, and even though I tell myself, That's stupid—it's not getting blown up you need to worry about right now, I can't help it.

I thought I was getting better.

"Are you feeling sick?" John asks.

I shake my head. "No. Just don't like sitting in a car in traffic, that's all."

"Almost there."

We get off the main street finally. Turn down a little lane lined by old grey walls with red doors, peaked roofs coyly hiding behind them, revealing just a glance, and I catch a glimpse of the bright moon through a tree—I don't know what it's called, one of those trees you see everywhere here with the narrow limbs and tangles of thin twigs that stretch toward the sky, like they're trying to break through the smog and the bullshit to nourish themselves somehow—and it hits me like a wave, how in spite of how ugly this city is, sometimes it's still beautiful.

WE PULL UP IN front of a grey wall. A uniformed valet swoops in and takes John's keys.

I heave myself out of the car. Pain arcs up my wobbling leg, and I'm suddenly light-headed. I stare up at the sky, blinking, looking for the moon through the smog. The streetlamps light up the dust, making the air seem to sparkle, like somebody threw yellow glitter into the sky.

"Are you all right?" I feel John's steadying hand on my arm. And I'm remembering the night we met, how he tricked me. I was dizzy that night, too, walking with him. I remind myself why that was. What he did.

I pull my arm away. "Yeah. Fine."

"Yili . . ."

I turn to face him. He looks confused, he looks concerned, he looks like he actually gives a shit. But hey, I've been wrong about that before.

"What?"

"We can just go home if you like." He sounds so earnest saying this. So honest.

"Yeah? And then what? I get arrested for killing some girl I don't think I ever even met?"

"I can take care of it. You don't need to—"

"I *do* need to," I snap. "I need to take care of myself. I need to . . ." I get hit by another wave of dizziness. Swamped. I steady myself against the wall. "Let's just go to this dinner, okay?"

What the fuck is wrong with me?

A panic attack. It's like I used to get, when I wouldn't leave the house, when I'd freak out in the supermarket, or in a car, or . . . well, anyplace. But I'm better. I've been handling things. Look at what I've done the last two years. Look at the shit that got thrown at me. I survived it, right?

Why is this happening now?

There's a double red door with brass studs. A red wood beam threshold. We step across it. On the other side is a broad court-yard and, across it, what looks like a small, Tibetan-style temple: ornate upturned roof with scalloped yellow tiles, red screens and walls and columns. Pillars of light rise at even intervals, like they're another row of columns holding the place up.

It's your head that's doing this, I tell myself. There's nothing wrong right now. I'm not going to get blown up. It's just a feeling. Like what the army shrink used to say: *Feelings are transient. You let yourself feel them, observe what they are, let them go.*

"Just because I feel this way now doesn't mean I'll always feel this way," I mutter.

"*Ni shuo?*"

"Nothing," I tell John. "Nothing important."

There's a flagstone path leading up to the temple, lit here and there by lanterns on iron posts. A little stone bridge that arches over an artificial stream. And finally, as we walk up a couple of broad steps that lead to the entrance, a bronze sign with a cutout character lit from behind: 茶.

Tea.

I sure hope they have booze.

YEAH, THE WHOLE PLACE is gorgeous and expensive: ancient wood, hand-crafted furniture, mood lighting, a Buddha statue here and there, perfectly placed paintings—calligraphy mostly. The patrons also look like money. It's quiet, unlike most Chinese restaurants, the kind I go to anyway, with some traditional music plinking in the background.

The hostess leads us to a private room.

A low, round table. Seated at its head are Tiantian and Mrs. Tiantian, Dao Ming. Tiantian's wearing another expensive jacket with a mandarin collar that doesn't quite fit right over his dumpy frame, Dao Ming some Gucci/Pucci/whatever dress. She smiles tightly in my general direction, which I guess is an improvement over calling me a bitch. To their left sits the older guy from the party with the sad eyes and the sharp suit, the one who led Dao Ming out when she had her little meltdown. I can't remember his name. She called him "Uncle," I think.

To the right, Meimei. Tonight her hair is loose instead of slicked back, and she's wearing a silk outfit, an embroidered red robe and flowing pants, that looks like something from a Chinese historical soap opera. "Oh," she says, "you've brought a friend."

"Yeah," I say. "I . . . uh, mentioned it to Vicky when she called to set this up. That John would be coming. This is John. Zhou Zheng'an."

John steps forward. *"Hen gaoxing renshi nimen."* Very pleased to meet you all. Which I'm pretty sure he's not.

I look at him, and he has a smile on his face and a sort of glitter in his dark eyes.

Strike that, he's probably really looking forward to opening up a whole can of whoop-ass on one or more Caos.

Speaking of, no sign of Gugu.

Tiantian makes a sweeping gesture at the empty chairs across from him. *"Qing zuo."* Please sit. "I have ordered some special tea to start our dinner."

Oh, great. Fucking tea.

We sit. I try to turn the grimace on my face that comes from the pain in my leg as I get down on that low chair into a smile.

I'm next to Meimei. John's next to me. There are two more empty chairs to his left.

Introductions are made. John smiles and nods politely. The last to introduce himself is Uncle.

"Yang Junmin," he says.

There's the slightest flicker of recognition on John's face, quickly covered up by a polite smile.

"John's a consultant," I say.

John nods vigorously. "Yes."

"Really?" Meimei says. "On what kinds of projects?" She seems amused.

"Various kinds. I work with relevant government departments. To help obtain necessary permissions."

At that, Uncle Yang's eyes narrow, and I hear this tiny snort. And I get this sudden flash: Celine at the party, telling me how Dao Ming is *hong er dai*, "second-generation red."

And this guy is her "uncle."

There were all kinds of government officials at that party, I'm pretty sure.

I get that creepy-crawly feeling, like a spider's walking up my spine.

What are the odds that this guy's someone pretty high up?

Meanwhile John's continuing his earnest, slightly clueless routine. It doesn't fool me anymore, but objectively it's a pretty good act.

"I think this project, it is very exciting," he says. "And a way to make China shine on the world stage."

Tiantian leans forward. He likes this idea, I can tell. "In what way?"

"There are many valuable and important works in your father's collection. If you can build a first-class museum for them, it can help show China is a world cultural power."

Tiantian slowly nods. "Though it is better to emphasize Chinese works. Chinese traditions. Create a showcase for our own culture."

So is Tiantian actually interested in the museum project? And is that a good thing? Because it's not like I actually want to *do* any of this.

"That's a good idea," I say. "But first we need to deal with the collection that's already there. Right?"

"Of course."

"Is the tea coming?" Dao Ming asks abruptly.

Dao Ming has her forehead resting on three tense fingers, her thumb tucked under her cheekbone. Her fingers are long and skinny and white, like ivory.

Uncle Yang nods. "Yes. Just wait a moment." He lifts a hand. *"Fuwuyuan."* It's funny, he hardly raises his voice. But immediately a waitress hustles into our private room. *"Women xianzai yao he cha."*

We want to drink our tea now.

THE TEA IS ALL fancy. It's Tieguanyin, which I'm pretty sure is Chinese for "really fucking expensive."

"Name means 'Iron Goddess of Mercy,'" the waitress explains to me in English. "Is one of very best oolong tea."

She goes through this whole big production: First we have to look at the tea and say how pretty it is and how nice it smells. I mostly nod and leave that to the others. Then she puts the tea in a pot and "rinses" it with hot water that she pours out of a brass kettle with a long, skinny spout. She pours from a couple feet off the table, so the water splashes everywhere. This is normal, I guess. Then she pours it into our cups, but we're not supposed to drink that. She pours more hot water into the teapot, this time from a normal height. Our cups get emptied onto the outside of the teapot. Finally she pours the tea into these tiny porcelain cups: not to drink, to smell. And you're supposed to put your larger, drinking teacup over that to capture the smell.

"*Long feng cheng xiang*," Tiantian says, intoning this with his eyes half closed like it's some kind of blessing.

"This means 'dragon and phoenix in fortunate union,'" the waitress explains.

Somebody bring me a beer.

WELL, OKAY, FOR TEA it tastes pretty good. Kind of smoky and smooth in a way that rolls off my tongue and slides down my throat.

"The purpose of tea ceremony is to encourage relaxation. And pleasant discussion." Tiantian wags his finger at me. "It does not matter in a teahouse who is rich and who is poor. All can speak frankly together."

I'd be on the "poor" end of this equation. Thanks for rubbing my nose in it, asshole.

"Huh," I say. "That's very interesting."

A sudden movement from Dao Ming catches my eye. She's tossing back her cup of tea like it's a shot of tequila. "We should order," she says in Tiantian's general direction. "Otherwise we could wait for Gugu all night."

"We can wait a while longer. The Tieguanyin is good for several more pots."

"Our guests are hungry," she hisses.

"Perhaps some *dianxin*," Uncle Yang murmurs. Which is Mandarin for dim sum.

Tiantian's hand thrusts up. *"Fuwuyuan,"* he calls out.

It's Uncle Yang who's the big dog here, I'm pretty sure.

HALFWAY THROUGH OUR APPETIZERS, Gugu stumbles in. Yeah, I'm pretty sure he's blasted. Marsh is at his side, a steadying hand on his back.

"Sorry I came late," Gugu mutters, landing on the chair next to John.

Tiantian's mouth tightens; he sits up in his chair, and I think he's going to start something with Gugu.

Instead he pulls back and says, "We are just about to order dinner."

Gugu's eyes are swollen, and he leans back in his chair like it's the only thing holding him up. "Let's get some wine." He raises his hand. *"Fuwuyuan!"*

The waitress rushes over.

"A couple bottles of Bordeaux."

"What kind?"

"I don't care," Gugu snaps. "Something good. Just bring it." He closes his eyes.

John bobs his head. *"Ni hao.* I'm Zhou Zheng'an. I am Yili's friend."

Gugu forces his eyes open to look at John. He manages a nod. "Nice to meet you."

Marsh is still standing behind Gugu. John's focus shifts to him, his eyes sharp, before he softens the predator look with a friendly smile. "And you are?"

"Marsh Brody." He slides into the chair next to Gugu. "I'm a friend of the family."

★ ★ ★

I HAVE TO SAY it's a little weird when I'm one of the more sober people at a gathering like this. Everybody's slugging down this crazy-expensive wine like it's Yanjing Draft, everybody except for maybe John, who's really good at taking a gulp when everyone's watching and taking minimal sips when they're not.

Normally I'd be all over keeping up with the Caos in the drinking department, but this whole evening has me spooked. Nothing bad's happened yet, not that I know of anyway, but I feel like something bad's hovering just overhead, like one of those dreams I have sometimes when a jet drops out of the sky and comes crashing down on top of me.

I'm sitting there thinking this when Meimei leans over and refills my wine.

"Thank you," I say.

She puts down the bottle and rests her elbow on the table, her head on her hand, posed like a model in one of those old Hong Kong cigarette ads. "So is this your lover? He's pretty good-looking."

"I . . . uh, he's a friend."

She laughs. "I see. Of course, friendship can take many forms." Her hand stretches out in my direction. She picks up her wineglass, fingers closing gently around the stem, all the while smiling at me.

Is this some kind of come-on?

I take a gulp of wine.

Maybe Meimei's just plastered. She's been giggling a lot, which at least would make her a happy drunk. Unlike Tiantian, who has this pissy expression on his face as he wags his finger in Gugu's general direction, and Gugu, who's doing his best sullen-teenager impression. Meanwhile Dao Ming looks like she's wound herself up a few notches tighter, which can't be good—I can see the tendons in her neck standing out from here.

As for Marsh, he just leans back in his chair smirking, at one point wiping wine from his lips with his fingers.

I can't quite get a read on Uncle Yang. He's flushed and sweating, the only real giveaway that he might be drunk. Smiling tightly, occasionally nodding or chortling as Gugu and Tiantian argue about something—I can't hear it well enough to figure out what. I just catch phrases here and there. Tiantian saying, "Why do you want to make something so common? Copy Western trash?"

Gugu laughs. "So I make a film and it's common. We should serve the people, right? Chairman Mao said that. The people *like* common things. Stupid entertainments. Why not give them what they want?"

Tiantian catches me watching them. He forces a laugh. "Maybe you can see our problem," he says to me. "We have different tastes. So how can we work together for this museum?"

Meimei lifts up a hand. "Don't forget about me."

"It's not possible to forget you, Meimei," Uncle Yang says, sounding maybe a little too jovial.

"*Women xuyao yige . . . yige dongshihui . . . danshi . . .*" I switch to English. Easier. "We'll have a board. You'll vote on things. But you'll hire a professional director and staff to actually run the place."

"And we tell them what to do?" Tiantian asks. I get the feeling he likes the idea of telling people what to do.

"Well . . . it's better if they tell you. I mean . . ." I think about the nonprofit that Harrison set up, the one that I supposedly run. Ha, ha. "We need to have a mission statement. That's something you guys have to agree on. And then you let the people you hire do their job. You kind of guide each other."

"Democratic centralism," Gugu pronounces with a snort, falling back in his chair. Oh, yeah. He's really loaded.

"I don't know, maybe?" I say. "It's more like unless you want to be running the thing day to day, you need to tell the staff what the mission's about, and then you have to step back a little. Make sure they're doing it, but let them do it. If that makes sense."

"You know what else Chairman Mao said," Gugu says abruptly. He wags a finger. "That the superior man should help the common people. Unless there are too many common people. Then common people just become a burden on the superior man." He giggles.

Uncle Yang is listening to this really hard. I'm not sure how much English he speaks. Gugu catches his look and repeats in Mandarin what he said about Mao and superior men and the little people.

"*Ah, wo mingbai,*" Uncle Yang says. I get it. "But Chairman Mao was very young when he said that. Of course, his thinking evolved and deepened. He said we should be guided by the wisdom of the common people."

"What is the wisdom of the common people? Make money, that's all. That's all anyone cares about in this country, right?"

"Some of us care about higher things," Tiantian snaps. "About China's culture and place in the world."

"China's culture." Gugu snorts. "What culture? *This?* This is fake. All fake. Just something you can buy if you have the money. Anyway, what do common people know about this or care? All they want is someone to fuck and an indoor toilet to take a shit."

"Gugu," Uncle Yang begins, and I hear the warning in his voice.

"Don't you start," Gugu says. "Like *you* listen to little people. You just want them to shut up and do what they're told." He turns to the rest of the table and flings his hand in Uncle Yang's direction. "Our wise leaders know better."

"Ah, so tiresome," Meimei mutters next to me. She's smiling, though. Watching the show.

"Okay, buddy," Marsh says in English, clapping Gugu on the shoulder. "Why don't we take this down a couple of notches? Sorry, everybody," he says to the table. "*Duibuqi.* We had a . . . a meeting with some investors before this. Lots of toasts. You know how it goes."

"Sorry," Gugu mumbles. "Sorry. I was speaking nonsense. *Wo jiu qiu niubi.*"

And for a minute I think everything's going to be okay.

"I am curious," John says out of nowhere. "How do you all know about what common people want? Your circumstances are not . . . not common." He, too, is smiling. He repeats this in Mandarin for Uncle Yang's benefit.

"My parents were peasants from Anhui," Uncle Yang says. "So of course I know." There's an edge to his voice that sounds like trouble.

"But this"—John gestures, palms out, at our pricey private room—"this is very far from a village in Anhui." John smiles at him. He sounds so polite. "So I think you have done very well."

"Our country has done very well," Uncle Yang says between clenched teeth, with the kind of smile that looks more like a grimace. He seems to catch himself then and continues, in a friendlier tone, "Of course, we still have much progress to make, so that all Chinese can benefit more."

"So I'll make my movies, then." Gugu leans back in his chair and closes his eyes. "They will be stupid, and common, for the common people. I entertain myself, and they are entertained. Everyone knows his place. Everyone should be happy."

John stares at him. I can see a nerve twitch in his jaw, and I think, There's a high potential for this all to go to shit, right about now.

"I wonder sometimes how much common people's lives are worth," John says. Very evenly. Like he's talking about the prices of . . . I don't know, cell phones, or purses, or cooking oil. "Just recently I hear about a poor girl, killed and dumped in trash like she is worth nothing. Do we really have respect for that common person?"

For a moment there's a silence that's as heavy as an explosion. I see their faces, all of them frozen in mid-expression, like somebody hit PAUSE in the middle of the scene.

Yeah, John just dropped the bomb.

"You are all disgusting," Dao Ming hisses.

CHAPTER THIRTEEN

"WHAT THE *fuck*, JOHN? What the *fuck* was that? And don't tell me it's . . . it's killing the monkey to frighten the snake or something."

"Something like that."

"Are you fucking crazy? Oh, wait. You totally are."

I'm sitting in John's car, and I'm shaking. With anger, with fear, with whatever's left after an adrenaline rush. My leg has started to throb.

I don't like being blown up.

"I cannot fucking believe you did that. Do you know who's going to get shit for this? Me. Not you. They don't even know who you really are!"

"They have my card," John says. He's keeping his eyes on the road as we head back to Gulou. Doing that overly calm thing that pisses me off.

"Oh, yeah, your fake card with your fake name and fake business on it!"

Now he does look over at me.

"You want to catch them, right? Get justice for this girl?"

I have a flash again, of the picture Inspector Zou showed me, of that bruised, swollen face. And the thing is, I do. I want someone to answer for what was done.

"Yeah. Yeah, I want some justice. But . . . these people—do you understand who we're dealing with here?"

"Yes. The Caos, one of richest families in China. And Yang Junmin. He was governor of Hubei, then party chief. Next he was party chief in Zhejiang. Now he is also member of Central Politburo. He is a powerful man. But if he is corrupt, then he needs to be exposed."

John's on a mission, all right. Straight into the kill box.

Jesus, this is a fucking nightmare.

"How is this gonna expose them? The only people it exposed are you and me. That we know about the dead girl."

"You saw their faces. They know about her, too."

I think about that scene. How everything stopped. Try to picture their expressions. Uncle Yang, eyes narrowed, and Tiantian, stunned, both staring at John. Gugu, eyes closed, like he was in pain, or maybe just really loaded. Marsh, patting Gugu on the back, eyes flicking up at me. And Mcimei?

"Very sad," she'd said lightly. "So many bad things can happen to poor girls in the city."

"It is a problem with modern society," Tiantian pronounced.

And everyone went back to eating.

Yeah, it seemed like they knew something. But how could anyone be sure? I mean, murdered girls dumped in a pile of garbage isn't exactly polite dinner conversation.

"I will protect you. You must know that," John says, and he sounds like a freaking Boy Scout, he's so earnest.

"I wouldn't need protecting in the first place if you didn't keep fucking with my life!" I just want to punch him, but he's driving, so I slam my fist into the seat next to me. "I swear to God, I am so done with men. And women. And people! Fuck it, I'm going to live out in the country with my dog."

"You know the only way to help you is to find out who kill this girl."

"You could've told me what you were planning, instead of sandbagging me like that! Thanks for making it real clear to me what you really care about."

I mean, at least I know.

There's a long silence as we turn down the alley to my apartment.

"I am sorry," he says. "But I did not plan. I just was . . . I just was angry."

"Why? Why does it make you so angry?"

We pull in to the parking lot of my building. John shoves the transmission into park, and the tires squeal.

"People like that . . . they take everything. They give back nothing. They use people like . . . like toys. If they break the toy, they just throw it away. They ruin this country. They ruin everything."

"But it's personal for you. Isn't it?"

That muscle in his jaw works. I think he isn't going to say anything, or say that I'm just imagining it.

He nods. "Yes. Maybe, a little."

"You gonna tell me about it?"

"Maybe some other time."

We sit in the car in silence.

He sighs. "Still . . . you are right, I should not have said what I said."

"What do we do now?"

"Wait and see."

"Wait and see if Uncle Yang sends out a hit man?"

"Someone will stay outside your apartment. You don't have to worry."

"Oh, because there's nothing that makes me feel safer than some underpaid nark from bumfuck Shanxi or wherever watching over me."

"Yili . . ." He does that thing where he scrunches up his face, like he's getting a headache, and I think, Good. Because I want him to lose it. I want to make him mad.

Instead he just shakes his head and says, "I'm sorry."

I let out a long sigh, my anger emptying out like a deflating balloon. I just don't have the energy to be mad anymore.

But I have to do more than just "wait and see."

"Betty," I say.

"Who?"

"One of Gugu's friends. She was at the party. I called her after it, just to make sure she wasn't . . . you know, dead. I swear she was scared. Maybe she knows something."

Or maybe it was a total coincidence and she'd just had a fight with her boyfriend.

"Okay. We can talk to her, then. I'll call you."

"When?"

"Tomorrow."

I shrug and open the car door. "Okay."

John stops me with a hand on my shoulder. "Yili, please . . . do not do anything without me."

"Right. Because it went so well when we did something together."

WHEN I GET UPSTAIRS to my apartment, it's dark, even though it's only ten fifteen. There's a note on the fridge from my mom: *"Mimi and I are at Andy's. Come over! The tortillas came out great!"*

No way, I think. After that dinner I don't have any appetite left, and though I'd kind of like to be hanging out with the dog, I don't have the energy to make up some story for my mom about how great the evening was.

I crack open a beer and collapse on the couch.

I should change out of these fancy clothes, I think. Instead I just sit there on the couch, my thoughts in a whirl, and I can feel myself spiraling down.

Let's see. DSD on my ass. Check. Lao Zhang coming back to town. Check. PSB looking at me for a murder. Yep. And now I'm in the sights of some Party bigwig, plus Sidney's three kids.

And oh, shit, what about Sidney? Would he know about what happened tonight?

Okay, I tell myself, okay, calm down. If you murdered a girl, would you want your dad to know?

You would if you thought he could fix the problem for you. Oh, shit.

From inside my fancy little leather bag, my phone makes that bamboo text tone. I don't even want to look.

But I do. It's my landlady. She lives someplace near Wenzhou, so almost all our communication is by text. I try to communicate with her as little as possible. Last thing I want to be is the pain-in-the-ass *laowai*.

YILI, NI HAO. SORRY BUT I MUST RAISE RENT STARTING IN 1 MONTH. NEW AMOUNT IS 10,500 ¥.

Which is, oh, almost double what I'm paying now. More than I can afford, even if I could sell Lao Zhang's art again.

On my craptastic disability pension? I could maybe afford the bathroom.

But hey, at least my landlady isn't trying to kill me or have me arrested, right?

At least not so far as I know.

I have to wonder about the timing here. Uncle Yang or Tiantian couldn't have moved *this* fast to fuck with my life, could they?

It's probably just a coincidence. Rents have been going up like crazy in Beijing.

Still, how much more jacked up could things get?

The Suits could make an appearance, I guess. That would be one awesome FUBAR party.

I take a slug of beer, wishing I had something stronger in the house. Well, I have Percocet. This just might be the time for one.

I thumb back to the list of messages out of habit, just to make sure I didn't miss anything else, because I do that sometimes.

I see Celine's name there, and the message underneath: LETTERSFROMTHEDEEPYELLOWSEA.COM. Her website.

Maybe you can learn more about modern Chinese culture.

And she was at the party.

Couldn't hurt to take a look.

Celine's blog is in English. That's interesting, I think. English language blogs don't get as much attention from the censors as Chinese language do. Which would make sense for the kind of China *Sex and the City* stuff I figure she's doing from that "Yellow" in her blog title.

It is so boring sometimes, being a young girl in a city like Beijing. If you are not a member of their class, then you must be more attractive and more clever in your flattery when you are trying to get ahead in this place.

It's best not to settle for a man your own age. They don't usually have good jobs or incomes. Your best bet is to find a local official who is looking for a girlfriend. This has many advantages. For example, a parking place when you want it. Getting your phone and Internet hooked up quickly, making sure you breathe filtered air. Taking you to restaurants you could never afford yourself and ordering an emperor's feast, with fine French wine to wash it down, and you must eat it, you must eat it all. Telling you not every girl deserves this.

This is what it means to taste the new life, in the new society. We must gather it into our mouths, rip into it with our teeth, and taste its raw, warm blood.

Ooh-kay. That was not what I was expecting from Celine. I was thinking more, lots of designer brands, parties, booze, drugs, and hookups. Not all . . . whatever this is.

She posted this entry tonight, it looks like.

I scroll down to the one before.

It is so wonderful to have tradition to fall back on. To fall into, into its cold, hard grip. Of course, you can have it your way, soft, fresh, and young, whatever you can afford. You don't have to return it in perfect condition. Tradition is your foundation as well as your excuse.

The time stamp says she posted it two nights ago. Three nights after Tiantian's party.

I feel that prickling on the back of my neck I get when I'm close to something I want to know but that I know is dangerous. And I'm wondering just what Celine saw, that night at Tiantian's place.

CHAPTER FOURTEEN

So many girls think they want a rich lover. It is true this is a cruel country to be poor in. But I know a girl who has a tuhao *boyfriend, and she is not so happy. She can never feel secure. He buys her nice gifts, but he can buy anything, including other girls. He only wants to fuck her now and again, and it is all for his pleasure, not for hers.*

But the parties, she likes the parties. She likes the presents he gives her, the designer bags and the jewelry. She likes riding in his Lamborghini, she likes being seen with him. He is important, and if she is with him, then she must be important, right? But she knows she is not. She is nothing. She is just another thing he bought, and when he gets tired of her, he can just throw her away.

Tonight I will go to a party with my friend and her rich boyfriend. We can drink the best champagne, we can take E or K if we like, and we can dance on our private dance floor for hours and hours, and everyone will admire her for her good fortune. But if I ask her if she is happy, I know how she will answer.

THE DATE ON THAT entry lines up with Gugu's party, the one at Entránce.

I skim a couple of others. Cynical, funny descriptions of

Beijing's privileged class, of parties and expensive champagne, of designer clothes and bags, of sex and drugs. But nothing that's quite like those two posts at the end.

I wonder if Betty's the girlfriend and Celine's the observer or if Celine's the girlfriend and she's just describing things like they're happening to someone else. Sometimes it's easier to think about things that way.

There's a place to sign up to receive blog posts by email. I do that, using a Yahoo! address that isn't linked to my real name—at least I don't think it is. You never really know. One thing I've learned is that nothing you do is really private anymore, if someone wants to find out bad enough.

Should I call her? It's after 11:00 P.M. Probably not late for Celine, given all these late nights with the rich folk she's blogging about.

I find her on my messages and press CALL.

A burst of music, some Mandopop. "*Duibuqi, nin bodade yonghu zanshi wufa jietong, qing shaohou zai bo.*" Sorry, the subscriber you dialed is busy. Please try again later.

I disconnect.

I decide to write a text. Something simple.

I READ SOME OF YOUR BLOG. I ENJOYED IT A LOT. I'D LIKE TO TALK TO YOU ABOUT IT.

And I hit SEND.

AFTER THAT I CHANGE into my sleeping T-shirt and sweats. Toss my party clothes into the hamper. I am so done with all this shit. I pad around the living room, beer in hand, thinking if I get arrested or deported, at least I won't have to look for a new apartment. Because I'm going to *have* to get a new place. No way around it.

I guess it won't be so bad. Hardly anything here is mine. Most of the furniture came with the apartment. I've got some kitchen stuff, a computer, a TV, a few pieces of art. I could move to a smaller place, easy. I don't really need this much room. There's my mom to think about it, but truth be told, she's practically living with Andy as it is. I'm tempted to ask her how this squares with the whole Christian thing, but she told me once she has a weakness when it comes to men, and I guess if Christ forgives us our sins, hers are pretty small in the scheme of things. Hey, I remember when I was going through my Christian phase, I wasn't exactly chaste.

For all the bullshit we've been through, she's a good person. I know that. And the crazy thing is, she's happier than I'll probably ever be.

Sometimes you just have to go for it.

I'd go for it if I had a clue what "it" even was.

I CAN'T FALL ASLEEP.

I keep hearing things, sounds out in the hall, random creaks, and I think I should've gotten Mimi from Mom and Andy. She'd keep watch for me. Because no matter what John says, no matter who he has staking out my place, Uncle Yang's budget for hit men is probably bigger. As is Tiantian's. Or Gugu's. And let's not forget Meimei and crazy Dao Ming.

The wind's howling, too. Coming from the north, and they say the dust will come with it.

I lie in bed and wonder how can I suggest to my mom that she just move in with Andy already. It has to be safer for her with him than living here with me.

Even if she'd be just across the hall.

Maybe I can talk them into a vacation. Preferably out of the country.

I'm finally drifting off when I hear the chime of an incoming text. I fumble around for my phone.

Celine.

My pulse picks up. I get that feeling again: I'm on the track of something. Weird thing is, I'm starting to like it.

GLAD YOU ENJOY MY BLOG. SURE, WE CAN TALK ABOUT IT.

GREAT, I type. WHEN?

NOW?

OKAY, I type. I'LL CALL YOU.

BETTER TO TALK IN PERSON.

This does not strike me as a great idea.

IT'S PRETTY LATE, I type. HOW ABOUT TOMORROW?

I'M BUSY TOMORROW. COME TO MY APARTMENT TONIGHT. I'M IN CAOCHANGDI, YOU KNOW CAOCHANGDI?

Caochangdi is a Beijing suburb just northeast of 798 Arts District, a little village that used to be a commune and turned into an art center all its own, thanks to Ai Weiwei building a bunch of studio spaces there. It hasn't gone completely upscale the way 798 has, so there are some actual working artists there, galleries, too.

SURE, I type. I KNOW IT.

SO COME.

IT WILL TAKE A WHILE, I type. MAYBE WE SHOULD JUST TALK ON THE PHONE.

I DON'T WANT TO TALK ABOUT THIS ON THE PHONE.

ABOUT WHAT?

ABOUT THE PARTY. ABOUT WHAT HAPPENED.

I don't reply. I just stand there staring at the screen of my iPhone.

YOU WANT TO KNOW ABOUT IT, RIGHT?

OKAY, I finally type. SEND ME YOUR ADDRESS.

HERE'S THE THING.

I may be a fuckup, but I'm not totally stupid.

I never actually talked to Celine. She, or whoever was texting, didn't answer the phone and then wouldn't talk to me. Who knows if it was actually Celine at all, or if this is even her address? I'm just supposed to hop into a taxi and run over there after midnight?

I don't think so.

But I do want to know.

I'll go tomorrow, I decide, in the daytime. Do some recon before I go all knock-ops on her door.

If it was her, and she wants to talk to me, she'll talk to me. If it was somebody else? They won't be expecting me. Or maybe they'll be gone.

I'M OUT IN THE kitchen at 7:00 A.M., which for me in recent years might as well be oh dark thirty. With all the dust in the air right now, it's still darker than it should be.

I'm sucking down some coffee when the doorknob rattles. I hear Mimi's whine, so it's probably Mom and not one of Uncle Yang's hit men.

I wander out to the living room with my coffee as Mom and Mimi come through the door.

"Oh, hi! I was just . . . walking Mimi." She's a little red-faced. Like I care that she's semi–shacking up with Andy.

"Thanks."

Mimi's dancing around, ready for breakfast. She dashes over to me, stands up on her back paws, and braces her front legs on my pelvis, runs back to my mom. One of us is bound to feed her.

"So windy out today," Mom says.

"Yeah. Supposed to be a dust storm coming."

"Well, good thing we got our walk in already, right girl?" Mom ruffles the scruff around Mimi's neck. "You're up early," she says to me.

"I have a . . . a meeting. To look at some art."

I go back to the kitchen to heat up my coffee and give the dog some food. Also to avoid my mom. Because I have to say something, right? Let her know there might be some bad guys out there with me in their sights and that she's better off being out of range.

But where would I start? And do I want to deal with the resulting freak-out?

"So what are you guys up to today?" I ask.

"Well, we're going to visit a few more potential locations for the restaurant." She grabs a mug and pours herself a little coffee. "One of them's near Workers Stadium. The other's by Dongsi Shitiao."

"Oh, cool," I say. "Because . . . there's maybe going to be some work going on in the apartment today. So I was hoping you could take Mimi and . . . not be around. Because, you know . . . workers don't like dogs."

Her forehead wrinkles. She takes a sip of coffee and gives me a sideways look. "If you're going to have workers in and out of here, wouldn't it be better if I kept an eye on things?"

Well, okay, that was not one of my better lies. But it's way too early, and I'm only on my first cup of coffee.

"Normally, yeah." I take a big gulp from that cup, scalding my throat in the process.

"Okay," I say when I've stopped coughing. "Here's the thing. I need for you and Mimi and Andy to not be around the apartment today. There's this kind of . . . weird situation I'm involved in, and . . . it's just really better if you're not here."

My mom rocks her head back a little. "Oh. Sure. I understand if you need your place to yourself."

She gets this sly smile on her face. "Are you still seeing John?"

Oh, so *not that!* I want to scream.

Instead I say, "Yeah. Kind of."

NOT GOOD ENOUGH, I tell myself, over and over, hugging a pole on the subway out to Caochangdi. Yeah, I might've kept her and Andy and Mimi out of my apartment for a day or so, but is that really going to protect them from Uncle Yang or the Caos?

I've got to tell her the truth, or some version of it anyway.

I will, I tell myself. I will. Just as soon as I deal with Celine.

I MAKE IT TO Caochangdi around 8:30 A.M.

I figure a party girl like Celine probably doesn't get out of the house too early. I sure had a hard time getting here. For one thing, the subway only gets you as far as Liangmaqiao, and from there it's a bus or a taxi. I opt for the taxi. Easy enough to find at the subway stop. The way back I might not be so lucky.

Finding anything in Caochangdi is kind of a hassle. Most of the streets don't have names. The address I have is just "Focus Space, 草场地村, 468-3，艺术区内, C区内." Which is basically "No street name, just a number, Inner Arts District, C Section, Caochangdi." I've never heard of Focus Space, but that's not saying much; things are changing fast in Caochangdi like they are nearly everyplace else in Beijing, with all kinds of construction and new galleries popping up everywhere, plus a sudden increase of Audis and Beemers parked in front of them. I do know, sort of, where the Inner Arts District is, which is more than the taxi driver did. So I had him drop me off at a gallery complex I've been to before. Someone will know where this place is. I hope.

THE GALLERY'S NOT OPEN yet, but the little coffee shop/bar attached to it is. White walls and concrete floors like the gallery, decorated with posters from various exhibitions they've put on. I could use another cup of coffee anyway. I order an Americano from the girl with the spiky, blue-streaked hair behind the counter, and then I show her the text from Celine.

"Do you know where this is?"

She studies it and nods.

THE WIND IS STILL howling, and the air is so thick with yellow dust that I hardly cast a shadow. I feel the sand hitting my face, and my teeth are crunching grit. I take out a bandanna and tie it around the lower half of my face, bandit style, like I used to do in the Sandbox. I'm jumpy like I was back then, too. Outside the wire you never knew what was going to happen. Of course, *inside* the wire plenty of bad shit happened, too, like my getting blown up, for example.

Focus, McEnroe, I tell myself. Don't get lost in those times. Don't start seeing stuff that isn't there. Focus on the here and now, because you don't know what you're walking into.

Supposedly the place is about fifteen minutes away on foot: *You just go down this big road, then at the second cross street you turn right.* Here's hoping.

I've reached the second cross street, so I hang a right. A small road, narrow, not paved. A cluster of shops, mostly two stories, cement and white tile, clusters of wires droopily strung from one side of the street to the other, the wind making them swing and snap. Art supplies, a couple hole-in-the-wall restaurants, cell phones, groceries. A bike-repair shop. Not a lot of people out, but who would want to be out here right now, swallowing dirt? A stray dog trots down the street, tail low, finally taking shelter in a doorway.

I keep walking. The sky looks like something out of a science-fiction movie, all yellow, an alien planet. A plastic bag floats by like an airborne jellyfish, a paper cup tumbles into the road. The businesses thin out. I pass a newer-looking redbrick complex, stark squares and skinny windows, obviously some kind of art space. But not the one I'm looking for.

New apartments. Half built, only ten stories, not the kind of crazy high-rises you see everywhere in China, with a design that mirrors the art space.

Funny. This isn't where I would've pictured Celine living, in an art village like Caochangdi. Sure, it's pretty hip, and I get the feeling she's into that, but not in the center of things for Beijing, hard to get to, and hard to get out of if you don't have a car. Though maybe she does—I mean, I have no idea. I don't know much of anything about her, other than what I read on her blog, and that she hangs out with Gugu and Marsh.

Gugu, whatever else he is, he's got his pretentions, right? Not that he's the upholder of Confucian virtues, like Tiantian fancies himself, but that he's a creative guy. An artist of sorts, even if he says he's only interested in making trashy movies. The kid who Sidney wants to manage his art collection. Maybe Gugu hangs out here, and it's where he met Celine.

Stuff I think I'll ask her about when I see her.

Here's what looks like an old factory or a school: grey

wall with thick pillars on either side of the entrance, painted white concrete buildings, faded gold calligraphy announcing whatever it used to be—okay, that says FACTORY—and a newer signpost with placards for the various galleries and studios inside it. Some brass, some professionally printed, others deliberately hand done.

And there's Focus. I almost miss it because it's done in these overlapping typefaces that are different colors and seem to make the word shift and blur. Cute.

I walk in the direction of the sign.

The path takes me past old concrete and brick buildings, some plastered, some raw. All kinds of flyers and posters pasted up on the walls, layers of them, for exhibits, for bands, for film showings. I pass a life-size wooden tank, with faces and gargoyles and I don't know what carved into it, along with the block letters VICTORY! in English. A little farther down the path, some giant calligraphy statues that spell out 为什么? "Why?" A couple of people with scarves wrapped around their faces scurry across the grounds, looking for shelter. The wind isn't getting any better. Dust hits a window with an audible rattle; a tin sign on a wooden stake topples over and scrapes against the pavement.

Finally a grey brick building with the same graphic as the signpost by the gate—FOCUS—bolted to the wall next to double metal doors. I do a little recon. One small smoked Plexiglas window to the left of the entrance. I don't see anything useful, just high ceilings and some statue shapes I can barely make out.

Weird. It looks like a gallery. Celine can't really live here, can she?

I don't see a doorbell or anything like that. I jiggle the door handle. Unlocked.

Okay, I think. It's nine fifteen. A little early for a gallery, but not out of the question. Just because it's the middle of a howling dust storm, that doesn't mean there's anything so weird about my being here, right?

Right.

My heart's doing double time as I open the door.

If the gallery's open for business, it doesn't look like it. It's dark, with just some dim yellow light filtering in through the skylights. Enough for me to make out the shapes I glimpsed from outside.

Bodies. Limbs and trunks and heads. I let out a gasp, then tell myself to get a grip. They're too big to be human. They're doll parts. Giant doll parts that look like Chinese Barbies. Like a rubbery pink Barbie torso that towers over me, then another wearing a sailor blouse and a skirt that ends that just above its swollen pink crotch. There's a pair of legs, one bent backward at the knee, like my friends and I used to do when we were kids. Arms, hands with painted red nails. Heads. Blank eyed. Cascades of shiny plastic hair: black, blond, and red.

Why couldn't it have been fluffy kittens and puppies, you know?

I pull the bandanna I'm wearing down around my neck. *"Ni hao,"* I say. My voice cracks a little from all the dust. *"You ren zai zheli?"*

Anyone here?

No one answers.

To my left there's an alcove with a desk and a computer, behind it shelves with books and exhibition catalogs. The computer's off. At the back of the gallery, a doorway, a dark rectangle. Blue light flickers from inside—a TV?

I hesitate. Listen. Howling wind, things creaking and thumping, the crackle of grit hitting glass.

None of it's coming from in here. I don't think.

Okay, McEnroe, I tell myself. You have one of two choices: keep looking or turn around and walk away.

I almost leave. It doesn't feel like anyone's here, and the whole thing's off anyway. This can't be where Celine lives. The text messages last night, whoever sent them wanted me to come here. But why?

It's that question, the "why?" that makes me keep walking. Which is pretty stupid. Because one of the answers I come up with would inspire a sane person to get out, right now.

I'll just go look in this next room, I tell myself. That's as far as I'll go. I'll check it out, and then I'll leave.

Sometimes I'm really a dumb shit.

It's a smaller gallery. Dark because there's no skylight. A bedroom, I guess, a girlie, Barbie kind of bedroom: pink and red, anime eyes and hearts on the walls, lit by a huge flat-screen TV playing some Chinese soap with the sound turned off. It smells like somebody took a dump somewhere close by.

Over on the bed, there are more larger-than-life dolls. The first is another Chinese Barbie. She's lying on her back with her legs spread. There are three others, all men. I guess you could call them Ken. Unlike Barbie, they're clothed. Two are Chinese Kens. One's a Westerner. They stand there surrounding the bed, seeming to stare at the doll lying in it.

My eyes move right, past the bed, past the giant stuffed Hello Kitty.

Next to the Hello Kitty, propped up against the wall, at first I think it's another doll.

Celine.

Oh, shit.

CHAPTER FIFTEEN

I KEEP IT TOGETHER. I was a medic, right? So my first reaction isn't to bug out. I hustle over there and kneel awkwardly next to her.

Even in the TV light, I can tell she's dead. Her eyes are open, her mouth slack, her lips cyanotic, and there's a line of dried white foam running down from one corner. No obvious wounds. Is that white powder around her nose? I put two fingers on the side of her neck to check for a pulse, just in case. The skin's cold. As lifeless as the Barbies.

If I were doing this by the book, I'd do a couple other things—get a mirror and make sure there's no breath moving, check the fingers for the degree of rigor, check for blood pooling—but no fucking way that's my job right now.

That's when I do freak. I scramble to my feet, faster than I knew I could, back out of the room, and then haul ass out of the gallery.

"WHY DO YOU NEVER do what I tell you to do?" Yeah, he's pissed. What a surprise.

"Not the time, John."

I'm out of the gallery complex and hustling down the street, back toward the center of town and, I hope, a taxi to get me the fuck away from here.

"Did anyone see you?"

"I don't know. Maybe. But I had a scarf around my face because of the dust."

"Good for cameras anyway. Cameras don't work well today. Any inside?"

"I didn't notice."

I hear that sharp exhalation of air that might be a curse.

My steps are slowing down. I think what's the point of running? Running where, back to Beijing?

"Maybe I should just go to the police. I mean, she's been dead . . . I don't know, at least eight, nine hours—it's not like anyone could say that I went there just now and killed her."

"Not a PSB case anymore."

"You mean it's *your* case? What happens if your boss finds out you're freelancing? That you're doing this on your own?"

"Nothing for you to worry about."

Which is bullshit, of course, but I don't have the energy to fight about it.

"You talked to Inspector Zou?"

"Not yet. Today."

By now my steps have slowed to a halt. The wind's whipping around like crazy; a gust tumbles over a trash can, and there are papers and leaves blowing everywhere.

"What do you want me to do?" I finally ask.

"Just go home. And stay there."

For once I'm inclined to do what he says.

I HAVE A LITTLE bit of luck at least: There's a taxi dropping somebody off at the gallery complex where I got directions this morning. I have him take me to the Liangmaqiao subway stop—I figure I'll get home faster on the subway than I would in a taxi going through rush-hour traffic.

As it is, the subway ride's long enough to give me plenty of time to think. Too much time. I keep seeing Celine's face lit by the flickering TV, her open eyes, her slack mouth. Just what I need, another fucking thing like that in my head.

God, you're an asshole, I tell myself. I mean, she's *dead* and you're not, so suck it up and drive on. And it's not like I really knew her, but she was smart, smarter than I realized, and she cared about things, and now she's paid for it.

Okay, I don't know for sure that someone killed her. If I had to guess, I'd guess an overdose of some kind, and who knows? Those texts last night could actually *have* been from her. She could've gotten really wasted and decided that she had to talk to me right *now* about what she saw at the Caos' party, because, you know, wasted-people logic where it just couldn't wait for the morning. In which case it really sucks that I didn't go out there, because if I had, maybe she wouldn't have died.

Maybe she was into something and did a little too much, and it's just a weird coincidence that she was at a party where a girl died and that she was writing about the lifestyles of the rich and heinous on her blog.

Yeah. Right.

By the time I get off the Number 2 subway line at my Gulou stop, I'm sweating, streaking the dust on my face and leaving blotches of mud on my bandanna when I wipe my forehead. First thing I do when I get home, I say to myself as I ride up the escalator, first thing I do is tell my mom. Maybe not everything, but enough to convince her and Andy to get the fuck out of Dodge for a while. No bullshit story about how I need the apartment private for me and my boyfriend, Creepy John.

I have to scare them enough so they get out of the kill zone. I don't know if Andy has a passport or not, but just go to Hong Kong or something—he can go to Hong Kong, right? And Mimi, what do I do with Mimi? Can they take her to Hong Kong?

As for me . . . maybe it's time to call the embassy. Not that they can help much if I actually get arrested for something. Or that they'd necessarily even want to. I don't know how much of the trouble I caused over Lao Zhang and the Uighur last year stayed between me and my private-contractor friends at GSC and how much of it turned into official US government trouble.

I guess I could call Carter, my contract-spook frenemy at GSC. GSC gets a lot of outsourced US intelligence work. Or it's an actual CIA front, for all I know. The distinction is pretty fuzzy these days. Maybe Carter could give me some intel.

I doubt he'd actually help me much. Last time I tallied things up, I kind of owed *him*.

I think about what I might be able to trade. He's into horse-trading. It's mostly the only way I can deal with him. I can't count on hitting him in his tiny guilt complex, not again. Not on something like this.

It's your own fucking fault, Doc. I can hear him saying it already.

Outside, it's brighter than I was expecting. The wind's died down, the dust settling onto the sidewalks. I blink a few times and head south on Jiu Gulou Dajie, toward the *hutong* that leads to my apartment complex.

Okay, think of a good lie to tell Mom. Or an acceptable version of the truth. Maybe, *I've got some Chinese gangsters after me. Because . . . No time to explain. Just get out of town.*

I've reached the entrance to my alley. There's a new black Audi parked there, pretty much blocking the way. The license plate is white instead of blue, with a big red *V* on it right after the 京 for "Beijing." Military plates, I think, which means they get to park wherever they like. Half of those plates are counterfeit anyway, and the ones that aren't, you always see them on Audis and Beemers and even Porsches. Way to "Serve the People," asshole.

That's when I stop in my tracks. New Audi. Military plates. Blocking the entrance to my *hutong*.

I turn on my heel and head back up the street, fast as I can without actually running. Maybe they didn't see me.

I hear the click of a car door, footsteps hitting the ground, and now I am running, which is crazy, because I can't run fast. And whoever these guys are, now there's one on either side of me, and they're jamming hands under my armpits and grabbing my arms, and one of them says, *"Bie zhaoji."* Don't be nervous.

Right.

"Let go of me! *Fang wo zou!*"

"Don't cause trouble. Just come with us," the one on my left says.

"Hey!" I yell. "I don't know these men! Somebody call the police!"

I say this, and there's an old, shoulder-hunched auntie staring at us, granite faced. A couple of college kids, who get out their cell phones and start recording. A street sweeper in a Day-Glo vest freezes, broom and dustpan in hand.

The guy on my right punches me in the face.

Nobody does anything as the men drag me back toward the Audi.

CHAPTER SIXTEEN

TWO GUYS IN FRONT, one guy in back, next to me. I blink, trying to clear the fuzz from my eyes.

They might be driving an Audi with military plates, but none of the three guys is wearing any kind of uniform. Just slacks and sport coats or bomber jackets. They're all young, though, with buzzed hair and military vibes.

The guy next to me opens up my little canvas bag, gets out my iPhone, and powers it off.

I probe the area around my right cheek and eye and temple with my fingertips, wincing.

"Sorry," the guy on my right says. "You should have done what we said."

"Who are you?" I manage, my voice shaking.

He doesn't answer.

My ears are still ringing, but my head's cleared some. Enough for me to panic. They could be taking me someplace to kill me, for all I know.

You can't lose it, I tell myself. If you're going to get out of this, you have to keep it together.

My heart's pounding in my throat. I think, I'm sitting by the rear door—do I open it? Take my chances? I look out the window, try to get my bearings. We're on the Second Ring

Road. It's a freeway, sort of, but the traffic's so bad a lot of the time, that if it slows enough . . .

The rear door has to be locked. They wouldn't have missed something like that. I haven't ridden around in Audis much. If I pull the handle, will it unlock? Or does it have some kind of child safety lock on it?

I take a quick glance at the guy to my left. He's staring at me. He's lean and cut and looks like he moves fast. I know he hits hard. I'm pretty sure he's not going to give me a chance to try to find out.

These aren't Pompadour Bureaucrat's people, I don't think. His crew flashed IDs the two times they picked me up. And the plainclothes team didn't have nearly this nice a car.

So someone else. A Cao? Uncle Yang?

Military plates, I'm guessing Uncle Yang.

I am in some serious, big-time shit.

WE DRIVE NORTH ON the Jingzang Expressway, then west on the Fifth Ring Road. I tell myself they aren't taking me somewhere to kill me. Using an official car to kidnap me in broad daylight, on one of Beijing's more heavily touristed streets? It doesn't seem smart.

On the other hand, guys this high up can get away with all kinds of dumb.

Assuming it's Uncle Yang I'm dealing with.

We keep going west, past the Summer Palace, past temples and golf courses, heading toward the Fragrant Hills. The Fragrant Hills has some of the prettiest scenery in Beijing, people tell me. All the time I've lived here, I've never been. Until now. And this isn't looking like a sightseeing opportunity.

We're off the highway now, going into the hills. There are trees everywhere, pine trees and cypress trees, other kinds I don't know what they're called. It doesn't even look like Beijing, except for the yellow dust that's still hanging in the air.

The road winds around, and I glimpse walls and gates, the top of a pagoda. The park, I guess. We keep going and finally turn off onto a smaller road that heads up into the low hills. More gates and walls. Hotels? Villas?

We turn up a drive, iron gate sliding open as we approach.

It's a two-story building, stone, with these sorts of round towers at the four corners, topped by round red roofs, the bastard child of a Chinese manor and a French château. The driver parks the car, and the guy in the passenger seat gets out and opens the rear door.

"*Zou, zou,*" the guy next to me says. "*Xia che.*"

Out of the car.

I get out, clutching the doorframe for support, bad leg cramping, stomach churning, shaky as hell. Suck it up, I tell myself. Try to walk like you aren't so scared you're gonna puke.

Or go ahead and puke on the asshole who punched me. Serve him right.

UNCLE YANG WAITS FOR me in his office.

He's sitting behind a big, modern desk with a new computer on it, examining, or pretending to, some official-looking papers. He barely looks up when I enter. Just puts the papers back into a file folder that he lays on his desk.

"You can go," he says to the guy who escorted me here. "Sit," he says to me.

The guy goes. I sit.

Uncle Yang makes a further show of tapping a few keys on his computer keyboard and staring intently at the screen.

Finally he turns to me. "Who is Zhou Zheng'an?"

My mouth is dry. I swallow once. "He's . . . a friend of mine. A consultant."

"What does he really do?"

I take a moment to think. If I tell him who John really works for, will that protect me?

Or will it just screw John?

I stare at Uncle Yang, with his sad, baggy eyes and sharp suit and absolutely no sign of sympathy or warmth whatsoever.

"You have his card," I say. "Why don't you ask him?"

Uncle Yang stares back. Drums his fingers on the top of the desk, just a single riff.

"He said some very strange things at dinner. Why?"

"I don't know," I say, which is kind of the truth. "I think he was just making conversation. He's very concerned about conditions in modern society." Yeah, I say that. It's a phrase in Chinese that I can always remember.

"Really." His voice is flat. It's not a question.

"Look," I say, "he's . . . my boyfriend. Just recently. So I don't know everything about him. I just, I didn't want to go to the dinner by myself."

"He upset my sister's daughter," Yang snaps. "Dao Ming is not well. I don't like seeing her upset."

"I'm sorry to hear that."

His cheeks redden; I see sweat start to bead on his forehead. "This is a very complicated time. Do you have any understanding of this?"

The 18th Party Congress next year, maybe that's what he's

talking about, when the old leadership gives way to the new. Different factions and players jockeying for power now. Whatever his side is, getting connected to two dead girls isn't going to help his position any, or his allies'.

But if I bring it up, will that get him all defensive? Piss him off even more?

So I just nod, slowly.

He stares at me. And in case I'd somehow managed to forget that this is one powerful asshole who could smash me like a little bug, the look he's giving me now reminds me.

"Tell your 'boyfriend'"—yeah, he practically puts that in air quotes—"to contact me directly. I don't want to have another conversation with a foreigner."

I nod again.

He picks up the folder on his desk, makes a show of opening it, picks up a paper and pretends to study it. Does this mean I'm dismissed?

He lowers the paper. Gives me that look. "But if I have to talk to you again, I will. I suggest you make sure that he contacts me. Do you understand?"

I nod. What else can I do?

He picks up the paper again. "Go," he says to me with a wave of his hand.

I push myself up from the chair and hobble out.

The guys who brought me here are lounging in the living room, which is big and white and marble, with gold highlights. Typical. There's even a white grand piano. I wonder if anyone who lives here actually plays it.

My kidnappers sit on the couch, eating sunflower seeds and drinking Cokes, watching an NBA game on a big flat-screen TV, fist-pumping as a shot hits the basket.

I'm thinking maybe I'll just walk out of the house and down the drive and get to the road and just keep on walking till I find a cab or a bus that can get me back to Gulou.

Then the guy who punched me stands up.

"I need to return home now," I say.

He nods.

THEY DON'T EVEN TAKE me all the way home. Instead they drop me at the subway station by the Old Summer Palace.

Assholes.

I get on the subway. I'm drenched with sweat—the back of my shirt is soaked with it—and I'm shaky enough that I just lean against the wall and clutch the rail to keep from falling over.

I walked out of Uncle Yang's McMansion *this* time, but the next time maybe not.

Phone. I pat the side of my bag. It's still there. I reach in and get it out.

Powered up now.

I saw them turn it off.

I stare at the screen. Yeah, I have a password. Yeah, the lock screen is on. But I have to figure they got all the information off it, or tried to anyway, and for all I know, they could have hacked it, too. I mean, I wasn't there very long, but who knows with this stuff? Maybe it's as simple as installing an app.

I power off the phone.

I FIND A BIT of space by the accordion wall that connects two cars, watch the ads and animated safety messages on the little video screen: Don't walk on the tracks. Don't set yourself on fire. Right—and I try to think it through.

This is a very complicated time.

Uncle Yang is a high-level official jockeying for power in the middle of a leadership transition. And knowing how these guys play, no doubt he has some powerful enemies.

Uncle Yang was at a party where a girl died. And John essentially called him and all the Caos out on it.

Clearly John's not on his side.

Then there's Marsh. The family friend. Is he working for somebody else? Maybe one of Uncle Yang's enemies? Yang's and Sidney's families are connected. What hurts one hurts the other. Is that why Sidney wanted me to check up on Marsh? Or was that just because he's an asshole who's a bad influence on his son, like Sidney told me?

Who is Zhou Zheng'an?

Good question.

WHEN I GET HOME, Mimi greets me at the door, dancing around me and making happy little yelps. Mom and John are sitting at the table sipping tea.

"Oh, hi, hon," my mom says.

"I thought you were going to stay away from the apartment today," I say, and I know I don't sound calm.

"Well, sorry," she says with an eye roll. "Actually, I was at Andy's, and John came and knocked on the door."

"Yes." John half stands, then sits back down. "Yili, did you have some trouble getting home?" He's smiling, but there's that nervous twist in his voice that he can't quite cover.

"Yeah." I go into the kitchen and grab a beer. "I was delayed."

"John thought the two of you were having lunch, so he was worried when you weren't here." My mom's looking me over, giving an extra glance to the beer in my hand.

"Beer, it's not just for breakfast anymore," I say. I sit down at the table, pop open the bottle, and pour myself a glass. Mimi sits at my side and rests her head on my thigh.

My mom leans in closer. "What happened to your eye?"

"I ran into something."

"John and I were just talking about restaurant locations," she says, trying to make nice or, more accurately, make normal.

"Yes." John nods. He turns to Mom. "I think . . . Dongsi Shitiao very nice area. But not so many people walking by. Not like Sanlitun. Maybe that is better?"

"I'm not so crazy about Sanlitun," Mom says with a frown. "I think someplace that's a little quieter might be nicer."

I chug about half my beer, wishing it were stronger.

"Yili, are you ready to go to lunch now?" John asks.

I shake my head.

"Is something wrong?" my mom asks. The way she's looking at me, she *knows* something's wrong.

I laugh. "Yeah. You might say that."

I catch John's eye, and he's giving me a warning look. The one that means, *Don't say anything.*

I glare back. He doesn't get to have an opinion this time.

I face my mom. "Okay. I can't really explain the whole situation right now. It's complicated. And it's bad. So I'm just gonna tell you a bullshit story about . . . I don't know, Chinese gangsters in the art market, and we're having a business disagreement, so this isn't a good place to be right now."

"Yili—" John starts.

I hold up a hand. "Don't." I turn back to my mom. "Can you and Andy go someplace for a week? Like Hong Kong? Maybe take Mimi with you? She's got her papers. Right, John?"

John gets that scrunched-up look for a second, then nods. "Yes. I can help arrange."

Through all this my mom's watching me with her mouth slightly open and a confused expression on her face.

"Are you talking about actual Chinese gangsters?" she asks.

"I'll explain it all better later, I promise." I slug down some more beer. I'm thinking it's Percocet time.

"This isn't fair," she suddenly blurts out. "You're always hiding things. You know my life's an open book, and I get that hasn't always maybe been a good thing for you, but you never share *anything*. You just . . . you just keep it all to yourself, and you won't let anyone help you—"

"You know how you can help? By just fucking doing what I'm asking you to do, okay?" I pour out the rest of my beer and slam the bottle onto the table. Brace my hands on the edge of the table and push myself to my feet. "I'm gonna change my shirt," I mumble, and I limp off to my room, banging the door closed behind me.

I dig around in the top dresser drawer for my main Percocet stash. Get out the bottle, pop it open, and tap a pill onto my palm.

I hear a whimper and a scratching at the door: Mimi.

I hobble over and let her in.

"Sorry, pup," I whisper, scratching her neck where the thick ruffle of fur is. "You don't like all this yelling and drama and stuff, do you?"

Her tail thumps on the floor.

I look at the Percocet in my hand. My leg doesn't really hurt that bad right now. It's more like I just don't want to feel this shit.

I have maybe fifty pills left. Sounds like a lot, but it's not, not really, and what you don't want to have happen is to keep taking them, run out, and then have to go cold turkey. I've done it before. It's nasty.

I split the pill in half and put the other half back into the bottle.

When I come out, I'm wearing a shirt that doesn't smell like stale sweat, and I'm feeling a little calmer. I guess I should apologize or something. I've got to figure out how to keep my cool better.

Or I could stop getting kidnapped and/or beaten up by assholes. That would probably improve my mood.

John's still sitting at the dining-room table, thumbing the screen of his smartphone. As soon as he sees me, he puts it down and stands up, like he's thinking about coming to me and giving me a hug or something.

But he doesn't. He just stands there, uncertainly, his hands clasped loosely in front of him.

Which is a good thing, because I pretty much want to smack him.

"Where's Cindy?" I ask. My mom's nowhere in sight.

"She is fetching Andy." His hands fall to his sides. "Can you tell me what happened?"

When I finish my story, John looks grim. The only thing he says is, "I see."

He strides over to the kitchen window, the one with a view of the courtyard parking lot. Stares out. I get the feeling he's taking an inventory of every car, every person, every object, looking for threats.

"You see something?"

"No. Does not mean no one is there."

"Shit." Because it hits me like a bucket of ice water. "They could've seen you come up here."

He nods.

I think of something else. "Could they . . . ? Could this place be . . . ?" I point to my ear. "Can they hear us now, do you think?"

"I don't think so. Not this quickly. I check before." He sounds like he's trying to convince himself.

You probably bugged the place yourself, I want to say, but I don't.

John goes over to the TV and turns it on. Finds a loud variety show and cranks the volume. Cartoon sound effects and high-pitched screams of teenage girls fill the room.

"Maybe best thing for you to go with your mother to Hong Kong," he mutters.

"No way."

"Why? You are better off in Hong Kong than Beijing." He's all certain, the big man who knows best. Better than I do anyway.

"Because they're watching me, John," I say, and I know I sound really pissed, because isn't that obvious? "I go with Mom and Andy, they're gonna know about it and follow us there. I stay here, Mom and Andy can go on their own, and maybe no one will notice 'cause they're busy watching me. Maybe they won't even care."

His expression wavers, just a little, because he hadn't thought of that, and he knows that he should have.

That's when my front door rattles, and Mom and Andy walk in.

Her eyes are red, the lids puffy. Great. I made my mom cry. Andy is close behind her, solid, slightly padded, like she could fall back on him if she had to and she'd be okay.

"*Yili, ni hao,*" Andy says, like this was any other day. I'm starting to see why my mom likes him. When everything's going batshit, there's something to be said for a guy who doesn't seem to rattle, even if the calm is coming from his faith in Brother Jesus of the Righteous Thundering Fist.

"Hi, Andy. I'm sorry," I say to my mom. "I didn't mean to . . . I just . . . Things are really screwed up right now."

"I guess I get that." She sniffles a little. "Why do you have the TV on so loud?"

"Because, uh . . . just because."

"*Heibang* can be big problem," Andy says with a nod.

Is he really buying my story about gangsters? I wasn't even pretending to be serious about it.

"I have car," he continues. "We can drive to see my family in Xiamen. Xiamen is very pretty. Mimi can come, too."

I hesitate. I'd feel better if they got out of the mainland altogether. But Xiamen's only a couple hundred miles from Hong Kong, there's all kinds of flights and even boats that go to HK from there, and if they just go to visit Andy's family, maybe it wouldn't attract as much attention as crossing into Hong Kong. They could get away with not contacting the local PSB for a couple of days to register my mom, and it's not like the different provincial authorities always talk to each other. Maybe it would be safe.

Has to be safer than Beijing anyway.

"Okay," I say. "Thanks. I appreciate it."

"This isn't exactly how I wanted to meet your family, Andy," my mom says with a little smile.

He slips his hand into hers. "I know my family like you very much."

She blushes.

IT DOESN'T TAKE LONG for Mom to pack a suitcase and for me to gather up another bag with Mimi's food and dishes. Mimi's dancing around, all excited, stands up on her hind paws and rests her front paws on my hips, her doggie hug: road trip!

"Wish I could go, too," I mutter, hugging her around the neck.

Mom's just coming out of the bathroom with her Dopp kit. She sees me playing with the dog and hesitates by the door.

"You know, you can tell me the truth," she says quietly, so John won't hear. He's pacing around the living room, scowling at his phone.

"I really can't," I say. Not about this.

Not about a lot of things.

WHEN SHE'S READY TO go, Andy comes over to carry her bag, which is just a little wheeled carry-on, but she's kind of got her hands full with Mimi and the tote bag with Mimi's things.

We're all standing around the door, me and John on one side, Mom and Andy on the other, Mimi prancing in place between us.

I can tell my mom's trying not to be upset. She's got a smile on her face and everything. "I'll call you or email you as soon as we get there," she says.

"Actually . . . don't. I mean . . ." How to put it? "I'll get in touch with you in a couple of days. Unless you have a problem, and then call me right away. Not that you'll have a problem or anything."

She nods.

"But . . . when you do go online? Make sure you always use the VPN. The thing I downloaded for you so you can log on to Facebook."

Her face twists, and I can tell she's about to lose it. She gathers me into her arms and hugs me tight, and she's crying now. I hate that. I pat her on the back, and I hold my breath, and I tell myself, You have to keep it together, you can't lose it, too, because I'm scared if I do, I'll break down completely. Curl up into a little ball and just wait for someone to come and put me out of my misery.

Finally my mom lets go. Steps back and glares at John.

"I don't know what your story is, John," she says, "but if you have anything to do with the problems my little girl is having? I'll come back here and I'll kick your ass."

"I . . . I," John stammers, and then falls silent. Looks away. "I will take care of her," he says.

"You'd better."

Yeah, like he's done such a great job so far. But I don't tell my mom that.

"NOW WHAT?"

Mom and Andy and Mimi have left. It's just John and me, circling each other like a couple of wary cats.

He stops and massages his forehead, as if he's trying to pull out a solution with his fingers. "We should go. I can take you someplace. Someplace safe."

There are all kinds of things I want to ask, questions swirling around in my head so fast that I can barely separate one from another.

First and foremost, how is he going to keep me safe from a guy who apparently has the fucking *PLA* to do his dirty work?

But there's no time for that right now.

I hustle into my bedroom, grab my daypack, my laptop, a light jacket, a T-shirt, and clean underwear, my Percocet, the old iPhone I keep because I can buy anonymous SIM cards for it, just in case something like this should happen, and my Beanie squid, for good luck.

God knows I'm going to need it.

CHAPTER SEVENTEEN

"LET ME CARRY YOUR bag."

"I can carry it myself."

John grits his teeth. We're in the elevator heading down. An ad for cognac plays on the little flat-screen TV by the door.

"Right now we just pretend we are boyfriend and girl-friend," he says. "Boyfriend carries girlfriend's bag."

"Whatever," I mutter. I hand him my daypack. "Are we gonna hold hands, too?"

"We should act like nothing's wrong."

"Why? What difference will it make?"

"Just . . ." He hisses through his teeth. "Just do what I say, for once."

Fuck you, I think really loud.

"CAN WE GO OUT another way?" he asks when we reach the ground floor.

"What about your car?"

"Better to just leave it here. In case . . ."

In case someone bugged it, I'm guessing, while John was talking about restaurant locations with my mom.

"Yeah," I say. Behind my building there's an alcove where they keep a couple of dumpsters and a little yard that has a long bike rack crammed with rusting Giants and a few old Flying

Pigeons and some battered electric scooters. It's enclosed by a cinder-block wall with shards of glass embedded in the top, but there's a little gate with a triangular metal tube barrier that no one watches and you can slip through if you want, which has never made sense to me, but whatever.

"This way."

We exit onto a tiny *hutong* that runs perpendicular to the alley off Jiu Gulou Dajie. If we hang a right, we can head up to Xitao Hutong and over to the Gulou subway station or keep going north to Deshengmen and the Second Ring Road to catch a cab. Or we can head south, to Gulou West and Houhai. Plenty of cabs there, too.

"South," John says.

"Why?"

"Other way is where car would go, maybe to get on Second Ring Road or Jiugulou Dajie. Or to go on subway. This way maybe they don't expect us to go."

"Okay."

We head south, down an alley lined with grey brick walls. There's a worker with a bicycle cart hauling empty Yanjing Beer bottles who looks up as we pass. He has a PLA-green cap pulled low over his head, but I can see his eyes, staring at us.

"So where are we going?"

"A safe place I know. Where Yang Junmin can't find you."

"A DSD safe place?"

John shrugs.

"Because your boss wants to nail my sorry ass to a wall, so how the *fuck* is some DSD off-the-books shithole where you lock up dissidents you don't like *safe*?"

Okay, I'm yelling. But it's been a really lousy day so far.

"He is not my boss," John mutters, his jaw tight.

"Oh, great, here we go with the man-of-mystery routine again."

We're getting close to Gulou West. We turn a corner, down another little alley, past one of those tiny shoe box–size stores that sell beer and toilet paper and snacks.

And see two guys heading toward us. Young. Buzz cuts. Sunglasses and fake leather jackets.

"Keep walking," John murmurs.

"Just . . . ?"

"Keep walking." He places his hand flat on my back for a moment, urging me forward.

My heart's racing. I feel the pain shooting up my leg, and I tell myself, I can do it, I can keep walking, just walk right on past these guys, we'll make it to Gulou West, grab a cab, and get the fuck out, and we're just about even with them when one of the guys bumps his shoulder into John, hard.

"Watch where you're going," the guy snarls.

John lifts his hands, chest-high. *"Duibuqi,"* he says. Sorry. He takes a step back.

That's when they rush him.

John drives the heels of his palms into the first guy's jaw, shoves a knee into his groin. First guy goes down, but as he does, the other guy drives his shoulder into John's side, a foot-ball tackle, and they hit the ground, scrambling and punching and kicking, knocking over a crate of empty Yanjing Beer bottles.

One of those rolls in my direction. I pick it up. Hold the bottle in both hands. Wait till I have a clear shot. And smash it over the guy's head.

It's not like the movies. The fucking thing doesn't break. But I hit him hard enough that he collapses for a moment, lifts his hands to the back of his head like a reflex, and that gives John enough time to roll away and slam his heel into the guy's ribs a few times. I hear a sound that might be one of his ribs breaking, and I shudder, I can't help it.

Thankfully, he goes limp. He's breathing, and he's conscious, but the fight's gone out of him.

John scrambles to his feet, my backpack still on his shoulders.

I hear a tinkle of glass, and a beer bottle rolls past my feet. Turn and see a middle-aged woman poking her head out of the doorway of the tiny shop.

"Duibuqi, gei ni tian mafan le," John says. Sorry to trouble you.

And we hustle ourselves down the alley, leaving the two guys moaning on the pavement.

"You'd think Uncle Yang could afford better thugs."

John shrugs. "They are not bad. I am simply better."

I roll my eyes. "Well, you had a little help."

"I did." He gives my hand a squeeze. "You were very good."

The two of us are making like boyfriend and girlfriend, riding on the subway out to John's safe place, wherever that is. Just laughing and touching each other, like we're an actual couple.

There's a part of me that knows I should be asking those questions, such as where are we going exactly, but I'm so wired and buzzing from what just happened that I'm mostly just thinking about how good it feels leaning into Mr. Badass next to me here.

"What about your car?" I ask.

"What about it?"

"Can't they use it to find you?"

John whispers in my ear: "Not with the plates on it. Fake."

"Smooth."

"The next station is Sanyuanqiao. Sanyuanqiao is a transfer station. All passengers, please prepare for your arrival." I half listen to the recorded announcements, wondering as I always do who they got to do the English—the way she says "transfer," all nasal like she's from New Jersey or something always cracks me up.

"We can get off here," John says.

"We going to the airport?"

He shakes his head. "We just look for a taxi."

We take the long escalator up to the surface, emerging into dusty yellow skies.

RIDING IN THE CAB, I'm not sure why, but everything feels heavier somehow. We were having fun on the subway, celebrating that we'd beaten the bad guys. Now the boyfriend/girlfriend act is over. We're sitting next to each other like near strangers.

We're out in that patchy no-man's-land close to the airport. You can't get here on the subway; the Airport Express doesn't make stops between Sanyuanqiao and the terminals. Not that there's much here. Just the highway and scrubby fields and skinny trees, the occasional factory.

We pull off the highway. Close to the interchange, there's this massive concrete building painted a yellowish shade of beige. It's about three stories, and I would've taken it to be a factory or a school of some kind that was built in the Soviet days, except for the fountain out in front surrounded by a circle of yellow-beige concrete columns and topped by a yellow-beige concrete ring. That and the rooftop sign that spells out AIRPORT HARMONY GARDEN HOTEL.

"Wait a second—" I say as we pull in to the drive.

John shoots me a look. "We can discuss in a minute. *Ni keyi dao houbian ting che*," he tells the driver. You can stop around the back.

I'm liking this less and less. I'm thinking maybe I should just stay in the cab and have the driver drop me someplace else. But I don't.

John pays the guy, and he gets out, and I slide out after him.

We're in a small parking lot behind a secondary building, a ragged tennis court to one side. "Wait here a moment," John says. "I have to make an arrangement." He trots off toward the main building. I stand there, pissed at myself for going along with him. The two times that Pompadour Bureaucrat had me picked up for tea, it went something like this. Some crappy hotel on the fringes of Beijing. Going upstairs through a side entrance. Never checking in and not knowing if I'd be checking out anytime soon.

But this is different, I tell myself. This is John. I don't know exactly what his deal is, but he seems to care about me, right?

There are two guys playing tennis in the late-afternoon sun. One wearing jeans, neither very good. I watch them play, the guy in jeans swatting with an awkward hop at a ball that sails past his head and a giggle when he misses.

I stare at the cracks on the tennis court, at the frayed net.

Finally I turn and see John jogging toward me.

"Okay," he says. "We can go inside now."

EVEN THOUGH THE HALL is dark, I can see stains in the worn brown carpet, that the faded white walls are dingy with decades of cigarette smoke. It's a lot like the hotels Pompadour Bureaucrat had me brought to, except worse, maybe because there's so much more of it. The halls are wide and strangely empty. Maybe it's off-season for detaining dissidents.

We pass only one person, a thirtyish man in a cheap leather jacket and dark slacks, Ray-Ban-style sunglasses perched on his forehead. He and John exchange a glance, or am I imagining that? He sure looks like a low-rent undercover nark anyway.

John stops in front of a room close to the end of the hall. Gets out a key card. I hear the little whir as it unlocks. He steps inside, and I follow.

A faded yellow runner over a greying quilt on a bed that I already know is a thin foam pad on top of plywood. Dusty beige curtains. The whole place stinks of mildew.

John stands there, an uncertain look on his face.

"So," he finally says. "You can stay here awhile. I will take care of things."

"Awhile? How long? And what things?"

"Just . . . a day or so. I come back for you."

"Jesus," I mutter. "So you're just gonna leave me here while you go do whatever it is you're gonna do?"

He gives a little half shrug. I guess that's all the answer I'm going to get.

"You need to eat some things, you can go to the canteen. They put it on room. You can . . . you can go to . . . to *jianshenfang*, to . . . to gym." There's this weird helpless note to his voice. That's when it hits me.

"You don't really have a plan, do you? Awesome."

"I can manage something. You must trust me."

"Oh, must I?" I plop down on the bed. The mattress is hard enough to send a jolt up my spine.

It's not like I have a lot of choices. I don't have a working phone—well, I have one with no minutes and another that I'm pretty sure is hacked. I do have my laptop, though. I unzip my backpack and pull it out.

John lets out a short, sharp sigh and shakes his head.

Of course there isn't going to be Internet in a secret black-jail detention hotel room.

"Fine. Whatever."

"Yili—"

I hold up my hand. "Don't. Just . . . just go. Go manage something. I'll wait here."

He stands there a moment longer, like he's looking for something from me. I have no idea what.

"Sorry," he mutters, and leaves.

Yeah, you should be sorry, buddy, I think. I may not know John's whole story, but how is he going to deal with a pissed-off Uncle Yang?

I hope the TV works. Maybe there's an American movie on CCTV-6.

I fiddle with the remote. Nada. Just a black screen.

"Fucking great."

There's a teakettle at least. I can make myself a cup of coffee. I usually have a couple of Starbucks VIAs in my messenger bag.

I pull the bag out of my backpack. Slip my hand into the outside pocket. Feel around for the little tube of coffee.

That's when my fingertips feel something else through the rough canvas fabric, something in the small interior zip pocket. Something round, like a coin. Except it doesn't feel exactly like a coin somehow. Too thick.

I unzip the pocket and jam two fingers inside, feeling for the thing. I find it and fish it out.

Yeah, it looks like a coin. An old one-yuan model. And yeah, they're heavier than the modern version. But not like this.

I stare at the rim. Is that a seam down the middle?

Yeah. It is.

I don't know what this thing is for sure, but if I had to guess, I'm guessing it's a bug—or some kind of tracker.

Fuck, fuck, the fucking fuck.

I try to think it through. There was plenty of time when I was having my little session with Uncle Yang for one of his men to plant it. But John, he would've checked, wouldn't he? I mean, he knows all about this stuff, right? Granted, things happened pretty fast—maybe he slipped up.

Or maybe he put it there.

I have absolutely no way of knowing.

"Shit."

I dump everything out of my bag. Press my fingers against the fabric, feel all the pockets, the seams. Pull all the money and cards from my wallet. I don't find anything else, at least nothing I can spot.

I scramble to my feet. Go into the bathroom and put the little disk on the counter. Flush the toilet. Then I turn on the shower. It's streaked with rust and black mold, and I have time to think, at least I won't be using *that* thing.

Because all I do know for sure is I need to get out of here, right now.

CHAPTER EIGHTEEN

I CLOSE THE DOOR to the hotel room, backpack slung over one shoulder, like I'm just going out for a little stroll. Like maybe to the restaurant for a beer and some dumplings.

I look down the hall. That guy we passed before, the one in the cheap leather jacket and Ray-Bans, is loitering by the stairs, doing something on his smartphone.

There's probably a stairwell at the other end of the hall, but I can't see it from here. I'm a lot closer to this one. If I'm trying to act casual, does it make sense for me to walk away from the stairs right by me, to the opposite end of the hall?

I draw in a breath and head toward the stairs I can see. Ray-Ban Guy glances up from his phone, then back down to his screen. I'm going to have to walk right past him.

If he's someone John knows, if he calls John, maybe that's not so bad, I tell myself.

But what if he's one of Pompadour Bureaucrat's men? What if he doesn't trust John? What if John's just abandoned me here in this dump and isn't coming back, because he doesn't have any way to fix this mess and I'm the one who's going to pay for it?

Dumplings and beer. I'm just going out for dumplings and beer.

I've reached the top of the stairs. Ray-Bans doesn't move.

Should I offer to bring him back a bowl of noodles? Would that be casual or just weird?

I keep my eyes forward and step down. As I do, something on his phone squawks. I stumble a little, grab onto the railing.

He's playing Angry Birds.

I hop unevenly down the stairs.

OUTSIDE, THE GUYS WHO were playing tennis are just coming off the court. Laughing, not sweating. One of them swats the other lightly on the ass with his racket.

If there are taxis, they'll likely be out in front of the hotel, maybe picking up or dropping off. But do I want to risk going there? If that bug/tracker thing belongs to Uncle Yang, could they already be here, watching? Waiting for me to make some kind of move?

For that matter, they could be parked out here, in this lot, close to the building.

I take a couple of deep breaths, tell myself I can't panic, that I have to keep it together. I do a scan of the parking lot. Only a few cars. They're all empty.

Okay, I tell myself. Okay. You're all right for now.

There's a feeder road running alongside the back of the tennis court. I have no idea where it goes. But if it doesn't lead past the hotel entrance, maybe that's good enough.

I head toward it.

I DON'T KNOW HOW long I walk, since neither of my phones is working and I don't own a watch. Long enough for the throbbing pain in my leg to feel like someone's stabbing my thigh with a barbecue fork and for my feet to feel like they're bruised. There's nothing much on this road, mostly trees with

their white-painted trunks that were probably planted for the
'08 Olympics and a few fields and redbrick farm buildings that
haven't been swallowed up by high-rises and car dealerships
and factories.

Finally the road runs head-on into a bigger one. A town.
A couple of new hotels with "Airport" in their names among
clumps of older white-tiled storefronts. A restaurant, battered
red lanterns swaying in the wind.

I see an available cab pulling away from the restaurant and
raise my hand.

He stops in front of me. I get into the backseat.

"*Qu nar?*" he asks. Where to?

It occurs to me that I have no freaking clue.

I HAVE HIM TAKE me to Haidian, near Beida. I know the
area pretty well, and it's a place where being a foreigner doesn't
attract much attention, what with all the colleges around here.
Plus, there's a Number 4 subway stop near the east gate of the
university, and that line goes all the way to the Beijing South
Railway Station.

Because yeah, my first instinct, as usual, is to get out of town.
But I'm trying to be smart, trying to think things through, and
I don't know if that's such a great idea.

Won't running make me look guilty? Another black mark
against me for Inspector Zou? Has John even talked to him?
I've got to find out.

And then there's Uncle Yang. How far does his influence go?
How many guys can he afford to have running around keeping
an eye out for me? Or . . . I don't know, electronic surveillance
stuff, is he tied in to that? I can still buy train tickets without
showing my passport—they'll start requiring that in a couple

of months, I've heard—and I can avoid using my *yikatong* card on the subways and just pay cash, but there are surveillance cameras everywhere in Beijing.

Who is actually watching?

First things first. I need to get a new SIM card and minutes for my old iPhone. Try to get in touch with John, find out if that was his bug or Uncle Yang's. Ask him if he's talked to Inspector Zou.

After that . . . I don't know.

I have friends. People I can ask for help. My ex-boss, British John, lives not too far from here.

But there's the other side of that, what happens to the people who help me. British John got enough shit because of me a year ago. Do I really want to drag him into something again?

Then there's Harrison. If anybody's got the juice to help me out, it's him. Though Harrison told me that he's no match for the Caos.

The Caos. Shit. I can't keep avoiding Sidney. Eventually he's going to catch up to me, and when he does . . .

I don't know exactly how deep the connection between Sidney and Uncle Yang goes, but they're both from Anhui, and Sidney's son is married to Yang's niece, and someone's got to be greasing the wheels for Sidney high up in the government, and someone's got to be supplying Uncle Yang with those really expensive suits, so . . . yeah.

Pretty deep.

If Uncle Yang's unhappy, I have to figure Sidney's pretty unhappy, too.

Which brings me back to calling the embassy. They won't necessarily help me if I'm in trouble with the police here, but they might be interested in intel about high-level politics and murdered girls. And then there's Carter, who'd be the guy to broker that kind of deal.

But am I ready to take that step? Because once I do . . . well, there are all kinds of consequences. Like probably closing the door on my life here.

Am I ready for that?

What kind of life will I have if I do?

There's nothing for me in the States. No job. No marriage. No future. Just a shitty disability pension that won't cover my rent, plus all the psych meds and Percocet I want.

But going up against Uncle Yang and the Caos . . . If nobody I know has the *guanxi* for that, what makes me think *I* can handle it?

I'm messing with tigers here. With dragons.

I BUY A NEW SIM card and minutes at a newspaper vendor and fire up my phone.

It's a new number, so no new messages, except for a few spam texts that appear almost immediately. I'm going to have to go someplace with Wi-Fi and get onto my laptop to see who's been trying to reach me. God knows how many emails Vicky Huang's left me by now.

First thing I do is call "Zhou Zheng'an" at "Bright Spring Enterprises."

No answer. Voice mail with a woman's voice saying, "You've reached Bright Spring Enterprises" and to please leave a message. Very slick.

I hang up.

I'm not too surprised that John isn't answering his phone. Uncle Yang has this number, and you can track someone on a cell phone, right?

Maybe they can hack the voice mail, too.

I switch off my phone.

Email.

I walk down the tree-lined street, past university walls and gates, until I come to a smaller lane with little shops and cafés.

First thing I do is buy another SIM card. I'll use the first one to call numbers that might be tapped.

Second thing, I find a little café/bar advertising free Wi-Fi and grab a table.

Another typical Beijing joint: small, wooden tables, a couple fake plants, some random decorations—in this case the top half of a male mannequin wearing a Mao cap and a Rolling Stones T-shirt—specials written in English and Chinese on a board with Day-Glo chalk, selling some form of pizza and burgers and sandwiches.

I order a Yanjing Beer and one of the pizzas, because by now it's almost 6:00 P.M. and I can't remember if I've had anything to eat today. I don't think I have. When the pizza comes, it's pretty bad—canned tomato sauce and plastic cheese—but I wolf it down. Get out my laptop, start up my VPN, and close my eyes so I don't see the emails coming in. I'm not ready for Vicky Huang, or the Caos, or the Beijing PD, or my mom.

When I open my eyes, I launch a browser and go to the Yahoo! account that's not linked to my real name—at least I hope it's not. And I type John's email in the address box. Not the Bright Spring email. The other one he gave me: "Jinhuli."

Cinderfox.

On the subject line, I type, *"From Little Mountain Tiger."* And then I write, *"Either you or Uncle left something in my bag. I couldn't wait to find out who."*

I stop. Take another slug of beer. I don't know what to say. There's too much in my head: Did you talk to Inspector Zou? Did you find out anything about Celine? Are you going to fix this shit? Save my ass?

Because I'm all alone, and I don't know what to do, and I'm scared.

I don't type any of that.

"Write me back. Leave me a number where I can reach you. We need to talk."

After that I take a big gulp of the Yanjing and start reading email.

Five messages from Vicky Huang. The first few are variations on *Mr. Cao is interested in your report. When can you meet?* The last one says, *You must contact Mr. Cao right away. He urgently needs to speak to you.*

Here's one from Meimei: *Did you know your phone isn't working?* ☺ *If you have a problem, maybe I can help. Call me or write.*

And here's one I didn't expect at all. From Marsh Brody:

> *Hey. Well, you really know how to liven up a dinner. What's the deal with your friend? I bet he's even more fun at parties. Tiantian and me are heading south to Movie Universe to do some shooting on our film. Why don't you join us? He's actually really interested in this museum thing. Here's the info.*

Movie Universe. I've read about this place. Huge outdoor sets with reproductions of the Forbidden City and the streets of old Hong Kong, and it's out in the middle of nowhere, someplace south of Shanghai.

And what do you know, here's an email from Tiantian:

Dear Ellie, I think you have a misunderstanding recently of the situation with our family. I would not like you to have a bad impression of us. Perhaps we can meet to discuss. I think your museum proposal has merit. Please call me to schedule.

Weird. It's like all the Cao kids want to make nice with me. I have my doubts that this is actually the case.

So what do I do? Keep avoiding Sidney or call him? If I call him, what do I say? *Hi, one of your kids, or maybe your political patron, is a murderer?*

Maybe the killer is Marsh. That would be so much more convenient.

I'm thinking about this, and another email comes in.

The subject line is *"Letters from the Deep Yellow Sea—My Decision."*

I feel a prickling along the back of my neck, up and down my spine. She's dead. Celine's dead. So what the fuck is this?

I have written things for a while now that I do not publish. Because I know they could cause me trouble and I am scared. I am also selfish. I like the life I have, even when it seems very silly. But now after what I saw I must speak the truth. When you read this I will be gone from Beijing. Maybe from this world. That's okay. I think there are better worlds we can't see. This one sometimes is so ugly.

Okay, I tell myself, okay. I subscribed to her blog feed. She set this up to autopublish. Simple enough.

Everyone knows the rich move their money overseas. So they can send their kids to some fancy American university. Buy their winery in France. Everyone knows about this. But it is not just the rich. It is our leaders. They set up phony companies overseas to hide their money. You know this, too, but I can prove it.

I have this sudden flash, of Celine offering me one of her Panda cigarettes with her little half smile.

They do this in ways that maybe aren't against the law, but they still don't want the people to know about it. Regardless, they can use the law any way they want. For you and for me, the laws have different meanings.

No one took her seriously, I'm thinking. I know I didn't. All the while she was there, in the middle of all that wealth and power, taking notes.

But sometimes their money is just dirty, and then they must clean it. They have all kinds of ways to do this. For example, I know one leader who has a friend who invests in art.

Well, shit. I have a pretty good guess where this is going.

It is so simple with art. Another friend in a foreign country buys the art for you. You pay him too high a price. The friend gets some of this money and gives you back the rest. The other money goes into a bank account overseas. The money is now clean. So simple! No one knows how much this art is really worth.

I'd be surprised if Sidney hadn't been doing something like

this. Is there a rich Chinese person who doesn't have money stashed overseas?

The big question is, does Uncle Yang? Because the whole trend of high-level officials and their families getting super rich and taking their money out of the country is really pissing off the *laobaixing*, the common people.

＊

But that is just a small thing compared to the other things. There is so much more I can say. How the leaders help the rich get richer. How the rich give money back to the leaders.

I can tell you about companies overseas. These companies are just fakes. Ways to open bank accounts. Places to hide money. This is how the leaders and the rich help each other. The leaders relax the laws so that the rich can move their money to these places. The rich give the leaders money. Help their relatives and children become rich. Even the foreign companies help. Paying money to relatives of leaders, for 'consulting' and things of that nature. It is just to try to gain influence. Everybody knows this.

Here is a company you should know about, in the British Virgin Islands: Favorable Wave LTD. If you can find out who really owns this company, I think it is very interesting.

I'm sweating now. This is not shit that I want to know. I don't need to know it. So Uncle Yang and the Caos are corrupt—this is news? But the details—those can get you killed.

What do I do with it?

I can send it to John. Maybe it will give him the kind of ammo he needs to get us out of this mess.

Or maybe it will just be more fuel for his vendetta.

And if I completely throw in with John, if this blows up my relationship with the Caos . . . is that smart?

I forward the email to another address, the one I used to write John aka Cinderfox. Then I delete it from my inbox and sent mail. I know it's not gone, not really. The best I can do is hope that no one decides to look.

And now *I* have to decide. What do I do next?

I can't go back to my apartment.

I can't go to any hotels, because I'd have to show my passport.

I might be able to get out of town on a train or a bus if Uncle Yang isn't watching. But then what? Where would it make sense for me to go?

Maybe it's time to call my old pal Carter and see if he can fix things for me with the American embassy so they'll protect me. I've got two dead girls and an offshore company to trade. That should be enough.

But then there's my mom. And Andy. What happens to them if I pull the plug on my life here? Can I bargain to take them with me? Would they want to go?

What would any of us do?

If it was just me, I swear to God, I'd get my ass out of here and go hide someplace where the living's cheap and I could just . . . I don't know, just *be*.

Where *is* that place anyway? I don't have a clue. Does it even exist?

And it's not just me. It's my mom. It's Andy. It's people I work with, like Lucy Wu, like Harrison Wang.

Okay, well, maybe not Harrison. He's got the resources to take care of himself.

But there's Lao Zhang, who says he's coming back to Beijing.

Plus, there's Creepy John. If I bail and his bosses find out he's been protecting me . . .

If I bail, are they all going to look guilty?

On the other hand, if I stay and end up going down, will they be any better off?

In the back of my mind, it's like there's this worm turning over, whispering in my ear: if I'd never met Lao Zhang, I wouldn't be in this mess.

But what kind of life would I have? The way I'd been going before I got involved with Lao Zhang was nowhere but down.

There's no time for what-ifs, I tell myself. Not now.

"Fuck it," I mutter. I pick up my phone and dial Vicky Huang.

I don't know what I'm going to say to her. Depends on what she says to me. Just try to stall, I guess. Give John a chance to do what he's going to do. Maybe I can hide out at Harrison's place in the meantime. You can't beat the coffee.

Vicky doesn't pick up, which surprises me until I remember that I'm calling from a number she doesn't know. Instead I hear a loud burst of a cheesy orchestral arrangement of "My Heart Will Go On" (of course) and a beep.

"Hello, Vicky, it's Ellie. Ellie McEnroe. Sorry for the delay in calling you. I . . . uh, had some phone problems. Anyway, you can reach me at this number."

I disconnect. Drain the rest of my Yanjing and lift my hand to have the waitress bring me another. Maybe I'll pop for the Rogue Ale instead, even though it will most likely be stale. I'm already so nervous my hands are sweating, and I nearly drop my pint glass.

It takes all of a minute for Vicky Huang to call me back.

"Where have you been?" she demands. "Why do you always have this trouble with your phone? Maybe you need new one."

"Yeah. Well. This time I dropped it on the subway tracks. So I definitely needed a new—"

She cuts me off. "Mr. Cao is very anxious to talk to you about your findings. Very anxious."

"Right, well, we're still meeting to discuss—"

"Mr. Cao wants to talk to you now."

And with that she hangs up.

I'm just taking my first sip of Rogue Ale when the phone starts playing System of a Down's "Hypnotize," the default I use for an unknown caller. Blocked. Sidney's private number, presumably.

"Hello, Ellie!" He sounds unexpectedly cheery.

"Hi, Sidney. Uh, sorry for the delay in getting back to you. Stuff has been—"

"I am hearing strange things. Some very strange things."

"Yeah. Well. It's . . ."

What do I say?

"Kind of a mess."

"Yang Junmin is asking me what I think about you. I tell him you help me with getting the Zhang Jianli artwork, and I ask you for some help with family business. He doesn't like this very much."

"I'm sorry to hear that," I say, which is a stupid thing to say, but it's about all I've got right now.

"I tell him of course I don't know everything about you. So maybe there is some problem I don't know about."

Oh, like the ones where the DSD is on my ass and the PSB has me as a murder suspect?

"The *problem* is, your son Tiantian had a party, your other kids and Marsh and Uncle Yang and Dao Ming were guests, and a waitress ended up dead."

Because fuck it. What else can I say at this point? Either he already knows or he's going to find out.

There is a long silence on Sidney's end.

"I see," he finally says. "So who has killed her?"

And I can't tell if this is the first time he's heard it or if he already knew.

"I don't know."

"But you have an idea."

"No. I really don't. It could have been anybody. Anybody who was there."

"Then you can help find out."

I did not just hear this.

"What?"

"Of course, if the killer has no connection to my children, then it does not matter. You don't have to worry."

"You want me to find out who killed her? Sidney, this is . . ."

Crazy.

Slow down. Remember, you're dealing with a billionaire who can swat you like you're a crippled little ant.

"Sidney . . . I'm not a detective. I don't know how to do what you're asking me to do."

"Of course you can!" He sounds like one of those amped-up motivational speakers you see on late-night infomercials. "Just continue to do what you do before."

"Which is . . . what? I mean . . . what do you mean?"

"You can just spend some time with my children. They all like you very much."

I don't even know where to start with this.

Stall, I tell myself. Just stall. Then, when you get off the phone, bug out to Harrison's place, hole up, and wait for John to get in touch.

Assuming that he does.

"Okay," I say. "Sure. I can do that. It might take me a day or two to deal with things here, but—"

"I think you must act quickly. You must . . . strike while the iron is hot." He sounds very proud of himself for coming up with this phrase.

"Okay," I say. "Will do."

I have this vivid picture in my head of Harrison's penthouse, of his very comfortable guest room, of packaged silk pajamas, good meals, fine wine, awesome coffee, and beautiful art. Just get there, I think. Hide.

"Oh," Sidney says. "I should tell you. Your mother has come for a visit."

CHAPTER NINETEEN

It takes me a moment to absorb this.

"You kidnapped my mother?"

"Ellie." Sidney sounds hurt. "How can you say such a thing?"

The nice thing about being really pissed off is that rage tends to push the fear away.

I take a deep breath. I need to calm down, and I need to be smart. Because I can't reach through my iPhone and strangle Sidney. There's no app for that.

"Sorry," I say. "It's just that I don't understand. My mom's in Xingfu Cun?"

"Yes. She and her friend have some car troubles. On the road."

I try to piece this together. I know Sidney's MO. I experienced it a couple of months ago.

"So . . . you had people following my mother. And when they had this 'car trouble'—"

"I invite your mother and her friend to come for a visit." He sounds very happy about this. The jovial host. "Because of course I want to meet your family. Since you have met mine."

Silence. I'm not sure how to fill it.

Finally I say, "Is my mom close by? Because I'd like to talk to her for a minute."

Another pause.

"Of course!" he says. "She is just in the dining room. Having a snack."

And he puts me on hold.

A blast of an old-school Chinese patriotic folk song from the fifties, full orchestra and a woman with a high nasal voice warbling at a glass-breaking volume fills my ear. I wait. It feels like forever, but it's probably more like two minutes. Then:

"Ellie? You there?"

It's Mom. She sounds anxious. I can't tell if she's scared.

Me, I am so pissed off that I'm ready to head down to Xingfu Cun with a black-market AK and do some serious damage.

"Yeah, it's me. Are you okay?"

"Oh, yeah. We're fine. Andy's here, and Mimi. We were just having a bite to eat."

She *sounds* fine anyway.

I calm down a notch. "Okay. Listen, you don't have anything to worry about. Sidney is . . . a little different, but he likes having guests."

"Is he one of the *arte bandidos* you were talking about?" she says in a low voice. I figure Sidney's got to be listening.

"I, uh . . . Kind of. It's complicated."

"Okay. Don't worry, hon, everything's fine. Mr. Cao's been very nice. The food is delicious. And that wine, what was that wine, Mr. Cao?"

"Call me Sidney!" I hear in the background. "It is Bordeaux. Château Margaux."

"Yes, really tasty!" Her voice drops again. "Are *you* okay?"

"Yeah," I say. "You have your phone?"

"Hm-hm."

"Okay. I'm going to call it from my new number. You have any problems at all, you call me."

"Oh, don't worry, hon. We're having a lovely time. *Y puedo cuidarme de mí misma,*" she adds.

And I can take care of myself.

"Oh, it means 'Have a safe trip,'" I hear her say, presumably to Sidney.

Kick ass, Mom, I think.

"You do what you need to do. Just be safe, okay? And call me as soon as you can."

"I will," I say. "You, too."

For a moment there's silence. Then Sidney.

"So you see your mother and her friend are having a very nice time in Xingfu Cun," he says. "Tomorrow we can play laser tag. Or maybe karaoke."

"Great," I say.

"And you go to meet my children." This, in case I had any doubts, is not a request.

"Will do."

"And you can call me each day and tell me about these meetings."

"I can do that. But you need to do something for me."

"What?" He sounds impatient. Like I've got no business asking him for anything.

"Get Yang Junmin off my ass. You want me to do this, I can't be worrying about him getting in my way."

There is a long pause. I hear footsteps, I think, and a door close. Sidney, getting some privacy maybe.

"Ellie, I am sorry," he says, and it sounds like he really means it. "I can only have so much control over Yang Junmin. I can tell him you and I are friends and you help me with this art business. But sometimes he does not listen."

I stare at my bottle of beer and think it's time to drink some more. The one thing I counted on was that Sidney and Yang were "lips and teeth," as they like to say here, as close and inseparable as brothers. That Sidney gives Yang money and Yang helps him make it. But if Sidney can't control him . . .

Maybe they aren't as close as I thought.

"Okay," I say. "Do what you can do. Just . . . take care of my mom. And Andy. And my dog."

"I can do that. I like your mother, very much. She is . . . *haoxinren*, you know this word?"

Good-hearted.

"Yeah. She is."

His voice drops to a whisper. "You see, I think it is better for her to come here. Xingfu Cun is a very nice place. And safe."

AFTER I GET OFF the phone with Sidney, I sit in the café a while longer, drinking my beer. There's no way I can be sure, but I'm wondering if I've gotten things backward with Sidney. Sure, he wants me to do what he wants me to do. Yeah, he's willing to strong-arm me to do it. And he has people killed. I know this from personal experience. Plus, the amount of money he has and the way he uses it are sometimes pretty gross.

But he also saved my life, and even if that was because he needed something from me, I have to appreciate it, since I'm still alive and all.

Maybe he was telling the truth, in his own way. He might have "invited" my mom to Xingfu Cun to give me an incentive to hang out with his kids. But maybe she *is* safer there with everything that's going on.

I can't be sure. But it would really help me keep on going with this mission if I could believe that.

★　★　★

So what do I do next?

I want to stay off Uncle Yang's radar, to the extent I can. That means I'd better put off any meetings with Tiantian. I didn't get the feeling he and Yang are all that close—and if Tiantian's been banging other women, who knows, they might not be on good terms at all. It's one thing for rich and powerful men here to have mistresses. More of them do than don't. *Ernai*, "second wives," are a status symbol, like a Rolex, and if you can fit more than one on your arm, more power to you.

But Uncle Yang seemed very protective of his sister's crazy daughter.

Besides, if I had to pick a least favorite Cao, it would probably be Tiantian.

Though it's a close call.

Which brings me to Gugu. I have to figure, logically, that if one of the Caos killed that waitress, odds are it was either Tiantian or Gugu. Okay, I guess it's possible that Meimei could be some kind of crazed psychotic killer, but beating and choking a girl to death like that? I figure it would take a lot of rage, the kind of anger that makes some men attack women, not to mention the strength to do it.

Though Dao Ming seems pretty pissed off. I can't rule her out.

So . . . Gugu. He gets off on playing baby and sucking milk from a wet nurse for hire. Could he also get off on beating up a woman? It doesn't seem to go together to me, but then what do I know about how crazy head cases think? I can't even figure out my own crazy head.

He's got some anger issues, though. No doubt about that. And he drinks, a lot, plus who knows what else he's using?

Put those things together and you can't always predict what happens.

And Gugu comes with Marsh. I still don't know what I think about that guy. He's kind of a creep. I wouldn't trust him with my daughter, if I had one, with my money, if I had some, with my dog, or with my back turned. Or with my mom, given her generally terrible taste in men. He kind of reminds me of one of her boyfriends when I was in middle school, now that I think about it, the one who was super charming and treated her really well and then stole her credit cards and split.

I've never seen Marsh get really mad, but maybe he's the kind of guy who's good at hiding that part of himself.

Then there's Meimei. She's weird. Not because she's maybe gay or bi and not because she may or may not have been hitting on me. There's just something about her that feels off. The way she reacts, or doesn't react, to stuff. Her whole fascination with my being a soldier, being outside the wire, finding that "admirable."

Which isn't that unusual, I tell myself. Lots of people think it would be cool to play soldier. Most of them have only played the video game.

There's nothing very admirable about what I did in the war, or the war I did it in.

But maybe I'm overthinking all this.

I look up Meimei's number in my online address book, and then I text it.

IT'S ELLIE. YES, HAD SOME PROBLEMS WITH MY OLD PHONE. THIS IS MY BACKUP. CAN YOU GIVE ME A CALL? I'D LIKE TO TAKE YOU UP ON THAT OFFER TO HELP.

Then I sip my beer and wait.

I don't trust her, at all. I'm just hoping I guessed right that she's the least lethal. To me anyway.

I'M STILL DRINKING MY stale Rogue when the phone rings.

"*Wei?*"

"Ellie, is that you?"

Meimei.

"Yes. Thanks for calling."

"Where are you?"

"Beijing."

She chuckles. "Yes, I assumed so. Where in Beijing? I can come to pick you up."

I hesitate. If I'm wrong about her . . . well, I'm pretty much SOL. But I placed my bet. All I can do now is let it ride.

"Haidian. Near Beijing Daxue." And I give her the address.

I'VE SWITCHED TO YANJING Beer because of the "beer-flavored water" factor. As much as I'd like to get really loaded, I know I'd better not. I don't know what I'm getting into with Meimei.

I'm about done with a draft when she saunters into the bar. She's wearing what looks like a vintage embroidered cowboy shirt, sky blue with red and yellow roses, skinny jeans, and cowboy boots. Snakeskin, I'm pretty sure.

"Cute bar," she says, dropping onto the chair across from me.

I shrug. "I guess."

"I think it is maybe . . ." She purses her lips. "More authentic than some other places, like the restaurant we go to before."

More authentic? I have no idea what she's talking about.

"Or maybe you are," she says, smiling at me.

Great.

Why is it the last few years I feel like I'm always playing a game where I don't know the rules and I don't even know what the object is?

I sip my watery Yanjing Draft. Think, I tell myself. Here's this woman. This girl. I mean, she's younger than I am. She's worn a different costume every time I've seen her. Like she's trying on different identities. Maybe she doesn't know who she really is.

Maybe in the core of herself, there's nothing there.

I shiver a little, because people that are empty inside that way, I've met them.

"Yeah, you know, keeping it real and all," I say.

She's studying my face. "What happened to your eye?"

"Frisbee accident. I was playing with my dog. You want a drink?"

"Sure."

I wave to the waitress.

"Just whatever you are having," Meimei says.

"*Zai lai liang bei zhapi,*" I tell the waitress.

Two more beers.

"So," Meimei says, after the beers come. "Have you been staying busy since we met for dinner?"

That has to be a joke, right? The way she's smiling at me, it must be.

"Yeah," I say. "Running around a lot. You?"

"Oh, not so much since we had dinner. Just . . . visiting with the family."

"I thought Gugu went out of town," I say. "To go work on his movie."

"Oh, sure." Meimei sips her beer. Her nose wrinkles. "He left this morning. Early."

I think about it. I don't know when Celine died; I didn't stick around long enough to check her out too closely. But I'm guessing she'd been dead awhile by the time I got there this morning.

So last night. Not too early—I'm assuming that gallery is open during the day—someone would have found her, right? It could have been before dinner, I guess. Gugu and Marsh arrived late, now that I think about it. But probably after.

Everyone was pretty drunk by the end of that dinner, though. Maybe no one killed her. Maybe she just OD'd.

"Penny for your thoughts?"

"Your Uncle Yang's pretty pissed off at me," I say.

"Oh? Why?"

"You don't know?"

She pauses, as if to consider. "I think actually he was mad at your friend." She rests two fingers on her cheek, tilts her head to one side. Stares at me, that little smile on her face, but without the usual amusement behind it. "Do you know why that is?"

Man, that game we're playing? Whatever it is, I think she's better at it than I am.

"I guess Yang Junmin didn't like some of the things John had to say."

Meimei nods. "Yes." She puts on a thoughtful expression, like this is something she's just now considering. Which I don't believe, not for one second.

"It was almost as though your friend accused Yang Junmin of something," she says.

So what do I do? Tell her I know about the dead girl at Tiantian's party?

She must suspect that already, right?

I wave my hand, all dismissive, trying to match her performance. "It's just his way of making conversation. John's got kind of a thing for justice. Maybe he's a little suspicious of powerful men."

"And you say he is a businessman?" She chuckles. "Funny. Not so many businessmen are concerned with justice. Just with making money. And keeping that money safe."

"He's an unusual guy."

"Apparently so." She glances around the bar. "And he is not here?"

"He had some . . . some meetings."

"I see." She puts her elbows on the table and her chin on her fists. "So what can I do for you?"

"I need a ride," I say.

"You want to go to Movie Universe?"

"Marsh invited me to come down and visit the set. Of their film."

"I didn't know you are interested in films," Meimei says, chin still resting on her fists.

"I thought it might be fun. Plus, you know, Gugu and I, we still need to talk."

"About the museum project."

"Yeah. Right."

"Okay." She sits up straight. "So we can go together." A smile. "I can even invite Tiantian. So we can all have this discussion."

"I . . . maybe we should just keep it simple for now."

"But it's a long drive. We should just fly. I can get a car in Shanghai."

"You mean, on your dad's jet?"

She laughs. "No. That's in Xingfu Cun. By the time he can get it here . . . Even my father has some trouble just flying to Beijing without a flight plan. Other places, sure, you can just go, fly a *hei fei*, but not Beijing."

A black flight. I know about those, from back in the Sandbox. Off the books.

"For a jet it's faster to get a flight plan than for small planes, but still . . ."

Who knows how Sidney got me out of Shanghai so fast a couple of months ago, but I'm guessing it involved substantial amounts of money.

She sighs. "So silly. In a year or so, I think these rules will change. Many people in China want their own planes now, and to fly them when they want."

"Yeah. Sure. Understandable."

"So we can just fly on a regular airline."

She checks her watch. It's a fancy-looking retro thing, all stainless steel with actual hands, two tiny dials set in the larger face. "I think there is still a flight at ten P.M. If we hurry, maybe we can make it."

"Yeah, well . . . I'd rather not do that."

"Why?" She chuckles. "Do you have a fear of flying?"

"I, uh . . ."

Think your uncle-in-law might be watching the airport, waiting to see if my passport pops up when I buy a ticket.

"Yeah. Flying. Not crazy about it."

"Maybe we can make the last train tonight to Shanghai, then. If I drive very fast."

I WILL SAY THIS for Meimei: she's a way better driver than Sidney. Or maybe it's just that there's enough traffic on the highway to the Beijing South Railway Station that she can't drive quite as fast as he did the time I rode with him. Still, she weaves her Beemer two-seater in and out and around other cars with some grace, without slamming on the brakes, like she knows what she's doing.

It's possible that the Percocet I swallowed with the remains of my Yanjing Beer might be affecting how I'm feeling about things, too.

"In a few months, we have the *gaotie*, the high-speed train, between Beijing and Shanghai. We can get back and forth in just four, five hours. That will be lovely!"

"Yeah," I say. "Looking forward to it."

WE MAKE IT ONTO the last train to Shanghai with seven minutes to spare, leaving Meimei's car in a VIP lot and grabbing two upper berths in a first-class car.

"Like a slumber party!" Meimei says, bouncing on the bed a bit.

"Yeah." I am really hoping for the "slumber" part of that equation.

"I can see you are tired," she says. "We can talk more on the way to Movie Universe. About the museum project." A pause. "Or whatever it is you really want to talk about."

I DON'T SLEEP MUCH. There's the usual middle-aged snoring guy on the bunk below me. My leg is aching, and I can't get comfortable. Mainly I can't stop the wheels turning in my head.

What is it that Sidney expects from me? How am I supposed to find out which of his kids had something to do with a murder?

I can hang out with them. Call Sidney every day. That's what he asked me to do. But I don't see how that's going to help me get out of this mess.

THE TRAIN ROLLS INTO Shanghai just after 9:00 A.M. There's a stretch limo waiting for us. A fucking yellow Hummer.

"I thought that would be better," Meimei says. "So we can relax for the trip. It is about five hours or so."

I hate Hummers. "Yeah. Thanks."

The driver's already out and opening the doors for us.

I climb inside, and it's insane. White leather bench seats with rolls for your back and neck. A bar across one side, made out of polished walnut, the kind with the coating so glossy you can see yourself in it. Giant TV screens. A huge moon roof. I mean, where's the disco ball?

"We have some breakfast," she says. "Just croissant and coffee and things. And champagne."

She sounds almost apologetic. I think I'm keeping a poker face, but maybe I'm not.

"Thanks," I say. "That all sounds great."

I sink back into one of the leather seats. They smell wonderful. Like money.

The coffee smells even better.

The limo's got these tables that pull out from under the seats, kind of like the tray tables on an airplane, with cup holders, too. I sip on my coffee and nibble on a croissant as the limo pulls away from the curb, and it's hard to even care that we're stuck in a line to get out of the underground parking garage at the Shanghai train station and that we sit in traffic on Shanghai streets and crawl along Shanghai freeways, because the limo's air-conditioning filters out all the exhaust, and the music, some techno-ambient shit, plays at just the right volume, and the seats are so comfortable, much better than on the train.

And yeah, I take a glass of champagne, chilled just right.

"I thought when you saw the car, that you did not like this kind of thing," Meimei says.

I hesitate. It's not like I want to share. But I've had a glass of champagne—okay, two—and not very much sleep. "It's just . . . Hummers."

"You don't like them?" She laughs. "Actually, I think they are not very good cars. I would never drive one myself. But the rental agency said this was the most comfortable car for a long trip."

"I've ridden around in one," I say. "Except it was a Humvee. Up-armored. They're military vehicles. That's what they were built for. For war." I wave my arm a little, at the interior of the car, all that leather and walnut and tinted glass. "This is just . . ." Now I laugh. "It's crazy. Making a war machine into . . . into this. It's some kind of sick joke."

I lean my head back against all that soft leather and I think it's all connected somehow, Humvees built for war getting turned into limos, or maybe it's that the Hummer limos need the war machines to exist. That's what they're built on, right?

"More champagne?"

"Sure. Why not?"

I KIND OF PASS out for a while. I mean, I sleep. I stopped drinking after that third glass, so it's not like I blacked out. But even though I know I'm supposed to be trying to get some intel from Meimei, even though I know I should stay frosty, I just can't stay awake anymore. Whatever adrenaline I had that got me through yesterday is gone, leaving behind an acid wash of exhaustion. My muscles ache. My head . . .

All I can think before I drift off is, I can't keep doing this. I can't do this anymore.

But I have to.

Suck it up and drive on.

Too bad I'm not the one driving.

CHAPTER TWENTY

I DOZE STRETCHED OUT on the white leather seat for
the next few hours, slipping in and out of dreams that most
of the time I can tell my head is making, the low hum of the
engine mixing with the ambient music on the sound system. At
one point we stop and I bolt up, heart pounding. I was having
a dream, or a memory. Of riding in an up-armored Humvee.

I look out the window. We're at a gas station just off the
highway, a flat road under hazy, yellow-grey skies.

I lean back against the seat. I wish we'd get going. I liked it
better when we were moving.

"Do you want some lunch?" Meimei asks.

I shake my head, thinking she means the restaurant next to
the station, a low, white-painted concrete building that you
find at gas stations like this, serving dishes swimming in oil in
battered white plastic bowls to long-distance bus passengers on
their twenty-minute break. "Only if you do."

She mimes a shrug. "We have some things packed, if you
want them."

"Oh. That sounds good. But . . . I think I'll use the *xishoujian*, long as we're here."

I hoist myself up with an assist from the handgrip that runs
above the window, lean against the side of the Hummer for a minute, waiting for my leg to stop cramping enough that I can walk.

I hobble off to the head.

What I do first when I get there is pee, in the stall with the lone Western toilet, because the leg's hurting enough that I'm not sure if I can manage a squat. Also, the stall has a door.

After I pee, I get out my old phone, swap the SIM card, turn on the VPN, and go to the email account I use to talk to John, aka Cinderfox.

I see the forwarded email I sent, the one from Celine, detailing corruption and offshore accounts.

And I see one from Cinderfox:

"WHERE ARE YOU? CALL ME AT THIS NUMBER."

I call. He picks up.

"Wei?"

"It's me."

"Yili, why . . . ?"

"Because someone bugged my bag."

"Bugged?" He sounds confused.

Shit. He doesn't know what that means, and I can't remember the Chinese equivalent.

"Put something. In my bag. To spy. A microphone. Was it you?"

"*Yige qietingqi?* No." A pause. *"Wo cao."* Fuck me.

"Yeah."

"Where are you now?"

"South of Shanghai. Going to a place called Movie Universe. Uh, Dianying Yuzhou."

"But . . . *Why?*" He sounds so frustrated. I can just picture him standing there clutching his forehead like he's getting a really bad headache.

"To keep an eye on the Cao kids."

A moment of silence. Then, "You should not . . . You . . . *Why?*"

"Because my mom is a guest of Sidney's, okay?" I snap.

I hear a sharp intake of breath.

"Your mother . . . If he has done something . . ." He sounds furious. I kind of like him right now.

"She's fine. But I need to see this through. You want to find out who did it, right?"

Funny. He asked me almost the same question.

You want to get justice for this girl?

"Yes, of course. But this is not safe for you."

"What *is?*"

That's when I hear a swarm of footsteps and chatter—a bunch of women entering the bathroom. A bus must just have pulled in.

"Look, I have to go. I'll call you later. There's other things . . . We need to talk."

"Yili—"

"Later."

I hit the red button. Swap SIM cards.

Yeah, we need to talk. About what he's been doing, if he's found out anything about Celine's death, if he's gone to Inspector Zou and pulled DSD rank on him. The thought makes me shudder. Uncle Yang's on John's ass, too. Right now he doesn't know how to find him. But if John's outed himself to Beijing PSB, if he's asking questions about people connected to the Caos . . .

Who knows what could happen?

I HOBBLE BACK TOWARD the Hummer, squinting in the hazy sunlight.

Meimei leans against the car, striking a pose. Waiting for me.

"Are you feeling all right? You took a while."

"Oh, yeah, you know. *Yidianr la duzi*. But I'm fine now."

She stares at me through her designer shades. Why do I get the feeling I'm not the only one playing detective here?

"Happy to hear." She gestures toward the Hummer. "Ready to go?"

"Sure," I say. "Hey, we have any of that coffee left?"

Because whatever the game is, I'm pretty sure it's on.

WE DRIVE ANOTHER COUPLE of hours, through plains with checkerboard fields and clusters of skinny five-story buildings topped with weird silver—I don't know what they are. Weather vanes? Antennae? Decorations? A bunch of globes of different sizes topped by crescent moons, skewered on a pole like some aluminum *chuanr*. I've seen them before, and I've always wondered, but I've never gotten around to asking anyone about them.

"You know, that was a crazy party at Tiantian's place," I finally say.

I might be imagining it, but I think her coffee cup pauses for a second, just before it hits her lips.

"Was it?"

I do my best sincere chuckle. Which is probably not very good.

"Yeah. I mean . . . I saw some kind of weird things."

She sips. "Such as?"

"Oh, just . . . people having a little too much fun. You know? And it was still pretty early when I left. I'm guessing things just got crazier."

"Oh," she says, and she seems to settle back into her seat. "Yes, I think I left right after you." Then she laughs. She doesn't sound too sincere either.

"Yes, people like to have fun," she says. "And . . . it can get crazy sometimes, when you can do whatever you want."

We pass through a city I've never heard of that feels like it goes on forever: an anonymous collection of apartment blocks, skyscrapers, commercial buildings, a stretch of luxury-car dealers, Lexus and Mercedes. This part of China, there's a lot of small manufacturing. Maybe they specialize in something here, like shoestrings, or bra hooks.

Then the countryside again. Green fields. Those five-story, skinny houses with the silver ornaments on top. Low mountains in the distance.

Finally we roll into a town. No skyscrapers here. Just low-slung businesses in beat-up concrete and white tile, dusty, uneven streets. Knots of people going about their business, buying shoes at a run-down shop with SALE! signs, lining up for snacks at an open window: Bowls of noodles. Steamed buns.

Sure doesn't look much like Hollywood.

We head out of the main drag. The street widens, the buildings thin. Now we're in an area with what look like warehouses or small factories, lined up like Lego bricks. There are billboards with photos and drawings of traditional Chinese furniture. Maybe they make it here.

In the middle of all this cinder block and corrugated metal is an expanse of gleaming red-and-grey marble.

"Not a very good hotel, but the best one in this town," Meimei says.

"Cool," I say. I hope she's paying.

"Do you have anything you want to drop off?" she asks.

"No, not really."

I mean, all I have is my little daypack with my laptop, a few pairs of underwear, and a clean T-shirt. Not a lot to carry. And I don't leave my laptop in a hotel unattended. Ever.

"Then, after we check in, do you want to go to the filming base?"

"Sure," I say. "Yeah, that sounds good."

IT LOOKS LIKE WE'RE going to a theme park, or to some huge temple complex: high red walls, a row of ticket windows topped by a peaked tile roof, signboards with maps of the area and prices of various attractions, a huge expanse of parking lot. People, almost all Chinese, wait in lines to buy tickets. They make money here off tourism, like Universal Studios, I guess, except there's no Jurassic Park ride.

"We can't take the Hummer inside," Meimei informs me. "But we can have an electric cart, I think."

I nod. I'm kind of distracted. I had to show my passport to register at the hotel, and it's never been clear to me if there's some kind of central database where all that information goes.

If it's just local, I should be fine. But if it's national?

What are the odds that Uncle Yang would be plugged into that system?

It's probably just local, I tell myself. For all the *hukou* and ID checking they do here, you're always reading about how people wanted for a crime in one province hide out in another, because the different PSBs don't talk to each other.

Nobody's that organized. Not China. Not the US.

Yet.

The driver lets us off by this big red gate that looks like the entrance to the Forbidden City off Tiananmen Square, except no giant painting of Chairman Mao. My written Chinese sucks, especially when it's traditional characters, but I recognize this set of gold characters on blue: MING/QING IMPERIAL PARK.

Inside the white arched entry are steel rails guiding visitors into several different lines: TEAM PASSAGE, INDIVIDUAL PASSAGE, and VIP CHANNEL.

That last one would be us.

Inside, a wide expanse of browning grass gives way to a bricked path leading up to a red gate that is a dead ringer for the Gate of Heavenly Peace at Tiananmen. On the way there are stalls where you can shoot fake machine guns or arrows at targets, a sort of bumper-car ride where the lone guest reclines in his little car and texts on his cell phone, giant cardboard cutouts of famous movie stars that you can pose next to. Tourists cruise around in pedal-powered carts with yellow canopies.

We get an electric golf cart. I let Meimei drive.

"So where are they filming?" I ask.

"Further away. In the old Qing/Ming village section."

"What's the movie about, do you know?"

"Not really. I think maybe they are using a story taking place in the past to comment on the present." Meimei raises an eyebrow and rolls her eyes. "So common."

We cruise up the path past the fake Forbidden City. It looks pretty good from a distance, but when you get up close, you can see the peeling paint on the red walls, the concrete in place of marble walkways, crumbling plaster on the "brass" statues.

Meimei has to stop several times to study a map—"I've never been here before," she tells me, and this place is big. The fake Forbidden City has courtyards and palaces and galleries like the real one; there are temples and guard towers, an imperial garden with giant rocks and artificial streams. A couple of times we pass groups of tourists dressed up in court costumes, posing for photos. I hear a blare of recorded music, a show going on to entertain the visitors, "Qing soldiers" on horseback performing in a dirt arena—but parts of the complex feel deserted. You'd think there'd be a squadron of teenage security guards in polyester uniforms, but no.

Finally we hum past a big crane thing, and I see giant lights with petal-like flaps on tall stands, translucent white sheets stretched on rectangular metal frames to diffuse the light, two cameras on dollies. Meimei pulls the cart up against a wall, and we get out.

A village set, grey brick buildings. Crews carrying messenger bags and wearing belts weighed down with equipment and walkie-talkies move lights. A makeup girl adds some dirt to the face of an actress wearing bloody rags and helps her to her feet. The actress takes her place by a fancy-looking gate—the front of a mansion, it looks like.

"*Zhunbei!*" a woman with a megaphone yells. "*Ji zhu!*"

Get ready. Start cameras.

"*Kaishi!*" Begin. Which I guess means "Action" here.

Another woman slaps one of those film clapboards, the kind you see in every movie or TV show ever made about Hollywood.

The actress stumbles through the scenery, breathing hard, like she's being chased and doesn't have the energy to run anymore.

Then, from the opposite direction, a white guy in an old-fashioned suit strides into frame. Sees the girl. Grabs her arm. Slaps her across the face.

It takes me a minute to recognize him, because he's got on a blond wig and a fake handlebar mustache. Marsh.

She falls to the ground, sobbing. Three guys run in from the direction she came, like they were the ones chasing her: two guys dressed like early-twentieth-century Shanghai gangsters and another in a uniform—maybe he's supposed to be a cop. They swarm the girl and pull her to her feet.

"*Ting ji!*"

Cut.

Everyone relaxes. One of the "gangsters" gives the girl a friendly pat on the shoulder and says something I can't hear. She laughs loudly.

"Hey!"

It's Marsh. He's spotted me. Gives a little wave and ambles over.

"Glad you could make it."

"You're an actor?"

He guffaws. "Nah. But we needed an evil Western imperialist, and the guy who was gonna do it bailed. Got a gig pretending to be an American partner in a Chinese start-up, to impress the Chinese clients, you know, for meetings. Guess he spends most days wearing a suit, watching movies, and playing video games on his laptop."

He looks me up and down.

"You want a part? I'm supposed to have a wife. She's dreadfully unhappy and addicted to opium. I bet you'd kill it."

I don't tell him to go fuck himself.

And people say I have no self-control.

"No thanks."

"Hello, Marsh," Meimei says. "I think you make a very good imperialist."

He does a half bow. "Thanks. Hey, we could find a part for

you if you want. There's usually some girl who likes wearing pants in these movies."

"Hmmm." Meimei smiles at him. "Perhaps, if this part is well written, I might consider it."

"Gugu around?" I ask.

"Yeah." Marsh cocks his head to one side. "Over there, by the herbal-medicine store."

I limp down the fake Qing town street, past the light stands and the cameras.

There's Gugu, sprawled in a director's chair. He's wearing sunglasses and another one of his overpriced hipster outfits, engrossed in what looks like a script.

Hovering at his side is Betty, definitely among the living, wearing that same rhinestone-studded Ed Hardy trucker hat with the skulls and roses she had on at Gugu's party.

Betty, who sounded terrified when I called her the day after Tiantian's party. Whose friend (frenemy?) Celine is dead.

I think I need to have a conversation with Betty.

"*Gugu, ni hao*," I say.

He looks up from his script, seeming annoyed by the interruption, until he recognizes me. "Oh, it's you," he says.

He sounds a little friendlier than I expected. At least he's making an effort to put on a decent act.

Betty, on the other hand, looks startled and wary. She blinks a few times. Like maybe I'm this hallucination that she hopes will vanish.

"Hi, Betty," I say. "*Hao jiu bujian.*" Long time no see.

She nods, too quickly.

"I'm happy you could come down," Gugu says. "And sorry that we haven't yet had a serious talk about my father's museum."

Well, this is a first—I think Gugu is actually sober.

"Maybe on this trip," I say. "Later, when you're not so busy."

He nods. "Yes. After we finish filming for the day, we can discuss."

I wonder, does he know about Celine? I mean, assuming he didn't kill her, does he know that she's dead? Do any of them?

"Hey, Guwei!" One of the crew, a young guy with a shaved head, pierced ears, and a visible tat on his forearm, jogs over. *"You yige xiao wenti,"* he says, leaning over the chair—there's a small problem. He goes on about something involving an actress and a location that I can't quite make out.

Betty sidesteps away from Gugu, then turns and double-times it down the fake Qing street, away from Gugu's set.

Whenever people want to get away from me, I figure they know something they'd rather I didn't find out about.

"Hey, I'll get out of your way and let you do your work," I say to Gugu. "Looking forward to catching up later."

He nods, distracted, and turns back to his conversation.

I take off after Betty.

So here's a big problem with me playing Nancy Drew: just about anybody who's in decent shape with two good legs can run faster than me.

Not that Betty's running, exactly. But she's walking really fast, and I almost lose her in a crowd of costumed extras heading up the street. Luckily, the rhinestone trucker cap stands out in a crowd of Qing-dynasty peasants hauling baskets and carry poles across their shoulders.

I make my way through the extras, up the street, and see Betty take a turn down an alley to the right.

"Hey!" I call out. *"Deng yihuir!"* I'm jogging now, my chest already burning from the smog. "I need to talk to you. About Celine."

I see her at the end of the alley. She half turns, pauses, her eyes wide with an emotion I can't read—fear? grief?—and for a moment I think she's actually going to talk to me.

Instead she pivots and takes off.

I almost throw in the towel right there. Because I can catch up with her later, right? But I don't. Because . . . I don't know, I'm pissed off. I'm tired of not having any answers, and I don't want to wait anymore.

Besides, now I see she's wearing these stupid platform versions of Chuck Taylors, and that means she can't run all that much faster than I can.

The alley leads into another village street, this one with a temple and a teahouse and a sign for something called the "Ningbo Cathouse." Old Shanghai cigarette ads are pasted up on the walls. Maybe we're out of the Qing dynasty now? There's a little production set up here, nowhere near the scale of Gugu's, just a single camera and a diffuser and two actors, a young guy lying on the ground with a bloody shirt and a girl cradling his head in her lap, weeping. A small group of tourists in matching baseball caps stand around, watching the scene. No one pays any attention as I jog past after Betty. Maybe it was a rehearsal.

I see her circle the temple, running awkwardly in her goofy platform sneakers. My leg is cramping up, my daypack's bouncing against my back, and my lungs are screaming for some breathable air, but I am catching up to her, and I am not giving up.

I reach the back of the temple. There's Betty not too far ahead, going down a street flanked by a low grey wall on the left and an artificial lake on the right. Across the lake I see a giant hot-air balloon. Don't ask me what dynasty *that's* supposed to be from.

Up ahead, the path we're on dead-ends into another wall, a taller one this time, like maybe we've reached the rear of the lot, a road running along in a T intersection, one way along the "lake," the other heading back into the sets.

I am so close now. "Hey, I just want to talk to you!" I gasp as she starts to turn left, toward the sets. She totters a bit on an uneven flagstone, and I think, I am going to catch her, and she's going to talk to me, and I'm going to get some answers, finally.

That's when one of those bicycle carts wobbles down the road from the opposite direction, the two teenagers driving it giggling and swerving and taking selfies, and I have to throw out my arms to keep from running into it, and my palms bang into the frame, sending shock waves up to my elbows.

"Fuck!"

"*Duibuqi, buhao yisi,*" one of them says, looking like she's actually sorry, while the other giggles with her hand over her mouth.

"*Mei shi,*" I manage. It's not important.

I steady myself, take a deep breath, cough a few times, and hobble off.

Up ahead there's a big signboard with arrows pointing in all different directions: IMPERIAL PALACE, PRINCE'S GARDEN, MING STREET, OLD GUANGZHOU. No sign of Betty.

"Shit," I mutter. If I had something to throw, I'd throw it.

But I've got time. She's here with Gugu. Where's she going to go?

She can't run forever.

CHAPTER TWENTY-ONE

I TAKE ADVANTAGE OF the walk back to Gugu's set to call John. He picks up on the third ring.

"You are okay?" he asks.

"Fine. You?"

"*Xing.*" Good enough.

"Did you find out anything about who killed anybody?" I mean, I'm not picky at this point.

"A little. The girl, the second one, she died from some drug. *Baifen.*"

"Heroin?"

"Yes, I think so."

"What about Inspector Zou? Have you seen him?"

A pause. "It is complicated."

"Complicated, how?"

A longer pause.

"I think maybe Yang Junmin interferes with the case."

I feel a prickle of cold sweat. Not that it's a surprise. You'd expect a guy with his clout to try to control the investigation.

That's not the part that's got my heart thumping hard right now.

"Did you go to see Zou? Does he know who you are?"

Because you also have to figure that Uncle Yang's keeping a

close eye on things. That anyone coming around asking about the case is going to get noticed.

"No. I have some contacts in Beijing PSB. They cannot say who. Only they hear Zou Qishi no longer controls the investigation."

"Good."

"Good?"

"I mean, that you didn't see Zou."

"I will speak to him when it's time."

I shouldn't have to lay it out for him. If anyone knows this stuff, he does. But he's the one who blew everything up that night at dinner, when he met Yang Junmin.

"John, look . . . you need to stay away from this."

A snort. "That is a funny thing for you to say."

"Yeah, hilarious. Okay, I don't know what faction is what and who's fighting who, or any of that. But I do know this guy's a *da motou*, that there's a leadership transition coming up, and if he finds out you're with the DSD? That's not stirring the pot, that's throwing dynamite in a firecracker factory. Do you *want* that kind of shitstorm coming down on your head?"

Another pause.

"Not yet. I have to first line up the ducks."

This just gets more awesome by the minute.

I RECAP IN MY head as I limp up the Qing Village street toward Gugu's production.

John is on some crazy crusade to bring down Yang Junmin. Why, I don't know, and I'm not sure I really care. What I *do* care about is my ass, and though he swore on a stack of Little Red Books that he's going to fix my PSB problem, and I think he believes that he means it, the shit John's stirring up could swamp both of us.

I'm going to have to handle this on my own somehow.

I look at it this way: Sidney asked me to investigate his kids. To find out if any of them are involved in a murder.

Sidney's a powerful guy, and even if he can't control Uncle Yang, he might have the pull to get me off the PSB's list of convenient suspects.

So I'm doing what Sidney asked me to do. I'll try to figure it out. If I do what he wants, then the way I look at it is, he owes me.

Okay, he's sort of holding my mom as a hostage, and that was a total dick move. Or maybe he's keeping her safe from Uncle Yang. I'm guessing it's a combination of both.

But knowing Sidney, either way, if I help him, I think he'd be willing to do me the favor.

Speaking of.

I swap SIM cards and call him.

"We have a wonderful time! First today we golf."

"Golf?" I don't think my mom has ever played golf.

"Yes. Her friend likes to golf. Your mother give it a good try. It was very much fun. Tonight we can sing some karaoke and watch movies. My home theater is very nice."

"That's . . . great. Listen, I just want you to know, I'm with Gugu and Meimei now. So I'm doing what you asked me to do. Spending time with them."

"What have you learned?"

Don't snark at the homicidal billionaire kidnapper, I tell myself. "I just got here," I say. "I'll call you as soon as I find out something important."

"What about Tiantian? Will you see him?"

"I, uh . . . yeah. I will. Soon."

"Good."

How I'm going to handle the whole Tiantian issue, I have no idea. I don't want to go anywhere near him. Because with Tiantian comes his wife, Dao Ming. And with Dao Ming comes Uncle Yang.

MY MOM SWEARS THAT everything's fine. Golf was fun, "and tomorrow I guess we're playing paintball." She lowers her voice. "I think Sidney might be a little lonely."

It's possible, I guess. Though he could afford to buy himself as much company as he wants.

"How much longer do you think . . . ? I mean, we're having a nice time and all, but . . ." .

"Soon," I tell her. "I just need to . . . line up the ducks."

THEY'RE SHOOTING IN A different place when I get back to the set, around the shops in the village street. The crew moves light stands and diffusers, checks makeup and wardrobe of the actors. I don't see Marsh. Maybe he's done being an evil imperialist for the day.

What I do see, up ahead in the "town square": a parked black BMW sedan. Standing next to it is Tiantian.

I skid to a stop. Turn and walk as fast as I can without running until I reach the alley that goes alongside one of the "shops." Turn the corner, hug the wall, and peek around it.

Tiantian's talking to a guy with a clipboard. I look for Yang Junmin and Dao Ming, but I don't see them.

I do see a guy by the driver's side of the car: buzz cut, military vibe, plainclothes, doing a slow survey of the set.

I don't know if he's one of Uncle Yang's helpers, but I can't afford to assume that he isn't. I scurry down the alley and then around a corner along the back side of the shops.

NOW WHAT?

I'm hiding out in one of the courtyards of the "Imperial Palace," just inside a big hall with red columns and a gold-painted throne up on a dais, surrounded by carved screens, brass incense burners, and giant character signs. Tourists dressed in Qing costumes pose for photos—there are racks of costumes to the right of the throne and a small line of customers waiting to change and have their pictures taken.

Who narked me out to Tiantian? I figure his showing up here is no coincidence. I'm guessing Meimei—she's the one who knew I was coming, who even made a joke about inviting Tiantian along.

But she might have called ahead. Marsh and Gugu didn't seem surprised to see me. Either one of them could've called Tiantian.

If Tiantian's brought Uncle Yang's soldiers with him, there's no way I can stay here.

But if I leave and I don't have any answers for Sidney . . . that's not going to go over very well.

Though I can't exactly figure out what Sidney's game is.

If I tell him that one of his kids is a murderer . . . what would he do with that information?

I watch a young guy slip a robe over his Paul Frank–branded jeans with the little monkey face on the back pocket.

Betty, I think. She knows something. If I can get her to tell me what it is, maybe that will be enough for Sidney.

I dig out my phone, the one I haven't turned on since I

left Uncle Yang's place. I'm going to have to risk it to retrieve Betty's number. I assume it's been hacked, but I don't really know what that means. If I turn it on, will he instantly know where I am?

If that's one of his guys with Tiantian, then he already knows.

I turn it on, heart hammering as it boots up.

I grab a pen from my backpack and scribble the number on my palm.

Then I power off the phone and retrieve my backup. Punch in Betty's number and text: THIS IS ELLIE. YOU CAN TALK TO ME OR YOU CAN TALK TO THE POLICE OR HOW ABOUT INTERNAL SECURITY? THEY'RE LOOKING INTO TIANTIAN'S PARTY. CALL ME OR I'LL GIVE THEM YOUR NAME.

A minute later she texts me back.

NOT SAFE TO TALK TO YOU.

YOU'RE NOT SAFE NOW, I type. LOOK WHAT HAPPENED TO CELINE.

I wait for a return text. For a minute, nothing. I think maybe she isn't going to bite.

Then: WHAT HAPPENED?

YOU BETTER COME TALK TO ME, I type back.

I'M SITTING ON A bench outside the hall wearing a gold Qing-dynasty robe over my jeans and T-shirt and a hat with an embroidered band, dangly beads, and a crown that's a cloud of wispy feathers when Betty shows up.

She's looking around and not spotting me. Which is good, because I don't want to be spotted. I might not look Chinese, but at least I look like a tourist.

"Hey." I lift up my hand.

She does a little double take. Lifts her own hand to her mouth and almost giggles before I guess she remembers there's some serious shit going on here.

She approaches the bench, her fingers clasped in front of her, her feet turned slightly inward, wobbling a bit on her platform Converse sneakers. Stands in front of me. I can see the tears gathering in the corners of her eyes, along the lower lids.

"You better sit down," I tell her.

She does, on the bench next to me.

Now that she's here, with her Ed Hardy baseball cap and skinny jeans and designer sequined T-shirt, I don't know what to say. She looks like a kid. A little kid, on the verge of crying, her lower lip trembling. Like she knows she's going to hear something bad, but she's still hoping she's wrong.

"Celine's dead." Because just get it over with. There's nothing I can say that would make this news any better.

She squeezes her eyes shut and nods.

"They think it was heroin. *Baifen*," I add. "Did she do drugs like that?"

Betty shakes her head, her eyes still squeezed shut. Then she says, "Maybe, sometimes. But not a lot."

Well, that's the way it goes with heroin, right? You don't do it regularly, you don't do it a lot, you encounter some good, relatively uncut shit, and you die.

"She died the night before last," I say. "At a gallery in Cao-changdi. Do you know anything about that?"

Betty gasps and chokes back a sob. Nods.

"You better tell me," I say.

She looks around, like she's making sure no one can hear us. There are a couple of other costumed tourists clowning around by a guardian-lion statue, taking pictures of each other. They aren't paying any attention to us.

"Gugu and Marsh pick us up to go there," she finally says. "Celine knows the owner. Sometimes she work there. We go because Gugu want to look at this new art. He say he want to learn about it. But he is already very tired."

"Tired. You mean drunk?"

She hesitates and nods.

"What time?"

"Maybe ten."

So after dinner. Yeah, Gugu was pretty drunk.

"Who else was there?"

She shrugs. "I don't know. Some people. Like a little party."

"So what happened?"

"We just . . . Gugu doesn't want to stay. He is too tired. Celine and Marsh say they are having fun, so . . ." She sobs for real this time. "We just leave them there."

Celine and Marsh.

She's crying now. "I didn't think . . . I didn't think anything bad . . ."

"But something bad happened at Tiantian's party. And you know about it." Now I'm pissed off. "Come on, Betty. Don't bullshit me."

"I just . . . hear bad things," she whispers.

WHAT SHE TELLS ME is this:

It got late. Most of the guests went home. A few men stayed. "They have girls for them," Betty says.

"Where was this? Where in the *siheyuanr*?"

"I was in the front north house."

The main house. Where the bigwigs were hanging out.

"I see a few of those men go across courtyard to that east house."

Where Gugu was. Where I left Marsh.

"I want to leave, but I come with Gugu, and I don't know where he is. If I can find Celine, I just leave. But I cannot find her. So I wait. Play games and watch video on my phone."

"You were alone?"

She nods. "I think maybe I fall asleep for a while." She squeezes her eyes shut. Shakes her head back and forth like she's trying to shake the bad thoughts out of it.

I know how that goes.

"I hear screams," she says, whispering again. "A girl's screams. A man, shouting. He is angry."

"Could you tell where it was coming from?"

"The back house, I think."

Tiantian's man cave.

"She keeps crying, but not so loud. She . . . she moans. Then I can't hear her anymore."

I have a sudden flash of those photos of the dead girl, of her battered, swollen face.

"Okay," I say. "What happened next? What did you do?"

"I run," she says. "I just run. I get to the gate of the *siheyuanr*, and I know if I am running, maybe the guards will stop me. So I walk."

"And they let you out?"

"Yes." She pauses to get a Kleenex out of her little Gucci purse. Wipes her nose. Not a country girl, no blowing her snot onto the pavement for this one.

"I just walk as fast as I can away from that place," she says. "I get to Yonghegong, to a taxi, and then I think, Celine. I leave my friend behind. I am . . . terrible."

"You were scared."

Because I know what it's like. I know how it is to be young and dumb and in over your head. And I'm still beating myself up for what I did.

For what I didn't do.

"I call her," Betty says. "She does not answer. I don't know what to do. So . . ." She hangs her head. "I just go home."

I'm sweating under the embroidered band and dangling beads and cloud of feathers of my goofy fake Qing hat. I take it off and lay it on the bench next to me.

"Did you talk to Celine after the party . . . about what happened?"

"Yes. She calls me. Very late, almost morning, but I am so glad to hear her voice."

Betty's crying again. She covers her face with her hands.

"She tells me yes. A bad thing happened. She tells me I should be very careful around the Caos."

Now Betty's doing a quick, nervous scan of the perimeter again. Searching for bandits.

She looks at me. "Especially Tiantian," she says.

"Oh, well, that's just great." I throw up my hands. "So why are you here?"

Betty rolls her eyes like I am too impossibly stupid. "Gugu wants me to come."

"You think if you stand by your man, he's gonna marry you or something?"

She flinches at that. Bingo.

Anything's possible, I guess.

"Look, I know you're gonna do what you're gonna do, but if I were you, I'd get out of here and I'd stay out of Beijing for a while. You don't want to be in the middle of all this."

"Gugu can protect me from his brother," she says.

Here's hoping. Assuming Gugu's hands are clean and it's not just Tiantian she needs to worry about.

That's when I get one of those sudden drops in my gut, that sickening rush, because I'm the one who needs to worry, and I've been sitting here too long.

"Good luck with that." I push myself to my feet, wait for my bum leg to stop spasming, just trying to breathe through it.

"Please think about what I said," I say when I can.

She nods.

I pick up my fake Qing hat and start to walk away.

"Celine say something else."

I stop. "What?"

"She won't willingly let them just do this thing. She says she cause them trouble. She . . ." Betty ducks her head. "I don't know how to say."

"Tell me in Chinese."

"It's old-fashioned, what she says." Betty clasps her hands together, like a schoolgirl sitting at a classroom desk, and recites: "*Shanyou shanbao, eyou ebao, bushi bubao, shihou weidao.*"

I remember this one.

Good will be rewarded with good, and evil with evil. If the reward is not forthcoming, then the time has not yet come.

I finish it: "*Shihou yi dao, yiqie dou bao.*"

When the time comes, you'll get your reward.

"Yes." She frowns. "But I think this is stupid."

"Why?"

"Celine is good. She should get a good reward. But she does not."

★ ★ ★

I'm walking as fast as I can to the exit. At least I hope that's where I'm heading. The signs aren't very good, and this place is huge. I'm close to the back of the complex, paralleling the high grey wall with guard towers that looks like it would encircle a Ming town. It's close to 5:00 P.M., and I'm wondering what time they kick the tourists out. I'm not seeing anybody back here. No tourists. No film crews. No staff. It's so quiet. That's something you don't get a lot of in China, silence. And it's making me nervous.

I arrive at a metal signboard with a bunch of different destinations: ANCIENT CULTURE STREET. SHAOLIN MONKS TEMPLE. NINGBO CATHOUSE.

And NORTH GATE EXIT. The arrow for that points in the same direction as the Shaolin Monks Temple.

The "temple" grounds are deserted, too.

They did a good job with the place, I think. Close up, I'm sure you could tell the difference, but from a small distance it looks like a typical Chinese temple complex: red walls and wooden shuttered doors, eaves painted blue and green and gold, green roof tiles. No Shaolin monks, though. No signs of life at all, except for a cawing of crows and the beating of their wings.

I walk through a gate and into a hall with painted wooden statues of gods and demons. I've never been too clear on which is which.

On the other side of that building is a courtyard, and at the back of that is a large towerlike pagoda on top a quadrangle of stairs. I exit the hall, doing my one-step-at-a-time routine down the nine flat steps, and head toward the pagoda.

I'm about halfway there when something tugs at my foot. I look down and see that my shoe's untied on the bad-leg side and that my other foot's stepping on the lace.

I prop my foot on a rock, boosting it up with an assist by locking my hands behind my thigh. Bend over and retie the shoe.

And hear an echo of footsteps.

I jerk upright, stumble a little as I step down on my bad leg, and run.

Yeah, maybe I panic. But given how bad I run, I don't have the luxury to stop and look and see who it is.

I bolt down the path, jink left behind a giant fake iron incense burner, peek around it.

There's a guy coming out of the first hall.

The light's not that great, and I can't really see much about him, just a guy, a little stocky, short hair, short work jacket, walking steadily down the stairs. Tiantian's driver? I have no idea.

I'm not going to take a chance.

I don't know if he's spotted me yet. It didn't seem like he had.

There's a path that rises up and curves around to the left side of the pagoda, with some tree cover. The main path goes straight up the middle to the entrance.

Okay, I tell myself. Okay. Go left.

I run, Qing robe flapping.

If he's chasing me, he'll catch up. I need to find a crowd. I need to find the exit. Just get myself out of here.

I reach the pagoda. And see that behind the pagoda there's a little more garden, some trees and giant rocks, and then there's a temple wall.

The edge of the lot. No exit.

I turn to the pagoda.

At the base of the steps, I see something I don't expect.

An entrance cut into the steps, rust-red iron gate swung

open, stairs leading down. Framed like an Egyptian tomb, with a sign above saying GUESTS STOP! in English and something about no smoking in Chinese.

Well, what else can I do?

I head down.

CHAPTER TWENTY-TWO

I T ' S   N O T   C O M P L E T E L Y   D A R K . There are work lights here and there, casting a dim glow that lets me see concrete pillars, stacked scenery flats, odd bits of props and equipment, a costume rack, spread out in this huge space running under the pagoda and beyond—it has to be over the size of a football field. Nobody's working down here right now that I can see, though. There's a small square of light on the other side.

I peel off the robe and toss it over a costume rack, throw the hat in its general direction. It's not like I really care about the deposit.

I head toward the square of light.

I'm about halfway there when I see that it's an exit, only this one has its rust-red metal gate closed. Doesn't mean it's locked, I tell myself. But if it is?

That's when I hear footsteps. Behind me, I think. With the echo it's hard to tell.

Could be anybody. Could be the guy. Could be a worker. I start jogging toward the exit. Not a full-on run, an "I'm working, gotta get somewhere" trot. To my left there's a couple restaurant-freezer-size metal things painted submarine grey. Generators? They hum. A bundle of cables the thickness of a python runs from them along the floor to the right.

Okay, they have to be going someplace. Like out of here.

What I can see by the work lights is that the cables run over to the far wall and into a corridor. I can't see where that goes.

I jog alongside the cables.

When I get to the far wall, I see that the corridor slopes gently up, a long ramp into sunlight. The cables snake up with it.

I reach the top, and I stand in the entrance for a second, blinking in the late-afternoon light, and there's a volley of gunfire.

"*Ting ji!*"

I fall back against the wall, and I almost go to the ground before I get a grip: It's a set. This is a film. The cables lead to lights and cameras. Between them I can see a half dozen actors dressed in Republic-era police costumes and one guy, presumably the revolutionary hero, all dropping their guns to their sides and shuffling around, waiting for the next take.

I circle the area of the action, a square in what looks like an Old Hong Kong or Old Guangdong set. As I look back, I see the stocky guy with the work jacket approaching one of the crew, a young woman with dyed pink hair who is carrying a clipboard. He has a couple rifles propped on his shoulder. Maybe he picked them up under the pagoda.

Not a bad guy. Just a crew member delivering props.

"It's only a fucking movie," I mutter.

I need to find the exit and get out of here before it turns into something else.

I FIND AN EXIT. It's not the way I came in. Smaller, without the crowds and tour buses. Across the street is a line of beat-up two-story shops: a noodle joint, a little convenience store, and a drugstore. Beyond that, another busier-looking street. No cabs in sight.

I walk over to the convenience store and buy a bag of spicy peanuts and a bottle of water. "Please, can you tell me, how do I get to the train station?" I ask the clerk.

"No train station here. You have to go to the city for that."

Which is how I end up first on a shuttle bus next to a twenty-something girl whose suitcases are piled where my feet should be, then on a city bus so crammed with people that I can barely lift my arm to drink my water, old metal sheets rattling over every bump, diesel fumes leaking in through the cracks. I look around at the riders on the bus: office workers, *nongmin* peasant farmers, students, a couple old aunties, some guys in oil-stained coveralls, a few little kids, ordinary people just trying to get through the day, all of us squeezed together in this jolting, shuddering tin can, and I think, Far cry from a fucking Hummer limo, right?

But maybe this is where I belong. Maybe even where I'd rather be.

I JUST MAKE THE last train to Shanghai, a two-and-a-half-hour ride that will get me into Hongqiao station around 10:00 P.M. I have no idea what I'm going to do when I get there.

I'm thinking I panicked, and maybe I should've stayed at Movie Universe. I don't know that Tiantian's driver was connected to Uncle Yang—he could just be a driver, like that film-crew guy was just a film-crew guy.

I've been so cranked up for so long that I'm thinking movies are real and seeing bandits that aren't there.

Maybe Tiantian just wanted to talk to me, and Sidney sure as shit expects me to talk to Tiantian.

I lean back in my seat, which isn't bad—this is one of the new fast trains. Close my eyes. Think about what I know.

Celine saw something bad and told Betty to watch out for all the Caos, but especially Tiantian.

So does that mean Tiantian killed the waitress?

"The waitress." I can't even remember her name.

Celine promised that she'd cause trouble for the guilty. That they would get what they deserved. Eventually anyway.

I think about that one. Who's causing trouble here? That would be me. And John. John because I got him involved.

And why am *I* causing trouble? Because my card was found on the body of a dead girl.

If my card hadn't been there, would the body ever have been traced back to the Caos?

Maybe that wasn't about implicating me in a murder. Maybe it was about my weird skill set of pissing people off and causing trouble without meaning to.

Lastly: when Betty left the art gallery with Gugu, Celine was still alive and Marsh was there with her.

Why was I at Tiantian's party in the first place?

Because Sidney asked me to look into Marsh.

You don't know that Marsh killed Celine, I tell myself. She could've OD'd on her own, without his help.

I don't know anything for sure, but what do I think?

I think Tiantian killed the waitress and Marsh killed Celine.

But here's the part that doesn't fit. Why would Marsh care enough about protecting Tiantian that he'd kill Celine to do it?

So what do I do now?

Once I get to Shanghai, I've got the same problem I had in Beijing with staying off Uncle Yang's radar—if I check in to a hotel, I have to show my passport. Maybe I'm being too paranoid about that, but as we all know, it's not paranoia when they really are following you, right?

I could crash in a bathhouse. They're not what you might think; there's a side for women and a side for men and meeting rooms where you can meet up and hang out if you want. I've done it before, gotten a massage, sweated in the steam room; I could see an acupuncturist or even get a facial and just kill time in one of the meeting rooms in a bathrobe and slippers, doze in a reclining chair in front of a TV broadcasting the latest Korean soap.

I could call a friend. I have a few in Shanghai. Most notably Lucy Wu. I trust Lucy. Well, as much as I trust anybody. What I don't want to do is get her dragged into my shit.

She already is pretty tangled up in a lot of it. She's my partner in selling Lao Zhang's work. She's his friend, I'm pretty sure one of his exes. That stopped bothering me a long time ago.

I start thinking about it all again, though, about me and Lao Zhang, what we ever really were to each other, what it all means, and then I shake myself. This is not the time.

Okay, I can find someplace to crash tonight. At Lucy's, at a bathhouse, whatever. But ever since Tiantian's party—ever since I got sucked into Sidney World, really—I've only been able to think about what I do next. Where I go. How I get out of whatever fucked-up situation I'm in at the moment. I need to think beyond "Where am I going to sleep tonight?"

I need to draw this thing to a close, one way or another.

So what are my choices?

Do I call one of the Caos and start this circus all over again? Hang out with Gugu and Meimei and wonder when Tiantian's going to sic Uncle Yang on me? I mean, what are the odds that I'm going to find out any more than I already know? That Tiantian's suddenly going to break down and confess all or that one of his siblings will rat on him—that is, if they know anything about what happened.

Fuck that. I'm done.

Like always, I think about running.

But there's my mom and Andy and Mimi, on their forced vacation in Xingfu Cun.

Whatever I do, I have to get them out of there first.

"HI, SIDNEY."

"Ellie. Do you have news for me?"

"Yes, I do." I pause. Stare out the window at the dark landscape, the anonymous towns and half-completed high-rises passing by like ghosts of some imagined future.

"Here's the thing," I say. "We need to talk in person."

"This is not difficult. You can come to Xingfu Cun."

"Yeah. I will. No problem."

I stare out the window some more. Think, I'm on a train to nowhere.

Time to get off.

"I'll come to Xingfu Cun, and I'll tell you what I found out. But you need to let my mom and her boyfriend and my dog be on their way."

There's a long silence.

"I already tell you, I am just keeping them safe."

"I know. And I appreciate that. I just . . . I don't want them involved in this."

"Okay," he says. "You can tell me where you are, and I can send the car or the plane. Then you can come to Xingfu Cun, say hello to your mother before she leave."

"How about this? You send your car or your plane. When I meet it, you let them go."

Another stretch of silence.

"If this is what you want," he finally says.

"I do."

"I only hope you have something interesting to tell me," he says.

Yeah. So do I.

I END UP CALLING Lucy Wu.

I don't want to get her in trouble. I really don't. I tell myself one of the reasons I want to see her is to give her the debriefing. If she stays involved with Sidney, she should know what she's stepped in.

I tell myself that, but the truth is, I'd like to see a friendly face before I go off to confront Sidney in Xingfu Cun.

I call on my safe number. She's not going to recognize it, so who knows if she'll answer?

But she does. *"Wei?"*

"Lucy, it's Ellie. Are you free later? There's some things I need to talk to you about."

CHAPTER TWENTY-THREE

"JUST COME TO MY apartment when you get here," Lucy had said. "I'm already home."

I've never been to Lucy's place. We're not that close. Most of the hanging out we've done has been at her gallery and at bars or restaurants.

I take the subway. I don't want to risk a taxi and a driver who could maybe identify me and tell someone where I go.

Lucy lives close to the French Concession, on a smaller lane lined with shade trees and mostly older, two-story buildings: yellow and grey, plaster and brick, with shops on the bottom and apartments on top. Scalloped roofs in places, old-fashioned wood-framed windows and doors that open onto tiny balconies bristling with laundry poles that have inside-out pants hanging from them like banners. Run-down and kind of charming, the lighting mostly soft and small. Every time I see a neighborhood like this in a big Chinese city, I wonder how long it will last before it gets *chai*'d, knocked down and replaced by anonymous, disposable high-rises.

"I'll meet you out in front," she'd said. "Call me when you're close."

When I get there, to a two-story yellow-plastered building with a wooden banister and a jumble of half-story structures on the roof, Lucy Wu is already there, coming out of a wine shop next door, wearing pajamas.

This is actually a Shanghai thing, running errands on the street in your pj's, something the government campaigned against during the Shanghai Expo last year because it's "uncivilized," but the campaign doesn't seem to have affected things much. Somehow I wouldn't have expected Lucy to do it, though. Hers are the kind both men and women wear, two-piece blue silk with white piping.

"Oh, hi," she says when she sees me. "I thought I should get us something to drink."

Sounds good to me.

LUCY IS SITTING CROSS-LEGGED on her couch, wineglass in hand. She leans forward like she can't quite believe it. "He kidnapped your mother?"

"Well, not exactly, but . . . kind of."

I've told Lucy the Twitter version. A girl died at a party, Sidney wants to know if one of his kids is involved, and chief murder suspect Tiantian's uncle-in-law is a scary-powerful government official.

And yeah, that Sidney kind of kidnapped my mom.

"Or he's protecting her. It's not totally clear."

"What are you going to do?"

I shrug. "Go down there. I'll call Sidney to arrange for a ride, and he'll let my mom and her friend leave."

Lucy looks genuinely worried. "Are you sure this is a good idea?"

"It's a *terrible* idea. I just don't happen to have a better one."

We both drink a few sips. Some Australian wine you see here a lot that's on the lower end of overpriced.

"This is really a bad situation," Lucy murmurs.

I look around Lucy's apartment. It's not a huge space; it's an old building with low ceilings, but the way it's remodeled and decorated—whitewashed walls with a few pieces of art, a comfortable couch, some cheerful clutter—it's really nice. The wall facing the street is almost all a grid of glass-paned shutters and doors. Right now they're shut, covered up by thin white curtains.

I'm thinking I shouldn't have come here.

"I'm sorry," I say. "I should have kept you away from Sidney. You don't want to be connected with him. He . . . he does stuff."

Lucy waves a hand. "I asked you to introduce us. He's a billionaire who buys a lot of art. Those are the customers who keep this business afloat. Some of them aren't the most pleasant people, to be honest."

"I guess."

"Are you really going to call him?"

I nod. "There's nothing else to do."

She suddenly straightens up. "Well, you should rest here awhile first. You look tired."

That's a diplomatic way of putting it.

"Take a shower if you want," Lucy continues. "Maybe I have some extra pajamas."

I feel like I should argue, but I'm too wiped out.

"Thanks," I say. "That sounds great."

I DON'T TAKE A long shower, but it's enough time to think about the things I didn't tell Lucy. Like about John. And about Celine, and her blog, and that offshore company.

When I come out of the shower, dressed in my jeans and a clean T-shirt, in case I need to make a quick exit, Lucy is brewing some tea at her kitchen bar.

"There are some other things," I say.

"Oh, please don't tell me that."

Like she can cope with a murdered girl and a crazy billionaire, but one more thing might be stretching her patience.

"First off . . . Jianli says he's coming to Beijing."

Lucy draws back. "Why?"

"I don't know. He wants to do some kind of performance piece."

"But that's a *terrible* idea," she says, and she's somewhere between shook up and disbelieving. "Maybe even worse than yours."

"Yeah," I say. "I don't know if he's there now or not. I haven't seen him."

She flops onto a barstool. "This is very bad timing."

"No kidding."

I hesitate.

"This next thing . . . I think it's a big deal. Like maybe you don't want to know, because it's trouble."

Lucy sighs through gritted teeth. "I'm starting to think I should take a trip to Vancouver."

"That might be a good idea," I say, and I mean it.

"So what is this other thing?"

"It has to do with Yang Junmin. I don't know for sure, but I think he's tangled up in some kind of power struggle with the upcoming leadership change."

Now Lucy scrunches her eyes closed. "I don't think I want to have anything to do with this," she says.

"You don't," I say. "But maybe . . . if something goes wrong,

I don't know." I shrug. I feel like a total shitheel. "It might be something you can use."

"I just want to have a nice gallery and promote good art," she mutters.

"Yeah. Do you have a printer?"

LUCY HAS A TINY office in a little room at the back of the apartment, next to her bedroom. I boot up my laptop, hop onto her network using the VPN, download the driver I need, and print out the email from Celine. Get an envelope from Lucy, fold the paper, and put it inside. Seal it.

When I go back into the living room, Lucy's sitting on the couch staring at her cup of tea. Maybe she's trying to read the tea leaves. I'm pretty sure she's sorry that she invited me over here tonight. I wouldn't be surprised if she was sorry she ever met me.

"I know you don't want this," I say, holding out the envelope. "But maybe, if you don't hear from me in a couple of days . . . could you get it to Harrison?"

She looks up and meets my eyes. Nods. "I can. I promise."

I SLEEP ON THE couch until stupid o'clock the next morning. Get up with the first light of dawn. Lucy's still asleep. I don't want to wake her. The best thing I can do is get out of her apartment before I bring some bad shit down on her head just by being here.

I find a notepad and a pen. Scribble, *Thanks for everything. And sorry.* I can't think of anything else to say.

I TAKE THE SUBWAY to the Bund. I don't want to meet Sidney's people anywhere near Lucy's place, and I don't know Shanghai that well, so why not the Bund? The hotel I like to stay at is close by, just north of where the Wusong River runs into the Huangpu, and there are some cafés I've been to over there, and now that I think about it, I haven't had anything to eat since a sandwich in Meimei's rented yellow Hummer and some spicy peanuts on the train, so I should probably eat something. At least have some coffee. So I can be awake when I ride to my doom.

Sidney's not going to kill you, I tell myself. I'm walking along the Huangpu now, restored nineteenth-century European buildings to my left, stately granite and marble, and on the other side of the river to my right, the gold-and-blue mirrored glass science-fiction skyline of Shanghai's Pudong District.

It's just that I can't predict how any of this is going to turn out. How he's going to react when I tell him I think Tiantian might have killed a girl, but I can't really prove it.

And then there's Marsh, who may or may not have killed Celine.

I don't really know anything for sure. What happens when I tell him what I suspect?

I just have a bad feeling, about all of it.

There's a coffeehouse up ahead. It looks open.

As good a place to wait as any, I guess.

I get a cup of coffee and a chocolate croissant. Walk out to the promenade that runs along the river and sit on a bench. Smell the river's mossy funk. Watch a boat cruise by. I don't know what it is, some kind of working boat, low-slung and rusting blue. The day's warming up—I can already feel sweat beading on my back.

A barge maybe?

I don't know shit about boats.

I swap SIM cards and call Vicky Huang.

CHAPTER TWENTY-FOUR

"Someone can pick you up in an hour," Vicky tells me.

I think I might have woken her up. Which feels oddly satisfying.

"Great," I say. "I'll be here."

"Mr. Cao is anxious to see you," she says.

The way she says it sounds like a threat.

"I'm really looking forward to seeing him, too," I lie. And I disconnect.

Then I call my mom.

"Hello? Ellie?" She sounds anxious.

"Yeah. It's me. Are you okay?"

"We're fine. Andy and I just came back from walking Mimi and doing tai chi."

"Oh, cool. So here's the thing. Sidney should be sending you guys on your way today. But . . . I think it might be a good idea if you don't go back to Beijing right now. Maybe you should just go visit Andy's family in Xiamen, like you planned."

"Well, sure. We can do that. But . . . what about you?"

And she sounds really worried now.

"I just have a few things I gotta take care of," I say. "Nothing to worry about."

There's a pause.

"I really wish you would stop lying to me," she says.

I feel this rush of . . . I don't know what. Anger? Love? Something. Emotion I don't have time for, whatever it is.

"I can't get into it now," I say. "Just . . . please go with Andy and visit his family. Okay? Because . . ."

I'm choking up, and I can feel the tears gathering in my eyes, and I don't have time for it. "Just do this for me. It would really help."

"Okay," she finally says.

"I love you," I say. "Pet Mimi for me." And then I disconnect.

THERE'S ONE MORE THING I have to decide before Sidney's men pick me up.

What do I tell Creepy John?

If there's anyone who could do some damage with Celine's email and that offshore company, it's John. But do I want him to?

I pull that trigger and it's going to have all kinds of consequences.

If I could trust him to keep the information safe and only use it if he has to, it could be ammo for me. I can tell Sidney and Uncle Yang, *I've got this on you, so leave me and mine alone.*

But I can't trust him. He's already shown me that he's willing to put me in danger to advance his agenda, whatever it is, with the way he mouthed off at Yang Junmin at dinner. Maybe he just lost his temper, like he told me. What's to say he won't lose it again? Or that whatever his game is, it's too big and important for him to not take advantage of ammo like that email.

I still should call him, though. Even if I'm not really sure why at this point.

"JOHN."

"Yili."

"You're okay?"

"Sure. Are you?"

"Yeah. I . . . I maybe found out something."

"Tell me."

"Celine's friend Betty. She said Celine saw something at the party. And that Celine told her she should be careful of all the Caos, but especially Tiantian."

"I can believe that."

"Why?"

"I check a little more on the Caos. I find out Tiantian likes to visit *santing*, the 'three halls,' see some girls there."

Bars, karaoke parlors, bathhouses, and the like.

"What, no *ernai*?"

John laughs, once. "Maybe Yang Junmin would not like that. But maybe Tiantian would not either."

"What do you mean?"

"I hear he can be cruel to girls. A second wife can maybe cause him some problems, if he beats her. A *xiaojie* who works at KTV place . . . maybe not so easy for her to cause him problems."

"And a *xiaojie* who works at a catering company . . ."

Yeah. A soft target.

The croissant I ate is sitting like a stone in my gut.

"That's one thing," I say. "The other . . . I'm pretty sure it was Celine who put my card on the body. She wanted to get me involved. I'm not sure why. Except she said to Betty that she wanted to cause trouble for the person who did this bad thing she saw. And she told me at the party that she'd heard some things about me."

Now John snorts. "If she wants someone to cause some trouble, you are the good person to call."

"Thanks a lot."

"Where are you?" His voice has suddenly changed. It's soft and serious.

"Shanghai. I . . ."

There's a new boat, and this one is easy: an open-sided cruise boat for tourists, two decks, the rails and struts painted red, the temple-style peaked roofs painted yellow, like a floating pagoda.

"I'm going to Sidney's place in Xingfu Cun," I say. "So I can tell him what I found out about his kids. He's going to let my mom and Andy go if I do."

"Yili, do not do this. Just wait. Let me go with you. Let me—"

"I can't wait. That ship's sailed." Whatever ship it is. Maybe a barge. I laugh a little.

"Nothing bad's going to happen," I say, even though my gut's saying otherwise. "But tell you what. If something does, which it won't . . . go to Harrison Wang. You know him. Right?"

A pause. "Yes. I know who he is."

"I made an arrangement to get something to him. If anything happens. You go to him and tell him I told you to. Tell him I said he should show you what I sent."

"Please, Ellie, just wait."

"Why? Something's suddenly going to change? I mean, what am I waiting for?"

Give me an answer, John, I'm thinking. Just give me one fucking thing to hold on to.

But he doesn't seem to have one, because all I hear is silence.

I see a new black Buick, cruising slowly up the road that separates the European buildings and the river walk. Headed in my direction.

"Nothing good's gonna happen if I wait," I say. "I'll call you as soon as I'm done with all this."

I SIT IN THE back of the Buick and try to chill.

I called Sidney, and he swore that Mom and Andy and Mimi would be leaving Xingfu Cun like he promised. I talked to Andy, just to make sure we were all on the same page. "Yes, we go to see my relatives in Xiamen," he told me. "No problem. We just pack the car now. They give us nice lunch to take along."

I heard Mimi barking in the background, a happy bark, heard my mom say, "Good girl!"

I didn't talk to my mom again. I already said good-bye once. They're fine, I tell myself. They have to be.

We drive a couple hours, maybe half of which is just sitting in Shanghai traffic, out into suburbs: flat, paved, hazy grey, factories here and there, remains of old towns and half-built new developments. Here's one that looks like a housing tract near where I grew up in Arizona, too many cheap town homes built too close together; here's another that's a fake English village.

Finally we turn off onto a small road that runs through some farmland. Green fields, these half-cylinder frames covered with opaque plastic sheeting covering rows here and there—greenhouses? Farming is another thing I know fuck-all about.

At the end of the road, there are a couple of structures that look like connex—shipping containers converted to something else, housing or offices—and what looks like a couple of aircraft hangars. Then I see the runway, and I can guess what's waiting.

Sidney Cao's private jet.

★ ★ ★

I'VE FLOWN AIR SIDNEY before: the flight attendant in the retro uniform with the white gloves, short skirt, and peaked hat, the leather seats, the endless selection of fancy food and expensive booze. I don't take advantage of it this time. I'm not hungry. I don't even want to drink.

I just want to get this over with.

An hour and fifteen minutes later, we land at Xingfu Cun.

XINGFU CUN IS SIDNEY Cao's personal ghost city, as far as I can tell: a collection of nearly empty government and commercial buildings and half-built housing developments, high-rises covered in green construction netting and bamboo scaffolding. The government building is a huge black granite dome that I like to think of as the CCP Death Star. The shopping mall is really special, too—it's this giant gold-painted pyramid thing that looks like a Mayan temple, or maybe an Egyptian one, architecture being another one of those areas I know fuck-all about.

I have no idea how many people live here or what they do. Maybe they all work for Sidney.

Vicky Huang is waiting for me when we land, standing impatiently on the tarmac next to her shiny Beemer SUV.

"So you are finally here," she says.

"Yeah, finally."

She looks me up and down. Sniffs. "Don't you have any other clothes?"

"I have a clean shirt."

I think.

"We can shop."

I hold up my hands. "No. Mr. Cao wants to see me. Let's not keep him waiting."

I can tell she's torn. She'd love to dress me up a little, but first things first.

"I will wait for you to change," she says.

I DUCK INTO THE hangar and change. I don't care if anyone sees me, and I'm not sure if the shirt I put on is any cleaner than the one I took off.

VICKY BARRELS HER SUV through the streets of Xingfu Cun, speeding down the avenues and swinging wide around the curves, which would normally make me nervous—that's how we drove in the Sandbox, pedal to the metal, tougher to hit a moving target and all—but there's hardly a car on the streets, hardly any people here at all. It's like we're driving around in some weird postapocalyptic movie, except with no zombies.

I lean back in the seat and try to clear my head. Just try to not think about anything at all. Like that army shrink told me.

Feelings are transient. You let yourself feel them, observe what they are, let them go.

I repeat it to myself a couple of times, but it doesn't take.

I want to not feel anything right now. That's what I really want.

SOON COMES THE LONG trip up the drive that leads to Sidney's mansion. Sidney's French palace. It's more decorated than a wedding cake—curlicues, marble and gold everywhere—and instead of a champagne fountain there's a real one, with statues of Greek gods and little cherubs. I can't believe that anybody actually lives here, but so far as I know, Sidney does. And down in his basement he's got an art collection that's the envy of major museums.

The butler answers Vicky's rap with the door knocker. Because of course Sidney has a butler. I'm only surprised that he didn't go all out and hire an English one.

"*Cao Xiansheng zai keting,*" the butler murmurs to Vicky. Mr. Cao is in the living room.

We walk down the long hall I've walked before, the one with the paintings of European lords and ladies hunting and eating and posing with little froufrou dogs, all hung in these massive ornate, gilded frames. The butler leads the way.

I check my phone for the time. High noon.

He's probably planning some crazy, over-the-top banquet lunch, I think. Expensive food and too much of it. That's just how Sidney rolls.

The butler opens one of the massive carved wooden doors that are painted a high-gloss white. Gestures for me to enter.

I step inside, and that's when I realize how wrong I was about lunch.

Sitting there in a semicircle, perched on the fancy French furniture, are the Caos: Sidney, Tiantian, Meimei, and Gugu.

Sidney rises.

"Ellie, thank you for coming." he says. "Now you can tell us what you found out."

CHAPTER TWENTY-FIVE

"I, uh . . . seriously?"

"Of course," Sidney says. He spreads his hands, at the room, at his kids, I don't know what. "Anything you say does not leave this room."

And that's supposed to make me feel better?

I look at them all. Tiantian, sitting rigidly on one of the mini-couches, hands covering his knees. Gugu, slumped and defeated. Meimei, leaning against the hard cushion and sculpted chair back in a pose of relaxation. I'm pretty sure she's not actually relaxed.

Sidney, meanwhile, just stands there, hands clasped in front of him. He isn't smiling like he usually is. There's no expression on his face at all.

I think of that guy I saw dying right in front of me a couple months ago, because of Sidney.

"Okay, fine. Whatever," I say. I don't even care anymore.

"There was a girl at Tiantian's party. One of the waitresses. I guess sometimes she worked late. Sold a little *doufu*. She was just doing what she could do, because she lived in a fucking box in a basement and she wanted something better."

No one moves.

"She ended up dead, dumped on a pile of garbage."

Now I turn to Sidney. Because he's the one who wanted to know.

"I think Tiantian killed her," I say.

"Why do you think this?" Sidney asks me, his voice low.

"Because he has a reputation for visiting *xiaojie*. And for hurting them."

Tiantian half rises from his chair, color flaring on his cheeks. "These are nothing but lies. You have no proof of this."

I shrug. "No one asked me for proof. That part's not my job. You know who *could* prove it, though?" I laugh. "Celine. She saw something that night. But she's dead, too. Did you know Celine was dead, Gugu?"

Gugu sits up, the blood drained from his face as if someone pulled a plug. "I . . . no."

I feel bad for a moment. I think he's telling the truth. And he may be a privileged asshole, but nobody needs to find out the way he just did that someone he knew has died.

But he's still an asshole, so fuck him.

"Yeah. Drug overdose. Right after you left that gallery party. Funny how that works. Maybe we can ask Marsh about it. He around?"

Gugu looks like someone slapped him across the face and he's still trying to absorb the blow.

Sidney nods, his eyes a little narrowed. Making a calculation. "Yes. He is here. But he is not family. First I think we can talk to Dao Ming."

Now we're having a real party.

THE BUTLER COMES IN and asks us what we want to drink. I ask for a beer. Sidney's serving Rogue Dead Guy Ale, and it even tastes fresh.

I drink it as we wait for Dao Ming to arrive.

Dao Ming's wearing black: black slacks and a short-sleeved black mock turtleneck. She stands in the doorway looking around the room, her eyes wild, like they're taking up more space than they were meant to.

Finally she sits in a chair that's catty-corner to Tiantian. As far away from him as she can get.

This time I say it in Chinese. "I know this. At Tiantian's party a *fuwuyuan* died. She served as a prostitute. I think Tiantian killed her. I don't know what the rest of you know."

"This is not true!" Tiantian snarls, the red on his cheeks getting deep and dark.

Dao Ming twitches in her chair. "He likes *xiaojie*," she spits out. "Don't lie," she says to her husband. "I know what you do. You do it with these girls. You do it all the time."

"I didn't . . ."

I roll my eyes. "Everyone knows you did."

"I did not kill her!"

"But you beat her, right? You choked her. You get off on that kind of thing. Don't you."

I am pretty sure Tiantian's going to bolt out of his chair right then and launch himself at me, and I'm thinking, Bring it on, asshole, but Dao Ming rises first.

"He broke the rules," she says, biting off each word. "He had these girls at our house. *Our* house!" She strides over to Tiantian and gets in his face, pushing and shoving him with each word. "That's not allowed! How dare you humiliate me that way? *How dare you!*" Now she slaps him across the face. He raises his hands to protect himself, and she just keeps hitting him.

Finally she stops. Like she's too exhausted to continue. He

remains frozen for a moment, his raised hands in front of his face, palms out.

She turns to me, still breathing hard, cords in her neck standing out like twisted wires.

"Yes, he beat her," she says. "He choked her. I found her, after. She was half dead, crying and carrying on. So I put her out of her misery. It was an act of mercy."

The beer roils in my gut, and I feel like I'm going to puke. I grab my pack, turn without a word, and I walk out of the room. No one tries to stop me.

CHAPTER TWENTY-SIX

I KEEP WALKING, DOWN the seemingly endless hall, into the entranceway, and out the front door. I walk outside onto the driveway, past the fancy-ass sports car parked there, until I get to a stone retaining wall that overlooks the long drive and the surrounding grounds. I stop there.

The sky's pretty blue out here, with only a little haze in the distance. I realize I don't know what the fuck I'm going to do now.

I just want to keep walking, but to where? It's a couple of miles into Xingfu Cun proper, such as it is, and I can walk that, gimpy leg and all, but what do I do when I get there? Are there buses out of Xingfu Cun? Taxis? Any cars for hire at all?

Will Sidney even let me leave?

I'm not there all that long before I hear slow footsteps on the flagstones behind me.

Sidney.

He looks apologetic. I hope that's a good sign.

"Is that enough?" I ask.

He nods.

"Can I go now?"

"Soon."

Soon. I don't know if I like the sound of that.

Sidney sighs. "Tiantian is my first child. My first son. He

should be the best. But . . . he has this jealous nature. Always. I think maybe because I am not rich when he is a boy. I work very hard . . . His mother . . ." He shakes his head. "She works, too. The relationship between us . . . is not very good. No one pays Tiantian very much attention."

"So he beats up on girls?" I snort, even though I shouldn't. "Not a great excuse."

"No. It is not."

He doesn't look mad. He looks like he's thinking it all over. "Meimei and Gugu have more gentle natures. I think because their mother is more gentle."

So there are two Mrs. Caos. Neither of whom seems to be around. At this point I'm not sure I care what that story is. Unless Sidney killed them and buried them in the backyard. That might be relevant.

"But Dao Ming, she is not good for Tiantian."

"You think? She's batshit."

"Bat . . . shit?"

"Sorry. *Fengkuangde.*"

"Yes. She is . . . not happy." He shakes his head. "I want to . . . to *fenkai* . . . to . . ."

"Separate?"

"Yes. Separate my family from Yang Junmin's family. But this is . . . a little complicated."

"Yeah," I say. "I kind of get that."

"I help give him power. He help make me rich. But . . . I do not like him. He does not like me."

"Then why . . . ?" I ask, before I can stop myself. Because really, do I need to know? But it's like there's a part of me that *does* need to. Like if I can make things make sense, then it means something. It's not all just some kind of sick joke.

"Do you know Wenhua Da Geming?" he asks.

"Cultural Revolution. Yeah." I know something about it anyway. Ten years in the sixties and seventies, when Mao decided to stir shit up, promote a "revolution" that was part idealistic crusade, part power struggle among the leadership, part score settling among ordinary people with generations of resentments. It got crazy bad. Almost a civil war in places. Most of the younger generations here hardly know a thing about it. Just like they don't know about the Great Leap or Tiananmen.

But how many people in the US know why we went to war in Iraq?

I'm getting lost in my own thoughts again, something I shouldn't do when I'm at a house containing at least several people with homicidal tendencies and in the presence of one who outsources.

"What about it? About the Wenhua Da Geming?" I ask.

"My family and Yang Junmin's family. We grow up in same place. Same town, very close to here. Our families . . . we are not friends. Then Mao start Cultural Revolution. Yang Junmin and I are Red Guards. We smash the Olds."

He smiles a little. "Making revolution is . . . fun. When you are young."

I get a shiver, right across my shoulders and the back of my neck.

"My Red Guards split from Yang Junmin's Red Guards. We are enemies. We hate each other, very much," Sidney continues. "But later, when all of that is over, we are still two young men from Anhui. It is time to rebuild China. So we work together. Now . . ." Sidney spreads his hands. "Here we are."

Here we are.

He starts to pace. "I try to build something. Something big. Something beautiful. Why? My children, they all are . . . terrible."

"Meimei and Gugu are . . . okay."

"They do not care, about what I build. They do not start families. They do not work. They simply want to . . . play." He's pacing harder now. Building up to something. I've never seen him lose it before. But I'm wondering if I'm about to.

"There is nothing left but to buy beautiful things," Sidney says. "Enjoy them in this life."

He stops suddenly. "Do you know something?" He jabs a finger at me. "You."

My heart jumps.

"Me?"

"You. Are. Right."

He whirls around, stretches out his arms toward his fake French château. "I can spend it all. When I die, I can leave it to the people. We can build this museum. Make it . . . great. Beautiful. For the people. I want everyone to see these things and learn about them. Let this art bring them some joy and good feelings." He drops his hands. "It is all I can offer."

"It's . . . a good thing," I manage.

"Thank you, Ellie." He bobs his head a few times. "Thank you, for helping me understand this."

Then, "Please stay for dinner. I can send you home after."

"Okay," I say. "Sure."

What else can I say? I'm all out of words right now.

I DECIDE TO TAKE a walk. If I'm stuck out here for dinner, I don't want to spend any more time than I have to with the people in that house.

I head around to the back of the mansion. There's a fancy garden, with trimmed hedgerows, flowers, and fountains. Beyond that, another low retaining wall and a gently sloping hill.

I walk out to the retaining wall. Unsling my pack. Take a look at more of Sidney's domain.

Off to the left, rows of what might be grapes. A vineyard, I'm guessing, given Sidney. To the right, I'm not sure what that is. Some tall hedges, some structures I can't quite figure out. Sheds? Another garden maybe.

I can't tell how big the grounds are. They seem to go on as far as I can see, but who can tell where Sidney ends and Xingfu Cun begins, right?

"Hey."

I jump. Turn. It's Marsh.

"We need to talk," he says.

"Oh. We do?" I'm looking for the quickest route out of here.

His hands are balled into fists, arms dangling at his sides. Pissed as hell, but not quite ready to beat the shit out of me.

"What the fuck, Ellie? Seriously, what the fuck?"

"What." I say it that way where it's not a question.

"You told the Caos I fucking killed Celine?" His cheeks are red. He's standing close enough where I can catch a whiff of scotch.

Can I walk away?

"No. I said she died right after Gugu left the gallery. It's not my fault you were still there."

He's breathing hard. Like he's trying to calm himself down. "Look, we need to help each other. You think Yang is going to trust either of us with knowing all this shit?"

I shrug. "Hey. I don't actually *know* anything. Do you?"

He paces a step or two in a tight little circle, clenching and unclenching his fists, running a hand through his hair, like he's trying to figure something out. I'm watching him, and I can't decide if he's dangerous or not.

I don't think I can get past him.

"Okay," he says. "You want to know what happened to Celine? I'll tell you."

I hesitate. I don't know for sure if this guy's a murderer or just a douchebag. But what I do know is that I want to know what happened.

The truth. The end.

He gestures at the low wall, slowly, like he doesn't want to startle me. "Let's sit."

"Let's not. If you're serious about this, you can take a step back. I don't want you this close to me."

Marsh lifts his hands. "Okay." Steps back. "Okay."

"So tell me," I say.

"Celine liked heroin," he says. "Said it made her feel like she lived in a beautiful world." He smiles a little. "She was kind of . . . dramatic. You know? I stayed behind to do some with her. Just a snort. We crashed out and listened to music for a while. I left. I guess she did some more after that. She just did a little too much. I used to think she was maybe suicidal. Maybe she was." He shrugs. "That's it. There's nothing else to it."

"Nothing? Nothing about how she saw a dead girl at Tiantian's party?"

"So what? So did I."

We just stand there for a moment, staring at each other.

"You want to know how it went down?" he asks.

I nod. I can't help it.

"The two of us were . . . just kind of hanging out. Celine and me. After it happened, Tiantian called Yang. He sent two guys to take care of the body. Celine helped them put some clothes on her that they brought over. Cheap-ass worker's uniform, like a supermarket smock or something."

I flash back to the photo of the dead girl. What the fuck is her name?

Wang Junyi. That's it.

"Here's the thing," Marsh says. He sounds calmer now. "They're gonna want to blame a foreigner. You've got Sidney in your corner. I've got Tiantian."

My heart's speeding up like somebody turned a dial.

"Tiantian?"

He nods. "Yeah. Gugu's my buddy, but I fix things for Tiantian. Help him move money around. The pay's a lot better."

"Okay," I say. "So we both have friends. How exactly do we help each other?"

That's when he laughs. "Yeah, you know what? I can't help you. But you can help me."

He's reaching behind him, into his waistband, and I already know what he's reaching for.

I snatch up my daypack by the straps and swing it hard, as his hand rises with the gun.

The weapon, some pistol, I can't see what it is, goes flying, but there's no way I can beat Marsh to it. I don't run that well, and he's bigger than I am.

There's only one thing I can think of to do.

I clamber over the low retaining wall and tuck and roll. Down the gentle hill, side over side, arms clasped over my chest, like I'm a kid playing a game, just rolling down the hill, collecting grass stains, except I'm going too fast, and I don't come to a stop until I slam into a row of grapevines and some kind of wire strung along them, my forearm absorbing most of the blow.

I pick myself up and look up the hill. I don't see Marsh, yet, but I have to figure he's going to get the gun and come after me.

I head for the tall hedges. They're like walls, one running along the side of the vineyard, the other perpendicular to it, facing the retaining wall up the hill. There's a gap between them, the entrance to the garden, or whatever this is.

I don't like going into terrain I don't know, into someplace I could get trapped, but I need to find some cover, and there aren't a lot of choices.

"What the fuck?" I mutter.

I can't figure out what this is at first. One of the sheds I saw, it's like this house or something, painted sand colored, and in front of it there's a life-size stand-up figure of a soldier, in full-on battle rattle, holding a rifle aimed at me. I look around, and I see a mock-up of a tank—I mean, it can't be a real tank, right? It looks pretty real, if a little old, metal rusting around the edges, done up in green camo. Behind that are concrete walls, crumbling in places, with black bursts around the broken places like they've been hit by mortars.

Weird thing is, there's these bright splotches of color on the soldier, on the building, on the tank. Orange, and neon green, and bright red.

Paint.

Oh, fuck. It's Sidney's paintball playground.

CHAPTER TWENTY-SEVEN

FIRST THING I THINK is, Keep going. Get through this maze, however big it is, and to the other side. At least there should be some cover along the way.

Second thought: painted in big stenciled letters on the big shed to my right is ARMY WEAPONS DEPOT. The door's open.

I've got a second to decide.

I haul ass into the shed.

Inside, I can see racks of protective clothes, pads, goggles, supplies. And paint guns.

Spread out on a table is a clutter of gear, as if the last players just left it there when they finished playing. Including a couple guns.

Somebody didn't field-strip his weapons, I think. Lucky for me.

I grab one. It sure doesn't look like the paint guns I played with a few times when I was a kid, which looked and felt like plastic toys. This thing resembles an AR-15, and it has close to the heft of one, too.

I pop open the hopper, and it's about half full of paintballs. I close the lid and pray the thing works. I don't have time to do anything else. I don't think Marsh rolled down the hill like I did, but it's not going to take him that long to jog down here.

I poke my head around the entrance. I don't see Marsh, but I think I hear him. I scramble across the courtyard, past the dummy soldier, to the tank. It's actual metal, not a wooden mock-up. Maybe PLA surplus or something. I duck behind it and wait.

Now I do hear Marsh for real: a crunch of footsteps on gravel. "Come on, Ellie," he says loudly. "I was just kidding around."

I risk a peek. There he is, standing by the soldier, scanning the area, gun dangling loosely from his hand at his side.

I stand up, brace the stock against my shoulder, put my finger on the trigger, and unload.

Clack, clack, clack! My first two balls miss, and Marsh starts to raise his gun arm; my third shot hits him in the chest, and he flinches a little as the burst of green paint spreads across his black designer T-shirt. His gun's level now, he's taking aim, gun turned sideways like he's seen too many stupid movies, and I fire again, semiauto, and I hit him right in the face.

"Mother*fucker!*" he yells, hitting a high note, and he's clawing at one eye, and I think, Good. And I fire a couple more times and get him in the face again.

I may have been a medic in the National Guard, but I shot expert in basic training.

"You fucking *cunt!*"

I hope I put his eye out. Muzzle up, I run, deeper into the maze.

MORE CRUMBLING WALLS AND "bombed" houses. The shell of a burned-out car. I zigzag through it. I don't know how big this place is. I don't know where it ends or if I can get out the other side. A jolt of pain goes up my bad leg every time my foot hits the ground; my chest is burning, and I can't catch my breath.

The course has opened up some, like it's the town square. Not as much cover. A couple more burned-out cars. A dry fountain. Buildings and walls along the perimeter. I need to get to cover, I think. That low wall at the back. I'll be able to see if Marsh is coming. Have a chance to keep running, if I can.

I make it to the wall, collapse behind it.

You can't stay here, I tell myself. You need to keep running.

I look back the way I came, and I don't see Marsh yet.

Maybe I *did* put his eye out.

I hear light running footsteps behind me.

I twist around, paint gun ready, and see Meimei.

"Jesus!" I hiss.

She drops down next to me.

"Go get help," I whisper. "Marsh has a gun. He's—"

And she's pointing a handgun at me.

This is it, I think. The end. I feel nothing but empty.

She flips the weapon around and holds it out to me, butt first.

"Take it," she whispers, her eyes bright. "It's loaded."

A revolver. A .38, I think.

Now I hear Marsh, or someone, coming across the plaza. Not running. Just steady footsteps.

I risk a glance. There he is by the fountain. He's wearing goggles now, his face and chest still splashed with fluorescent green paint.

"Stay down," I whisper to Meimei.

"What the *fuck*, Marsh?" I yell out. "What are you *doing*?"

"Hey!" he yells back. "Cool. Let's talk."

"Talk about *what*? How's this gonna fix anything?"

"They need someone to blame for that dead girl." His voice echoes across the square. Still moving toward me. Taking his

time, ambling almost. "Crazy Iraq vet with all kinds of problems, bad political associations—might as well be you."

Okay, I think. Okay. Let's talk. And keep talking. Let me get
a bead on where you are. So I know where to aim.

"You're gonna shoot me? How're you gonna explain that?"

I try to remember the terrain. A burned-out car. A blasted
concrete wall.

"You know they don't care." He's talking loud, but he
doesn't need to shout anymore. He's getting close. "Besides,
you're going to shoot yourself. That's where you've been heading anyway, right?"

"Fuck off!"

He laughs. "Hey, I was wrong. I *can* help you."

Come closer, asshole. Just a little bit closer.

"You just keep pushing," he says, "because you're hoping
somebody puts you out of your misery. Let me take care of it
for you."

I squeeze my eyes shut. "Fuck you."

"Come on," he says softly. Like a lover. "You want it to be
over. You know you do."

"Back the fuck off," I say between clenched teeth. "I
mean it."

Don't make me do it, I think.

"Or what? You'll shoot me with a paint gun?"

Close enough.

I hold the revolver in both hands, the way I was taught, one
hand braced against the other. Tell myself I am going to stand
up no matter how much it hurts. With the strength of my good
leg and all I can muster with my bad one, I spring up, pain
making my vision go white for an instant. See Marsh's dark
mass in front of me. Fire. Three shots.

He drops in his tracks.

Ears ringing, I limp around the edge of the wall, weapon ready.

He's lying spread-eagled on the ground, outstretched fingers grazing the butt of his pistol. I hobble over and kick the gun away.

I stare down at him. He looks up at me. Like he's confused about what just happened. I can see blood coursing out of a hole below his ribs. Somehow the blood looks blacker than his black T-shirt.

I take off my jacket and kneel down beside him, fold up the jacket, and press it into the wound, because that's what I was taught to do.

He gasps.

"Just lie still," I say. "Help's coming." I have no idea if that's true or not. I lift the goggles away from his eyes with my free hand and push them onto his forehead. I can see speckles of green paint on his nose and cheeks, swelling around one eye where the paintball hit.

The confusion in his face is fading. He gets it now. "You shot . . ."

"You asshole," I mutter. "Why did you make me do it?"

"I . . ."

His eyes roll up and to one side, like he sees something coming. Whatever it is, it scares him.

"You're gonna be okay," I say.

He nods a little. I hear it in his breathing now, a gargling sound as his breath passes through fluid and mucus that he can't cough up.

I hear a noise behind me. Meimei, watching intently.

"Get help," I tell her again.

I turn back to Marsh. I can see it in his eyes, the dimming of the light. A labored breath, then another.

He exhales, a last, long, rattling sigh. His pupils dilate. His bladder and bowels release, and I can't smell the blood anymore, just shit and piss.

"Is he dead?" Meimei asks.

"Yeah."

Meimei retrieves his gun. Stands up. For a moment I wonder if she's going to shoot me.

Maybe he was right. Maybe I don't care.

Instead she fires two times over the wall where we'd been hiding.

Then she crouches down, puts the gun in his hand, presses his fingers around the butt and the trigger, lifts his arm, and fires a third time, into the air.

"So there won't be any questions," she says, matter-of-fact. "You had to do it. You had no choice."

CHAPTER TWENTY-EIGHT

YOU KNOW HOW THEY say things happen in a blur? Not for me, not this time anyway. I remember all of it. But it's like I can't feel it properly, like I'm watching the whole thing through a pane of glass.

I killed a guy. Somebody I knew. Maybe he deserved it. Maybe I really didn't have a choice. But I could tell by the way he held his gun, he didn't know what the fuck he was doing.

I did.

"Don't worry," Meimei tells me.

"How are we going to explain this?"

"Easy. I was . . . target shooting."

"Target shooting?"

"Sure. My father has guns, as you can see. He likes to shoot sometimes." Her nose wrinkles. "He's not very good at it."

We're standing there by the body. By Marsh. I keep expecting people to show up, to come running down. I mean, there was live fire. Wouldn't somebody notice?

Maybe Meimei's target-shooting story is more believable than I thought.

"So . . . why did *you* have a gun?" I ask. "I mean, really. Don't tell me you were going target shooting."

"I saw Marsh leave, and I suspected something. So I took

one of my father's guns and followed him. When he went after you, I knew to go around another way."

She's a cool customer. Either she's telling the truth or she had her story worked out in advance.

"Where'd he get the gun? Marsh. One of your father's?"

She does a little shrug. "I don't know. But I think from Tiantian. You can get guns in China, if you know the right person. If you have money."

"And Tiantian told him to kill me?"

"I doubt if he told him that. Just to . . . take care of the problem."

I stare down at the body. Flies are starting to land on it, their buzzing louder than the ringing in my ears. "What do we do now?"

"We call the police." She looks like she's thinking it over, but I'm pretty sure she already has something figured out. "We say Marsh tried to kill you. I saw it, too. Perhaps he would have killed me as well, but you stopped him."

"Why? I mean, what do we tell them? *Why* was he trying to kill me?"

"What he told you. That he wished to blame you for that *fuwuyuan*'s death." She pretends to think about it some more. "We can say he admitted to killing her. And that I heard him confess this to you."

"You think the police are going to believe all that?"

Now she laughs, a light chuckle. "If my father wants them to, they will."

"And Tiantian and Dao Ming? They just walk?"

"Of course," she says. "What would you expect?"

Justice, I think. But truth be told, that's not what I expect. It's what I want. And I already know I'm not going to get it.

Meimei gets out her iPhone. "I'm going to call for help," she says. Her finger hovers above the touch screen. Then she stops and clasps her hands, the phone held between them.

"I will share something with you," she says. "Tiantian does not like my father. Or trust him. He is afraid that he won't receive my father's money and businesses when he dies. In Tiantian's mind, if someone must be blamed for this girl's death, let it be an associate of my father's. Especially let it be someone who tempts my father into spending his money on some crazy projects, like this museum."

I decide not to mention this new idea Sidney has to give away his entire fortune. "But he's a billionaire," I say. "It's not like the museum will take up all his money."

"True. But Tiantian can't see things that way. He's always been terrible at sharing."

She smiles. This time I think I'm finally seeing her real smile, and it's cold.

"Now Tiantian will never get what he wants," she says.

It hits me all at once that if anyone inherits Sidney's empire, it's going to be Meimei.

I DON'T KNOW WHAT to do with the gun. I don't want to carry it; I don't want to touch it anymore. But I can't just leave it lying around or tossed in the dirt. It's a weapon. It killed someone.

I killed someone.

You had to do it, I tell myself.

The gun is also evidence.

So I take it with me as we walk up the path that leads to the gardens at the back of Sidney's fake French palace, carrying it cradled in both my hands.

When we get to the house, Sidney is waiting for us on the terrace. *"Fashengle shenme shi?"* What happened?

"Marsh tried to kill her," Meimei says. "He might have killed me, too."

"But . . . why?"

"He works for Tiantian as well as Gugu." Funny thing, now I hear emotion in her voice. A ragged edge of anger.

Sidney starts to say something, I don't know what. Some form of denial, I'm guessing. But he doesn't get there. He stops himself, covers his face with his hands for a moment. *"Duibuqi, Meimei. Qing raoshu wo ba."* Please forgive me.

Maybe he's thinking about how he could have lost her.

He turns to me and just shakes his head. "I am very sorry, Ellie. This should not have happened."

THINGS GO DOWN THE way Meimei said they would.

The police come. Meimei puts on a little show for them. It's pitch-perfect: she's not quite hysterical, just slightly breathless, and shaken. "I still can't believe it," she says more than once. "He was completely crazy!"

As Meimei suggested, I tell them pretty much what happened, with a few key additions and omissions. They don't speak much English, so I tell them in a mix of English and Chinese, with Meimei filling in some of the Chinese details. They don't separate us to keep us from getting our stories straight. They don't even try. They ask me to write out an account of what happened and why, and I do that.

I went for a walk. Ran into Marsh. He said something to me about the dead girl. How he needed someone to blame. I was able to get away, distract him with the paint gun. That's when Meimei showed up, to go target shooting.

"I gave her the gun, because she was a soldier," Meimei tells the police. "I knew she could shoot better than I."

One of the policeman nods. "Americans all have guns anyway," he says to his partner. "Of course they know how to shoot."

I still have to wonder if Meimei set Marsh up. Pretended to make some kind of deal with him. Kill her to save yourself. Kill her and you can fix things for *me*, too.

I don't think she wanted me dead. But maybe she wanted to use me to kill.

Guess I'll never know, because it's not like I'm going to ask.

HERE'S HOW I GET out of Xingfu Cun.

John shows up.

It's been a few hours, late afternoon, the sun heading for the hills on the left end of the vineyard. The PSB is still here, more of them now, technicians or people pretending to be them who convoy down the hill to the paintball course, carrying cameras and evidence bags. A little while ago, I watched one of them bag the revolver I used. Now I'm standing out at the back of the garden watching them. Same spot I was in when Marsh found me. I'm finding it hard to believe that there's actually a CSI: Xingfu Cun, but I could be wrong.

Nobody's told me that I can't leave yet, but then I haven't asked.

"Ellie."

I turn, and there's John, dressed in his usual snug black T-shirt and black jeans.

"Hi," I say. "Thanks for coming."

He doesn't say anything. Neither do I.

"I talk to the police here," John finally says. "They say you cooperate well with them."

"I gave them a statement."

"I think it's okay if we leave now." John slips his hands into his front jeans pockets. "If you want."

"Yeah. I want to leave."

BEFORE I LEAVE, I figure I'd better have one last word with Sidney.

I find him sitting behind his massive carved desk in the wood-paneled room lined with bookcases, the room with the giant stuffed deer head. Maybe it actually is his office, and not just for show. Vicky Huang is there, too, sitting on the couch with her ever-present iPad, taking notes.

Sidney rises when I come in. Gestures at one of the leather club chairs.

I shake my head. "I'm going now," I say.

I'm a little curious to see if he tries to stop me.

"I am making certain arrangements," Sidney says. "I do my best so Yang Junmin won't bother you or your family."

"Thanks."

He shakes his head and waves his hands in that little brusque gesture that won't allow any discussion. "I cannot do business with him anymore."

"And Tiantian?"

Now Sidney sits back down. "He has made his choice," he says curtly. "He is not my child."

In spite of everything that's happened, in spite of feeling mostly numb, I still have this weird corner of sympathy for him. "Meimei's really smart," I say. "She could help you run things. And Gugu . . ."

What can I say about Gugu?

I think about how he was yesterday on the set, how focused

and . . . well, sober he was. I think about the night he went to the gallery, because he wanted to learn about art, even if he was too drunk to appreciate it.

"He's okay," I say. "He's interested in art. I think he'd like to work with you. If you'll listen to him sometimes."

Sidney doesn't say anything. He stares down at his desk, face dark.

I steal a glance at Vicky, who sits there utterly still. It's funny how a person as pushy as she is can turn into a piece of furniture when she needs to.

"If you're still planning on the museum," I say.

Now Sidney looks up. "Of course. Even more." He spreads his hands. "This will all belong to the people."

I think about the mansion, the art, the vineyards and private jet, a mostly empty "village," all that money, and I wonder what the people are going to do with it all.

I DON'T KNOW WHERE John got the car, a slightly beat-up black VW Santana. I don't think it could be his: not enough time from when I called this morning for him to drive down from Beijing to Anhui.

We drive a few hours to Hefei, the capital of Anhui Province, not saying much on the ride.

"What you tell the police," John says after a while. "Is that true?"

"Pretty much. Except Marsh didn't kill Wang Junyi. Dao Ming did."

He draws in a startled breath. "Dao Ming?"

"Yeah, after Tiantian beat Junyi half to death."

Another long silence.

"You shoot him?" he finally asks.

"Yeah. He had a gun. He said he was going to kill me, like I told the police." I look down at my hands, clasped loosely in my lap, and I can still feel the weight of the revolver there, if I let myself.

"Why did you go alone, Ellie? Why didn't you wait for me? I might have—"

"Yeah, well, you might *not* have," I snap back. "You might have brought Yang Junmin's army down on us."

Anyhow, I don't want to think about a different way it might have gone. One where I didn't kill anybody.

CHAPTER TWENTY-NINE

WE GET TO HEFEI. John leaves the Santana at a curb somewhere in the city. I don't know where. I've never been here before. It's another big city that looks like it grew too fast, with constant jackhammers and construction trucks and cranes, half-completed high-rises covered with green netting, giant earthmovers and huge pipes and gaping holes in the ground. Then we take a taxi to the train station, the usual clusterfuck of cars, taxis, buses, and people swarming in and around a space that isn't big enough to hold them all. I'm still too nervous to fly. I'll give Sidney some time to do whatever it is he's going to do with Yang Junmin before I get on a plane.

We make our way to the ticket hall. The lines aren't too bad, a sort of halfhearted mob that gets funneled into lines by aluminum crowd-control rails up by the windows.

"We can go back to Beijing together," John says. "Or someplace else for a few days. If you want."

"I have to go to Shanghai."

He elbows a guy who tries to cut in front of us. "I can come with you."

I think about it, and I don't know whether I'm being stubborn or smart or if I just don't want to be around anybody.

"If you really want to help me . . . go to Beijing, John. Let me know if you think it's safe for me to go back."

He's not happy about it. But at least he listens.

"Okay," he says. "I can do that."

I GET A TICKET on the last train to Shanghai leaving at 8:00 P.M., a fast D train that will get me to Shanghai Hongqiao station just after 11:00 P.M. John's train for Beijing doesn't leave until right before 10:00, and it's a long ride, nine and a half hours. The high-speed line's not opening till next year.

I almost wish my ride was that long, so I could just sleep on the train and dodge the whole hotel passport-registration issue one more night. But I'm hoping Sidney's already done what he said he would, that he's gotten Uncle Yang off my back already. I'm betting either Tiantian or Dao Ming has talked to him, too. Maybe both of them.

Who knows what any of them said? How it might make Yang react.

"You should take some food and things on the train," John says.

"What?"

We've gone inside the station proper, through the metal detectors, me with a daypack, John with a messenger bag.

"Here," he says, pointing to a convenience store next to a fast-food noodle joint.

"I don't need anything."

John rolls his eyes. "So just wait here."

He goes inside the convenience store. It's your basic rectangle, like a gas station mini-mart, except the long side is an exposed wall of Plexiglas.

I watch him go inside and walk purposefully down the aisles, grabbing things here and there, his image slightly blued by the thick Plexi, and I feel like I'm on the other side of an aquarium wall. Or maybe I'm the one who's in it.

He comes out with two plastic bags tied at the handles. "Here," he says, handing me the smaller of the two.

"Thanks."

"We can talk by the end of the day tomorrow."

"All right. Sounds good."

He stands there looking down and shifting back and forth, like he's trying to calm himself.

"Please take good care," he says, meeting my eyes. "I think you need some time to rest."

AFTER I SETTLE INTO my seat, I open up the bag. A giant cup of noodles. A bag of spicy peanuts. Some "biscuits," which might be crackers or might be cookies. A big bottle of water. Two cans of Snow Beer.

HALFWAY THROUGH THE RIDE, I call Lucy Wu. To warn her I'm coming.

"How about lunch? There's a soup-dumpling place near my apartment," she says.

"Okay," I say. I crack open the first of my Snow Beers. "If I don't make it . . . you know what to do with that thing I left you, right?"

A pause. "Yes. Right."

I FIND A CHEAPER hotel downtown off Huaihai Road, a "business-class" place called the Celebrity Garden. It looks like a thousand other Chinese hotels I've stayed in: marble-ized lobby, clocks on the wall set to Beijing, Moscow, London, and New York times, a room with a hard bed, a particleboard desk covered with plastic wood veneer, a desk chair, an electric teakettle.

I take the desk chair and wedge the top under the door-knob. Put the chain on the door. I don't know what difference it makes, really. A chair and a lock aren't going to stop Uncle Yang if he knows where I am, if he wants to bring me in.

I drink a bottle of beer. Watch TV. Doze off now and again. Think about what Marsh said.

You want it to be over. You know you do.

THE DUMPLING PLACE IS in the bottom floor of a ram-shackle two-story building draped with loose electrical wire and a painted wooden signboard for a menu, just around the corner from a glassy California Pizza Kitchen, a four-story art deco apartment, and something called "Privilege Banking," adver-tised in glowing white letters against a blue-lit aluminum wall.

Lucy beats me there. When I arrive, she's sitting outside at a white plastic table, perched on a white plastic stool. There's room for only three tables inside.

Our dumplings arrive in blackened, water-stained bamboo steamers, along with soup and a side dish of sliced green garlic and strips of marinated pork. I catch a whiff of steam from the first set of dumplings, and I'm suddenly starving.

We don't talk too much until the food is nearly gone.

"Sidney Cao is probably going to contact you about the museum project," I say.

Lucy wipes her lips with a square of tissue paper. "Oh?"

"Yeah."

I don't tell her much about what happened in Xingfu Cun. Just the part where Sidney wants to spend his fortune on buy-ing beautiful things to share with "the people."

"My," she says. "Well, of course I'd be interested in helping him spend his money."

"You need to really think about it. Sidney's trying to separate himself from Yang Junmin, but . . . I don't know. If there really is some kind of big power struggle going on with the leadership transition coming up . . . you just don't want to get caught out on the wrong side of that."

"I know," she says. "But the idea of a project like this . . . The things that could be created . . ." She stares at me across the table, and I can see the light in her eyes, the excitement. "We'll have to be careful, but if we keep some separation between our businesses . . ."

I shake my head. "I can't do it."

"But . . . why? You're the one who created this opportunity."

"I've been faking it this whole time. I don't know what I'm doing. And . . . I need a break."

"But you're smart," she insists. "You've already learned so much, in a short amount of time. Why not take advantage of chance like this?"

"I can't," I repeat. "I just . . ."

I look at her. It's funny to see her like this, no makeup, wearing light cotton pants and a girlie-cut New York Yankees T-shirt, eating dumplings at a neighborhood dive. Completely at ease, in a way I'll never be.

"You can do bigger things," I say. "I can't."

JOHN MEETS ME THE next morning at the Beijing South Railway Station, standing on the other side of the turnstiles that separate the arrival gates from the rest of the subterranean level of this massive complex.

"I came on subway," he says. "Traffic is terrible."

"Subway's fine." I've only got my daypack, and we're right by the subway concourse anyway.

"Where do you want to go?" he asks.

"Just back to my place."

We cram onto the Line 4 subway car, dodging gigantic wheeled suitcases and stuffed plastic grain bags, squeeze into the relative spaciousness of the vestibule connecting two cars, and I lean back against the wall and close my eyes until we get to Xizhimen Station, take the long jog to the Line 2, then just two stops to Gulou.

Finally we emerge from the long escalator into the smoggy daylight.

John walks with me through the tangle of jackhammers and piles of bricks, cars, and temporary walls and white construction dorms, until we reach the alley that leads to my apartment.

"What do you do now, Ellie?"

"Call my mom. Answer some email. Take a nap." I shrug. "I don't know."

"Do you want me to come with you?"

"No. I just . . . I know you've got things you need to do, and I'm . . . I think I want to just get some things done, like I said."

"If you're sure." He stands there with that slightly awkward, hands-jammed-in-his-jeans-pockets posture that makes me think he's a different guy altogether, the guy I thought he was the first time we met: kind of cute, a little clueless, maybe even sort of shy.

"I think it's okay," he says. "I don't think Beijing police or Yang Junmin will bother you now. But . . . I can't be certain."

"I know." I swing my daypack off my shoulders and zip open the main compartment. Reach in and get the envelope I'd given Lucy Wu, just in case.

"Maybe this is something you can use," I say.

I did a lot of thinking on the train. An offshore company that Celine knew about, that involved somebody at Tiantian's party. I thought about what she was likely to know and how she could have learned about it. She hung out around Gugu, and she hung out around Marsh. Marsh palled around with Gugu, but he worked for Tiantian.

I fix things for Tiantian, Marsh said. *Help him move money around.*

And who really needs help moving money around, way more than the son of a Chinese billionaire?

A high-ranking CCP official who needs to do it all off the books.

I hold out the envelope to John. "I'm not sure, but I think this might help you get Tiantian. And Yang Junmin."

He takes it. "Thank you."

"I'm just going to ask you to promise me something. If you use it . . . keep Sidney and his other kids out of it, if you can. Sidney's going to be in business with people I know. Besides . . ."

I think about Sidney's art collection, and I wonder: Will he follow through with it? Will he build a museum for regular people to enjoy? Give away his ghost city and his estate? Bring some beauty to people's lives, like he said he wanted to?

"They're . . ." I let out a sigh. "I don't know. They're not all bad."

John nods. "I promise." He folds the envelope and tucks it in his pocket. "I call you tomorrow. Or if you change number, you call me."

"Okay."

It's funny. I suddenly want to hug him and not let go. But I don't. Because now that he's finally seeing who I really am, I don't think he wants me to.

Anyway I don't deserve it.

CHAPTER THIRTY

THE APARTMENT LOOKS JUST how I left it. Some mess in the kitchen from one of Mom's taco experiments that's starting to smell. I clean it up. Make myself a pot of coffee. Think I should call my mom.

But I don't know if I can face talking to her just yet. How am I going to tell her about what I did?

Easy, McEnroe, I tell myself. You don't. Just like you never told her about what happened in Iraq, before you got blown up.

She doesn't need to know that stuff about me. What I'm capable of. What I'm not able to do.

So I text. HI, BACK HOME.

And then I strike "HOME."

BACK IN BJ. EVERYTHING'S FINE. PROBABLY A GOOD IDEA IF YOU STAYED WITH ANDY'S FAMILY A FEW MORE DAYS. IS THAT OK?

A minute later: WHAT HAPPENED?! U SURE UR OK?

FINE. JUST A MISUNDERSTANDING. ALL FIXED.

WE'LL BE HOME ASAP.

NO REALLY. STAY THERE A FEW DAYS. I

Think about what to say.

NEED SOME TIME TO

I stare at the screen. It's like I've finally run out of lies, but there's no truth to take their place.

WORK A FEW THINGS OUT, I finally type.

It's a minute or so before my mom replies. I imagine she's thinking about what to say. Or typing things and changing her mind.

OK. WE CAN STAY A FEW MORE DAYS. LOVE YOU.

LOVE YOU TOO, I type.

I CHECK MY EMAIL.

Shit, go away for . . . How many days was it? Whatever, there's a lot of email.

I delete the spam, the newsletters, the invitations to gallery openings, jokes sent to me by some friends in the US, also cute animal photos, even though I like to look at those. At least I'm not getting so many Jesus emails since my mom's actually living with me.

Here's one from my landlady in Wenzhou:

Just to remind you, rent rises in 1 month. If you want to continue lease, let me know.

"*Thanks for writing,*" I type back without even thinking about it. "*I'll be leaving. Best, Ellie.*"

It's suddenly clear. Just like that. I'll be leaving.

I KEEP GOING THROUGH my email. Just because . . . I don't know, I'd like to have an empty inbox. Leave things clean.

Here's a note from some buddies of mine from the Sandbox, Palaver and Madrid, with a new picture of their kid, who's over a year old now. "*So cute,*" I type. "*Thanks for sending.*"

Huh, here's an email from Francesca Barrows. She's this British art critic I met a year ago, when the whole craziness happened with Lao Zhang disappearing and the Uighur. I think she might be a part of the Great Community, but I never found out for sure.

> *It's been a while. Tried to call, but your number's not working. Can you give me a ring when you get this? A project's come up I think you might be interested in.*

Right. I delete the message.

Funny thing. Up next is an email from Sloppy Song. She's an artist I know from Mati Village, where I met Lao Zhang. I always figured she was in the Great Community, too. But it was kind of a "don't ask, don't tell" situation.

> *Hi Ellie, long time no see. Can you call me? Want to make sure you go to this new performance piece, I heard about it recently.*

Okay. I'm starting to get that buzz, that tickling up and down my spine. Especially when, after scrolling through a few more newsletters and petition requests, I see an email from Harrison Wang.

> *Call me as soon as you can.*

I don't have to go down too many more emails in my in-box before I see what prompted all this.

The email is from "Boar Returning from Mountain."

It has to be Lao Zhang.

> *Join me to fly a kite. Meet north of Mao's last erection. Tomorrow, 12 P.M.*

I check the date of the email. "Tomorrow" is today.

Mao's last erection—that's what some expats I know call the Monument to the People's Heroes. I told Lao Zhang that once.

The Monument to the People's Heroes, in Tiananmen Square.

I have an hour to get there.

You don't have to go, I tell myself. Whatever's going to happen, you can't stop it.

I'm done fighting.

I lean back in my desk chair. All I want to do is close up shop here. Go someplace peaceful. Just *be* for a while.

But I already know what I'm going to do.

"Just one more fucking time," I mutter.

CHAPTER THIRTY-ONE

TIANANMEN SQUARE ON A hot, smoggy Tuesday in May. A mega-mall parking-lot-size expanse of pavement. Chairman Mao's memorial hall behind me to the south. The National Museum and the Great Hall of the People to the east and west. The broad expanse of Chang'an Avenue and, across that, the entrance to the Forbidden City to the north.

In the middle the Monument to the People's Heroes.

They've chased the vendors out, the guys selling Mao singing lighters and Little Red Books; now they cluster as discreetly as they can by the entrances to the pedestrian tunnels that lead into the square. Tourists wander around, Chinese and foreign, snapping postcard shots and selfies. There are a lot of uniformed police and obvious plainclothes, too, single men with close-trimmed hair who don't seem to be doing anything besides watching other people.

Chinese have protested here for a long time, over a hundred years at least. Everything from mass demonstrations such as what happened in 1989 to individuals lighting themselves on fire. Seems like the government doesn't want to see anything like that ever happen here again.

Which is why, if I were already in deep shit and planning on doing some kind of political performance piece that was apt to get me in deeper, this would be one of the last places I'd think about staging it.

I get to the Monument to the People's Heroes at about ten minutes to noon. It's this giant . . . obelisk? I guess that's what you call it, on top of a platform of stairs, like a shorter, thicker Washington Monument sitting on a lopped-off Mayan temple. When the mass demonstrations happened in 1976 and 1989, this was the focal point, where people came to lay wreaths for Zhou Enlai and Hu Yaobang. They weren't just mourning those men, they were pissed as hell— about the rule of the Gang of Four, about corruption and their lack of say in how things were run—and tired of being silent about it.

They wanted different lives.

"Ellie."

I turn. There's Harrison Wang. He's wearing a white silk T-shirt and lightweight black pants. I think this might be the first time that I've seen him actually sweat.

"Hey."

"You got my email?"

I nod. "Crazy couple of days."

"You'll have to tell me about that."

He stares north, toward the Forbidden City.

I look around. I spot Sloppy and Francesca, on the west side of the monument. Francesca has a big camera, with a long lens. Nothing weird about that—this is a huge tourist attraction after all.

"We have other people with cameras and cell phones," Harrison murmurs.

"What's he going to do?"

"I don't know. But I thought we should be prepared to document it."

We stand there, waiting.

"Hey! Dude!"

There's only one person who calls me "dude." That would be Liu Chaoke, Chuckie, my former roommate, the hacker and gamer who introduced me to Lao Zhang.

He's wearing an oversize Green Lantern T-shirt and baggy shorts, and he's still thin and knobby kneed, though he's switched his old heavy-framed glasses to some rimless models.

"Dude," I say. I haven't seen him in over a year. And I can't help it—I give him a quick hug. He pats me on the back, as awkward as I am.

"How are you recently?" he asks.

"Oh, you know. Pretty good. You?"

"Same thing."

"What have you been doing?"

"Hacking for PLA."

This is kind of a surprise on the one hand, given Chuckie's problems with authority. On the other, I guess he's pretty good at hacking.

"Oh. So. How is that?"

He shrugs. "Boring. I quit."

Which doesn't surprise me at all.

It's almost noon.

Now I see a man approaching from the east side of the square. He's wearing shorts and a plain T-shirt and a scarlet baseball cap like he's a Chinese tourist on a group tour. He's carrying something, some kind of long, bright bundle, tucked under one arm.

Lao Zhang.

For a minute or two, I just stand there while he takes up a position slightly to the north of the monument.

I shake myself, and I limp toward him.

"Hey," I say.

He looks up. "Yili."

We stare at each other. I haven't seen him in over a year. All this time, everything that's happened, it's like he's turned into a symbol of something rather than a man.

Now we're standing in front of each other, and I really *see* him. He's thinner than he was. His hair's retreated above his temples, and he's shaved it close to his head, shaved off his goatee, too.

Mostly he just looks tired.

"What are you doing?" I ask.

"A performance." He indicates the bundle under his arm. "It's just a kite. I want to fly it for a while."

"Don't do it," I say. "Don't. You don't have to. You can still leave."

"I don't want to." He closes the distance between us. Rests his hands on my shoulders for a moment. "I never should have left you the way I did. It was selfish."

I want to hug him, but I'm afraid to. I don't know who's watching.

Besides, I'm pissed off. He comes home just to get himself arrested?

To leave again?

I step back. "Okay. Maybe you shouldn't have. How's this going to help?"

"It's just time, that's all." He starts to unroll the kite. "Time to step away from the computers. To act."

"You and what army? This isn't 1989. You see anybody out

here marching with you? They don't care. They're too busy trying to make down payments on their fucking Audis."

"I care. Let me do this." He unfolds the kite. It's a big kite, white with red trim, and I catch a glimpse of black characters and a fragment of English—DELETED, it says.

"You really think doing some kind of art piece is going to change things? Jesus. Your ego's bigger than I thought."

He pauses with his kite and smiles. "Maybe so."

It's making me nervous just standing here next to him. I glance to my right. Those two guys over there, are they plain-clothes? Are they watching us?

I glance around the square, and there are other people flying kites: kids and their parents mostly, and a few older men with fancy kites, like this is their big hobby. A unit of uniformed soldiers march by in cadence, and no one seems to notice. They're just part of the landscape.

"I'm going to move to the side a little," Lao Zhang says. "Wind is better there."

"Please don't do this."

"Take good care of yourself," he says. "I'm sorry for all the trouble I make for you."

He turns and walks away, holding the big kite under his arm.

You can't go after him, I tell myself. You can't. It wouldn't do any good.

He'll do what he wants to do, and it's not up to me to stop him.

I let him go.

When I get back to where Harrison is standing, Chuckie's gone. "Your friend said he wanted a better view," Harrison tells me.

I nod, throat too tight to let me speak.

Lao Zhang has taken a position about twenty yards in front

of the Monument to the People's Heroes. I get what he's doing. You frame the shot right, you'll get him with the monument in the background. I'm guessing some of Harrison's videographers know that, too, and are positioned accordingly.

I stay where I am. I don't need the perfect shot. I don't even want to watch this.

But here I am.

Lao Zhang puts his kite on the ground. Squats down and fiddles with it—he's tying the line onto the crossbar, I think. Stands, holding the kite in one hand, a reel for the string in the other. Stretches.

He holds the kite out in front of him, slightly above his head. Waits for a gust of wind and lets it go.

It takes him a few tries to get the thing up in the air, but when it does rise, it's as easy and gentle as anything that's going back to where it really belongs.

Up in the air.

I watch it rise. Lao Zhang reels in the string to keep it from going too high too fast. So we can all see what's written on it.

对不起，原文已经被删除

It's the message you get when you're surfing the web here or following links on Weibo, and whatever you were looking for got harmonized. Censored.

And in English:

SORRY, THE ORIGINAL TEXT HAS BEEN DELETED.

We all stand there watching. The kite bobs and weaves. It takes at least five minutes before a couple of those obvious plainclothes guys start pointing at the kite and yapping at each other about it. Like, *What do we do? Is this subversive? It* must *be, but we aren't exactly sure* why *it is.* One of them makes a call on his cell phone.

Then they march over to Lao Zhang and start asking him questions.

I watch him shrug. Continue to fly the kite. One of the plainclothesmen grabs the kite string out of his hands. Lao Zhang lets him. He knows it's over. The plainclothes guy reels in the kite. Snatches it out of the sky.

More plainclothesmen converge, along with a couple of actual uniforms. They're getting in Lao Zhang's face now, but he just stands there, all calm and Zen. Finally two of them flank him, grab his upper arms and frog-march him away.

I start to follow. I don't even think about it. Harrison clasps his hand around my wrist.

"Don't."

I stop. "I know. But—"

"We'll try to get the plates of whatever car they put him in, so we know who has him," Harrison says. "That's all we can do right now."

He stares out over the square. People still fly kites. Take selfies. It's as if nothing happened at all.

HARRISON TAKES ME OUT for a late lunch and drinks at a *hutong* restaurant that serves Malaysian food. I don't eat that much. I tell him what happened with me and the Caos. I tell him I can't do this anymore. "I just need a break, that's all," I say.

It's funny, because while I'm telling him all this, I'm not really feeling much of anything. I'm mostly staring at my plate of *nasi kandar* and thinking I should take it to go for later, because I can't eat it right now.

"Ellie."

I look up. Harrison's expression is one I haven't seen on him before. He looks . . . I don't know. Sad. Concerned. Like he actually gives a shit.

"We can manage a break. Don't worry about that. Do what you need to do."

I shrug. "Yeah. I will."

"Just remember, you have a place here." Then he does something really weird, for Harrison: he reaches out and covers my hand with his.

"What we're doing, it means something. It's important."

I laugh a little. "Yeah."

I STUMBLE BACK TO my apartment.

I'm thinking I'm not nearly drunk enough, all things considered. But I'm so far beyond tired that I don't even feel like drinking.

I'll take half a Percocet, I decide. Watch something loud and stupid on TV until I fall asleep. The way I'm feeling, it shouldn't take long.

Funny. The place looks so empty without my mom and Mimi. It's like I'm already gone. A ghost in my own apartment.

I pop open a Yanjing Beer. Collapse on the couch. Retrieve my Percocet stash from my daypack.

I open the bottle and tap a pill onto my palm. Think about it and tap a little harder. I keep doing that until I have maybe a dozen of them cupped in my hand.

I'm trying to calculate what happens if I take them all.

Would that be enough narcotic for me to just sort of . . . drift off? Or would I puke them up?

It's actually the acetaminophen you really have to worry about. That shit trashes your liver. So I take an overdose of

Percocet, and maybe all I manage to do is blow out my liver and die a slow, horrible death.

"Fuck it," I mutter. I pour the pills back into the bottle.

I drink my beer. I don't even make it to the end of the bottle before I sink down onto the couch and close my eyes.

WHAT WAKES ME UP is my phone ringing.

My hand finds it on the coffee table. As I pick it up, I try to remember which SIM card is in there. Is this the number the Caos have? Because I really don't want to talk to any of them right now.

Unknown number.

"Shit."

I hesitate for a moment, and then I slide the bar to answer. "*Wei?*"

"Ellie. It is John."

I feel . . . How do I feel? It's nice to hear from him, I guess. How much does he know about what happened today at Tiananmen?

"Did you hear? About Lao Zhang?"

"Yes. That's why I call." A pause. "I think there is a way maybe . . . to . . . to . . . have an influence. Over his case. And yours."

You know, seriously? I'm so done with this. I'm tired. If I'm not going to kill myself, then I just need to get away from all this bullshit. Go someplace peaceful. There has to be a place like that for me somewhere. Right?

"But . . . I need you to help," John says. "And . . . you must be careful."

I let out a sigh.

"Okay," I say. "What do I have to do?"

CHAPTER THIRTY-TWO

"Not really dangerous," John told me. "I make sure to watch. But . . . maybe he'll be angry."

"Maybe?"

"I take other pictures. But I cannot be seen. You just must take one. And he must know that you take it."

I can think of a lot of ways this could go wrong, actually. But I've gotten to that place where I've already surrendered.

Whatever happens, happens.

Strawberry Crème is another one of these overpriced Beijing nightclubs that I've done my best to avoid since moving here. This one's owned by Russians. You know you're getting close to the club because there are all these billboards with Russian women on them, draped in furs and diamonds.

Inside, it's a lot of black and red and gold: a foyer with a huge Plexiglas escalator that has the mechanics exposed, as long and as steep as a ride down to a Beijing subway. Giant paintings line the walls in gold-painted frames, a lot of fake eighteenth-century European stuff: kings and queens and half-naked nymphs. When I get to the bottom of the escalator, there's more red-and-black wallpaper and giant paintings hung from the ceiling as well as on the walls, so if you look up, you'll get an eyeful of pink nymph flesh, plus gold and crystal chandeliers. Look down and you'll see black leatherette booths with gold studs, giant samovars and hookah pipes sitting on tables here and there, and a dance floor with a disco ball and a small stage where go-go dancers are gyrating around poles, vaguely in time to the earsplitting music.

I do some recon, a quick sweep of the floor, checking out the guests. Mostly Chinese men, some Russian men, and a bunch of European women, most of whom are . . . If I had to guess, I'd go with "paid girlfriend"—younger than the men, wearing micro-miniskirts, low-cut blouses, and stiletto heels. There's a lot of vodka being drunk here. There's a lot of drinking period—it's not even midnight, and I'm already seeing dudes spilling their shots and draping themselves on each other.

I'm walking past one of the booths, and who I actually notice first is a Russian-looking man—trim, bald, wearing an open-necked silk shirt and a thick gold chain, lifting his shot glass in a toast and draining it in one gulp. He doesn't seem all that drunk, though. Unlike the Chinese guy next to him, whose face is bright red and beaded with sweat.

Pompadour Bureaucrat.

I get out my phone and snap a picture. Even though John told me what to look for, seeing it in person is so much better than I ever imagined. His shirt's unbuttoned, revealing white tank-top underwear stretched over a potbelly. He's leaning back against the back of the booth and laughing. One of those girlfriends for hire sits on his lap. She picks up a shot glass brimming with liquid and presses it against his lips, until he opens his mouth like he's about to suck it down. Instead she slips a finger in his mouth, and he sucks on that. I take another picture. She withdraws the finger and tilts the shot glass against his lips, and he switches to the vodka.

Which is when the not-drunk Russian guy notices me.

"What are you doing?"

I lift up my hands. "Who, me? Nothing." I quickly touch the photo to call up the sharing option and hit MESSAGE. Type "Z" to bring up the contact number John gave me on the phone today.

"Just sending this to a couple of buddies."

I hear a choking sound. It's Pompadour Bureaucrat, trying to uninhale his vodka.

"Ni hao!" I say. "I am so looking forward to drinking tea with you again."

I didn't think his face could get any redder. I was wrong.

He stands up, spilling vodka and knocking his temporary girlfriend onto the leatherette bench. "You! You, you . . ."

"Bitch?" I supply. "I get that a lot."

He lunges across the table, toppling a whole bottle of vodka and several water glasses. "Give me that!"

I guess he means my phone. "Sure," I say. "If you want. But that photo I just took? It's already gone."

I'm so busy gloating that I don't notice the Russian muscle until he's come around from behind the booth and has fixated on me, like a leopard. Or a jaguar. Whatever.

Oh, shit. I pivot and make for the dance floor.

The music's pounding, Russian disco, blue and purple strobes flashing in time, and up on the stage there's a chick with a white fur bikini writhing around one pole and a guy wearing a leather Speedo hanging off the other. I push on through, holding up my arms and waving them in a way that I hope looks sort of like dancing, weaving to the back of the dance floor, Russian Muscle not far behind me, crashing into the dancers like a bowling ball hitting the pins.

"Ellie!"

A hand circles my wrist and pulls me forward.

John.

"This way."

There's a door by the back of the stage. I plunge through it, led by John. A dark corridor. Then fluorescent lights, a glimpse of long tables and heaps of costumes, half-dressed women and men, the next act in the floor show. Past that, a long concrete staircase, lit by naked bulbs in iron cages.

I'm barely dragging my ass up all these stairs. "Come on, Ellie!" John says, his hand pressed against the center of my back.

"Okay. Okay."

We get to the top of the stairs. John pushes against a broad door, and we both stumble outside.

Halfway down the block is a new silver Toyota, right wheels parked up on the curb. John jogs ahead, unlocking it with the button on his key. He already has the engine started when I open the passenger door and fall into the seat.

I don't even have the door closed when he peels away from the curb, right wheels hitting the street with a jolt that sends a shock up my spine.

I slam the door shut.

"Holy shit," I gasp. "That was . . . awesome."

John turns his head to me. He's smiling as wide as I've ever seen him smile. "Yes," he says. "I thought you would enjoy."

CHAPTER THIRTY-THREE

"HE WAS VERY ANGRY." John tries to keep his serious face on, but the smile won't stop breaking through.

"I bet."

We're sitting in a *jiaozi* restaurant on Andingmen, chowing down on dumplings and vinegar peanuts with spinach. It's two days since I saw Pompadour Bureaucrat at Strawberry Crème.

"I tell him you send these photos to some of your friends. But you say you won't put them on Weibo or send to newspapers and websites if he stops bothering you. And stops bothering Lao Zhang."

"And?"

"Not sure," he says, spearing another dumpling. "Of course, he cannot tell me what he decides to do. He already lose a lot of face to me." The grin sneaks back. "But I think he will do as I suggest. This is a bad time to be accused of corruption. *Renrou sousuo* can cause him lots of trouble. He knows this."

Renrou sousuo, "human flesh search engine." Chinese netizens sick of corrupt assholes, who'd really enjoy spreading Pompadour Bureaucrat's photo through every corner of the Internet.

"Does he know you set him up?" I ask.

John shrugs. "Maybe he suspects. But he cannot prove it. He saw you take picture. Not me."

I get that hollowed-out feeling in my gut. I don't know exactly what power politics are like in the PSB and the DSD, but it can't be a good thing, having your boss or whatever he is to John suspect that you hold blackmail material on him. And being a guy who's done a bunch of things he hopes Pompadour Bureaucrat never finds out about.

How long can he walk this tightrope before he falls off?

"John . . ." I hesitate. I mean, who am I to give anybody advice about how to live his life? "I know you care about justice. About China . . . But working with guys like that . . ."

I'm probably going to piss him off. If there's one thing I know for sure now, it's that this guy has been on my side. But I still have to ask.

"How much of what you do is good?"

John chews on a dumpling, the muscles in his jaw working harder than they really need to. He swallows, like it's a hard lump to get down. "I don't know," he says. "I try to do good things. And China faces threats. I believe this. But . . ." He picks up another dumpling, shaking his head. "What I do, some of it I don't like. Sometimes I think I do it because I don't know how to do something else." He dips the dumpling in his soy/vinegar/chili mix, focusing on it like it's the important thing, as opposed to what he's talking about. "I don't know if you can understand," he says.

"I think I get it," I say.

AFTER WE'RE DONE EATING, we hang out on the sidewalk in front of the restaurant for a minute to say our good-byes. I'm going to hobble home on foot. John either has his car or took the subway.

Either way, we're going in different directions.

"What do you do next, Ellie?"

"Get out of town for a while. Just stop . . . being in this place I've been in." I shift back and forth from one foot to the other, trying to ease the spasm in my bad leg.

He hesitates. Slips his hands in his pockets. "Can I come and see you sometime? On your travels?"

I nod. "Sure. I'd . . . I'd like that."

We stand there for a moment, as if we're trying to take the measure of each other. After all this time, I still don't really know him, what makes him go, where the anger comes from, why he cares about me.

That last one's probably the biggest mystery of all.

"I see you soon, Ellie," John says. He turns and walks away, up the sidewalk toward the Second Ring Road.

HARRISON CALLS ME THE next day.

"I've gotten all the footage from Zhang Jianli's performance," he says. "We can have someone cut it together and start releasing it, if you believe the time is right."

I think about John's and my blackmail project and whether publicizing Lao Zhang's detention would help that or hurt.

"Let's give it a few days. It's his piece. Maybe he'll get a chance to cut it together himself."

I can tell there's a question Harrison really wants to ask, but he doesn't. "If you think so," he says.

"Just so you know," I say, "I'm leaving town on Tuesday."

"Next week?"

"Yeah."

"Do you have a destination in mind?"

"Yangshuo for a couple of days. I might visit some friends who run a bird sanctuary there."

"After that?"

"Maybe Yunnan. Somewhere the weather's nice and the air is clean."

A pause. "How long will you be gone?"

"I don't know," I tell him. "So don't wait for me. Do whatever's best for the foundation." We've got this charity where we donate money to set up art programs for migrant kids. I'm on the board, but it's not like I run any of that. I've hardly paid any attention to it.

"And your other clients?"

His voice is gentle, but it feels like a slap. I don't want responsibilities. I don't want to be reminded I have them.

"Lucy can handle it for now."

"All right. But you'll stay in touch. Won't you?"

"Yeah. Sure. I will."

"YOU'RE SURE THIS IS all you want to take?"

I've gotten it down to a little backpack and a small duffel bag. "Yeah," I say. "This is plenty."

"Well . . ." My mom clasps her hands in front of her. "We can keep some things for you at Andy's place." She turns to him. "Right?"

"Sure," he says. "We have room."

My mom's already picked over the kitchen and the DVDs. Most of the good kitchen stuff she'd bought anyway.

"Thanks. There's just a couple of boxes and some paintings."

I made a deal with my landlady to sell her my TV, couch, and bed. "Very convenient for new renters," she tells me. The rest of the furniture came with the apartment.

The framed paintings lean against the living-room wall. After a year of doing this art gig, I don't have that many pieces, just five, but I like them. Contemporary calligraphy, a take on a landscape, a satirical map-of-the-world print, a dreamlike image of a Red Guard on a swing, feet aimed at the clouds.

"What's this?" my mom asks. She's looking through the paintings, flipping them forward one by one.

I glance over. It's Lao Zhang's portrait of me, where I'm holding a scared cat and a snarling three-legged dog hugs my leg, against a backdrop of sand dunes and an exploding helicopter, and I look way stronger and smarter than I really am.

It's a cool painting, the one I care about the most, but I never hung it up. Who hangs up a picture of herself? That's just weird.

"Something a friend did," I say.

MY TRAIN TO GUILIN leaves around 3:45 P.M. from the Beijing West Railway Station. I was going to take a cab—the subway still doesn't connect up with the Beijing West Railway Station; it's supposed to happen later this year—but Andy offers to drive.

We're standing in my now-vacated apartment, the leftover furniture making it look like some kind of hotel suite where no one ever actually lived.

I start to turn him down, and then I take in my mom, who's hugging Mimi and telling her what a good dog she is.

"Hey, Mimi," I call out. She perks up and scampers over to me. Stands on her hind legs and rests her front paws on my hips. I bend over and ruffle the scruff around her neck. She loves that.

I can't take Mimi with me. I really want to. A part of me feels like I need some living thing around me, who cares about me, and since I just can't deal with an actual person right now, a dog would be perfect.

But it's not fair to her. She'd have to ride on the baggage car of the train. I don't know if I could bring her to most hotels or hostels. And I don't have a clue where I'm going, after Yangshuo.

More to the point, I don't know if I'm capable of taking care of anything. I'm sure not good at taking care of myself.

"Thanks, Andy," I say. "I'd really appreciate that."

WE GET TO THE train station really early, because the traffic didn't suck as much as I thought it would.

"I can park car, we can wait inside with you," Andy says.

"That's okay. Besides, Mimi wouldn't like it." Mimi and I sit in the backseat of Andy's newish Hyundai. Her head rests on my lap. She knows something's up, and she already doesn't like it.

"I don't like it either, girl," I murmur, staring into her gold-toffee eyes.

I think, Why am I doing this again? I can pretend it's just a vacation, but I know that's not what this really is. Why am I running away?

Because that's what I do.

Andy's gotten us through the tangle of cars and taxis over to the curb in front of the station plaza, up against a white traffic barrier, car horns going off in the haze of exhaust. Not a place where we can stop for long. Which is fine with me. I'm not good with long good-byes.

I get out. Lean in to give Mimi a hug and a scratch around the scruff of her neck. "You're a good dog," I say. "Be good for Mom and Andy, okay?"

I close the car door carefully. She puts her paws on the door-frame and sticks her nose through the cracked-open window.

Andy's gotten my bags out of the trunk. He lifts the pack so I can put my arms through the straps. Places the duffel bag on my shoulder.

"Thanks," I say. "And . . . thanks. For taking care of my mom."

Andy frowns a little, as if he's mulling that over. "I like your mom very much. But I think *she* takes care of *me*."

He reaches out and pats my hand. "You can come back soon."

"Sure," I say.

Two guys have trotted over. "Miss! Miss! Carry your bags?"

I shake my head. "I'd better get going," I tell Andy. "See you soon. And keep me posted on the restaurant."

I turn to go, and there's my mom. "Oh, hon," she says, wrapping her arms around me, awkwardly, because of the luggage. I pat her on the back. I want to give in, to let go, to just be a kid and have my mom take care of me, like when I'd have nightmares and she'd come into my bedroom and sing me a song, read me a story.

But I can't. I don't know how. The shit in my head won't dissolve the way those nightmares did once the light came on.

"You're going to be fine," she murmurs, like she was reading my mind. "It's all going to be fine."

"Do not tell me God has a plan," I snap.

She lets go of me. Puts her hands on my shoulders, gives them a gentle squeeze, and smiles. "I won't."

THE BEIJING WEST RAILWAY Station isn't one of my favorite places. A friend of mine once described it as "a Stalinist wet dream topped by a Chinese party hat," this massive upside-down horseshoe flanked by wings with a pagoda on top that feels like an evil Transformer crouching on the landscape, ready to start stomping its way through Beijing.

The inside's not much better. Three pairs of escalators cordoned off by Plexiglas and giant chrome tubes, like some kind of factory conveyor belts leading us all to be processed. I ride up one to the second floor, where the departure halls are, staring up at the giant information screen, video ads playing in the central slab between the slowly scrolling arrivals and departures. I'm surrounded by bright lights, lit-up plastic signs, neon. I wander down the hall, thinking maybe I should buy some snacks for the trip. Maybe I should sit down and have a beer. I've got plenty of time. It's only two thirty.

Finally I spot my gate, about two-thirds of the way down the hall. I glance inside. The waiting area is packed, as usual, the rows of plastic chairs occupied, people squatting or sitting on their luggage in the aisles.

Maybe I'll store my bags in one of the lockers. I've got a soft sleeper; it's not like I'm going to have to fight my way onto the train for a hard seat.

"Yili."

I turn, and there's Lao Zhang, wearing a white T-shirt and cargo shorts, like he always does when the weather's even a little warm.

I don't know what I'm feeling. It's like everything empties out of me.

"You're okay?" I finally ask.

He nods. "You have time for coffee?"

★ ★ ★

WE END UP AT a McDonald's, sitting at a bright orange plastic table covered with a thin slime of grease and the smell of stale french fries.

"How did you find me?"

"Your friend Harrison tells me you go to Guilin today. He didn't think you take the early train, and this is the other fast one. If not, the other two are later. So I just could wait."

It's a nice gesture, but I feel like I'm missing part of the story.

"When did you get out?" I ask.

"A few days ago." He sips his coffee and makes a face. Lao Zhang always did like good coffee, which this isn't.

I'm starting to feel something now. It might be anger. "Why didn't you call me?"

He shakes his head. He won't look at me. He takes another sip of coffee.

"I didn't feel good," he says.

I study him. If anything, he's thinner than he was at Tiananmen. The flesh around his eyes looks bruised with fatigue.

We got him out, but who knows what happened to him while he was inside?

"I'm sorry," I say. "Are you . . . ?"

I don't even know what to ask.

"*Hai keyi*. I'm okay." He fiddles with packet of sugar. Taps some into his coffee. "You just feel very small, when they take you."

I shake my head. I don't get it. "You knew what would happen if you came back," I say. "Why? Why did you do it?"

"I don't know." He shrugs and laughs a little. "I thought this system, it is completely corrupt. The Party is brutal, and cruel, and it only cares about its own interests, not about the *laobaixing.* The common people. If I believe what I believe, then I have to confront this."

And then he does look at me. He smiles. His eyes seem lost in their dark-circled beds. "Now I think maybe you are right. It is just . . . ego. Wanting to be a big man. Artists all think what we do is so important. But maybe it's only important to ourselves."

"No," I say. "No." And for once I'm sure of what I'm saying. "It *is* important. What you're doing . . . You're calling out the bullshit. Bringing it into the light. Helping people get together, because maybe they think it's bullshit, too, but they aren't going to be the first people to stand up and say it. Or they're not really sure what it is, but they see what you do and they go, 'Yeah. This isn't right.'"

He laughs again. "I don't think so."

"Look, if it wasn't important, they wouldn't have gone after you the way they did."

He sits there sipping his coffee. Thinking it over.

"I hope you are right," he finally says. "Sometimes I think they just don't want to take any chances. Easier to consider that everything is a threat. "

"You can't make people believe things forever, not when they see that every day they're being told lies." I'm thinking of John when I say this.

He nods, like his head's too heavy to hold up.

"Where are you going now, Yili?" he asks.

"Yangshuo for a couple of days. After that . . . I'm not sure."

He nods again. Sips his coffee. He looks so lost. He was the place that used to feel like home to me, if only for a little while. He's not that guy anymore.

But I'm not the same person either.

Now I do feel something. It's like I've been frozen and the blood's starting to circulate again. It hurts, in a way. But it's something.

"Come with me," I say. "We can just . . . go some places. Be together."

He smiles slowly, looking at me the way he used to, with the kind of warmth that made me seek him out on a cold day.

"I want to. But I can't." He tilts his head to the right. "You see that guy? At the table by the door?"

I glance over. Sitting there is a young guy with a shaved head, a compact build, some muscle underneath a tight T-shirt with a Nike swoop across the chest. Watching us.

"They tell me I can't leave Beijing for now," Lao Zhang says.

I feel the tears building up behind my eyes, and I can't stop them from falling.

"I could just stay," I blurt out.

"No. Don't stay for me." There's an urgency to his voice that's been missing till now. "Go and have a rest for a while. It's better if you're not in Beijing right now anyway. This"—his eyes flick toward the plainclothes guy in the Nike T-shirt— "won't last long if I don't cause problems."

"It's not fair," I manage, grabbing a paper napkin off the table to blow my nose. It's a stupid thing to say. Why do I even expect fairness anymore?

"I know." He looks at me, and I can see the old Lao Zhang there all of a sudden, like lit coals that were hiding under ash: the guy who's thinking about his next painting, his next performance. Maybe even about me.

"When you come back, I'll be here," he says.

★ ★ ★

I SIT ON THE lower berth of the soft-sleeper compartment. I have an upper bunk, but so far there are only two other people in the compartment, a stout older woman wearing a quilted black blouse embroidered with gold thread and a chubby kid in a Superman T-shirt who I'm guessing is about ten years old. Grandma and grandson maybe.

I'm drinking a Yanjing Beer, staring out the window, watching the familiar landscape roll by: half-built high-rises shrouded in green safety netting and smog, occasional fields, green struggling to break through yellow dirt, endless power lines. I'm trying not to think about anything. Just finishing my beer, and maybe another one, killing the time before I can fall asleep.

Grandma reads a magazine, grandson plays games on some little handheld thing, the two occasionally snacking on some sticky rice rolls with red bean paste and a can of Pringles.

Finally Grandma puts her magazine down. Yawns loudly, stretches. Turns her attention to me.

"*Ni shi naguo ren?*" What country are you from?

I almost laugh. This is going to be one of those rides, I bet. Next she'll ask me how long I've been in China, if I'm married, do I have any kids, and if not, why? It happens almost every time I take the train somewhere.

Oh, well, why not? It's an eleven-hour ride to Guilin. You have to pass the time somehow, right?

"*Wo shi Meiguoren,*" I say.

I'm an American.

ACKNOWLEDGMENTS

WRITING NOVELS MAY BE a solitary activity, but they never find their way into readers' hands without the work and help of a great many people.

My thanks to all the incredibly hardworking and dedicated folks at Soho Press and Soho Crime, a true independent voice for quality fiction. Publisher Bronwen Hruska, Associate Publisher Juliet Grames, Marketing Maven Paul Oliver, editor Mark Doten, Meredith Barnes, Rachel Kowal, Janine Agro, Amara Hoshiro, Abby Koski, Rudy Martinez: my appreciation and gratitude for your continued dedication to doing such great work.

A big thank you to copyeditor extraordinaire, Maureen Sugden, who goes above and beyond in her attention to detail both grammatical and story. Also many thanks to proofer Katie Herman (was there a better choice to proof this book? I don't think so).

Web designer Ryan McLaughlin, as always, a pleasure working with you.

I am truly fortunate to have an amazing circle of author friends, whose support and camaraderie make the bad times easier and the good times better: Purgatory, Fiction Author's Co-op, the Writing Wombats, you are all awesome. Special thanks to Dana Fredsti for the beta read! Also, to Tim Hallinan, for being one of the most generous and supportive writers I know. I want to be like you when I grow up.

I want to thank Nathan Bransford and the fine folks at CNET, past and present, who have helped me keep body and soul together over the last two years. Special thanks go out to Jennifer Guevin, Emily Dreyfuss, and Christine "Killer" Cain.

China friends and experts who have helped me get the details right and who have generously opened their homes to me: Richard Burger, Fuzhen Si, Tim Smith, Dave Lyons, Brendan O'Kane, Allison Corser, Karl Gerth, Peter Braden, and Dongmei Cao. I'm often asked why I keep going back to China. It's largely because of people like you.

I am about to do the most California thing ever: Thank personal trainers Tim Ehhalt, Kyle Hannon, and Nick Gombold. In all seriousness, I doubt very much this book would have been completed without these guys teaching me old-school weight training and keeping me moving. For all that we're told that writing comes from keeping our butts in our chairs, the best thing I have done for my writing work has been getting out of that chair and doing some serious sweating.

My mother gets a special shout-out in the dedication, but I have to thank my parents, Bill and Carol Galante, here too. Especially for all that Costco sushi. You know how to keep a writer going.

I'd like to express my gratitude to all the great folks at Curtis Brown, in particular Kerry D'Agostino, Stuart Waterman, Holly Frederick, Kerry Cullen, and most especially, my agent Katherine Fausset, who has been a rock when I've been in a hard place.

Finally, I want to thank all of the readers who have accompanied Ellie on her journeys. I hope you found entertainment, emotion, and some food for thought.

Beck